I0594190

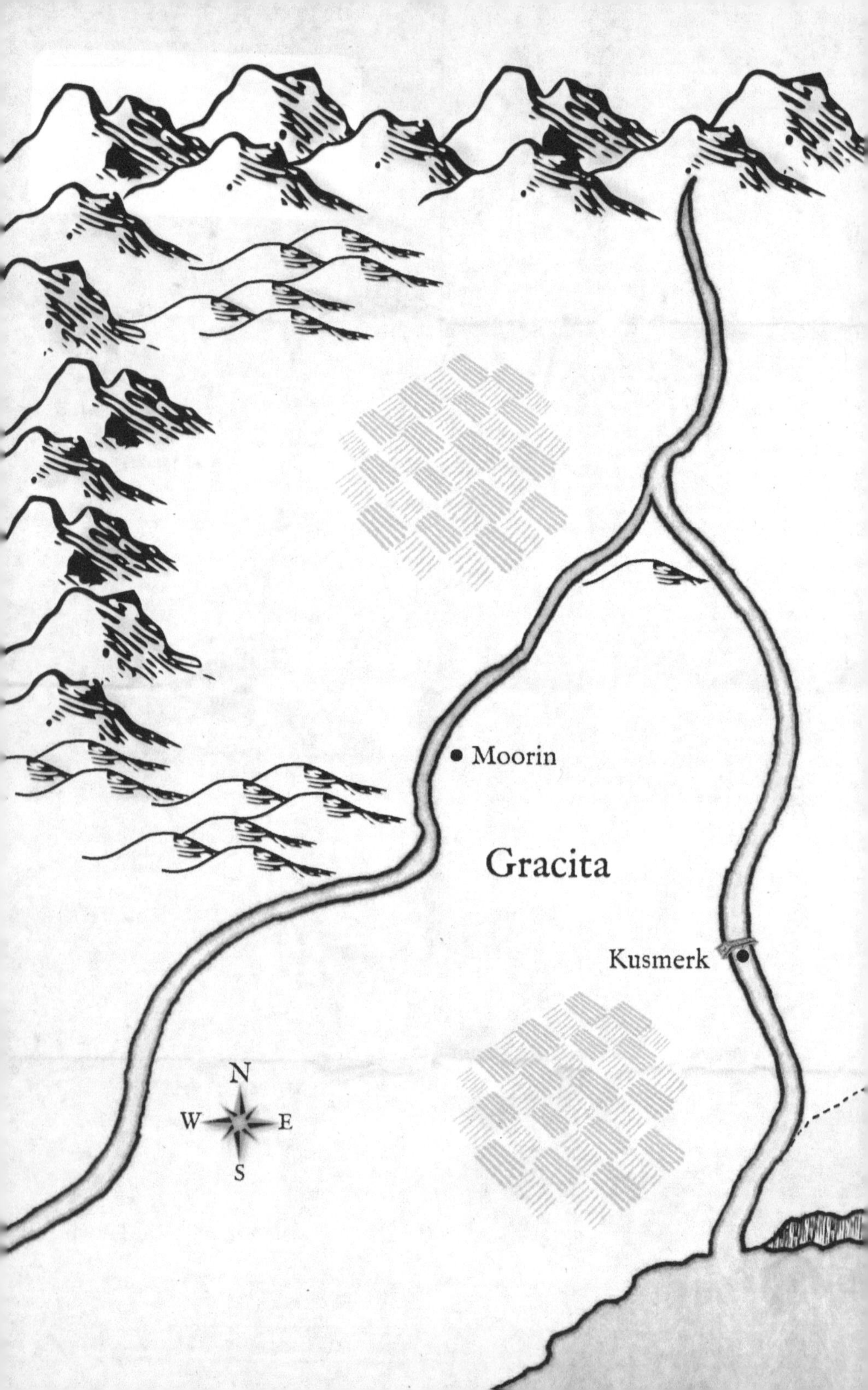

Moorin
Gracita
Kusmerk
N
W
E
S

Strong as Steel

Beatrice B. Morgan

AUTHORS 4 AUTHORS PUBLISHING

Marysville, WA, USA

This is a work of fiction. Names, characters, incidents, and dialogues are products of the author's imagination and are not to be construed as real. Any resemblance to actual events or persons, living or dead, is entirely coincidental.

©2022 Beatrice B. Morgan

All rights reserved. No part of this publication may be reproduced in any form without prior written permission from the publisher, except for use in brief quotations as permitted by United States copyright law.

Published by Authors 4 Authors Publishing
1214 6th St
Marysville, WA 98270
www.authors4authorspublishing.com

Library of Congress Control Number: 2022947441

E-book ISBN: 978-1-64477-058-0
Paperback ISBN: 978-1-64477-059-7
Audiobook ISBN: 978-1-64477-060-3

Edited by Rebecca Mikkelson
Copyedited by Renee Frey
Proofread by Brandi Spencer

Cover design ©2022 Practically Perfect Covers. All rights reserved.
Interior design by Brandi Spencer

Authors 4 Authors branding is set in Bavire. Headings and story signage are set in IM FELL English Pro. All other text is set in Garamond.

Strong

as Steel

Beatrice B. Morgan

Authors 4 Authors Content Rating

This title has been rated 17+, appropriate for older teens and adults, and contains:

- strong language
- intense violence
- brief sex
- mild alcohol use
- moderate negative fantasy drug use

Please, keep the following in mind when using our rating system:

1. A content rating is not a measure of quality.

Great stories can be found for every audience. One book with many content warnings and another with none at all may be of equal depth and sophistication. Our ratings can work both ways: to avoid content or to find it.

2. Ratings are merely a tool.

For our young adult (YA) and children's titles, age ratings are generalized suggestions. For parents, our descriptive ratings can help you make informed decisions, but at the end of the day, only you know what kinds of content are appropriate for your individual child. This is why we provide details in addition to the general age rating.

For more information on our rating system, please, visit our Content Guide at: www.authors4authorspublishing.com/books/ratings

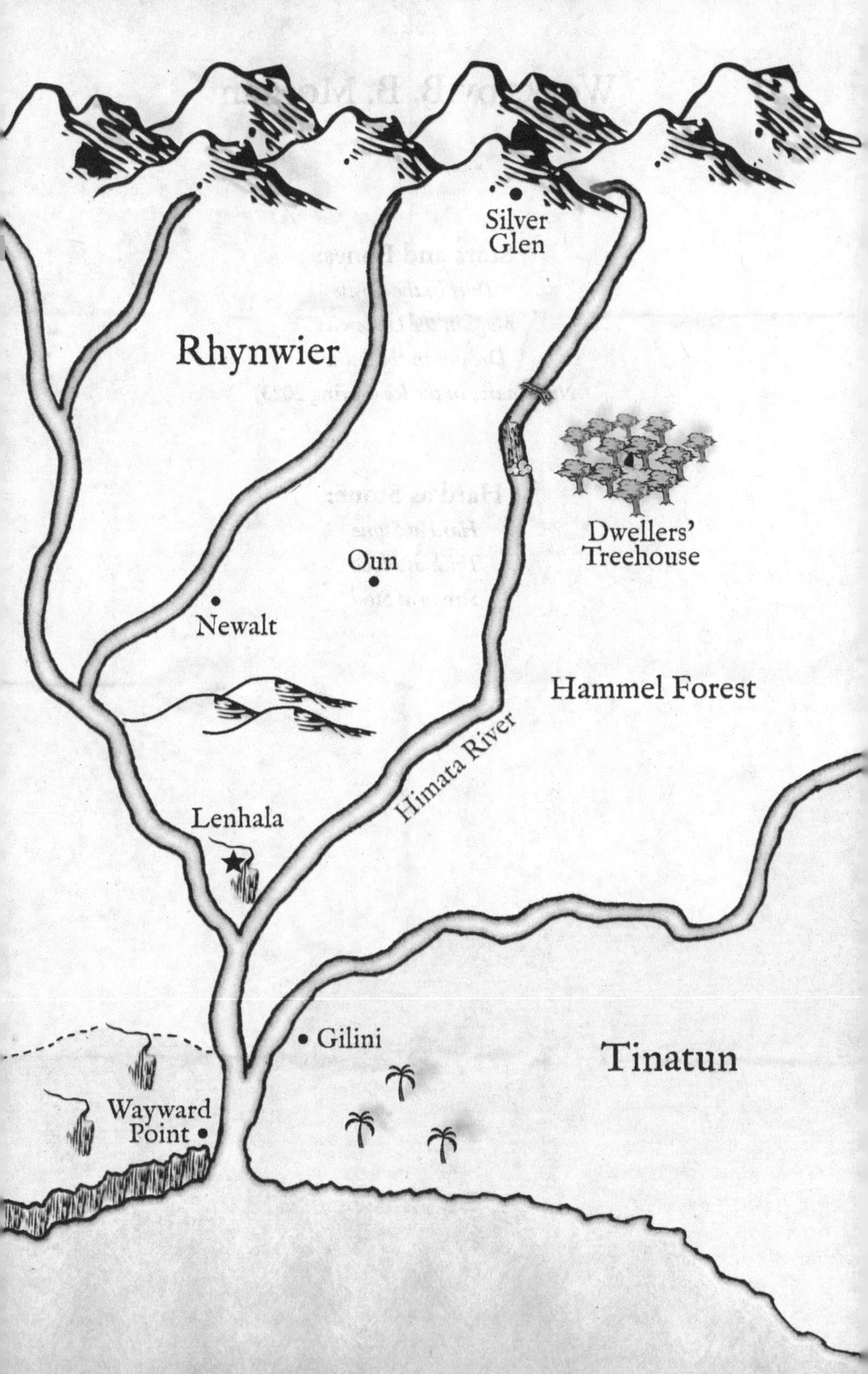

Silver
Glen
Rhynwier
Dwellers'
Treehouse
Oun
Newalt
Hammel Forest
Himata River
Lenhala
Gilini
Tinatun
Wayward
Point

Works by B. B. Morgan

Stars and Bones:
Thief in the Castle
Mage in the Undercity
Dreams in the Snow
Nightmares in the Ice (Spring 2023)

Hard as Stone:
Hard as Stone
Thick as Blood
Strong as Steel

Table of Contents

Table of Contents

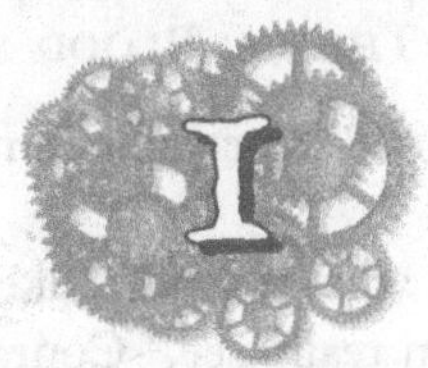

Raven Thane held a soft orange flame in her palm. It flickered in the humid breeze.

"A storm is brewing." Conrad's coal dark eyes were on the horizon, nostrils flaring as he inhaled the incoming breeze. "Smell that?"

"Smell what?"

"The rain in the air."

Raven inhaled. "It smells wet," she said flatly, focusing on the flame. It hadn't been easy at first to keep it stable and the same height, but she had gotten better in the last seven days.

"That's the perfume of a storm," Conrad said. "But we've got time before it blows in."

Raven glanced away from her flame and to the horizon. She hadn't quite gotten used to being in a sky city, or being able to see from horizon to horizon, or being able to look down on a floor of clouds, or having an endless sky of brilliant blue above her. Today, however, gray clouds bubbled below them and to the east. Not that the bubbling storm bothered her. Of all the things about the *Orion*, she loved the view the most.

She had almost gotten used to the fire she held in her palm. The blue base of the flame licked against her skin but did not burn her. She felt the warmth of it, but it didn't feel like real fire.

That's because it wasn't real fire. It was magic. Her magic. It felt unreal to think of it as magic, let alone her own. Her, plain Raven, a magician.

For the majority of her seventeen years, she'd had no magic, but thanks to her own naivety about the nature of magical items, she had unknowingly allowed the magic from the centrum of Altair's Augur to seep into her body. It had started as a fever, making her sicker and sicker, but she had conquered it. The magic had become hers.

Her friends had been helping her control it. Today, Conrad accompanied her on her morning trip to the Belt—the promenade deck of the *Orion*—to burn off the excess magic before it could build up and make her sick. It had been Princess Rosaria Whisehunt's theory, and so far it had worked.

The magic contained within the centrum had not been normal magic. It was wild and untamed, as Conrad said. He had the ability to see and sense magic in others, and sometimes she caught him looking at her, but not at *her*—at her magic.

She had asked him once what it looked like.

"It's not something I can really see," Conrad had said, tilting his head. "It's more of something I can sense...like how the heat radiates off stone or how the air blurs right before it rains."

She didn't really understand, but she hadn't asked further questions.

Every morning for the past seven days, Raven had gone to the Belt to burn off her magic. The first day had been trial and error, trying to bring the magic forth. Every day since then, she had held the flame in her hand. She felt it happening too. She felt it stemming the tide of the fever, calming it, sating it.

And without the fever threatening to burn her alive, she could feel the magic with a clearer mind. She could feel it working under her skin, within her bones.

"Are you nervous?" Conrad asked.

Raven glanced from the fire to him. His eyes held his usual mischievous glint, but also something else. She'd come to think of it as his form of worry.

"If I said no, would you believe me?" she asked.

"Not even a little."

"Then, there is your answer." Her magic fluctuated, and she shrank her flame in response.

"You're doing remarkably better." Conrad leaned against the brassy railing of the Belt. He tilted his head back and inhaled the storm-scented breeze. It fluttered through his long braids, clinking the golden beads together in disharmony.

"I've had several remarkable teachers."

"Oh," Conrad said, pretending to be embarrassed.

"Did you learn to smell storms as a pirate?" she asked, mostly to guide the conversation away from her and her magic. And she loved his pirate stories.

"I did," he said with a sigh. "That's one of the things about the ocean. You have maps, but they aren't as reliable as the stars. Maps are good if you know where you are. Stars will tell you where you are, what season it is, and where you are headed. The smell of the air will warn you of a storm before your eyes see it, and the smell of the crew will keep track of how long you've been on the sea."

Raven chuckled, and her flame responded with a flicker.

"Remember," Conrad said, stifling a yawn, "when you feel your magic start to pull, stop before it really pulls."

"Yes, sir." Raven let her flame shrink a little more. "I'm not there yet."

Conrad hummed but didn't respond. He'd done that several times in regards to her magic, that non-answer of curiosity. He knew a lot more about magic than she did, and she took every opportunity to pick his brain. She also took every chance to pry a pirate story from him.

"What about you, little bird?" Conrad hummed a note. "Word is, you've been avoiding the captain."

"I have not," Raven lied. "I've just…continually been in different parts of the ship than her."

He harrumphed.

Raven's conversations with Captain Bailey Luckett had been short and few. The air had turned awkward between them since Luckett confessed to being Raven's mother, who had abandoned her as a child to fly in the sky. Everything about the story made Raven's stomach churn—being abandoned, growing up thinking her mother dead, and finding out her mother had been flying around in the sky the entire time while Raven had grown up underground with nothing but daydreams.

And, if she were to be honest, a part of her was jealous and bitter that her mother hadn't taken her with her. How different would her life have been if she had grown up in the sky rather than a stuffy old silver mine with her overprotective father?

"You can't avoid her forever," Conrad said, a rehearsed line. "And she asked me to inform you that she would like to be friends."

Raven glanced at him over the flame.

Conrad shrugged. "Yes, she asked me to speak to you, and so I have."

"I will make sure to mention it."

"But onto more important things." Conrad pushed off the railing. "I'd say it's just about time to head inside if you want to see Zander before he goes under."

Her heart thudded at the reminder, and her flame flickered in response. It had been a long week for her, but a longer one for Zander. He had lost his left arm in their flight from Moorin, and today he would undergo the surgery to replace it with a mechanical one. Raven let her flame die out.

"Finished?" Conrad asked, eyes on the horizon.

"Good enough." She hadn't felt the gentle tug of depletion, and she suspected Conrad knew that, but he didn't argue.

They started toward the doors that would lead them down into the corridors of the *Orion*. As Raven followed Conrad inside, thunder rolled low and lazy in the distance.

Conrad and Raven parted ways, and she made her way to the hospital ward several decks below. Corin, the medic in charge of the magicians, greeted her with a smile.

"We were just getting settled in," Corin said. "Come on in."

He led her into the surgery room, all clean walls and bolted steel cabinets. Zander Winchester sat up in his hospital bed. The top half of his dark brown hair was tied into a topknot, the bottom half having been shaved that morning. A week of healthy meals had brought color back to his bronze skin. His sapphire eyes fell onto Raven, and a grin spread over his otherwise grim face.

Thalame stood at the bedside, arms crossed over his white medic's smock. He would be using his healing magic in the surgery, just in case. Thalame's eyes shifted to Raven, and then he went to the other side of the room to assist the medics. Raven took his place at the bedside.

"He's nervous," Zander admitted to Raven, his voice lowered so Thalame wouldn't hear him. "He plays tough, but he's been twitching all morning."

"Can you blame him?" Raven glanced to where Thalame stood with the medics, his back to them, his foot tapping on the steel floor.

Zander shrugged. "I guess not."

"How are you feeling?" Raven's gaze drifted over the clean bandages across his bare chest and the stump of his left arm.

He noticed her stare and shrugged. "I'm fine." He flashed her a crooked grin, though unease threaded his words. He swallowed, and that grin fell into a straight line. He motioned to his left shoulder and said, "Next time you see me, I'll have a new arm."

One of the medics appeared at the bedside, holding a glass of pale purple liquid. "Here she is." The medic motioned to the glass. "One order of knock-out juice."

"Looks delicious," Zander deadpanned. He accepted the glass and sniffed it. His nose wrinkled, he coughed, and the medic laughed.

Raven caught a whiff—it did not smell like anything a human should ingest.

"Drink it slow, like a fine scotch," the medic said. "Drink it too fast, and you'll wake up sooner than you want to. It's strong enough to knock you out and keep you out during the surgery and most of the day. Maybe tomorrow too."

Zander grimaced at the glass. He took a drink. "Bleh, that's disgusting. If I die during this, I want it on record how horrible the last meal was."

"I'll note it," said the medic.

Zander smirked at Raven, but she couldn't find the strength to smile back. Not with his surgery hanging over their heads. Zander was trying to make it easier on everyone, but her nerves refused to be helped.

"It's not funny," Raven said.

Zander's smirk flattened. He opened his mouth but then closed it. He glanced at the medics. Whatever he wanted to say, he didn't want the medics to hear it. He sipped the tonic instead, then sat the empty glass on the narrow table beside the bed. Already, his eyes looked glassy.

He reached across the bed and held his right hand out to Raven, palm up. Raven wrapped her fingers around his. The feeling of his warm callused hand against hers unsettled her nerves in an entirely different way—a pleasant way.

"I'll be fine," he whispered. "Thalame's here."

Raven nodded. Thalame wouldn't willingly let anything happen to Zander. But what if it was too much for him?

The medic team wheeled a tray to the other side of the bed. They had gathered what looked like torture devices, all sleek steel and sterile, made for slicing, prodding, and pinning flesh and human innards. The assortment made her skin crawl, and the feeling worsened when she imagined what Zander must have felt.

Whatever he felt, he held it in well. When his eyes gazed over the tools, his face calmed and hardened. Ready.

"Raven," Zander said.

She tore her eyes from the tools and met his. He squeezed her hand and gave her his typical smirk, but it lacked humor. He knew the risks of the surgery. He had known from the moment he'd agreed to it.

He blinked, and it took a moment longer for his eyes to open again. When they did open, his eyes had to refocus on her. "I loved you," he breathed.

The words slammed into her. She started to form her response, but they lumped up in her throat. The medical team circled the bed, hands gloved, faces masked.

The moment was gone, and it was time for her to go.

"I'll see you on the other side." Only after the words left her mouth did she realize he could have thought she meant the other side of death, so she quickly added, "of the surgery."

Zander chuckled. His grip on her hand slackened. He fought to keep his eyes open, and he held his unfocused gaze on her. As the tonic finally pulled him under, his breath came out in a whisper. He went under. His body relaxed: his eyes closed, the crease between his brows smoothed, his head slumped to the side, and his fingers released hers.

"Don't worry," said one of the medics, her voice muffled by the mask. "He'll be fine. We've done more complicated surgeries than this."

Thalame stood beside the medic, masked and gloved like the others. Raven left them to do their job and took up a post outside the surgery room. She took a moment to collect herself. She did feel better about having Thalame in the surgery. She had felt his healing magic firsthand. On the other side of the doors, the medical team mumbled to one another, and tools clinked against the tray—the surgery began. With nothing else to occupy her thoughts, Raven started to pace.

And she paced.

And paced.

The storm blew up, and Raven could no longer hear the sounds of surgery coming from the other side. Wind howled against the ship, whistling through the rigging and whipping against the thick leather balloons—the sound had startled her at first, as if the entire ship would tumble from the sky, but it held. She doubted the average storm could do any real damage to the *Orion*.

Rain beat against the hull, clinking against the metal parts and thumping against the wooden. Thunder quaked across the sky, the crack vicious and close, more violent than she had ever heard it. Each clap resounded through the ship and through her chest, making her heart skip a beat with each one.

Each clap reverberated within her magic too. It pulsed with the thunder.

But she hadn't the time to worry about her magic right now.

She paused in front of the hospital doors and pressed her ear against the seam. She heard the *click-click* of metal tools, the rustle of the medical team's sterile smocks, and the beeping, humming, and clanking of the dozen machines that kept Zander alive during his surgery.

Her legs itched to move again, her nerves already rattling with the lack of motion. She returned to her pacing.

Even now, hours after the surgery had started, she couldn't shake the look of Zander's face as the tonic had pulled him under. It was the look of someone trying to memorize a face he didn't think he'd see again.

There was a chance, the medics had said—as there was always a chance—that the worst could happen. Zander might not wake up. His body might reject the new hardware or see it as infection, causing his body to attack itself. Raven pushed those unhappy thoughts as far away as she could, though they persisted like an itch she couldn't reach.

"You're wearing a groove in the floor," came a soft female voice.

Raven halted her pacing. Princess Rosaria stood in the doorway, a cup of steaming tea in her hands.

Her short tangerine cloak looked marvelous against her olive skin. Her tightly braided dark hair hung over her shoulder. She wore a dress of silver and indigo underneath. Despite the simple dress, Rosaria held herself like a princess, shoulders poised, back arrow-straight, chin high but not arrogant. She stood like a queen before her court.

It came naturally, Raven supposed.

"Here," Rosaria said, handing Raven the tea. "You need this. And you also need a break from your worrying. Come on, walk with me."

Raven thought about protesting, but she knew her pacing wouldn't change Zander's fate. His life was in the hands of the surgery team. Raven accepted the tea and followed the princess into the corridor. Warmth seeped into her fingers. Not that she was cold; her nerves had been on edge since Zander's eyes had closed.

"Thank you," Raven said. The first sip of tea warmed the whole way down. Herbs, she guessed. Conrad had mentioned an herbalist on board and a greenhouse somewhere. It would have to be high to catch the sunlight.

The glass globes that lined the corridor glowed yellowish white, warming the rosewood and brass panels. The two girls walked down the corridor. Without the tea to hold, Rosaria laced her fingers together and held them over her stomach. The light glinted off steel pins tucked in her black hair. Raven had told her about the steel pins in her own hair, and Rosaria had taken to doing the same.

A girl uses every talent she has, the princess had told her.

"How long?" Rosaria finally asked.

"It's been five hours." Raven had kept count. Every minute. Every hour. Five hours of her standing outside, unable to help, unable to do anything but wait and hope and pray to the Three Sisters that Zander pulled through.

Rosaria glanced over her shoulder at the hospital doors, her eyes moving through her own worries and apprehensions. She and Zander had been raised together; she thought of him as her brother. Raven wanted to know what else the princess thought, but she worried her own fears would come pouring out of her mouth instead. So she kept it closed.

When her thoughts slipped into those fears, Raven felt the squeezing in her chest—a ghost of the loss she would feel if Zander didn't wake up. The feeling started in her chest and worked its way into every limb until she didn't think she could stand.

To stem her dark thoughts, Raven took a drink of tea. The herbal effects warmed her throat, soaking deeper than her skin, into her bones and tissues, soothing her. She knew the feeling—she had taken several tonics in the past seven days, either to calm the wild magic or to help her sleep.

"They said it would take five to seven hours," Raven said, though she knew Rosaria knew. She had been there for the meeting—they all had. Raven took another drink. If she asked the bartender in the cafeteria for something stronger, would he give it to her? Most of the crew had been or were pirates, so she didn't think he would mind. Most on board carried their own flasks.

"He will be fine," Rosaria said, her voice calming and reassuring. "He's Zander."

Raven gave her a smile, though it felt weak. By the look on Rosaria's face, it looked as weak as it felt.

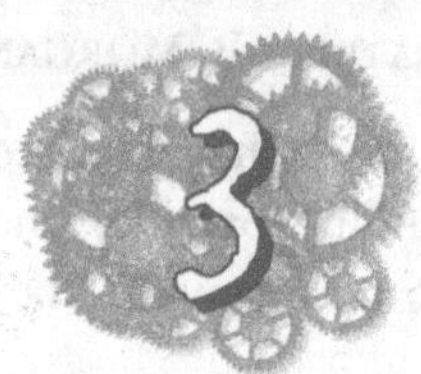

Rosaria led Raven down the corridor, the rain clattering, the thunder rolling, the wind howling. She led her up the wide stairs to the corridor above and to the stairs that would lead to the Belt. Rosaria tugged her up the stairs to the landing, but the double doors leading onto the Belt were closed for the storm.

Thunder cracked too close. Raven felt a tingle in the air as the lightning sizzled somewhere in the clouds.

Captain Luckett had assured Raven that the *Orion* had lightning rods to which the bolts were attracted and then redirected harmlessly. Rather than strike the ship and electrify the metal or burn through the leather or wood, the ship funneled the lightning to a coil, where the ship used what they could of it for power. What they couldn't use zapped into the air behind the ship, leaving a literal trail of lightning.

Rosaria, despite the storm, unlatched and opened the doors to the Belt. Unlike that morning when she had burned away her excess magic with Conrad, shutters had been drawn over the Belt to protect it from the storm. Scrolling wooden shutters arched over the Belt in sections, grayed with weather and time, secured together with small metal casings and hinges. The shutters shook in the wind; they rattled and trembled but held.

Every fifth shutter held thick glass though which the eerie stormy light flooded in, striping the Belt in dark blues and grays. Water dripped through the seams, hitting the lattice floor and vanishing, lost through the maze of tubes and pipes that gathered rain water and recycled it for whatever the ship or its crew needed.

Rosaria started through, walking underneath the center panel in the ceiling to avoid being dripped on. Raven walked with her, despite the tremor in her stomach that came with being on the Belt during a storm. Another part of her thrilled at how close the thunder sounded, how vicious the wind howled, and how angry the rain beat against the shutters.

On the other side of the portholes, thunderheads bubbled in dangerous shades of purple and gray and blue. The wind lashed through the rain, sending the rain in torrents. The lightning flashed between clouds, a constant barrage of light.

They walked along the Belt for a while, and then Rosaria asked, "What's on your mind?"

It occurred to Raven that Rosaria had brought her to the Belt, of all places, so that they wouldn't be easily overheard—granting her privacy, which hadn't been very easy to come by on the *Orion*.

"Too much to be healthy," Raven said with a sigh.

"Give me a few of your thoughts," Rosaria said.

Raven didn't want to start out talking about Zander, so she chose the second most occurring thought. "I don't know what to think about Luckett."

The princess gave a soft hum of acknowledgment, encouraging Raven to continue.

"I..." She sighed. She didn't know where to start. "I used to make up stories about who my mother was, who she had been. My father would never tell me anything, only that I had her eyes. I didn't grow up without a mother. I had my stepmother, and I love her like a mother. She raised me, treated me like her own." The words kept pouring out, faster and faster. "And now Luckett is here, my actual mother, who left me as a baby so she could go play pirate in the sky."

"You are bitter," Rosaria said softly.

"Of course I'm bitter," Raven snapped. "She left me to grow up underground, knowing that I would live the rest of my life there, washing dishes and making soap while she was flying around...doing whatever she does. I..." Raven sighed, releasing the pressure in her chest. "I wish she had taken me with her. I wish I had grown up in the skies."

"And you would be a different person." Rosaria nudged her arm. "Everything that has happened to you, your childhood, the mine, meeting Zander, everything that's happened in the past few months, it is all part of who you are today. If you had been raised in the skies, then you wouldn't have met Zander, you wouldn't have met me, and Sisters only know where you'd be. Maybe we wouldn't have met at all. You have made a difference in the future of both the kingdom and the empire."

Raven hadn't thought of it like that. "Still, Luckett wants me to just forget what she did? She wants to be my mother now, after all this time, and she wants to pretend like nothing happened?"

Rosaria paused by a porthole. On either side of them, the Belt stretched on. It went around the entire airship, and it didn't look like anyone else had come there to walk. According to the crew, a storm made for precarious flying. The crew stood alert, ready for anything, all hands on deck. No one had time to lollygag, as Luckett had said.

Despite her flaws, Raven admired Luckett's readiness and fearlessness. If she had grown up in the sky, would she be both of those things?

"I can't say I have advice for your situation," Rosaria said. "I'm not a parent either, so I can't help you understand what the captain is thinking or feeling." She sighed through her nose. "I don't remember my mother. I grew up with a caretaker and Mrs. Winchester. I used to think that since I had survived, and people thought I was dead, that maybe my parents had survived too. As I grew older, I started to realize the silliness of that."

Raven swallowed. Her problems suddenly felt childish. "You think I should give her a chance?"

"I think," Rosaria said slowly, "I think you should let her be herself. Maybe she isn't the world's best mother, but maybe she is trying to be a mother in the only way she knows how?"

Raven glanced at Rosaria. The princess gave her a sympathetic smile.

"Maybe one day I'll have better advice for daughters and mothers," Rosaria said.

Raven thought about mentioning Ezra Deacon, the Gray Elite captain whose estate Rosaria had been staying at. The two of them had gotten close during her imprisonment in Moorin. However, with Ezra's fate still unknown, Raven held in the thought.

They had left Moorin in a state of chaos. As the airships had sailed upward through plumes of smoke, Raven saw the destruction of that night. She hadn't forgotten the sight: fires everywhere, smoke trailing into the red, gray, and orange sky. The colossus automaton she had reduced to a pile of molten metal, the remains a speck of white-hot goo on the street.

And everyone had seen her do it too. The Gray Elite would have it out for her now.

Gossip from the city had been less and less. With the Gray Elite on high alert, their spies couldn't get into or out of the city easily, and with the *Orion* flying away from Moorin, they had fewer chances to gather information.

"And you're worried about Zander too," said Rosaria.

Raven didn't have to respond. Everyone knew how worried she was. She had gone to Zander's hospital room every day the past week, sharing meals, explaining all that had happened, and just spending time with him.

"When Zander was ten, he and Baxter and I were playing in one of the parlors," Rosaria began. "Zander climbed one of the bookshelves almost to the ceiling. He fell. Sliced his leg open. He started to cry, but then he saw how worried Baxter and I were, and suddenly he was too tough to cry. He didn't want us to worry about him, so he played it off as no big deal. That is what he is doing now. He knows we're worried about him, and he's trying to be a tough guy so we won't worry. Namely you."

Raven blushed.

Zander's voice resounded in her head with the last words he'd breathed before he'd gone under, *I love you.*

Twice he had said those words to her—when he woke up the first time, and now again before his surgery. She hadn't said the words back to him the first time. She had been too stunned, too relieved to see him awake.

And if he didn't wake up...

"It will be okay," Rosaria said, giving Raven's hand a squeeze.

She desperately wanted to believe Rosaria, but it did not calm the quiver in her gut.

They walked in silence while the storm banged and rolled. Tea long gone, Raven swung the empty cup in her free hand. She was thinking about Luckett and her father when she heard footsteps thudding behind them. She reached for the ebony-handled dagger she had always kept in her boot, which she now kept openly strapped to her middle. Rosaria tensed. Raven closed her hand around the hilt of her dagger and unsheathed it as she twirled to face—

Thalame ran toward them. He stopped just out of dagger distance, bent over on his hands and knees, and gasped for breath. Sweat shimmered on his brow and neck. His white smock was spotted with blood.

Raven's heart and lungs fell into her ankles, yanking her breath with it. "What happened?" she gasped, knuckles turning white.

Thalame waved off her concern. He caught some of his breath and then leaned against the railing. He wore no panic on his face, no fear or worry. "He's fine," he said, voice croaky. "He's awake. He's groggy as hell but awake."

Her heart jumped into her throat, swelling twice its size.

Thalame motioned to the dagger. "Planning on using that?"

"I heard footsteps, and I panicked," Raven admitted. She sheathed the dagger.

"Better prepared than sorry," Thalame said. "I ran up here to tell you that Zander's asking for you, mate."

Raven took off down the Belt.

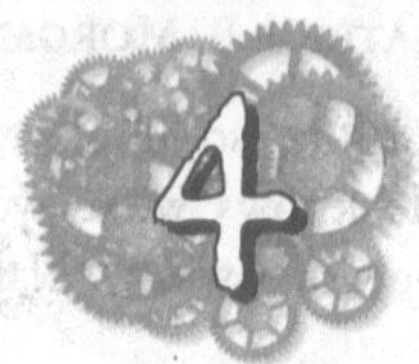

Raven ran. She didn't look back to see if Rosaria or Thalame followed. Zander was awake! By the time she reached the recovery room, her lungs heaved for breath, and a stitch in her side threatened to rip open. Sweat stuck her shirt to her back.

Corin met her at the door. Blood spotted his smock, more than Thalame's. A lot more.

"There you are." He gave her a tired smile. "Come on in."

Raven tried to ball her fists in her skirt, an old nervous habit, but she wore trousers. Instead, she steeled herself, leveled her shoulders, and walked into the recovery room. It smelled like blood, metal, and antiseptic. The mixture churned her stomach. The medics stood on the far side of the room, cleaning the bloodied tools in a wide basin. By the sterile stench, they used more than just soap and water.

Zander had been moved behind a white curtain on the other side of the room. Raven tiptoed closer. He lay on his back amid clean gray linens. His bronze skin had paled with the surgery. A fresh blanket covered everything below his navel, and looking at him like this, she could tell he had lost weight in the past week. His stomach flattened, and the bottoms of his ribs showed. Most of the bandages on his chest were gone. Zander's new left arm lay on a special table beside the bed. It had the shape of a human arm, only instead of skin, it had panels of shined brass and steel, and rather than bones, it had gears and wires. It was jointed at the elbow and wrist to mimic the human range of motion, and complicated little joints made up the five fingers. A salve had been heavily applied where the metal met the skin of his shoulder.

She traced the arm with her eyes several times, then met Zander's stare. His sapphire eyes focused on her, as focused as he could be—a film covered his awareness.

"Your name was the first thing on his lips," said Corin as he stepped around the curtain. He inspected the salve on Zander's shoulder.

Zander didn't look at Corin. He didn't acknowledge that he knew he was there. His eyes remained on Raven.

"The surgery went remarkably well." After applying another layer of the salve, Corin vanished around the curtain.

Raven stepped up to the bedside.

Zander's sleepy eyes searched her, and a lazy smile stretched over his chapped lips. "Hey," he said, his voice dry and weak.

"Hey," she said. The fingers of his limp right hand twitched, and she gently curled her fingers around his. "How are you feeling?"

"Like I'm a floating head." A crease formed between his brows. "I've got legs, right?"

She tilted her head toward his legs. "Yeah, I'm pretty sure that's what those are."

"Are you sure? You might be looking at something else." Zander chuckled, a one-note huff of air through his intoxicated lungs.

Heat rushed to her face, but the retort rolled off her tongue—maybe it came from all the time she'd spent around Conrad in the past week— "No, I'm certain those are your legs. I doubt you're that big."

Zander's sleepy smile widened, and his eyes wore a mischievous glint.

Her face heated more. She cleared her throat, and before he could add to the lewd joke, she nodded toward his mechanical arm. "Does it hurt?"

Zander slowly turned his head toward his left arm. For a long moment, his eyes scanned the metal, his shoulders to his fingers. "It's nice," he said at last. "I can't move right now. Not for a few days, they said. It will take a while for my body to figure out what happened or something like that." He turned back to her and smiled. "The engineer that built this baby said there's a blade hidden in the wrist, a compass in the palm, and a place for bullets in the bicep."

She scanned the metal panels. None seemed like they opened, but she didn't know what to look for. "Convenient," she said. "Does it have a snack compartment?"

Zander studied it a moment longer, an appraising look on his face. Even in the short time since she'd arrived, the glassiness of his eyes had ebbed. "I don't know," he said. "Maybe."

"Are you sure it doesn't hurt? Not even a little?" Raven asked, skeptical of his answer. It looked like it would be painful. Thalame had told her a little of how the procedure worked, attaching nerves and bolting bones and... It gave her a chill to think about.

"No," he said. "They gave me a shot of something after I woke up. I can't feel anything right now. That's why I asked about my legs. I can't see them or feel them."

She looked to his metal fingers. When the shot wore off, would he be in pain?

"Rae?" Zander's brow furrowed.

She blinked, and water smeared across her eyelashes. She quickly wiped at her eyes—she hadn't realized she'd teared up. "I'm fine," she whispered. "I'm glad you're okay."

"Thalame said you were pacing in the hall." Zander ran his thumb along hers.

She nodded. She squeezed his hand. Seeing Zander awake and alive opened something in her chest, something that had been coiled tight far longer than a week. He would live. Everything would be fine.

"What are your plans tomorrow night?" Zander asked, grin tilting to the side.

"I...uh, dinner? Maybe train a bit with Thalame. Why?"

His grin widened. "Want to grab something to eat? Maybe eat together somewhere?"

She blinked. "Like a date?"

"Exactly like a date," he said. "Only you know, there's likely going to be other people around, and it won't be as romantic as one of those hideously uptight and expensive restaurants in the city. It'll be a little more pirate-themed."

"I do have a soft spot for airships," she said, smiling back at him. "And I think I know the perfect place."

His brows rose in question.

"I'm not telling you. You'll have to wait and find out."

His smile widened. "I'm looking forward to it."

With shaky, limp fingers, he brought her hand to his lips. It wasn't the most graceful maneuver, but she blushed all the same.

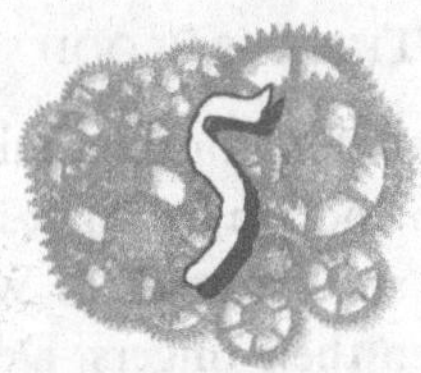

Raven returned to the hospital the next morning to see Zander sitting on the edge of his bed. His mechanical arm hung in a sling, the hand and fingers limp. Zander's eyes found Raven immediately, and his bored face stretched into a grin.

"Come here," he said.

She came to stand at the bedside. Zander motioned to his mechanical pinky—it twitched. He flashed her a triumphant smirk.

"Did you do that?"

He nodded.

"The rest of the arm will take time," Corin said from the other side of the room. He walked over and set a jar of taupe salve beside Zander. "If the skin on your shoulder gets irritated, rub this on it. The skin touching the metal will eventually callus, but until then, there's salve."

"Thanks," Zander said. He took the jar and tucked it into the pocket of his trousers.

"You know," Corin said lightly, "a night of observation might be in your best interest."

Zander glared at the medic. "No. Everything went fine, and I'm sick of this place."

Corin chuckled. "I'm kidding. You're free to go. If you start feeling like something's not right, come back and see us."

"Yeah, yeah." Zander scooted closer to the edge of the bed.

Raven stood on one side and Corin stood on the other. Zander set his socked feet on the floor. He wobbled once, gained his balance, and took the first step toward the hospital doors. A few steps into the corridor, and Thalame appeared at his other side. They walked first to the room Thalame had been staying in, which Zander would now be sharing with him. Raven stood outside while Zander changed and washed—when the boys reappeared, Zander had clean hair, fresh trousers, boots, and a simple shirt with baggy sleeves that hung halfway down his arm.

"I've got some things to take care of," Thalame said, walking down the corridor with a nonchalant wave of his hand. "He's your problem now, Raven."

"Feel better?" Raven asked Zander.

"It's a wonder what a bath does for the soul," he said.

He let out a content sigh and ran his right hand through his loose hair. He held his hand out to her, and she took it. Water from his hair clung to his hand and squished between their fingers. Despite it, a tingle ran up her arm at his touch.

"Would have been better without Thalame waiting on the other side of the shower curtain," he added lowly.

"You'd rather have to figure out how to dress yourself with one arm?" Raven eyed his mechanical fingers. "I suppose I could find you a dress to wear instead."

Zander sighed. "A dress might have been worth not having another man help me put on my pants."

She chuckled and said, "I'm sure Conrad would have helped."

Zander frowned. "No."

Raven wanted to tell him that she would have helped, if only to make him blush, but even the thought of saying the words aloud brought a mild blush to her cheeks. If she were to say them, her face would burn. And Zander might take her up on the offer when he needed to change.

"The others have prepared a little surprise brunch for you," Raven said.

"Thalame may have let it slip," Zander said. "He knows I hate surprises."

She knew too, but it hadn't stopped her. "Just remember to act surprised. I'm supposed to be bringing you."

"Lead the way." Zander glanced down both sides of the corridor. "You know your way around better than I do."

Raven guided him down the corridor at a leisurely pace. Zander hadn't been out of the hospital since they'd boarded the *Orion*, but she had told him all about the ship. In the first few days, it was all she had talked about. Zander hadn't shushed her, letting her go on and on about the corridors and decks and tangled maze of ladders and lifts and catwalks.

Zander paused by one of the portholes. Dark gray clouds whisked by. The worst of the storm had blown away and left streaks of brilliant blue between the straggling clouds. Far, far below, the world stretched on in blurry greens, grays, and blues. In the far distance, mountains rose in shades of purple and grayish blue.

"Is being in a sky city everything you thought it would be?" Zander asked, taking his eyes from the clouds and looking at her.

"It has been so far," Raven said. "I've heard all manner of sky pirate stories from the crew." She frowned. "Except flying through the storm. That was a little lackluster."

"No cloud dragon attacks?"

She blushed. In one of her favorite books—one she had left in Silver Glen—storms were caused by illusive cloud dragons. To fly through a storm could provoke an attack, and only the toughest, bravest, or foolish pirates flew through storms.

"No," she said. "None of those. But I suppose I'd rather not be attacked by ancient magical beasts while hovering miles over the earth."

The sun broke through the clouds, dappling over the lower clouds and dashing them in gold and yellow.

Raven cleared her throat. "I don't know if you have heard," she started.

Zander's brow rose.

"But Captain Luckett is my mother."

Zander's brows shot to his hairline. "What? You're kidding."

She shook her head. "No. My locket used to be her locket." She lifted it from under her blouse. The gold shone in the sunlight. "That's how she knew who I was. Malik saw me with the locket and told her. Luckett won it in a game of dice when she was twelve, a game in which she cheated."

Zander whistled his astonishment.

"And Malik is apparently my half-brother," Raven added.

Zander shook his head in disbelief. "Sisters. I've known Malik since I became a Wraith. He's your brother?"

"What's he like?" Raven slipped the locket back under her blouse. It no longer held the centrum, but wearing it hidden had become habit. She liked feeling the metal against her chest. "I haven't spent much time with him. I...might have been avoiding him and Luckett."

"He's a seeker for the Wraiths." Zander leaned against the rosewood paneling. "That means he can detect magic in others. I didn't think he left Wayward Point. He's the one with connections. He knows people everywhere, has spies all over. He's something like the Wraiths' spymaster."

"Spies?" Raven asked.

"Contacts, friends, pirates, smugglers," Zander explained. "When I was training, he was the one I asked questions. I always thought of him as the one who knew everything, or knew where to find the answer. He's also serious as death, ridiculously smart, quiet, and a bit, uh, sensitive. The opposite of Conrad."

At that, she laughed. "Is being sensitive a bad thing?"

"No," Zander said quickly. He cleared his throat. "Just a thing. But let's get back to the important topic. Luckett is your *mother*? Your mother is a pirate captain?" He laughed. "That explains where you got your stubborn streak and your bizarre interest in airships."

The conversation dwindled. Raven met Zander's eye, and she felt three words rise in her throat. Three words she needed to say.

She swallowed and said instead, "The others will start to wonder what's taking so long."

She tugged him down the corridor, and he didn't object. Those three words jumbled in her throat. The timing didn't feel right. She had never said those three words to anyone other than her father, stepmother, and her half-sister, Lena.

Raven had grown up hearing her father and stepmother reciting those words to each other every day—Raven had grown up with love. She thought she understood it and how it worked, but then Zander had said those words to her. Now, the very concept of love felt like something unreal and impossible. Since those words, every time she thought of Zander, it felt like ribbons tightening on her ribcage.

How could he say those words to her after all the problems she had caused? If it weren't for her, he would still have two arms.

They walked down the corridor and started down the next and the next, and then familiar voices drifted out of the lounge at the end of the corridor. Their friends.

Zander pulled her to a stop. "Raven," he breathed.

"I'm sorry," she blurted, though she had said those two words over and over to him in the past week. Her eyes fell onto his mechanical arm. "I should haven't acted like a child."

"Raven," he said, his voice deep and velvet soft. "It's okay. We're here now, and everything's going to be fine. There's nothing we can do about the past. It's done."

She blinked at him. She motioned to his mechanical arm. "Is this your idea of okay?" she said, her voice high and squeaky. "Moorin all but burned to the ground, and Sisters only know what the Gray Elite think of us now, and then there's the Wraiths, who probably think—"

Zander's lips met hers. His kiss was chaste, just enough to silence her worries.

"It's fine," he breathed, his lips hovering a hair's breadth away from hers. "It's not a perfect situation, but it is what it is. There's nothing we can do to change what happened. We deal with it. We move on. We punch through walls with our new metal arm."

She frowned. "Is that your plan?"

"It's one of my plans." He smirked, hooking his right arm around her waist. He couldn't pull her too close with his metal arm in a sling. "But we will be okay. I won't push you away again. It's obvious that you don't need me to protect you anymore."

She sought solace in his eyes and found it. Steadiness. Forgiveness. "I did save your ass this time," she whispered.

His smile returned, wider than before. Something in her chest broke apart at the sight, broke into a thousand pieces of white-hot ooze.

Rosaria's voice fluted through the corridor, followed by Thalame's. Zander and Raven both jumped. His metal arm jostled. They stepped apart just as the door to the lounge opened and Thalame stepped out. He had words on his tongue, then spotted Zander and Raven.

"Don't tell me you broke it already, mate," Thalame said, grinning.

Zander blinked and looked at his limp left arm. "I have to be able to use it in order to break it," he quipped.

Rosaria and Conrad stuck their heads out of the doorway.

"There you are," Rosaria said, giving them a cheerful wave.

Sensing the moment gone, Raven pulled Zander to the lounge. Rosaria patted the couch she sat on, and Raven and Zander joined her. The others had gathered for tea, cookies, and sandwiches. Like the rest of the upper deck, the lounge had rosewood and brass paneling, hardwood floors, and brassy glass globes shining with yellowish light. The rosewood furniture had been bolted to the floor and angled around a large coffee table.

It had been a while since they had gathered in one place without planning or scheming. The change of pace was nice.

"Look who's up and walking," Rosaria said to Zander.

"Give me a week," Zander said.

"And you'll be jogging?" Raven asked.

Zander shrugged and accepted a cup of tea from Rosaria. "What have I missed?"

They took turns telling Zander stories from the past week on the ship and what news they managed to get from Moorin and Lenhala. The Crusaders were mostly pirates and smugglers, but the Wraiths had spies all over the continent. They didn't have solid news. They could only speculate on the movements of the Gray Elite since the dramatic retrieval and subsequent escape—as Conrad called it.

"It's not every day the most wanted person in the empire flies away while the Gray Elite are scratching their heads," Conrad said, winking at Raven.

Conrad's version of that night sounded more like a fantastic adventure, full of whizzing rockets, bursts of colored sparks, and purring airships. Due to his injury, Zander had missed that part. Raven had been mostly out of it, but as Conrad told the story of that night, she started to doubt whether they had experienced the same night. She didn't ask; Conrad's version of the night made her sound dangerous and exciting, as if she had cleverly planned her escape and remained a step ahead of the Gray Elite.

"We've got the entire city talking about us," Conrad said, grinning wide. He leaned forward and plucked a cookie from the tray. "The girl who melted an automaton already has bards composing songs of her outlaw life and pirate associates. Some say she could swoop down at any time and set the world on fire."

"Swooping makes it sound..." Raven hummed her disapproval.

"They've also upped your bounty," added Thalame. He tipped his tea to Raven. "That makes you twice the wanted girl you were. They've thrown Zander and me into the heat too." He glanced at Conrad, who awaited Thalame's next words eagerly. "Turns out, Conrad here already had one on his head."

Conrad didn't look surprised. "Piracy does have its drawbacks."

"I've sent word to the treehouse," Thalame said to Zander. "Ivy will've heard about the mess by now, and I don't want them thinking we're dead."

Raven tapped the side of her teacup. She hadn't seen Ivy in what felt like forever—she had so much to tell her. Ivy maintained a healthy chain of spies for the Dwellers—freedom fighters who lived in the forest of Rhynwier. Thalame was a Dweller too, and he would know how to get word to her.

"Here's the next question." Thalame bent forward, shoulders hunched. He looked ready to pounce. "Do we use the Gray Elite's confusion to rest up and plan our next move, or do we use their confusion against them and use this time to hit them again while they're weak?"

"Trouble is, we're weak right now too." Conrad tipped his half-eaten cookie toward Zander. "As much as I'd love to march in and kick the dragon while it's down, I think the more intelligent move would be to wait."

Zander glanced down at his mechanical hand. A shadow passed over his face.

Raven raised her brows at Conrad. "That sounds like a reasonable decision." She put a hand to her heart in pretend worry. "Are you feeling all right?"

"It could be the thin air up here." Zander tore his eyes from his hand and looked clinically at Conrad. "I've heard it does strange things to the head."

Conrad grinned wider. "Then, we're all snorting the thin air."

Zander laughed and opened his mouth to speak—a series of bells pierced the air. An alarm. The bells started somewhere in the belly of the ship and rang through the speaking tubes that traveled to every room and office and mechanical closet.

Since their escape, Raven had heard a dozen different bells. A bell for dinner. A bell for incoming weather. A bell to signal the start or stop of an engine. A bell to signal the need for a medic, and another bell to signal where the need is. A bell to signal the officers to the captain's office. But these bells hadn't yet rang through the ship.

"What does that one mean?" Raven asked.

Conrad stood. All humor faded from his face. "An enemy ship is approaching."

Raven, Zander, Rosaria, and Thalame followed Conrad through the *Orion* and toward the air docks tucked underneath the ship. The rosewood and brass of the upper decks became the oak and steel of the lower decks, and then they came to a wide set of iron double doors. Wind whistled through the seams. Conrad pulled the crank, and the heavy doors opened.

At once, chilled wind rushed up to meet them, a residual beat of the storm. The doors opened onto a sturdy mezzanine of thick steel that circled the perimeter of the air docks. Steel walkways, held aloft by thick cables and rigging from the roof of the air docks, connected the mezzanine to the maze of the air docks—hundreds of narrow catwalks, rope bridges, and ladders connected the leveled berths.

Hundreds of air ships docked, varying in size and function. Some were small and painted sky blue, others were thick and equipped with multiple guns, and some were large and windowless. The air docks gave off a gentle rumble, a mixture of the wind, engines, and commotion of the docks themselves—from the engineers and mechanics in varying states of repairing and cleaning, and from the constant creaking of the rigging.

They weren't the only ones that had come to see the incoming ship; it seemed most of the free crew had come.

Conrad navigated through the air docks, and the others followed. Raven tried to copy his fearless posture, but the view left a wobbly feeling in her stomach. The clouds formed a floor far below them, but she knew her body would fall right through. The steel railing only helped a little. Zander's presence behind her helped a little too.

A strong wind blew into the docks, rattling the rigging and shaking the catwalk. Raven gasped and grabbed both sides of the railing. The wind passed, and the catwalk stilled. Raven's heart continued to pound.

"It's okay," Zander said in her ear. He held onto the railing too.

Raven blew out a breath—Conrad hadn't hesitated, and she jogged the several steps the wind had cost her.

"We've got procedures in place in case of a man overboard." Conrad glanced over his shoulder at her. "Don't worry, little bird. If you fall, we'll dive to catch you."

"And then we'll both be falling."

Conrad waved off her concern. "For a little while, but then we will be back on the ship."

"But—"

"We've got pilots standing by at all hours, waiting for deployment," Conrad explained. "See those ships over there?" He pointed to the small single-passenger ship painted sky blue. "They're the nimblest machines in the air. If you jumped right now, they'd catch you before you hit the clouds."

"And you know this for certain?" Raven asked.

"I am one hundred percent certain." Conrad paused at the uneven intersection of three catwalks and leaned against the railing. "I've both fallen and piloted to save someone from falling." He winked. "Yes, it is terrifying. For both parties. A little more so for the pilot."

Raven blinked at him. "Saving someone is more terrifying than falling to your death?"

"Yes." Conrad nodded. "When you are falling, it is your life you are going to lose, and the feeling of falling is a bit exhilarating. But when you are diving to save someone from falling, it is someone else's life you stand to lose. When you are the one who is going to die, you won't have to live with the guilt of failing."

"Oh. I hadn't thought of it like that." She looked down at the clouds. She had trouble envisioning it.

"I understand." Zander glanced at Raven, guilt darkening his face. "Saving someone else is more stressful than being the one who needs saving."

She frowned. He was clearly talking about her. She started to say something, but her words fell short. Being trapped in an automaton's chest had been stressful; being thrown into the *Chjelhu Tal* and fighting for her life had been stressful; not knowing if the fever would burn her alive in the night had been stressful; but witnessing the colossus strike Zander had been worse. Standing outside the surgery room, knowing she could do nothing, had been worse.

Had he felt the same panic when she had vanished from the treehouse? She met his eyes and saw a ghost of that panic, the worry.

She started to apologize again, but Conrad interrupted, "See?" Snapping his wrist toward Zander, he winked at Raven. "You just need more experience saving Zander."

Zander frowned, and Raven offered Conrad a laugh.

"I'd rather not be either," Raven admitted.

Zander nodded. "As would I."

More Crusaders made their way into the air docks. Even with all the extra bodies and footsteps, the catwalks barely swayed. Crusaders lounged on the rope bridges, looking comfortable standing so far above the ground with so little keeping them from falling.

"What's happening?" Raven whispered to Conrad.

"I don't know," Conrad whispered back. In a normal tone, he added, "The alarm signaled an enemy ship approaching, yet no further signal has come. The enemy ship has not yet posed an obvious threat."

"We're just waiting to see what happens?" Zander asked.

"Oh, don't you worry." Conrad grinned at Zander. "You can bet there are at least three Vultures circling, ready to take down the enemy ship." He motioned to where vicious-looking airships rested—spiked and painted black and red, made for offense.

Over the whistle of the wind, the buzzing of an airship sounded. The chatter around the air dock silenced, and more than a few Crusaders drew pistols. Many on the lower walkways held daggers and short swords—ready for a fight. Raven felt oddly unprepared, but then she remembered her magic. She would never be without a weapon or unprepared for a fight again. That knowledge settled her rattling nerves.

The heavy iron doors to the *Orion* opened, and Malik hurried into the air docks. Despite his quickened steps, he moved like a prince about to greet a visitor, but with the caution of a lion stalking prey. The Crusaders parted to let him pass. As the captain's son and a seeker for the Wraiths, he warranted their silent respect.

Malik hurried onto the catwalk on which they stood. As he passed Zander, he said, "Follow me."

Zander didn't hesitate. His gaze turned predatory, and he followed Malik toward an empty berth. Conrad grabbed Raven's hand, and they fell into step behind them. Malik didn't acknowledge them. Rosaria and Thalame remained on the catwalk.

"What news?" Zander asked Malik.

"It's a Gray Elite Buzzer," Malik said quickly, lowly. "Its pilot has asked permission to dock. He says he's got magicians on board seeking asylum and that he's been shot."

Raven tensed; beside her, Conrad did the same.

"What's the plan?" Conrad asked.

"Captain's given permission to dock." Malik cast a glance around the docks at all the crew armed and ready. "And she's given permission to shoot at the first sign of trouble."

Conrad sighed. "I love when she gives the shoot-first order. Makes life easier."

"We're not shooting first," Malik corrected. He gave Conrad a stern glare. "We're asking questions first, and depending on the answers, we shoot second."

They turned onto a downward angled catwalk toward the empty berth, and as they turned onto another, Raven glimpsed steel at Malik's waist. A pistol.

The buzzing grew louder. From below the *Orion*, an airship of white steel appeared through the clouds. It didn't fly as smooth as the others—gunfire had peppered its starboard side, and the front window had been cracked. As it came into the berth, it swayed, and its engines sputtered. Malik stood stone still as the air dock crew rushed to tie the ship off and hook it into the rigging. Crusaders moved into position, pistols and crossbows aimed at every side of the Gray Elite ship.

Malik stood in clear view of the door, stoic as a king greeting his enemy. Raven tried to stand like him. If they shared half of their blood, could she muster that same regal grace? Or had he inherited it from his father?

The airship's engine died, and the door opened with a hiss. Crusaders stood firm. A gangplank shifted into position, and a young man stepped out of the ship with his empty hands stretched in front of him. Blood spotted his shirt and trousers—the wound on his shoulder still bled.

"Don't shoot," he said, voice hoarse. Behind him, several other faces appeared. None were armed, all were wide-eyed and afraid. They wore dirty, tattered clothes of refugees. One small girl hugged the waist of an older girl, tears glistening in her eyes.

Malik stepped forward. "You're a magician." It wasn't a question.

Raven understood then why Malik had hurried to greet the ship. As a seeker, he could sense the magic in other people. She glanced sideways at Conrad, who had the same ability. He too, was staring into the ship with an intensity she'd come to recognize as his seeker abilities at work.

The young man nodded. "Yes."

"You seek asylum from the Gray Elite?"

"Yes, please, sir."

Malik looked the man over. He glanced once at Conrad—something passed between them, an agreement. Malik looked back to the young man. "Exit the ship," he said. "My friends here will escort you to a safe place."

"Thank you," he breathed as he limped down the gangplank.

The young man was not the only one wounded. Most others had cuts and bruises and poorly wrapped wounds. They carefully exited the ship one at a time, under the watchful eyes of the Crusaders, none of whom had lowered their weapons.

"What in Minerva's name happened?" Conrad asked, his tone not as serious as Malik's. Malik glared at him, but Conrad pretended not to notice.

"We were attacked when we tried to escape," said another of the magicians, who wore a bandage around his head and his right eye. The bandage looked to have once been part of a shirt.

"The pilot's been shot," said one of the magicians, pointing toward the cockpit.

As the magicians crossed onto the docks, the first young man started back in for the pilot, but Malik put a hand to his shoulder.

"We will get him," Malik said.

The magician didn't argue. A handful of Crusaders escorted him and the others up the catwalks and into the lower deck of the *Orion*.

After all the magicians had disembarked, Conrad walked up the gangplank and into the ship. Malik stood by the gangplank, watching his every move. Conrad turned toward the cockpit, hand on a dagger. He vanished from sight. Raven stood close enough to Malik to hear his sharp intake of breath.

"Well, I'll be damned." Conrad's voice echoed off the steel insides of the airship, a laugh on his words.

"Conrad," Malik said, a warning.

Conrad stepped back into view, a second person leaning heavily on his shoulders. The young man had indeed been shot. Blood had soaked through the left breast of his Gray Elite uniform. His blond hair was dirty and specked with blood, the knees of his pants torn, and his head hung. He looked ready to collapse.

"Looks like we've got ourselves a defector," Conrad said as he and the officer started down the gangplank.

"Or a spy," said someone behind Raven.

They made it to the docks, and a team of Crusaders made their way into the airship. The officer gasped and looked up, and Raven felt her breath leave her throat the same time Zander's did.

It was Ezra Deacon.

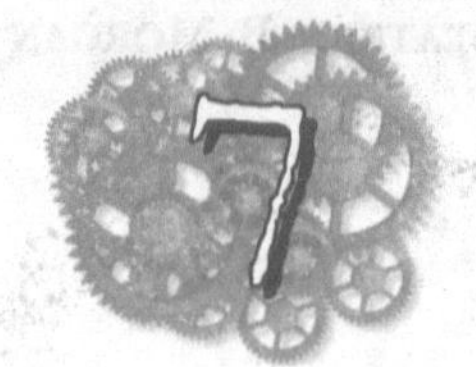

Raven couldn't believe her eyes. Ezra Deacon had defected? Rosaria, a catwalk above them, let out a fearsome shout—her voice silenced the muttering of *spy* and *defector* and *throw him overboard*. Rosaria started down the catwalk—the Crusaders parted for her. She marched, fearsome as a queen, determined as a general.

Halfway to Conrad, she shouted, "Ezra!"

At the sound of his name on her voice, he looked up. Ezra's bleary eyes sought her through the crowd, but he couldn't focus. Rosaria grabbed his face in her hands and forced his gaze to hers.

"Ezra?" Rosaria asked, her voice softer than it had been a moment before. "You're okay?"

He tried to give Rosaria a smile. With every passing moment, he looked closer to fainting. His peachy skin had faded to a frightening white, his hands shook, and his breath shuddered.

"Define *okay*," Conrad said. "Considering there is a bullet lodged somewhere in his chest, I'm not sure he would agree with you. I certainly don't."

Rosaria paled.

"Get out of the way," came Thalame's sandpaper voice. He shouldered his way down the catwalk and pressed his hand against Ezra's bleeding chest. Ezra didn't seem to register his presence. "Yup, bullet wound. Didn't hit anything vital, but he's lost an unhealthy amount of blood."

"And he still managed to pilot a Buzzer," said Conrad.

Ezra mumbled something too low for Raven to hear—Conrad chuckled.

"Boy's got a point," Conrad said. "Either fix him up or throw him overboard. End his suffering."

Mumbles surfaced on the surrounding catwalks. Several murmured to throw him overboard. Raven's heart hammered, and Rosaria frowned. Luckily, those who knew Ezra stood closest to him.

"Take him to the hospital," Rosaria ordered. The sound of her voice silenced the mumbling. "At once!"

"You want to take in this traitor?" came a pirate's objection.

Rosaria whipped her head around to see the pirate who'd spoken. "Yes," she said, any indication of doubt or fear gone from her voice. A queen spoke, not a dethroned princess.

All eyes in the air dock looked to her, and Raven felt a warm jealousy for Rosaria—she would have crumbled under all the stares. Her knees felt weak just standing this close to the center of attention.

Rosaria continued, "This young man is no traitor to us, but to the Gray Elite. Because of him, hundreds of magicians have escaped execution and imprisonment at the hands of the empire. Because of this young man, I am standing here." She turned her head to Conrad, her shoulders straight, her spine rigid, her chin up. "Take him to the hospital, and make sure his injuries are tended to."

"Yes, Your Majesty," said Conrad with a graceful dip of his head. His coal eyes glittered. He had said her title a little louder than he normally would have, to remind those around them who she was and who she would become.

Conrad and Thalame hoisted Ezra between them and started up the catwalks. Rosaria walked behind them, determination unmistakable on her face. Raven and Zander backed into the railing to let them pass, and Ezra's glossy eyes glanced up—his eyes met Zander's. Confusion, relief, and surprise passed over his pained expression, and the same mirrored on Zander's. As the procession passed, Zander and Raven fell into step behind the princess.

When they passed through the doors and into the lower deck, Zander whispered to Raven, "What just happened? What don't I know?"

"Ezra's been helping magicians escape the Gray Elite for years," Raven whispered back. "He smuggles them out."

Zander's surprise lifted his eyebrows nearly to his hairline. "He's done what?"

"He's been working alongside several turncoats within the Gray Elite ranks as well as a few smugglers and pirates," Conrad added.

Ezra grunted unintelligibly.

"We'll get more answers out of him when he's not dying," Thalame said pointedly.

The walk to the hospital seemed longer than it should have, and once again, Raven waited in the corridor. This time, however, Zander and Conrad waited with her. Thalame had gone into the surgery with Ezra. Rosaria paced in front of the closed surgery doors.

"I didn't realize how stressful it is to be locked outside and waiting," Rosaria said, her voice small and rushed. She stared at the floor as she paced, fingers fidgeting with the end of her braid. "I apologize for not being well prepared to handle it."

"You did just fine." Raven grabbed Rosaria's hands and pulled her to a stop, forcing the princess to meet her gaze. "Ezra has a gunshot wound, and Thalame had a decent meal earlier. He'll be fine."

"It's not like he's missing a limb," Conrad quipped.

Raven glared at him over her shoulder.

"This whole time," Zander said, hand to his temple, "Ezra has been helping magicians?"

"Yes," Conrad, Rosaria, and Raven said together.

Zander sighed, the information not fully wrapping around his mind. "I didn't know," he mumbled. "I could have helped him. We could have helped each other."

"He suspected you were a Hawk, but he didn't know you were a Wraith," Raven told him. "As far as either of you knew, you were on opposite sides."

"When in reality, they were on the same side." Conrad's smile turned up. "Funny how these things happen."

Malik came through the doors of the ward where the magicians had been taken, wearing his usual frown. The bangles on his left wrist clinked as he shut the door behind him.

"Anyone die on the way up?" Conrad asked lightly.

Malik's frown deepened, and he let out a quick, agitated sigh.

Raven, standing between Malik and Conrad, noted the glance that lingered between them, unspoken and unreadable. She had the worst feeling of having intruded on something private.

"According to the magicians' story," Malik started, "Ezra Deacon was planning their escape when the Gray Elite raided the safehouse where they were hiding. They barely made it out. Originally, Ezra was supposed to merely see them off, not to go with them, but those plans changed when the Gray Elite opened fire."

"They're all magicians?" Zander asked.

Malik nodded. "Every one. I've placed them under care for now. When they have rested, I will speak to them again. They also bring disturbing gossip that the Gray Elite have been shipping magicians south rather than executing them, though there are no records of this."

"The Gray Elite are saying they're executing magicians, but they're sending them south instead," Zander said grimly. "That sounds bad."

"South, as in...?" Conrad let his words trail off and waved his hand through the air.

Malik met Conrad's stare. "South, as in the magicians didn't know exactly. Somewhere in Tinatun. A few of the refugees claim to have overheard Gray Elite whispering about shipping magicians south."

"Why ship them south to kill them?" A fearsome chord struck Raven's chest. . "Unless...they aren't killing them. Could they be hiding them somewhere?"

"It's hard to tell," Malik said. "Those who go south never return."

"Magic isn't common in Tinatun," Conrad added. "The farther south you go, the rarer it is. Some of the far southern islands think magic is a myth."

"Then why...?" Zander rubbed his face with his good hand. "It doesn't make sense. We need more information."

"I agree," Malik said. "It doesn't make sense, but it doesn't matter. Whatever the Gray Elite are doing, the Wraiths will protect magicians. It's our sacred duty as Wraiths."

Conrad and Zander nodded in agreement, none too enthused.

Footsteps approached, and the surgery door opened. Thalame leaned out. His skin had paled with the use of his healing magic—he must have done more to Ezra than he had to Zander.

"He's awake and talking," Thalame said, his rough voice reflecting his exhaustion.

Rosaria didn't wait for permission; she rushed in first. Malik calmly followed.

Conrad meandered to the door and leaned to whisper to Raven, "This is going to be interesting."

The recovery room hadn't been designed for so many visitors, and Raven stood with her arm flush against Zander's. Ezra was sitting up in the hospital bed, bandages wrapped around his bare torso. Rosaria claimed her seat at the bedside and took Ezra's hand in both of hers. As Malik came around the other side of the bed, she held his hand tighter.

"He's not done anything wrong," Rosaria said to Malik.

Malik met her regal gaze with his own, his expression hidden behind a stoic mask. A beat passed between them. "I understand your concern," Malik said to the princess, every word careful, elegant, and vicious. "But I reminded you: you are not my princess. Your commands mean nothing to me or the majority of this crew."

Rosaria glared; Malik glared back.

Conrad leaned closer to Raven and mumbled loud enough to everyone to hear, "Pirates."

Malik broke his glare with the princess to glare at Conrad, who then winked.

"Ezra," interrupted Zander, who grasped the railing at the foot of the hospital bed. "What the hell happened?"

Ezra exhaled, the breath stable but stalled. "I could ask the same of you," he said, his words hesitant. He pointed toward Zander's mechanical arm.

"You first," said Zander.

"Fair enough." Ezra nodded. "I went to prepare another shuttle of magicians out of the city. Since your escape" —he glanced at Raven— "the Gray Elite have been in a frenzy. There have been several rebellions, not just in Moorin but in Lenhala, of magicians and magic-sympathizers. The Gray Elite ordered a block-by-block search for magicians. I tried to get them out before they were found, but...my father found out. I don't know how. Someone on the house staff, I think. Father tried to keep me from leaving, and that's when I knew something was wrong. I managed to get away, but as they were loading into the airship, Gray Elite stormed the safehouse. They opened fire. The pilot panicked and ran, and I took his place. I was shot in the process. After getting through the clouds, it was smooth sailing."

"I was expecting a shootout with the Gray Elite," Conrad added. "A bit more drama."

Ezra shook his head. "But my father will know that I've defected," he said, glumness overcoming his face.

"You turned traitor years ago," Conrad reminded Ezra. "This just means you're officially one of us. Wanted outlaws—saving magicians and making sure the Gray Elite stay on their collective toes."

Ezra's eyes fell on Zander's new arm, and a crease formed between his brows. "I'm not sure that's a comfort right now."

"Oh, this?" Zander twitched the little finger of his new arm. "I got this because that Colossus of yours nearly sliced my arm off."

Ezra winced. "It wasn't my Colossus," he said darkly. He glanced to the trashcan where his bloodied Gray Elite uniform had been thrown. A yellow striped sleeve hung over the edge, spotted with red. "I'm not Gray Elite anymore."

"Ah, the gloomy look of one recently thrown into the outcasts," Conrad said with a dramatic sigh. "I remember those gloomy days. Don't worry, it goes away with time and a few strong drinks."

Ezra offered Conrad a smile. "Good to know." His gaze shifted to Raven, then Zander. His smile faded. "There is something else. Something I overheard my father say. I didn't think I'd get the chance to tell you, but I guess the Sisters had other ideas."

"What?" Zander and Raven said together.

"My father," Ezra started, "he's planning—"

The doors burst open, and Captain Luckett stormed into the room. She wore her pristine crimson coat with black cuffs and brass buttons, a white blouse, and a black corset with golden strings. Her tricorn hat perched to the side. She had clearly dressed to impress. She marched into the room, fierce light brown eyes pinned on Ezra. She stopped beside Malik and looked down at Ezra like something rotten.

"This is Deacon's brat?" Luckett demanded.

Ezra reddened. "That would be me, ma'am."

Luckett blinked, then let out a bark of a laugh. "Ma'am," she repeated. Her smile vanished. "It's *Captain*, boy."

"Yes, Captain," Ezra said without hesitation.

"I see he's got that Gray Elite etiquette," Luckett said. "A bit refreshing after dealing with pirates and their attitudes." Her glare passed over Conrad, who looked sheepishly behind him. Finding no one, he turned back around, surprised, and pointed to himself. Luckett ignored him and returned her stare to Ezra. "What's the urgency, boy?"

"My father is planning something, an assault." Ezra looked again at Raven. "He knows now that you were in Moorin. Everyone knows about the Colossus you turned into molten metal."

Raven bit her lip. She'd been worrying about that. Would Deacon put the pieces together himself? She glanced sideways at Zander. He wore the same worry in his eyes.

"Something went wrong," Ezra said, a crease between his eyes. "I-I don't know what, he flew in from Lenhala a few days ago in a strange calm. He didn't seem upset by the Colossus, he seemed...fascinated. The emperor is calling the attack on Moorin an act of war by Rhynwierian rebels."

A stone fell into Raven's stomach.

"I overheard my father talking in his study. They are planning retaliation in the north," Ezra continued, "but I don't know exactly where.

One of the servants came up the stairs, and I couldn't listen in without being seen."

Ezra continued to talk, but Raven had stopped listening. Her skin went cold, the floor wobbled beneath her feet, and she latched onto Zander's arm to keep from tumbling over.

"Retaliation in the north," she breathed, halting whatever Ezra had been saying. She met Ezra's gaze.

Understanding widened Zander's eyes.

Words tumbled from Raven's lips. "Could he be talking about Silver Glen?"

"Full steam ahead," Captain Luckett bellowed into the speaking tubes tucked into the corner of her office.

"Aye, Captain!" came the response.

A heartbeat later, the engines roared, and the *Orion* pushed faster through the clouds. Raven stood in front of the window that overlooked the bridge. Clouds rushed by the bow, fluffy white and wispy gray. The storm had moved on, a bubbling mass of purple clouds in the distance. The crew worked in seamless harmony; the pilot steered from his raised seat, the navigator pinned a map of northern Rhynwier to her wall, and the engineer sat on the other side, watching gauges and dials and levels of power that Raven didn't understand.

Raven had gone with Luckett to the bridge. Thalame and Zander had gone to see a mechanic about Zander's arm—something about a checkup. Thalame implied the mechanics expected the arm to have broken somehow in the first few hours, and Raven had chuckled at Zander's frown.

"We'll be in Silver Glen by tomorrow evening," Luckett said. "Luckily, we've been heading north anyway. If the weather holds, we might make it there by tomorrow afternoon."

Raven's stomach trembled. If the Gray Elite attacked Silver Glen... The little village wouldn't stand a chance. They had little defense aside from old pistols and a few hobbled-together crossbows. All the people she'd grown up with, her father, stepmother, Lena... She didn't want to think about what might happen to them if the Gray Elite attacked.

Raven jumped when a hand touched her shoulder. Luckett stood beside her—in their translucent reflections in the window, their similarities showed. They had the same eyes and heart-shaped face. The weight of her mother's hand felt strange and sudden, intrusive but oddly comforting.

"Don't worry," Luckett said in that motherly tone she used when she spoke to Raven, softer than her captain's bark but not as soft as Raven's stepmother's voice. "The Gray Elite might have some powerful ships, but none can outpower the *Orion*."

"I will take your word for it," Raven said.

They stood a while in silence, or in as much silence as the bridge allowed. The wind whistled against the window, the engines rumbled, and the maddening networks of pipes and speaking tubes hummed, hissed, and clanked—the airship continually thrummed.

It felt strange to stand here with her mother, as if this is what Raven should have been doing her entire life. Is this how things would have been if Raven had been raised on the *Orion*?

"What are you thinking about?" asked Luckett.

"What would be different about me if I had been raised here with you rather than in Silver Glen with my father," Raven said plainly.

Luckett hesitated. The hand on her shoulder twitched. Raven turned toward her, expecting her words to have found a sensitive mark, but Luckett didn't look at all aghast by the question. If anything, she looked curious.

"Hmm," Luckett hummed. "I wouldn't have kept you up here as a child. The *Orion* isn't child-safe, and small children would just get in the way."

Raven blinked. "What? You would have left me anyway?"

That struck something in Luckett, and for a brief moment, her eyes softened. It vanished as fast as a lightning strike. "You would have been under better care in Wayward Point," she said. "That's where Malik stayed until he could take orders and take care of himself. He was nine when I allowed him on the *Orion*, and even then, I had him working with others.

"Nine?" Raven hadn't been a very cautious nine-year-old. She had been in constant trouble with her father for skipping chores or sleeping during lessons or wandering into parts of the mine without worry of falling down lost shafts or getting lost.

"Malik has always been a very serious boy, and he took orders to heart. Never joked or tried funny business. Not until he met that Conrad." Luckett made a disapproving sound.

"You don't like Conrad?" Raven prepared to defend him; she had grown fond of him.

"Oh, don't get me wrong," Luckett said quickly, "the boy is a great pirate and an asset to the Crusaders. He's intelligent and clever, and he's got a mind for the seas, but..." Luckett inhaled, pulling whatever words she had to say back in.

"...but what?" Raven asked.

Luckett looked at Raven with many unsaid things behind her eyes.

Raven had her own suspicions about what those things were. "They had something, didn't they? Between them."

Luckett sighed, and her shoulders slumped. "They did," she admitted. "Malik told me about it." She chuckled halfheartedly. "I used to worry about Malik bringing back these airheaded floozies who couldn't string a sentence together. Instead, he comes back with that scoundrel. I'm afraid he got that from me. I never had good taste in men. Until your father, of course. The best man I've ever met, even if we didn't get along. Had a good heart and a good head. I just hope you got some of that. My list of good qualities isn't very long."

"You changed the subject," Raven said. Not that she had minded the compliment.

Luckett's brows rose. She looked at Raven, a beat passed, and then she let out a sigh. "Caught me," she said. "You're not as easy to distract as these pirates. A few compliments go a long way."

"Don't try it twice." Raven frowned.

Luckett chuckled; then her face became serious. "Fine, though I don't know how much of it is mine to tell. Conrad has a heart that belongs to the sea and to himself, and he broke Malik's more than once. I've told him to move on, but that's easier said than done. And I know how—"

The office door opened, and Malik strolled inside. At the sudden silence, he stilled, looking between his mother and his half-sister. His straight-line mouth fell into a frown. "What?"

For a long moment, neither of them spoke. Malik's frown deepened.

"How's Ezra?" Raven asked.

"Better." He came to stand beside Raven at the window. He stood straight, shoulders back and feet firmly planted. He crossed his arms over his narrow chest, and the daylight glinted off his rings.

There, standing between Luckett and Malik at the window, seeing their reflections side by side, Raven spotted the similarities. They all shared a nose.

Raven took a step back, eager to leave the awkwardness. "Well... If there isn't anything else, I should be going. I promised Zander we'd have lunch," she lied.

Luckett laughed. "I think you got that from me too."

"Got what?" Malik asked.

"A horrible taste in men," Luckett said plainly.

Malik's frown deepened. "You *were* talking about me!"

Luckett shrugged.

Malik's entire face turned a shade of pink. "Mother!"

"What? She's your sister," Luckett said dismissively, and Malik glanced at Raven.

She felt her own face redden.

"It's not like she'll think any less of you for having piss-poor tastes. If anything, I think she'd understand."

Raven let herself out of the office and hurried down the corridor before Luckett could embarrass either one of them again, though she couldn't help the smile that stretched across her face.

A corridor below, Raven nearly walked into Rosaria. The princess carried a tray of tea and cookies—for two.

"I thought Ezra could use a pick-me-up," Rosaria explained.

"Like a date?" Raven asked.

Rosaria didn't blush. Instead, she considered it. "No, I'd rather save dating for more romantic settings, like beaches or ballrooms or rose gardens. This is simply lunch. What about you? Any lunch plans?"

By the way she said lunch, Raven knew she meant dates.

"No," Raven said. "But I'm going to see what Thalame and Zander are doing. They went to see a mechanic."

The girls walked together until they could no longer. Rosaria headed toward the hospital, and Raven headed toward Zander and Thalame's shared room. She knocked on the rosewood door—inscribed with the symbol of a lizard—and on a verbal note of approval, she let herself in. The two boys sat in the little seating area, examining Zander's metal fingers. His arm rested on the table between them. His little finger moved a fraction farther than it had that morning.

Raven sat on the couch beside Zander. "Does it hurt?"

"I wouldn't say it hurts," Zander said thoughtfully. "It feels more like it's numb. You know when you sleep on your arm and it's numb when you wake up? The feeling is slowly coming back with pins and needles and this strange... I don't know how to explain it."

"Give it your best shot, mate," said Thalame.

Zander inhaled. "It feels like my arm is made of metal."

Raven and Thalame glanced at each other. After a beat, Raven said, "It is."

"I'm aware. I told you I didn't know how to explain it." Zander touched the little metal finger. "I can *feel* the metal, like it's a part of me."

"Magic works in its own way," said Thalame.

"Magic?"

"Magicians have a better time adapting to mechanical limbs than anyone else," he explained. "I'm sure someone could have explained it perfectly about two hundred years ago."

Before the Gray Elite began their purge of magic and magicians. Raven sighed and looked down at the little finger of Zander's mechanical arm. How much knowledge of magic had they lost? How much would they be able to retrieve? The entire task felt impossible in a way that nothing else had.

"Speaking of magic," —Thalame leaned forward— "how is yours coming along, Raven?"

"Fine," she said. Thalame held his piercing gaze on her. Zander took his eyes off his hand and looked at her. "Why?"

"You're pale," Thalame said. "If I were to put my hand against your cheek, would you feel warm?"

She put her hands to her cheeks. Indeed she felt warm, but she didn't know if it was due to the magic or Luckett's embarrassing remarks.

Zander and Thalame both gave her curious, knowing looks.

"I might not have gone to the Belt this morning," Raven admitted. Thalame frowned, started to speak, and Raven quickly motioned to Zander. "I was busy, and then Ezra showed up, and now we're rushing to Silver Glen to save it from unknown destruction. I haven't had time."

She could feel the fever worming its way through her skin.

"Well," Zander said, standing, "we've got time before we get there. Come on, show me what you can do."

Thalame stood. "Oh, it's a sight."

Raven felt a pitting of excitement and dread. She had the feeling of having been ganged up on, but she stood and slid her hand into Zander's outstretched hand, and the three of them started toward the Belt.

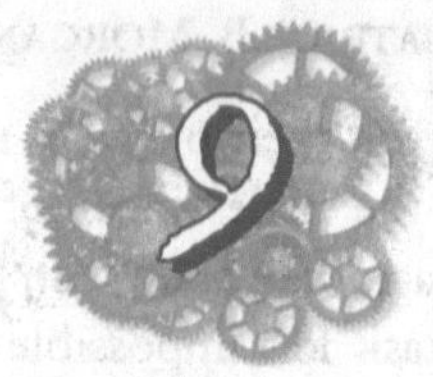

On the Belt, Thalame and Zander stood back while Raven summoned her magic—it burst from her palm in a bright yellow flame. As the flame burned, the bright yellow faded into red-orange, and the intensity of her fever diminished. The breeze whisked the top of the flame, curling it.

This high, the breeze felt cool, not the balmy breeze of summer as it would have on the world below.

"Will it always be like this?" she asked.

"Can't say," Thalame said, shrugging. "Normal magic doesn't build up like yours, at least not that I know of. And your magic is far from normal."

Zander appeared at her side. The red-orange flame reflected in his sapphire eyes and glinted off his arm. "This is what nearly killed you?" he asked, his voice soft but lined with guilt.

The flame sputtered.

Zander opened his mouth but closed it again. He looked at the flame in her hand, brows furrowed, eyes unreadable.

"It wasn't that bad," Raven said.

"Conrad told me how he had to paint the rune on your skin to keep the magic from eating you alive." Zander lifted his eyes from the flame and met hers. He wore no arrogant smirk.

She knew he would see through any lie, so she didn't bother to. "There were moments when I thought I was going to die," she said.

Zander flinched at those words.

"There were times when I didn't think I would wake up. I thought I would burn alive in my sleep. I didn't. I woke up every time. If it hadn't been for Conrad... I owe him a lot."

"So do I." Zander put his hand underneath hers. His calloused fingers brushed against hers, and with a feather-light sensation, tendrils of shadow drifted up her hand and intertwined with her flame. The red-orange of her flame and the deep plum, indigo, and black of his shadow combined into an unearthly sight; the two stems of magic burned together in a ghostly charcoal flame.

Raven couldn't describe the sensation—Zander's magic against hers felt like a cool breeze, like stepping into a shaded lagoon. The flame didn't feel hot or cold; it just existed.

"I didn't know you could do that," she said.

"It's not unheard of." Thalame appeared on her other side, eyes on the flame. "Sometimes magicians can combine their magic. Some combine better than others."

"It depends on the magicians," Zander added. "They need to trust each other."

She glanced away from the flame and met his eye. Trust. She hadn't flinched when he put his hand under hers. She hadn't worried about him being so close or about his magic spilling over her. She did trust him. And he trusted her, it seemed. Even after they had spent a considerable amount of time not trusting each other.

She burned through her magic with Zander's shadows surrounding it. When she let her flame die out, his shadows vanished as well. Rather than remove his hand, his fingers folded over hers.

She started to speak, but noticed the painful grimace on his face.

"The tattoo?" Raven asked.

He nodded and let go of her hand. "Mine's nearly gone." Zander turned and lifted his shirt. On the taut skin of his lower back, the swirling rune tattoo had faded to a pale gray. The skin around it had reddened.

Most Wraiths had the same tattoo. It burned off the extra magic that would otherwise attract the magic-detecting automatons. Unfortunately, the rune also burned the skin around it. The more magic, the worse the burn. Zander and Thalame both had been using their magic more, and by the look on Thalame's face, his own rune had paled.

"There's plenty of tattoo artists on board," said Thalame.

"No." Zander shook his head, letting his shirt fall back. "If we're going into war with the Gray Elite, I want all my magic. You should too. We'll need quick healing out there."

Thalame frowned. "I'd rather stay out of the fighting, mate."

"Oh, come on." Raven felt much better now that her wild magic had been defused. She hadn't even realized how much pressure had built up. "Don't you want a little excitement?"

Zander chuckled. "You're spending too much time with Conrad."

"That's bad for your health," said Thalame. "And ours."

Raven laughed as they headed back into the upper deck for lunch. Truthfully, she would rather stay out of war too. But the thought that they—a team of outcasts and magicians and pirates—could overthrow the Gray Elite empire and restore the kingdom tingled in her stomach. They could change the world if they wanted to, and she wanted to.

There were risks, but she would rather risk everything trying to change the world than cower for the rest of her life.

The *Orion* raced through the clouds and through the night. Raven found it hard to sleep, knowing she would be in Silver Glen soon, knowing she would face those she had left. Anxiety needled against her mind—she felt a glimmer of what her mother must have felt when she saw Raven for the first time.

The next morning, the air had changed. It had lost the summer heat and gained an ice-brimmed breeze—the cooler air from the mountains. The early morning sunlight stained the clouds bright blue and gold. Raven could see the distant peaks, bruised purples and faint blues and grays. It reminded her of when she used to stare at the southern horizon and pretend the clouds were far away mountains, full of adventure and mystery and magic.

Raven stood on the Belt, her magic flame flickering against the breeze, and gazed down at Hammel Forest. It stretched so far. It hadn't seemed so big when she and Zander traveled through it. How many times had she climbed her tree to gaze at the endless forest and dream of what lay beyond it? How many times had she stared at the sky, looking for airships and sky cities?

She felt a squeeze in her chest—she silenced her flame immediately. Wooziness overtook her senses, and she grasped onto the railing to steady herself. She hadn't been paying attention to her magic; she had gotten lost in a daydream. Luckily, no one else had come with her to the Belt. She didn't feel like listening to Thalame's scolding or Conrad's teasing or Zander's worry. The woozy spell passed. Her lack of sleep the night before likely had something to do with it too. Conrad had briefly mentioned how sleep rejuvenated magic better and faster than any potion or tonic.

"What are you doing up here?" came Zander's voice through the wind. He appeared beside her. He had tied his hair behind his head, and the wind whipped the loose strands behind him.

"Trying not to lose my mind," Raven said halfheartedly.

"Nervous?"

"Oh, no, not at all," Raven said, her voice light. "Why should I be nervous about seeing my father, who I left without a word?"

Zander shrugged, though his eyes trailed to the north. He couldn't hide his nervousness either.

"Going through your magic?" he asked.

"I'm already finished."

His brow raised.

"I've been here since just past dawn."

Zander whistled. "Let's go back inside." He nodded toward the doors and flashed her a wolfish grin. "I know something that might take your mind off it."

She glared.

He laughed. "Not that. Something else."

He took a step toward the doors, and she heaved a sigh and followed.

Something else turned out to be a long cargo hold in the lower decks that Zander and Thalame had set up like a shooting range. Three portholes allowed in the buttery morning light, tinting the discolored metal walls. The floor looked to be made of several different types of metal—steel and bronze and a strange bluish metal she'd never seen before.

Zander pulled Birdie from the holster—an awkward motion with his left arm in a sling.

"Is it going to affect your aim?" Raven asked.

"I don't know." Zander aimed Birdie at the targets on the far side of the room, set up at different lengths. He pulled the hammer back. "Give me the count."

She blinked; she'd nearly forgotten about that. She stepped into his peripheral and raised her fist into the air, splaying her fingers.

"Five," she said, and lowered her thumb. She counted down—putting down a finger each time—until only her index finger remained in the air. She hesitated before she put down her finger, mostly to annoy him, but he did not complain. She closed her fingers into a tight fist—the first bullet exploded from the barrel.

Bang! Bang! Bang!

Three targets, three bullet holes.

"Oh, I guess it hasn't affected my aim," Zander said haughtily.

Raven scoffed. "How is watching your target practice supposed to help me?"

"Because you're next," he said. "Come here."

She blinked—he had removed his hand from the trigger and held Birdie out to her. She gawked. "You're letting me touch her?"

Zander sighed. "I know, strange how things happen. Now, come here before I change my mind."

Raven took cautious steps to where Zander stood. He never let anyone else shoot Birdie. She was a beauty of a pistol, dark steel and red leather. Raven gently folded her hand around the grip. Zander stood behind and adjusted her fingers.

"Don't put your finger on the trigger until you're ready to shoot," Zander said in her ear. "Be careful not to get pinched by the hammer. Hurts like hell."

He adjusted her stance, talked her through aiming, and then released his guiding hand from hers. Raven looked at Birdie. The pistol had always been a strange extension of Zander, the prized possession he never went anywhere without, and he had let Raven hold her. It had demolished a wall between them she hadn't realized existed, and a different form of intimacy grew in its place.

"Ready?" Zander stepped into her peripheral, a safe distance away. He held up five fingers.

"Yes."

"Five." Zander started the countdown, and when he held his fist in the air, she pulled the trigger.

The kickback surprised her, and the bullet flew wide. It landed in one of the crates against the back wall.

"Try again," Zander said, no teasing in his voice.

She did—her second bullet missed, so did her third and fourth. Her fifth struck the edge of the target. Her sixth hit.

Zander laughed. "See? Practice."

"I'm glad to know it's not a natural talent of yours," she said, gazing sideways at him.

He smirked, and as he showed her how to reload Birdie, he told her about his time in the Gray Elite Academy. They trained for years to learn how to shoot with deadly accuracy, how to clean a multitude of guns, and how to handle aiming in combat.

"By the time a cadet graduates, they can hit a bullseye in the dark," Zander said. "Or so that's the plan."

"Can you?" Raven asked.

With a precise jerk of his wrist, the chamber slammed back into place. He shrugged. "Can't say. I've never tried. Seemed like a waste of bullets."

He set Birdie back in her hand, and this time, she only missed once. Granted, she took a lot longer to aim than he did. When she had emptied the chamber, she glanced at Zander—he was looking back at her with an expression of longing, of pride. He blinked, and the expression vanished.

"Hmm? See something you like?" Raven placed her free hand on her hip.

"I see several things I like," Zander said, sauntering over. "But it would take too long to list them all."

He slid Birdie from her grip and leaned his mouth toward hers. She leaned in to meet him—the door to the cargo hold creaked open.

"Ah, there you two are," came Thalame's dry rasp.

Zander sighed and straightened. He flicked his wrist and started to reload Birdie. "Great timing."

"No problem, mate." Thalame grinned like he knew. He carried two wooden practice swords over his shoulders. "I thought we'd see how much you learned while you've been gone. Feeling up to a combat lesson?"

Raven shrugged and held her hand out for the sword.

"Oh, and new rule," Thalame started, "no magic allowed."

Raven hadn't learned anything new since she had last trained with Thalame, and it showed. He didn't comment on it. Zander stood to the side—the medics and mechanics forbade him from any activities that might endanger his new arm. He focused instead on cleaning Birdie.

The morning went by in a blur. Raven tired herself out—but it didn't alleviate the anxiety tugging on her lungs and pushing on her ribs.

They shared lunch with Conrad and Rosaria, who then joined them in their practice room. Rosaria sparred with Raven—and won. Growing up with the Hawks, Rosaria had been trained in combat—she whispered to Raven how she had beaten Zander when they were younger, much to his fury.

"That's because I went easy on you," Zander said, having overheard. "I didn't want to hit you."

Raven half laughed as she slumped against the wall underneath the portholes. The sunlight had grown brighter in the afternoon.

Rosaria snorted. "So you say."

"That sounds like a fine excuse." Raven shared a knowing glance with the princess.

Zander scowled. "Just give me a few weeks. I'll show you."

Rosaria glanced down at his mechanical arm. Sympathy shadowed her eyes for a moment, then the brightness returned. "I doubt you'll be any better this time around."

Raven didn't see much of Malik, and she assumed he either didn't want to be around them or had other duties. According to Thalame, he had been spending a lot of time with the refugees, going over their options.

"He knows people," Zander chimed in. He took a long drink from his canteen. "All over the continent. He can get people to either end without the Gray Elite catching wind."

Conrad dropped his voice, adding, "Rumor has it, he's on the hill to becoming the next grand master."

"I wouldn't doubt it," Thalame said. "The Wraiths trust Malik. He'd be a good leader."

Raven sat on the floor, catching her breath; she didn't have the energy to ask them what they were talking about. Raven didn't know what all a seeker did, but Malik always seemed busy.

As the sun sank toward the west, a series of bells sounded. Raven's heart jumped into her throat.

Destination sighted.

Raven followed Conrad to the air docks. Standing on the catwalks, she watched Silver Glen appear through the thick forest, a spotting of wooden roofs and dirt paths. Her village rested at the base of the mountains, ramshackle and half-reclaimed by nature. She couldn't see the entrance to the mines from the air docks, but she could see the fake tree that served as their Lookout Tower. The bell would have been rung by now, and everyone in Silver Glen would know about the approaching sky city.

The *Orion* slowed. Its engine calmed, and the fans kicked on, allowing the sky city to hover.

Luckett wanted Raven to be the first to make contact. Silver Glen knew her, and her father would be less likely to shoot her on sight than a stranger. So Raven followed Conrad along the catwalks to a medium-sized airship of pale steel and yellow wings. Zander followed a step behind.

Conrad climbed into the cockpit of the airship, and Raven stepped into the hull. Zander gave her an encouraging nod—he offered no words of comfort. He looked as nervous as she felt.

"I'm sure it'll be fine," Conrad said as he started the engine.

Raven didn't have it in her to speak. Her nerves rattled like she'd swallowed crickets. She slumped into the passenger seat behind Conrad, where she could see through the front window.

A team of Crusaders unhooked the airship from the rigging. The ship swayed to the side, and then fell. Raven gasped—the sensation of falling fizzed from her toes, along her bones and skin, and to her scalp in a few short seconds—and then the ship's engine roared and started forward. Conrad steered them on a gentle downward slope, wearing a wide grin.

"You could have warned me about the drop," Raven said, breathless. The sensation ghosted over her skin.

"But then your reaction wouldn't have been genuine," Conrad whined.

The airship descended, and with every passing moment, her heart thudded harder. Silver Glen grew larger. Raven spotted a gathering outside the lopsided wooden structure that served as an inn and trading post. Among the villagers stood her father, tall and wide and imposing. He stood with his arms crossed, and he wore a deep frown. He and the others watched the airship land on a stretch of dirt and grass that had once been a sheep pen. The engines blew dust and old leaves into the air behind it.

Conrad idled the engine, and the lack of sound only made her thudding heart that much louder. Raven stared at her father through the window. He took a step toward the airship, the others held strong behind him. None of them looked happy or welcoming. They looked threatened and ready to defend their home.

"Feeling good?"

"I feel like I might vomit," she said.

"Do that outside, please." Conrad frowned. "It takes weeks for the smell to go away. Seriously, puke outside."

She fumbled with the door's latch. It finally came open, and she took a deep breath as she took the first step outside.

Her father was walking toward the ship, hand on his pistol, ready to shoot. As his eyes fell on her, he stopped. Their eyes met. The angry, suspicious frown fell away from his face, and disbelief replaced it. Her heart stopped and sped up at the same time. He looked the same: short brown hair, strong jaw, and imposing stature. Raven took a shaky step toward her father, and then another. She stopped in front of him, and for a long moment, neither moved nor spoke.

And then her father dropped his pistol and wrapped his arms around her. The embrace knocked the air from her lungs. Her feet left the ground, and he spun her—just like he had when she'd been small. Her feet met solid ground again, and her father held her tight for a long moment before he released her.

"Raven," he breathed. He cupped her cheek. Tears lined his eyes—Raven blinked twice. She had never seen her father, the strongest man in the village, cry. "You're alive."

She had no response. Any words she'd had vanished at the sight of her father's watery eyes.

He embraced her again. One hand cradled the back of her head as he let those tears fall into her hair.

"Dad," Raven started. She didn't know how to continue. She'd expected him to shout, to scold, to point out all the things she had done wrong. She'd expected guilt, and she felt it—tremendously so—even more so than had he yelled. She returned his embrace, albeit awkwardly, and managed to say, "I'm sorry."

"I'm sorry," said her father. He said it twice more before he released her. He set his hands on her shoulders and held her at arm's length, his grip gentle as if he feared she would vanish again. His eyes were puffy and red. "Where the hell have you been? Mel told me she sent you out, but we assumed you'd be back in a few days. No one heard a word. I thought you'd been taken. I thought you'd been killed. I didn't know what happened. I..." He sighed. His eyes hardened into the look she had expected. His grip on her shoulders tightened. "Then we got word the Gray Elite had put a price on your head and that they were hunting you down."

"They are still hunting her down," said Conrad. He stood beside Raven, just outside of her father's reach. His familiar lilted words felt so strange in Silver Glen, beside her father's harsh tongue and calloused words.

Her father frowned at Conrad. He took in Conrad's assortment of daggers, his tunic and trousers, his dirty leather boots, his waist-long braids, and golden necklaces. Raven knew what her father likely wanted to say—something about men and long hair—but he held in his words.

"Who are you?" her father asked.

"No time for that." Conrad looked to Raven, motioning for her to continue.

Her father started to argue, but Raven cleared her throat, stealing his attention back. "Right," she started, clapping her hands together. "Do you have a minute? I need to talk to you about a few things."

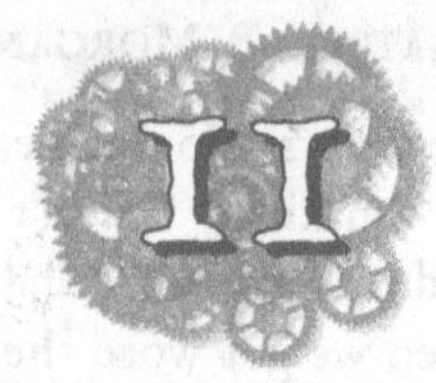

"*What?*" Samuel Thane asked his daughter, eyes wide and brows high.

"We need to evacuate," Raven repeated, holding firm under her father's gaze. In her mind, she pictured herself like her mother, shoulders back and head proud.

Her father stared at her, the news of the Gray Elite's impending attack still processing. They had gone to the trading post, and Raven told her father the quickest explanation of her adventure, boiling it down to the essentials. Her father sat back in the chair, watered-down ale in hand, listening with a blank face.

"We've received intelligence that the Gray Elite could be on their way here, right now," Conrad added onto the heels of her story. He stood behind Raven's chair, foot resting on the bottom rung. "And unless you don't mind them stomping around your home and bullying you for information, you need to come with us."

"I can't just leave my—"

"*All* of you," Conrad clarified.

Her father glared at Conrad. He hated being interrupted. "And where would we go? This is our home." He motioned to the shoddy trading post.

"I know," Raven said, a plea on her words. "It's not permanent. It's to protect you from whatever horrible fate the Gray Elite have in mind. They know I'm from here, and they would hurt you to hurt me, or hold you captive and torture you all to spite me."

Her father's frown deepened. "You've really gotten yourself into trouble."

"I'm eyeball deep in trouble." Raven shrugged. "There's nothing I can do about it right now. Like it or not, you are in danger, and I'd rather the empire not find any of you."

"Or this all might be a simple mistaken rumor," Conrad said, his tone light. "But it's better to be on the safe side, don't you think?"

Her father let out a grievous sigh and ran a hand through his hair. "Fine." He looked to the other villagers. "We evacuate, but we will return when it's safe."

Raven nodded. A weight lifted from her shoulders. Her family would be safe.

"All right, now that that's settled," Conrad started. "Tell your people to bring only the essentials. The *Orion* is stocked with the basics and food."

Conrad returned to the airship, and Raven went with her father to start the evacuation. Returning to the mines felt strange after all that had happened, and given the current situation, her presence did not go unnoticed. She caught more than a few odd stares and whispers on the way to her father's office—not unlike the days when they whispered of her rule-breaking. This time, she did not shy away from their stares. She held herself tall and strong, like her mother, like Rosaria, like Ivy.

Her father delivered his orders of evacuation into the speaking tubes in his office; they connected with every other important part of the mines—the workshops and smiths, the kitchens, the foundry. He didn't explain why Silver Glen had to evacuate; he promised to explain after the evacuation.

Standing in her father's office felt stranger still. The last time she'd been here, he took her off scavenging duty and put her on kitchen duty. She'd left in tears. That was the last time she had seen her father, and likewise the last night he had seen her. Guilt tightened in her chest.

Her eyes settled on a ticking bauble—the one he had knocked off in his rage that day. It's tail stick ticked.

"Raven?" came her father's commanding tone.

She snapped out of her daze.

He stood on the other side of his desk, looking at her. He opened his mouth to speak, but then closed it again. "Come on. We've got people to look after."

The next hour passed in a blur of confused faces, unhappy children, and worried whispers and questions. Everyone carried bags and satchels—bare essentials and prized possessions. Raven stood with Conrad on the surface as an airship ferried load after load of people from Silver Glen to the *Orion*. While they managed the evacuation on the surface, her father managed it from within the mines. Her father allowed only a few people out of the mines at once, as to not draw attention. From *whom*, he didn't say.

The people passed Raven and Conrad as they boarded the airship. Most gave her an odd stare of recognition; most blinked twice at Conrad.

Raven kept one eye on the sky as the airship came and went, carrying Silver Glen to safety. The empty skies made her nervous. How far behind were the Gray Elite? Were they on their way? Would there be a Silver Glen to return to?

"Raven?"

It was a voice she knew, and it took less than a heartbeat to find the familiar face and flaxen hair.

Raven's smile stretched. "Sweets!"

Sweets pushed through the crowd and wrapped her arms around Raven. It felt like ages since she had seen the other girl. They had been inseparable as children, and Raven hadn't realized how her absence had felt until she embraced her again. Sweets's blonde hair had grown out a bit, and she wore it in two braids on either side of her head. Goggles sat on top of her head, the lenses framed with decorative brass.

"Those are new?" Raven asked.

"That's right. You missed it." Sweets grinned and blush warmed her cheeks. "These were an engagement gift from Brent."

"Really?" Raven clapped her hands together. She had long suspected something more than friendship between her two friends, and the confirmation warmed something deep in her chest.

"We were worried like hell, you know." Sweets frowned at Raven, then looked up to the *Orion*-shaped shadow on the clouds. "I was starting to think you'd found somewhere more exciting to live. I guess I was sort of right. Your father was a mess. He tried to hide it, but we all knew how worried he was. We kept expecting you and Zander to show up one day."

The guilt that had somewhat unraveled tightened again. Raven tried to keep her face neutral, but Sweets nudged her. "I feel guilty as hell, don't worry."

Above, the airship ferry pushed through the clouds and steadily descended to the ground. The engine buzzed louder and louder.

"Oh, well, that's good." Sweets had to yell to be heard over the airship's buzzing. "And it's good to see you alive and well. I expect the full story."

"You'll get it," Raven said.

The airship landed, sending waves of wind through the tall grass and weeds all around it. Her father's booming voice commanded, "Let's move, move."

Sweets gave Raven's arm a gentle squeeze and then climbed into the waiting airship. Brent followed—he gave Raven a nod in silent greeting.

"All right," came her father's voice. "This is the last. The mines are empty."

"Are you sure?" Conrad asked. "I'd hate to come up a few people short."

Her father scowled. "Yes, I'm sure. I checked every room, as did my wife. There's no one left inside."

Raven had noticed but not registered the few people following her father out of the mines. Her stepmother and half-sister, Lena, were among the last out. Her stepmother was fussing over something, and then Lena's eyes shifted and met Raven's. Lena's eyes widened; she dropped her bag and threw her arms around Raven.

"Raven!" Lena started to cry. Raven hugged her tighter. "Dad didn't say you were here!"

"I'll tell you the whole story," Raven promised, "but later."

"We are running out of time." The casual humor on Conrad's face had faded with every ferry, edging on a seriousness that made Raven uneasy. He kept glancing at the sky too.

Lena shouldered her bag and accepted Conrad's hand as she stepped into the airship. Her stepmother followed—pausing long enough to give Raven a motherly stroke on the cheek. Her father boarded last. Raven took one last look at shabby structures and hidden mine of Silver Glen, then turned to climb into the airship—then she heard it.

A humming from the sky. A new, high-pitched humming.

She glanced at Conrad. His lips turned downward, and his brows creased.

"Hurry," he said to the pilot. "We're not alone in the skies."

The engine whirled. Raven climbed inside as the airship started to rise, and Conrad jumped on board with feline ease. He pulled the steel door closed and latched it. An uneasy mumbling came from the final passengers. Most had never left Silver Glen or seen an airship. The airship rose above the treeline; through the pothole, Silver Glen shrank and then vanished.

Raven leaned against the welded metal wall and released a breath.

"What's that?" asked her father.

"Shit," Conrad hissed.

Raven wrenched her eyes open. Her father and Conrad were looking through the front window. She pushed her way between them.

Her breath vanished from her throat.

Black dots spotted the southeast horizon, and they were growing large with every passing second.

"Sisters," her father breathed.

The dots multiplied. The closest had doubled in size. Raven swallowed.

"We're not alone," said the pilot, worry on every word. "Company from the southeast. And they're moving fast."

"I doubt the captain missed them," Conrad said.

"You got guns on this thing?" her father barked.

"It's a transporter," Conrad drawled. At her father's glare, he added, "That means no."

Her father growled. "What use is a ship without firepower?"

Halfway to the *Orion*, the distant dots became white and yellow airships.

"Buzzers," said the pilot.

"The Gray Elite were on the way." Conrad's voice lacked its usual humor.

Their airship pushed through the clouds. For a moment, the skies were clear, and then a dozen Buzzers burst through the clouds to the southeast. This close, the Gray Elite crest on the hulls gleamed in the sunlight.

"Hold on," spat the pilot.

Gunfire peppered the air. It echoed like broken thunder, and for a terrifying moment, Raven's world went gray. Bits of metal clattered against the transporter, her stepmother gasped and latched onto her father's arm, and Raven started to fall. Conrad grabbed her and held her upright.

Holes in the airship—daylight came through in beams.

Airships fell from the belly of the *Orion*. Engines roared to life and raced toward the incoming Gray Elite, streaks of bronze and steel against the clouds. Shrieking engines and gunfire shook the sky.

"We're hit," came the pilot's distant voice. "We've got injured."

Conrad leaned over the pilot's seat. "How bad?"

"We'll hold." The pilot gave it more speed.

Conrad pulled Raven toward him, and another pair of hands rested on her shoulders.

"You'll be fine," Conrad said.

Raven blinked. Blood smeared on her hands. Had she been hit? She didn't feel anything. They raced over the clouds, leaving the firefight behind. The engine under her feet whirled and choked; a tremor raved through Raven's chest.

Then she felt it—a sharp, hot pain on her abdomen.

"You'll be fine," came her father's voice this time.

She began to shake, and the color and sound returned to the world. It moved too fast, too loud. The ship docked in the *Orion*. A team hooked it into the rigging, the engines quit, and a Crusader opened the door.

"Medic," called Conrad. "Where's Thalame?"

Raven fell into the arms of a waiting Crusader. She could feel the blood leaving her body.

"Single file. Don't look down," said the pirate to the others, well-practiced words.

"My daughter—"

"Will be fine."

Raven felt the darkness on the edge of her vision, cold and clammy and breathless. It pulled and pulled. Her stomach turned over. A cold sweat broke out over her skin.

She fell under.

Raven came in and out. She felt warmth, like the midday sun on her bare skin. She heard the distant call of gulls. She heard chimes, sweet and gentle and low-toned. She heard voices, muffled by walls. She opened her eyes and found herself on the catwalks of the *Orion*. She blinked. The warmth remained, but it faded with every second.

Thalame knelt at her side, his eyes focused, healing her.

The catwalks buzzed with activity. The chaos of the gun fight raged below, popping and blasting.

"There we go," Thalame said. "Can you stand?"

Raven nodded. Thalame helped her to her feet. The pain had lessened considerably, though she felt the slick of fresh blood on her shirt and pants, and she felt it clotting in the threads.

The strange comfort of the dream faded, and the organized chaos and panic of the air docks returned. Her father and the others stood around her—they hadn't gone into the ship. They had waited for her. With her back on her feet, the procession continued into the *Orion*.

Raven leaned on Conrad as her family and the last of Silver Glen's people followed a Crusader along the catwalks, each looking down, except for her father. He cast his eyes around the air docks, nothing of surprise showing on his face. Of course, according to her mother, he had worked on an airship before. He'd be familiar with it all.

The Crusader led them into the lower deck. Inside the *Orion*, the gunfire sounded distant, but no less threatening.

"You were shot," Conrad whispered to Raven, low enough her father couldn't hear.

"I'm aware." The blood had begun to dry, and it pulled at her skin with every step.

Conrad smirked. "No, I mean you were shot a few minutes ago and bleeding profusely, and now you're walking like it didn't happen."

"Thalame's a skilled healer."

Conrad's smirk widened.

"What?" she hissed.

"I've never seen Thalame heal someone that fast, especially not with a wound like that one. It might have killed anyone else."

She opened her mouth, the words *I'm not anyone else* on the tip of her tongue at the same time a foreign bitterness clamped around her chest—she bit the words back. A strange sensation oozed through her skin, and she hadn't the words to describe it. The words and bitterness had not been her own—they had pulsed from somewhere else. She swallowed the words and the feeling.

"My magic, I guess," she whispered back.

Your magic?

Conrad gave her a suspicious, knowing smile.

The Crusader led them into the mess hall—the only place on the ship big enough to hold all the people of Silver Glen, aside from the cargo hold. People sat around the mismatched wooden tables. A few of the kitchen crew had brought out a cask of ale. As Samuel entered, the frightful murmuring calmed. Raven followed her father toward the front of the mess hall. She felt eyes shift to her, as they had in the mine. She held herself like Rosaria, regal and confident, despite the quaky feeling of intrusion in her stomach and the blood clotting on her clothes.

"What's going on outside?" one of the smiths asked. "We heard gunfire. A voice came over the air, saying something about enemy ships. What does it mean?"

Conrad leaned in to Raven and whispered, "It means we were none too early."

"Is Silver Glen under attack? Why?" asked someone else.

The panic returned, a fraction softer than it had been before.

Samuel held up his hand, quieting the panic in their voices but not their eyes. All in the room looked to her father. Raven spotted Sweets and Brent standing together, the girls from the kitchen, and the elders. Mel stood among them, looking solemn as ever.

"The Gray Elite have come to Silver Glen." Samuel's booming voice reached every part of the mess hall. "It was not a friendly visit. They came armed, as you've heard. We barely made it out in time. If not for my daughter and her friends, we would have been on the receiving end of that gunfire."

A murmur sounded at those words, and many eyes looked to Raven and Conrad. Conrad waved.

"But why?" asked her stepmother, her voice soft but strong. "What have we done to invoke the empire's wrath?"

Samuel hesitated, his eyes hard. He turned his attention to Raven, and within a few long heartbeats, all eyes were on her. Waiting for the explanation.

She swallowed, and with a nudge from Conrad, stepped up beside her father. "War is brewing." Disquiet met her words. She did not command the room like her father, but within the silence, it did not matter. "Silver Glen was likely only the first."

She felt gazes on her bloodied trousers and blouse and the dagger visible at her waist. Most women in Silver Glen wore dresses and corsets and did not arm themselves. They cooked, cleaned, and raised the children. Raven had grown up with disapproving glances and pitied stares, but it did not make it easier.

She couldn't admit that the attack had been revenge on her, that she had caused this, that she was to blame for their displacement. Yet she suspected they already knew.

She was saved from any more awkward talking by a knock. Malik entered the mess hall, rings catching the lantern light. Malik glanced to Samuel; Samuel glanced at him. Recognition passed over both their faces.

"The captain requests an audience," Malik said to Raven.

"Captain?" Samuel asked, the word venomous on his tongue. He looked between Malik and Raven, knowing. He rubbed his face and let out a groan of realization. "Son of a bitch."

Conrad smirked; Malik shot him a glare.

"What is it?" asked her stepmother, touching her husband's elbow. She looked between Malik, Conrad, and Raven.

Samuel looked around the mess hall. "I knew this hunk of junk looked familiar."

"You've been here?" she asked.

Samuel took a deep breath. "The captain is an old friend of mine."

Friend. Raven recognized that tone. Disgruntled and surprised—and by the look on her stepmother's face, she recognized that tone too.

"I'm coming with you to this meeting," Samuel said to Raven.

She nodded. "Okay."

Malik looked like he wanted to protest but didn't.

"Make sure everyone's all right," Samuel said to his wife. "I'll be back soon."

She nodded. "I'll take care of things here."

Malik led Raven, Samuel, and Conrad to Luckett's office above the bridge. No one spoke. Conrad looked delighted by the awkward air, and

Malik looked like he would rather be anywhere else. By the time they had entered, the gunfire had ended, and the *Orion* had started to move again.

Luckett stood by the speaking tubes, shoulders back, face calm in concentration. Her red coat had been thrown over the back of her chair. Her dark blue corset hugged her narrow waist, and a pistol and dagger hung off her hips. Voices were coming through the tubes, from all parts of the ship, reporting in.

"...all ships returned. A few casualties. Nothing major. No dead. Mostly minor repairs."

"...engines on full steam."

"Keep south," Luckett barked into the tubes.

"Aye, Captain!"

"What of the Gray Elite Buzzers?" Luckett asked into yet another tube.

"Scrap metal, Captain."

"Good." She leaned onto her desk. "Keep the ships ready in case the Gray Elite make a surprise visit."

"Aye, Captain."

"Captain," Malik said from the other side of the room.

"Ah, you're here," Luckett said, striding around her desk. If she looked surprised to see them all there, she held it in well. Her gaze settled on Samuel, then Raven. She leaned against the rosewood, arms crossed. "The Gray Elite followed us. We led them right to Silver Glen."

Raven's heart tumbled through her ribs. "What?" she gasped.

"You did what?" Samuel stormed toward the desk and slammed his fist onto the rosewood. "You led them to my doorstep?"

Luckett didn't look the least bit intimidated.

"We led them?" Raven asked, her voice a whisper. She had led the Gray Elite to her family's door. She might as well have introduced them.

Malik stepped closer to her. "It's not your fault."

Raven swallowed and added, "How?"

"Deacon's boy," Luckett said, annoyed. "He didn't do it on purpose, but the Buzzers followed him. I went to him first and accused him of lying. The boy looked about ready to pass out on me. He's a terrible liar. I'd bet gold that father of his knew he'd end up a turncoat and planted the information as a failsafe, knowing his son would turn to us."

General Deacon had again delivered a blow, and he had used his own son to do it.

"I suggest you not yell at him," Luckett said to Samuel, her words a warning. "I already have. Boy nearly cried."

Conrad failed to conceal a chuckle, earning him a glare from Malik.

"So," Luckett said, straightening. "Sam, how have you been?"

Raven's father looked like he might burst, caught between anger and disbelief.

"I've been damn swell, Bailey," Luckett said in a deep voice, an imitation of Samuel's. "Thanks for saving our asses back there and taking care of our daughter. You're the best." Her voice returned to her own cadence, and she said, "Oh, you're still the dashing type."

Samuel groaned and pushed away from the desk, from Luckett. He made a lap around the office, glaring through the window to the bridge, to the clouds parted by the bow. "This is your ship?" he asked without looking at her.

"She sure is," Luckett said. "Renamed her *Orion*. I thought it had a better ring to it, and besides, a new captain means a new name for the ship. It's tradition."

"What happened to Captain Elbert?"

"Dead."

"How?"

Luckett scoffed. "What do you mean 'how'? The man was ninety years old and drank a barrel of rum a week. I'm surprised he lived as long as he did."

Samuel heaved a sigh and stalked to the chairs in front of the desk. He sat without grace. "What happened?"

"Quite a lot," said Luckett as she meandered around her desk. She plopped into her ornate chair. She propped her boots on the corner and glanced at Raven. "It's quite the tale too. I struck a bad deal a few months back and landed in the Tombs. I thought I'd die down there when one day Raven shows up, melts the lock right off my cell door, and I make a quiet escape. Thanks to the madness on the surface, I was able to get back to the sky relatively unscathed."

Samuel sat in silence for a long moment. Then, he turned his gaze to Raven. "You melted a lock?" Each word was careful and unsure.

Raven sat in the chair beside his. "It's more complicated than that," she said. "But yes, I did. I, uh, might have left a few things out of the story I told you earlier. We were pressed for time."

"We have time now," said her father.

"I'll call for tea." Luckett jumped to her feet and delivered the order to the speaking tubes, her tone calm and pleasant, as if they hadn't just survived a gunfire storm, evacuated an entire village, and were hiding from an angry and vengeful empire.

Over tea, Raven explained everything, starting with the Cage Birds that had attacked her and Zander months before. She told him about the centrum and Altair's Augur and Zander's true intentions for coming to Silver Glen. She told him everything.

Her father did not speak. He listened—for the first time she could remember, he actually listened to her. His fingers were curled into white-knuckles fists, but he listened.

Of course, Conrad added his own tidbits into the story, flourishing his appearances, particularly at the arena in Wayward Point. Luckett stayed quiet, as did Malik. Both listened with the same intensity.

Telling the story, the whole story, felt easier than lying. She didn't have to stop and think of what she was saying or what she shouldn't say. It felt...alleviating to have everything in the open, and yet vulnerable at the same time.

When Raven's story came to an end, she took a drink of the tea she had made some time ago. It had cooled but still soothed her dry throat. She didn't think she had ever talked so much in her life.

"You're a magician now?" Her father hadn't touched his tea. He had leaned forward onto his knees, hands together, fingers laced. Raven had seen the expression plenty—it was his thinking face.

Raven summoned a flame to the palm of her hand. Samuel grimaced.

"And now the entire Gray Elite empire is hunting her for it," Conrad said lightly, perching on the edge of the desk.

"Thank you for reminding me," Raven muttered. She released her flame but held her warm hand against the teacup, heating the contents.

"You need to go into hiding," Samuel said sternly. Disapproval hung on each word. "Silver Glen would have been the best place."

"Not anymore," Luckett said. "It's been compromised."

"Thanks to you." Samuel glared at Luckett.

"Thanks to a clever son of a bitch in Moorin," Luckett snapped, glaring back at him. "The sky is the safest place. She's protected up here."

"She would have been protected on the ground."

"Nonsense. There's more firepower up here, not including her own."

"Raven doesn't need to fight."

"She might not have a choice. If she's attacked, she'll have to defend herself."

"If she's well protected, she won't have to fight."

"Some girls don't need protection. Some are very capable of protecting themselves."

"This isn't some pirate den, Bailey, we're talking about the Gray Elite. An empire."

"I'm well aware of the danger."

"Then start acting like it."

Raven cleared her throat loudly, bringing her parents' argument to an awkward end. Both pairs of burning eyes turned toward her. She knew then why her parents had not ended up together. They were both stubborn and looked in opposing directions.

"Raven left out the part where she melted a Colossus automaton into a pile of molten goo," added Conrad, a wicked smile tugging at his lips. "Turned the Gray Elite speechless!"

"You *what*?" Samuel asked, eyes wide and angry.

Raven turned a seething glare onto Conrad. He winked back at her. She had purposefully downplayed their dramatic escape from Moorin.

To her father, she said, "It was that or die."

"See?" Luckett motioned to Raven. "She is her own protection. She doesn't need a village of old-fashioned ninnies with clubs."

"That's not the point!" Samuel seethed.

"She's not a child, Sam. You can't lock her in a safe like some porcelain teapot."

"Stop!" Raven jumped to her feet. She slammed the teacup back onto the tray with enough force to slosh most of it out.

As she stood, the fever rushed from her feet to her head. The world wobbled. She felt herself tilt and grabbed onto the desk. She took several shaky breaths, and the world slowly righted itself, and the fever retreated. She blinked; Conrad's hand held her shoulder. Concern flashed in his eyes—eyes that were looking around her, not at her. At her magic.

"Raven—" her father started.

"Stop fighting about me like I'm not here." Raven looked between her father and her mother.

Luckett cleared her throat. "What do you think?" Samuel started to speak, but she held up her hand. "Let Raven speak for herself."

Spoken like a captain.

Samuel glared at Luckett before turning his attention to Raven.

Slowly, the fever receded to wherever it slept nowadays. Raven straightened, and Conrad pulled his hand from her shoulder.

Raven cleared her throat. "We can't change what's happened. The Gray Elite can't hunt us as easily up here as they could on the ground. Right now, I think it's best we stay above the clouds. And I can fight for myself."

Luckett grinned. Samuel frowned.

"I've been learning how to fight," Raven told her father. "I'm not as useless with a sword as I used to be."

Her father's frown deepened. "Sword? You've been sword fighting?"

"Considering she can shoot fire from her hands, a sword seems a bit nonessential, doesn't it?" asked Conrad.

Luckett nodded.

Samuel sighed deeply and hung his head. He ran his hand through his short brown hair and sighed again. "Fine."

"I know it's hard when you're not in charge anymore," Luckett said absently. "But try to be on your best behavior, Sam."

He inhaled like he had a lot he wanted to say, but he held it. He glared instead.

Luckett stood up and grabbed her red coat. "I've got to check on things below decks. Come on, I'll walk you back to the mess hall." She tugged on her coat and marched to the doors.

They followed Luckett into the corridor. Raven's stomach quivered, though having Conrad's effortless confidence on one side and Malik's silent strength on her other, she felt better.

"I aim to have proper rooms set up by tonight, but there'll be some crowding. Five or so to a room," said Luckett.

"That's fine," Samuel said. "We're safe. That's what matters most."

"Correct," Luckett said. "However, until we can restock, I'll have to place some rations on food and water."

"Understood," Samuel said.

The list of things went on, but Raven didn't entirely listen. She focused on the magic, the fever. Her parents' argument had caused it to spike, but it had since returned to its semi-calm state deep inside of her. She felt a ghost of that spike under her skin, pulsing against her, waiting to lash out. It felt...wild and violent, and she didn't know what to do about it. Conrad and Malik, both being seekers, would have sensed it too. Which is why, she assumed, they walked on either side of her.

They approached the mess hall, and her father let out a grunt of disapproval—a sound she knew by heart. She looked up to see what had caused it.

Rosaria and Zander stood in the corridor, talking to her stepmother and Lena. At the sight of Samuel, relief came over her stepmother's face. Rosaria and Zander both turned, and Raven felt the change. He stiffened, his fists curled, and his shoulders strained.

Within a heartbeat no one could have stopped, Zander and Samuel exchanged a heated glance; Luckett and Samuel's wife sized one another up with a shrewdness Raven had never seen in her stepmother; and Rosaria and Conrad observed it all with clever eyes. Both of them must have known the awkwardness of it all.

"You're alive and well," Samuel said to Zander, his eyes blazing. "Mostly."

Zander shrugged, jostling the fingers of his limp metal arm. "Mostly."

"I hear you're the reason my daughter up and left in the middle of the night and now has an empire hunting her down."

Zander started to spit something back, but Luckett held up her hand.

"Do your revenge shouting later," said Luckett, an order. She turned to Samuel's wife and added, "We'll have rooms for you all by tonight. I've given Sam the details, but I'll have more in an hour."

"That is good to hear." Raven's stepmother smiled, but she looked exhausted. "I think sleeping on the floor up here sounds much better than sleeping in a prison cell down there or dead."

"As would any sane person," Luckett said, her words aimed at Samuel.

Samuel huffed and started toward the mess hall. "Let me know when more details are available," he sharply said to Luckett.

"Will do." Luckett crossed her arms.

Raven's father, stepmother, and sister vanished back into the mess hall, but not without a sweet goodbye from Lena to Rosaria. The doors to the mess hall closed, and Samuel's booming voice could be heard reassuring his people.

"Your sister is a sweetheart," Rosaria said.

"Sister?" Luckett asked, brow raised.

"Lena is my half-sister," Raven explained.

Luckett let out a breath of relief and let her shoulder slump and her chin fall.

"Stressed, Captain?" asked Conrad.

Luckett rolled her neck over her shoulders. "Malik, my love, see how those rooms are coming along. Why don't you two help him out?" She waved her hand toward Zander and Rosaria. "Conrad, I'm sure there's something you need to do somewhere else. Raven, with me."

Her friends went one direction down the corridor, and Raven followed Luckett down the other.

They had gone a few steps when Luckett said, "Your father and I fought all the time, even when we were crazy about each other. I know it would have never worked out, but there's always that little bit of jealousy when you see an old beau with another."

Raven nodded.

"Was she good to you?" Luckett asked. "Your stepmother?"

"Yes."

"I'm glad to hear that," Luckett said, a different note in her voice. She paused in the corridor, and Raven paused with her. The portholes tinted the space in creamy daylight. "I know you are bitter at me for leaving you like I did, but believe me when I say you were raised much better than you would have been by me. I barely raised Malik. Sisters only know what would have happened to you. Knowing my luck, you'd have become some pirate heathen—given you survived to adulthood."

It took Raven a moment to recognize the strange lilt to her mother's words and the new look in her eye—it was remorse. Luckett met Raven's eyes—the light brown eyes they shared.

"Do you regret leaving?" Raven asked.

A beat passed.

"No," Luckett said, her voice soft. "I would have been miserable underground, and I've had some incredible adventures in the past sixteen years. I regret not being there for you, not being there when you became a woman or needed someone to tell you that life isn't always fair. I...regret not being the mother I should have been, to both you and Malik." She sighed deeply, and without the stern expression, she looked like a young woman. She absently toyed with the cuff of her coat. "I wanted to take you with me. I wanted to raise you. But I knew what kind of life you'd most likely have with me, and I knew what kind of life you'd have with your father. I thought by leaving you, I was making the right choice for you."

"Why not stay?" Raven asked, though she knew why.

Luckett half laughed. "I'd be useless in that kind of domestic setting. My spirit was meant for the skies. Not unlike yours, if what I've heard about you is true."

"There might be truth to that," Raven said.

"I'm sorry for what I've done, Raven." Luckett turned to her and extended her hand. "Can you forgive me?"

Raven knew she already had. Her grudge against her mother hadn't been deep to begin with. She pretended to consider it anyway. "I suppose I could." Raven gripped her mother's hand. "I do."

Luckett's remorseful expression turned into a grateful smile. "Then we've got a lot of time to make up for."

"And seventeen years of birthday presents," Raven added.

Luckett laughed, a deep and warming sound. "That's my side of the family coming out. Come on, why don't you come with me to see how those rooms are coming?"

Raven spent the afternoon with her mother as she coordinated her Crusaders. They organized rooms for the people of Silver Glen, made sure they had blankets and water, and Raven was glad for the work. It gave her something to do with her hands that didn't involve combat practice. Zander helped too, as much as he could with one arm, though he avoided her father.

By the time evening arrived and the clouds gave way to a starry sky, everyone from Silver Glen had a bedroll and something to eat. Raven was exhausted. Somewhere after midnight, she collapsed onto the couch in the room she shared with Rosaria.

Zander and Thalame had given up their room, and the two of them had brought bedrolls into the girls' room. They spread the bedrolls on the other side, both looking exhausted. Rosaria sat on the bottom bunk, chin resting in her hands. The globes burned low for the late hour, tinting them all in a shadowy yellow.

Thalame yawned. "We should sleep good tonight."

Raven felt the strain in her body, in every muscle and tissue and bone, pulling her toward the bed, toward the rejuvenating abyss.

"But before we crash," Thalame started. He came to sit beside Raven. "Zander and I have been talking."

"About you," Zander clarified. He sat in the chair opposite Raven. He wore no humor on his face. He started to lean forward, but his limp mechanical arm offset his weight, and he leaned back. "It's no secret the centrum gave you its power. Since we don't know what that means, we think it's best if we go see the Wraiths."

"The Wraiths?" Raven repeated, the word tumbling from her lips. The Wraiths, the mythical order of magicians that stretched back thousands of years, of which Thalame and Zander were part.

"They know more about magic than anyone else," Thalame said. "If anyone has an answer for what's happening to you, it'd be them. It's possible they might have some insight that we haven't thought of yet."

"Grand Master Deikun is a wise man," Zander added. "He knows magic like a sailor knows the sea. And because of your stunt in Moorin, I'd say it's only a matter of time until Deacon figures it out. For all we know, he might already have. All he'd have to do is open the box."

Raven nodded. The idea of meeting the grand master of the Wraiths made her stomach turn over, and going back to Wayward Point didn't sound very appealing.

But Zander and Thalame were watching her, waiting for her answer.

"You think the grand master could help me with my magic?" she asked.

Neither nodded, but neither declined the idea. Because they didn't know. She bit her lip. It offered a sliver of hope that she might not have to burn off her magic every morning or worry about the fever returning.

She inhaled deeply and said, "Okay. I'll go."

"I'm glad you agree," Thalame said. "Malik went to inform Luckett about the new course earlier this evening."

"You knew I'd agree?" Raven asked.

"No," Zander said. "We needed to get away from Silver Glen. We couldn't go north into the mountains. We couldn't stray into Gracita's airspace to the west. There's a Gray Elite stronghold to the east. So south was the most logical direction to go."

She frowned but gave up. She was too tired to argue about it. She was tired enough that she didn't know if there was anything to argue. "Fine," she said. "I need to get some sleep. I'll yell at you both in the morning."

"I've got the lights," said Zander.

Raven trudged to the top bunk, Thalame collapsed onto his bedroll, and Zander stood by the light switch. A few moments after Raven had pulled the blankets to her chin, the room went dark. The glass globes hissed out, leaving tiny pinpricks of light for a few seconds afterward. Zander's calm, steady footsteps retreated to his bedroll. As her eyes adjusted to the dark, she found two sapphires looking back at her from the other side of the room.

Zander woke up before the others. He'd never been one to lie awake, so he got up and slipped into the corridor. Portholes allowed generous sunlight, splashing the rosewood and brass. He stretched as much as he could with his new arm. He twitched his little finger—it moved a little more. Or maybe he just thought it did because he wanted it to.

He adjusted the sling around his neck and pushed the hair away from his face. He itched to move, so he started walking.

His feet took him to the hospital.

Zander let out a sigh. He knew what he should do, but he didn't want to. He cursed himself and walked into the hospital. There were few people in the hospital, mostly pilots who'd gotten roughed up during the fight. Zander made his way to the bed on the far side.

Ezra Deacon was awake, and his tired brown eyes focused on Zander.

The two friends stared at one another.

"You're a turncoat," Zander whispered.

"You're a Hawk and a Wraith," Ezra whispered back.

Zander shrugged.

Ezra half laughed. "Looks like we're both traitors now."

"Seems that way."

Ezra's sleepy smile faded, and he set a hard gaze on Zander. "I hear you're also something else."

Zander's heart squeezed. He knew what Ezra meant, but he couldn't bring himself to say it.

"You're the Revenant," Ezra whispered, not hiding his distaste.

A tense moment passed, and Zander didn't deny it.

Ezra gripped the sheets. His grip turned white-knuckled. "You killed my mother."

Zander couldn't deny that either.

Ezra wore hatred—a look Zander had never seen on the otherwise good-natured boy. Everyone had always loved Ezra, how kind he was, how friendly, how charismatic. Few had ever said such things of Zander.

"I'm sorry," Zander whispered. "I know an apology isn't going to fix anything, but it's out there."

"Why?"

"Because I felt like apologizing," Zander said. "Believe it or not, I feel bad about it."

"No, why did you kill her?"

Zander heaved a breath. "My father sent me to do it." He met Ezra's eyes as he said it. "According to the Hawks, she had been hiring mercenaries from Tinatun to bring back escaping magicians, the magicians the Hawks had smuggled out. They wanted it to stop, but the tipping point came when she hired assassins to attack Major General Taylor."

"I remember him," Ezra said. "They said he was smuggling drugs over the border."

"He was smuggling magicians out for the Hawks," Zander corrected.

Ezra sighed—understanding darkened his face. "Do you...remember it? That night?"

"I've tried my best not to remember details," Zander said. "I made sure anyone I went after was alone and that they died quickly."

"I was in the room, you know," Ezra said.

Zander tensed, though he held himself calm.

"When you killed her. I saw the Revenant, and I was too afraid to do anything to stop him." Ezra lifted his gaze to the ceiling. "If I would have, would you have killed me too?"

"I don't know." Zander didn't want to think about that question, and he didn't want to have to give an answer. "I'm not that person anymore."

"I'm glad." Ezra closed his eyes. "He was kind of a jerk."

"I've heard." Zander dared a step closer to the bed. "Are we still friends?"

"I'll have to think about it." Ezra sighed. "I've never been one to harbor grudges. It's too hard. It's so much easier just to be friends with people. But I've never found out that one of my friends killed my mother."

Zander nodded. Another of the patients started to wake. "I'll see you when you're out."

Ezra waved halfheartedly, and Zander let himself out of the hospital. Standing in the corridor, he didn't feel any better about the situation than he had before. Life was easier without everyone knowing about the Revenant.

He'd heard of magicians with power over memory. He'd considered hunting one down just to be rid of the horrible memories of the Revenant. Then again, if he didn't have those memories, he might make the same mistakes over again. Might as well live with the guilt and shame.

He started walking. He had no direction or end goal. He only needed to move.

On the lower decks, a familiar voice called his name. He turned, banishing the dark thoughts, to see Brent strolling down the corridor. A streak of grease ran from his cheekbone to his chin, and his magnifying goggles rested atop his head. His eyes settled at once on Zander's mechanical arm.

"I saw you earlier, and I couldn't help but notice this." Brent motioned to the arm.

"Stop fondling my arm with your eyes," Zander deadpanned. "What are you doing up so early?"

"I volunteered to help with the engine. It's incredible." Brent reached for Zander's mechanical hand, then realized that it was a part of him, and then asked, "Can I?"

Zander shrugged.

Brent examined Zander's metal hand. "I've heard about mechanical limbs, but I've never seen one," Brent said, his voice distant. "This is amazing, so intricate and artfully built... Can you move it?"

Zander twitched his little finger.

"Fascinating."

"There's a medic with a mechanical leg, and a pirate with two mechanical arms," Zander said.

Brent's eyes widened.

Zander jerked his chin toward the other end of the corridor. "Come on. I'll introduce you."

Brent's joy oozed into the air around him, and Zander did his best to soak some of it. They had a long few days ahead of them, and he would need all the optimism he could find.

Every morning, Raven went up to the Belt to burn off her extra magic. Zander stood with her, using his magic alongside hers, trying to burn away his tattoo. Without the rune's restraint, his magic would be stronger and faster, he said. According to Thalame, several of the other Wraiths were doing the same. They all felt the dawning of a war.

War. The word sent a shiver down Raven's back and shuddered through her flame.

With her magic stabilized, she worked with Conrad and Thalame, learning how to fight with daggers, swords, and her fists. Zander stood to the side in those sessions, and though he held a steady expression, his tapping foot gave away his impatience. Rosaria came and went. Like Zander, she had trouble staying still with so much commotion going on around them.

Malik spent as much time as possible with the new magicians, learning about their powers and helping them understand the gifts they had been forced to hide for so long. He had tasked himself with finding places for them to go before they arrived at Wayward Point.

Raven spent her afternoons with her mother, playing a game of catch-up. Raven told her about life in the mines, and Luckett told her about her years in the sky—all the places she had gone, the near-misses with authority, and how she came to be the captain of the *Orion*.

The evening meal happened wherever it could. With so many people needing to eat, the mess hall wasn't big enough. Raven, Zander, Rosaria, Thalame, and Conrad ate where they found room. Raven's favorite place was the Belt, if the weather held.

Two days into their flight south, Zander took his metal arm out of the sling. He didn't have full mobility, and it hung limp at his side, but Raven caught him wiggling his metal fingers near constantly. At his current rate, Thalame thought he would have near full control by the time they reached Wayward Point.

At night, he flexed his shadows.

"There are more of them at night," Zander told her on the night of the second day, after their dinner on the Belt. Dusk was quickly fading into twilight, streaking the sky gold and pink and indigo.

"I don't understand," Raven said, looking at the inky puddles at Zander's command. "These look different from what you did in Moorin."

"They are different," Zander whispered. He glanced around them. Thalame and Rosaria had gone to see Ezra. "I can command natural shadows, but I have my own shadows I can use."

The natural shadows jumped back into their proper places, and Zander summoned a miniature version of Raven, made of the undulating grays, blues, purples, and blacks—the same shadows that had encased her in Moorin.

"I only use these when I..." His words trailed away, and his eyes hardened. The little shadow figure vanished.

"When you were the Revenant?" Raven whispered.

"Yeah," Zander said. "It was my father's idea. As a stupid kid, I believed him. I thought my father could do no wrong. I thought he was one of the good guys, and I wanted him to be proud of me." He scoffed. "I didn't know how wrong I was until I met your old man. I started to wonder how my life would have been different had I been raised by a father like him."

"He would have made you cut your hair," Raven said, a laugh on her tongue. "He hates that haircut."

Zander pushed a hand through his dark hair. He kept the bottom half shaved and the top half to his shoulders. Raven had tied it up for him; he couldn't with one hand, and if he left it down, the wind on the Belt would tangle it.

"Well, lucky it doesn't matter what your father thinks." Zander leaned closer to her. "What do you think?"

She bit her lip. She took a long moment to stare at his hair. At her prolonged silence, he deflated.

"I can shave the rest and start over, I mean," he started, fingering the barely-there hair on the bottom half.

"Don't do that," she said at once, earning his surprise. Her face flushed. "I mean...it's not that I don't like it...it's just..."

"What?"

Her face heated. "Fine, I kind of like it."

Laughing, Zander pecked a chaste kiss on her cheek.

The next few days went by in a blur of preparations and activities. The *Orion* made a few stops, that is to say the main ship hovered above the clouds while smaller ships visited trading posts on the ground. They couldn't do all their trading at once, so they sent a ship down every few hours to trade at a different little town. Among them returned a familiar face—Niall, the Dweller's tinker and mechanic. He had gotten word from a scout, and he had been in Oun to greet the Crusaders.

Niall's eyes went wide at Zander's new arm. He asked technical questions about calibrations and adjustments and nerve conduits, but Zander blinked at him.

Niall had laughed. "That's a fair answer. Can you tell me where I can find the mastermind who built this beauty?"

"You know, I have a friend that I think you would get along with," Zander said. He shared a knowing look with Raven.

While Raven burned away her extra magic, Zander wiggled his fingers. While Raven and Thalame practiced hand-to-hand, Zander wiggled his wrist. Soon, he could lift his wrist halfway up his chest and move all five fingers.

"Can you use your magic with that hand too?" Conrad asked during lunch, eyeballing the mechanical arm with curious eyes.

And as it turned out, he could. Zander's mechanical arm guided Conrad's shadow away from him and formed a smaller version of him on the railing of the Belt.

A week into the flight, Raven woke up earlier than the others. The room was still dark, and the three sets of lungs puffed sleepy breaths into the cabin. Raven crept down from her bunk, grabbed her boots, her dagger, and her jacket, and slipped into the corridor. At the stairs leading to the next corridor, she sat down and slipped on her boots, slung the dagger around her middle, and tugged on her jacket. This time of morning, the Belt was empty. Most of the night crew was tending to the engines, the tanks, and the weather patterns.

Raven started along the Belt. The cool morning air whisked her hair against her cheeks. Wispy clouds glided along the Belt and through the riggings like ghosts. Dawn glowed an innocent blue, framing the spiky treetops of the eastern horizon. Most of the stars remained—the world caught between night and day, between this world and the next. The air smelled like rain but sweeter. She could smell the scents of the forest underneath them, soil and vegetation and faint perfume of wildflowers.

A ghostly cloud slid past her, grazing her with cool pinpricks of moisture. The cloud did not register her presence; it continued its way along the Belt.

Raven couldn't help the smile on her face. Never, not once, did she think she would get to touch the clouds. She brought her flame to life. The yellow light glistened off the passing clouds, burning through those that drifted too close.

The door to the Belt opened, and steady footsteps sounded against the metal.

"Getting some alone time?" Zander asked.

"I didn't want to wake anyone up," Raven said. Zander's presence felt as comforting as the heat of her flame, only deeper.

Zander sauntered to where she stood, hands tucked in his pockets. The wind pushed his loose hair around his face and shook the flaps of his jacket. Her flame reflected in his sapphire eyes, turning them shades of yellow.

"I'm getting better," she said. "Look." At her command, the flame grew brighter, hotter, and taller—then smaller and pale. She repeated in time with her breaths—she had discovered her breathing had a special rhythm with her magic a few days before, and she'd been practicing.

Zander smiled. "You know, when we left Silver Glen, I was worried about protecting you. Every time I turned around and didn't see you, I panicked. If something happened to you, it would be my fault." He chuckled. "And now you're the one protecting me."

She grinned, though her cheeks warmed. "When my father took me off scavenging duty and stuck me in the kitchens, I knew that I'd never get out of there. I'd never see the daylight again, or leave that little village, or ride on an airship or see a sky city." She let out a sigh, then laughed as she looked up at the sea of stars. "I knew the ground would be as close to the stars as I would ever get."

She reached out with her flame-free hand and touched a passing cloud. The mist touched her skin like a cool breath.

Zander smiled. "And here you are."

"And here I am," she repeated. She set her free hand onto the railing.

"The whole time you were gone, I felt like everything had been torn apart," Zander said. "I thought you'd somehow been tracked down and captured or killed, and I didn't even know where to start looking. I...had this nightmare where you'd fallen and broken something and couldn't walk, and no matter how hard I searched or how fast, I couldn't get to you."

Guilt tore through her chest. "I..."

"You what?"

"After those slavers saved me, I remember wishing that you'd feel bad about it," she whispered, looking at the flame in her hand. Guilt squeezed her heart. "I was mad. I didn't feel good. Those weren't my best moments. I... I'm sorry."

Zander stepped closer. "It's fine," he started.

"No, it's not fine." She turned toward him and doused her flame. "Zander, if we don't trust each other, how can we be together?" His eyes widened, and her heart jumped into her throat. "I want to trust you. I want to know I can come to you with anything and not be yelled at or thought stupid or dumb or useless. I want you to feel the same with me. No more secrets."

Zander swallowed. He wore nothing of his arrogance. He wore vulnerability, an exposure she had so rarely seen. "Okay." He nodded. "No more secrets. No more scheming without the other. You tell me what you're thinking, and I'll do the same." He tilted her chin up. "What do you want to know about me?"

"Everything," she said and meant it.

"That's a lot of information. Where do you want me to start?"

"I don't know." Suddenly, the six months she had known Zander in Silver Glen felt like nothing.

"I'm sorry I didn't tell you about being the Revenant," he whispered. "It's not something I want to think about. Looking back, I wish I'd told my father no. I wish I'd have just been a regular Hawk and a Wraith. The Revenant was something else I was running from when I ran away from Lenhala. I had planned on staying in Silver Glen. I wanted to leave all the nonsense about the Hawks and Wraiths behind. Until Thalame and I arrived in Moorin, I had planned to never be the Revenant again."

"How did it happen? Becoming the Revenant?"

"It was my father's idea," Zander said. "He pushed me to seek out the Wraiths. Because of him, I thought only of the Hawks and rebellion. I was young and reckless and arrogant, and I wanted to please my father. He dangled the idea of being a king in front of me, and I took the bait. I wanted to be the one who saved Rhynwier from the empire. I wanted my name etched into history." He leaned onto the railing and looked down at the passing forest. "I thought I was ready for it. I thought I was tough enough. After my first assassination, I cried myself to sleep. I had nightmares for weeks."

Darkness passed over Zander's face—he looked haunted. Raven felt horrible for bringing it those memories.

"I started to regret that part of my life, but I was in too deep with the Hawks. I didn't know how to get out," Zander said. "I thought stealing the centrum would prevent war. I thought I'd be somehow making up for all the horrible things I did."

"What's done is done," Raven said. "It's a part of you, and regardless, I..." *I love you. Say it. Just say it!* "And I accept all of you, Zander."

He gave her a ghost of his usual smile. She tried again to form the words she wanted to say, but they wouldn't come. A beat, and then Zander's metal hand cupped her cheek. She felt the cool metal plates of his palm, the subtle movements of the gears within his wrist and fingers, the adjusting of the joints.

"I can almost feel it," he whispered. He lifted his flesh and bone hand to cup her other cheek. "It doesn't feel the same, but..." His flesh and bone thumb ran over her cheekbone.

She reached for him, just to touch him, to feel him. She grabbed fistfuls of his shirt collar and pulled until her nose grazed the skin of his throat. He adjusted his hands to rest on her shoulders, hugging her loosely.

"Is there anything you want to tell me?" Zander asked, his breath warm on her temple. "I know you told me the story, but is there anything you left out?"

"I honestly don't remember," Raven said. "I've had to go over the story so many times now, I don't know who I told what or what I left out. It's all a blur."

"Then tell me again," Zander whispered. "Don't leave out anything. Not a single detail."

She tightened her grip on his collar. Underneath her hand, she felt his heart thumping.

The blue dawn had steadily grown brighter. As they stood there, the first rays of golden sunlight spilled over the horizon. The wispy clouds glowed yellow, each drop of moisture illuminated from within—glowing gold, everywhere. A heavenly otherworld. It warmed Zander's sapphire eyes and bronze skin. She met those eyes, and he hugged her closer.

He leaned in, and she met his lips with her own. This kiss was unlike any other. He had opened himself fully to her, and his kiss reflected it. He held her close, hand of flesh and its metal twin mapping the contours of her back. She hadn't bothered with a corset that morning. She wore only the blouse she'd slept in and her jacket.

When their lips and tongues broke apart, the sun had burned away a portion of the wispy clouds, leaving the sky a crystalline blue. Raven released her hold on his collar and flattened her hands against his chest. She started to talk. She told him everything he wanted to know—why she had left, where she had gone, and her thoughts during the entire ordeal, many of which she now contributed to her feverish state of mind.

Zander held her as she spoke, occasionally nipping at her ear and leaving small, tender kisses on her cheek and jaw, stealing her concentration and focus.

She told him how she had been sold by the scavengers and how terrified she'd been. She told him how Conrad had gotten her out and taken her to see Malik, how she had gotten a job aboard the *Marianne*, how she had thought she would die, how Conrad took her to see the Wraiths and then Ezra. When she told him about the dream she'd had about the Revenant, his lips on her jaw hesitated.

"You dreamed about me?" His voice drifted along her skin, hesitant and fearful.

"It was the night before you tackled me," Raven said. "I know it sounds strange. I hadn't seen the Revenant or your magic before, but I dreamed about it."

Zander smirked. "How close was the dream to reality?"

"Frighteningly so."

His grin faded. His brow creased, lips parted in thoughtful curiosity.

"Is it strange to dream about things and then have those things happen?"

Zander didn't answer for a long moment. He stared at her, thinking. "Magic does strange things," he said at last. "The Wraiths might know more about dreams and premonitions. But it wouldn't hurt to get examined." He spoke seriously, but his eyes roamed up and down her body. "It might be a sign of a deeper issue. I could examine you. There might be a physical marking of a magical curse."

She blushed, heat flooding over her skin. "I think I would have seen it by now," she said. "I do bathe frequently, you know."

"What if it's somewhere you can't easily see?" Zander's brows rose. The sunlight illuminated the pink blush that warmed his own cheeks. "Like your back."

She smacked him playfully on his good arm. "You just want to see me naked."

"Any human being with an interest in girls would want to see you naked," he said plainly.

She steeled herself. "Well then, you'd better be prepared to return the favor." Even as the words left her lips, her face burned like the fever had returned.

Zander grinned mischievously at her. "Oh, I would let you examine me any day of the week."

He leaned in, and she met him. Her tongue grazed his bottom lip when a male voice shouted from somewhere in the rigging. Another called back. A third sounded.

Zander sighed against her lips. Another day had begun on the *Orion*. Crusaders were climbing into the rigging, some strapped into harnesses and others not, doing their daily inspection of the balloons and the mechanics that kept the ship flying. Seeing Crusaders without harnesses made Raven's stomach turn over. They leaped from rigging to balloon like cats, never stumbling or hesitating.

The doors to the Belt opened, and passengers looking for fresh air further diminished the moment. Raven's slice of quiet now rang with murmurs.

Zander released a sigh, and his hot breath bounced against her lips. "Might as well go see what they've drummed up for breakfast today."

"I could use a cup of tea," she said, though she'd rather have his lips than a drink.

Halfway to the mess hall, someone cleared their throat. Raven and Zander paused and turned—Samuel stood in the middle of the corridor. He scowled at their linked hands.

"Morning, Raven, Zander," said Samuel tersely.

"Morning, Dad," Raven said. "Sleep well?"

"I've had better nights," Samuel said. "How about you, Zander? Sleep well?"

"I did." Zander cleared his throat. "All night, sir. Slept, I mean. In my own bed."

Samuel closed the space between them. He stopped within reach of Zander. He crossed his thick arms. "I heard a story, a wild story, that you and that other boy gave up your room and moved into Raven's room."

Raven felt Zander tense. Her father stood several inches taller than Zander and twice as wide.

"That is true," Zander said, speaking faster than normal. "Though there are four of us in the room, including Princess Rosaria. Between you and me, she's a bit of a prude. She wouldn't let anything unsavory happen on her watch."

"He's right," Raven agreed, though she lied. Rosaria had been the one to suggest the bed was big enough for two, insinuating Raven and Zander share one. Then she'd winked at Raven.

"Where I come from" —Samuel clenched his fists—"we marry the girls we fancy."

Raven laughed. She couldn't help it. It bubbled out of her throat without a second thought. Her father and Zander both looked as if she'd lost her mind.

"Is that true, Dad?" Raven asked. "Is that what you told my mother?"

Samuel blinked, and his gaze turned sheepish. "I meant—"

"You weren't married when I was born," Raven reminded him.

Her father blinked. Zander didn't dare speak.

"Raven," Samuel said, a different sort of terror on his face. "Please don't tell me you've already..." He hesitated, color draining from his face, and glared at Zander.

Something deep within gave her a boost of steely confidence she had never felt before, and she added, "No. I tried to jump him, but I was high on magic opium smoke, and Zander said no."

Her father inhaled sharply and pinched the bridge of his nose. "Sisters," he mumbled.

"I know," Raven said, softer. "Surprised me too. Turns out, Zander's not the arrogant, bumbling fool we all thought he was."

Zander scoffed. "Excuse me?"

"What? That's what I thought of you, so I only assumed other people thought the same."

"I'm not...those things," Zander said, brow furrowed.

"A little bit." Raven held up her index finger and thumb a hair's breadth apart. "You're a lot of things."

Zander frowned.

"Not all of them are bad," Raven added.

"Raven," said her father, a stern note back in his voice. "Relationships are serious, and trust me, babies are a hefty responsibility."

Raven blushed, and the confidence vanished from her voice. "I don't plan on bringing home grandchildren," she said. "Not for a very long time, at least."

Samuel cleared his throat. "Good. There are, uh, certain...precautions that can be taken to prevent—"

"Dad." Raven waved her hands between them. Her face burned red hot. "I would really rather not have this conversation with you."

Samuel cleared his throat. "Then, promise me you'll speak to your stepmother."

"I promise I will seek out my stepmother's counsel on the matter of contraceptives." Raven took equal parts embarrassment and glee at the twinge in her father's face at *contraceptives*.

"Good." Samuel cleared his throat and once again became the stern commander. "I'm glad we had this talk. I will see you later. And you" —he pointed at Zander— "mind yourself."

"Yes, sir," said Zander.

"Bye, Dad."

Samuel glared at Zander, a warning and a threat, and then continued down the corridor toward the mess hall. Raven lingered a few moments, wishing to put as much distance between her father and herself. At least for right now.

When her father had vanished from sight, Zander let out a breath and doubled over, hands on his knees. "Sisters," he gasped. "I thought he was going to hit me."

Raven chuckled. "I thought he was too." She looped her arm with Zander's and tugged him down the corridor. "But he didn't. Come on, I'm hungry. And now I've got to find my stepmother at breakfast so my father sees us talking."

At that, Zander's face turned a shade of pink. He gave a halfhearted, uncomfortable chuckle and said, "Remember, whatever bedroom advice your stepmother gives you, she's likely referring to your father."

Raven groaned; Zander laughed. She punched his good shoulder and said, "Just for that, you get to be my first opponent in training."

"Like you could actually hit me."

"I've got better motivation this time."

They continued into the mess hall to find it crowded, but not as crowded as it would have been for lunch or dinner. Zander sat with Thalame and Conrad, while Raven purposefully joined Lena and her stepmother—making sure her father saw them talking. Raven sheepishly brought up the subject of contraceptives, and her stepmother chuckled and gave her a motherly smile.

The conversation that followed was not nearly as awkward as Raven feared it might be; her stepmother gave her a list of herbal potions and mixtures, most commonly ginger and thistle, and Raven promised to stop by the ship's herbalist.

"Thanks," Raven said. "And make sure to tell Dad you told me."

Her stepmother chuckled; so did Lena—who had taken on a pink blush during the entire conversation and had taken much more interest in her tea.

After breakfast, Raven, Zander, Thalame, and Conrad headed to the lower decks for combat practice. Conrad had secured them a small cargo hold near the air docks. Crates and barrels lined the walls but left plenty of room for them. Due to the proximity with the engines, the air was hot and humid and loud. They kept the three portholes along the north wall open, but it didn't help. The only light came from the dull lanterns along the ceiling and the sunlight.

"All right." Thalame cracked his neck to the side. He motioned toward Raven. "Let's see what you've got today."

"Actually," Raven said, stepping to the middle of the room, "I told Zander he could try his hand today. He's been aching for a good beating."

Zander scoffed. He wiggled his mechanical fingers and flexed his arms. His mechanical arms moved slower than his real arm, but he had gained substantial range of motion.

Thalame chuckled and stepped to the side of the room. "Have at it, then."

"You're getting better," Conrad commented. "Must be the magic."

Zander stretched his metal hand toward Conrad and made a fist. His metal fingers clicked against his palm. He grinned. "Every day, I'm a little faster, a little stronger."

"Soon you'll learn to fly," Conrad said, unamused with Zander's dramatics.

"Stop talking, and start moving." Raven readied her stance. "Or are you just wasting time? Trying to get your bearings? Afraid to lose?"

Zander smirked. He sauntered into the middle of the room while Thalame hung back with Conrad. Raven took up a pair of practice daggers, as did Zander. She moved first—she flung herself at Zander, and he met her attack. Their wooden daggers clacked together, and they moved about the room. Raven had the feeling that Zander went easy on her. Thalame did, and Conrad did most of the time. They had trained for years to fight, but she could feel herself getting stronger, quicker, and more capable.

Luckett was right—she didn't need protecting anymore. She could fight for herself. Not just herself—she could protect her friends. Zander. Thalame. Rosaria. Conrad. Her family. The people of Silver Glen. The crew of the *Orion* who had risked their lives to bring her out of Moorin and then had raced to protect her family from the Gray Elite.

She would fight for them all, and she would protect them.

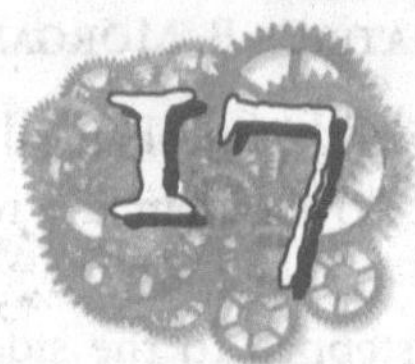

Ivaline Pemberton reclined on the cream-colored chaise. She propped her bare feet on a pillow to watch the fresh crimson paint on her toes dry. Her black heels sat on the floor, spotless as the day she'd bought them. She corked the bottle of crimson paint and set it beside her empty teacup.

Sisters, what a long day. Ivaline had attended brunch with the ladies of society in Lenhala, but her poor health had taken a turn—she'd left early to rest. None of the ladies questioned why Ivaline suddenly fell short of breath or lethargic, or batted an eye of suspicion when she requested to be taken home.

The first thing Ivaline had done upon returning home was rid herself of the damned corset and velvet dress and the stupid heels.

In truth, Ivy needed a break. She could only handle so much petty gossip and fruitless chitchat, and she neared her limit. She wore a simple day dress and had left the corset behind. Ivy felt marvelously better. Ivaline needed her rest—and Ivy needed several deep breaths—before she attempted Darlene's bridal shower in the Rose Gardens that evening. As much as she didn't want to, Darlene's husband-to-be worked directly under General Deacon, and Darlene had always had loose lips.

Ivy leaned back and stretched her arms above her head. A few more days of this drivel, and Ivaline would come down with a fever and a cough. She'd remain inside, resting, and Ivy would escape the city for the open countryside and rejoin her real friends, the Dwellers.

Even if the treehouse would be missing a few key players.

Through the windows of the lounge, the partly sunny sky made the towers of Lenhala glitter and shine, all steel and brass and colored metal. It was beautiful on the outside, but Ivy knew the ugliness on the inside. Backstabbing and lies and power-grabbing. She hated it. She missed the countryside. She missed her friends.

She leaned her head back. The sunlight glittered against the inlaid gold in the ceiling tiles.

What must it be like to see the open sky in every direction? She huffed out a quick breath. She was stuck playing the ninny while Thalame and Zander got to fly around the kingdom on a sky city. At least they'd found Rosaria and Raven. At least they had gotten out of Moorin. At least they remained safe.

Everyone was talking about Moorin and the girl who'd melted a prototype Colossus. Ivaline had been dining at the Twain estate that night, so she knew as little as everyone else, and she felt the same thirst for gossip. Ivy, on the other hand, had heard the truth from the scouts. Raven had melted the Colossus. Raven had magic now. Powerful magic too. It had something to do with the centrum, she knew it, but her scouts didn't know about the centrum or the augur.

And then her friends had vanished into the sky.

Ivy blew out a long sigh and inhaled the peppermint oil recommended by the healer. Another magician. Another member of the team to be more important than her. Of course, it didn't take much to be more important than Ivy. She spied, spread rumors and gathered intelligence, while the others could shoot lightning from their fingertips or walk through walls or command water.

And when the dam broke, a spy would be no good in the flood.

Not that she did much good. Spying kept her busy, kept the Dwellers current on rumors. Niall didn't need her bothering him in his workshop; Thalame and Zander didn't need her bothering them on their important mission to rescue the princess. She had thought—hoped—that she and Raven would stay behind while the others went to save Rosaria.

And Raven had left too.

Ivy didn't blame Raven. Not really. Raven had been miserable, but that misery had been something of a comfort to Ivy. She had been able to ease that misery, fix what Thalame's magic couldn't. But Raven had gone anyway. Ivy hadn't been enough. Again.

Footsteps sounded in the corridor. Ivaline didn't move; she didn't feel like it. Besides, she was supposed to be feverish and tired. For kicks, she coughed into her embroidered handkerchief.

A quick two-note knock hit the lounge door.

"A visitor, Miss Ivaline," drawled a servant.

"Who?" Ivy crooned softly.

"Miss Marie Kenara."

Ivy sighed dramatically and pulled a lacey fan from the side table. "I'll see her."

The door opened with a soft swish, and a pair of heels entered. The door shut. Marie's heels made their way through the room, sauntered around the chaise. Her dark hair had been done up in an elegant bun, her dark brown eyes lined with glittery kohl. She sat in the chair closest to Ivy, looking like a dream in black and gold silk. She leaned back and crossed her legs, flashing a strip of golden flesh that went nearly to her hip.

"You look like you have somewhere fancier to be," Ivy said.

"I had a brunch date." Marie smoothed her skirt. "But he's one of those 'all about me' types. I don't care how much he makes in a year. It's not worth putting up with that for the rest of my life. Or, his life."

Ivy shrugged. "They can't all be winners."

Marie grinned. "That's true. If every guy was like Ezra, well, the world would be a little better off."

Ivy schooled her emotions. Marie had dealings with the Hawks, but she was a Wraith first. For Marie to mention Ezra—she had news. Ezra had been involved in something. The Gray Elite claimed he had been caught up in the wrong crowd and dragged into one of the riots. Her scouts hadn't been able to bring her anything on him.

"I'm not sure Ezra still likes me." Ivy pouted. "I haven't heard from him since he went to Moorin. I hope he's not gotten hurt in the Riots."

Marie shrugged. "I hear he's gone north."

Ivy swallowed. North? The Gray Elite suspected the rebels had gone north. They'd dispatched Buzzers a few days ago. But, If Ezra had gone north—had he been on a Buzzer? Had he gotten out of Moorin?

Ivy let out a bored sigh. "That's fine, I suppose. We never went beyond friends, anyway." Not that she wanted to.

"I hear you tuckered yourself out this morning," Marie said, drawling her words. "Poor baby, socializing is such hard work."

"It is!" Ivy pouted. "All the talking and remembering things and planning." The pleasantries, nimble words, and crafted replies. "I don't know how girls do this all day!"

Sisters knew Ivy couldn't. She didn't know if Ivaline could handle it anymore. Spying had started out fun, but lately it had become exhausting.

"We take breaks. It's called cocktail hour." Marie laughed—a sound as graceful as the rest of her. "I've been thinking of relocating permanently to the south. Have you ever been to the southern coast? It's divine this time of year."

Ivy hummed thoughtfully. The southern coast—Wayward Point, home of the Wraiths. Outside of the Gray Elite's power struggle. Safe. Ivy caught the hidden meaning—a warning to get out of Lenhala, to get to safety.

Were the rumors of war true?

"I haven't," Ivy said.

"Oh!" Marie put a hand over her heart as if stricken. "The white sand beaches, the fruit, the free flowing music that never stops, the barely-dressed people. I don't know about you, but I could stand to be half naked for the rest of my life. And to drink from a coconut!"

Ivy thought about it. She wouldn't mind wearing one of those wispy dresses of cotton or just a swatch tied at her waist. Or nothing at all. She wouldn't mind feeling the sun over all of her.

"I think I could stand living on a beach," Ivy said with a sigh. She could do with a few months of peace and silence.

Marie scooted forward and joined Ivy on the chaise. "Come with me," Marie purred. She tugged on the loose ties of Ivy's day dress. "We can lie on the beach together, swim in the ocean, bathe in the hot springs."

Marie—like Thalame, Zander, and now Raven—was a magician. As a Wraith, she had spent time in the south. She knew of the Dwellers, but Thalame didn't trust her. He thought her shifty. Ivy did too, but she liked Marie—she had an unpredictable side. She knew of the Hawks too, but she hadn't openly chosen a side. Marie was loyal to herself first, and anyone else depended on her mood.

Marie leaned in to say something else, but as her lips formed the words, a swift two-tone knock sounded on the lounge door. Their tryst ended before it began.

"A visitor, Miss," said the servant.

"Who?" Ivy asked, her voice reflecting her irritation.

"General Oliver Deacon."

Her blood ran cold. Marie's eyes widened, and a fraction of her panic came through her painted mask. Ivy steeled herself quickly.

"Just a moment," Ivy called.

Marie slid to the end of the chaise, and Ivy quickly smoothed the bodice of her dress. She pulled a throw over her shoulders to hide her lack of a corset. Ivy leaned back into the chaise as any ill-feeling rich girl would do. She tried her best to hide her nerves. The general had never called on her before. He had come to speak with her father, but never her.

Something had changed. Something had happened.

And she would be the one to discover it and relay the information to the others. Lightning coursed through her nerves.

"Send him in," Ivy chimed.

The door opened. Heavy-booted steps signaled his approach. Ivy held herself still, but her heart thumped with each footstep. General Deacon stepped around the chaise, a fake smile on his face. He sat in the chair across from her. He looked so much like Ezra. Same chin, nose, and ears, but where Ezra's eyes were soft and sympathetic, the general's eyes were cold.

His cold eyes passed over Marie and settled on Ivy. "I'm sorry to hear you're unwell."

Ivy gave a curt nod. "Thank you for your concern, General," she said softly. "I'm sorry to say that I'm used to it by now."

Deacon glanced at Marie, his glare intent.

Marie cleared her throat and stood. "Pardon me, General. Ivaline, love, I will take my leave." She swept around the chaise and pressed a chaste kiss on Ivy's temple before she left. The gesture brought a wry smile to Deacon's mouth.

"Ah, young love," he said. "It's always beautiful to watch."

Ivy returned his smile with one of her own. She'd heard rumors of the sort of beauties he liked to watch. Men like him were the reason whorehouses had peepholes. The game between Marie and Ivy had never been anything more. Marie had a lover; Ivy had never met them. The game between Ivy and Marie was the smokescreen that hid anyone else.

"What do I owe the pleasure of this surprise visit, General?" Ivy asked. "My father would likely be more suitable company."

"Yes, yes, I have a meeting with him shortly, which is why I'm here," said Deacon. "But, as it is, he is running late. I thought I would come and see how his favorite child is faring."

"You flatter me." Ivy grinned anyway.

Likely, Deacon came digging for information. However, Ivy had never had an opportunity to dig Deacon for information. She could use this chance meeting to make this blasted trip into the city worth it.

Painting panic on her features, she said, "I've heard dreadful things from Moorin, General. Marcy's brother had the worst time getting across the border, and he spoke of riots and looting. It sounds terrible."

Deacon nodded grimly. He folded his hands together. "Moorin is in chaos right now. Rebels started a series of attacks against the Gray Elite. A group of magicians attacked one of the automaton factories, and with all the rioting, there is a shortage of automatons. The Gray Elite have apprehended several rebels, but there are many more out there." He offered her a kindly smile and added, "But don't you worry, Miss Pemberton. These are things soldiers worry about, not young ladies like yourself."

"It's hard not to worry when there are riots happening," Ivaline said, her voice quivering. She drew her arms up and loosely crossed them over her chest, making herself smaller, vulnerable. "I heard...I heard Ezra was there."

Deacon's kindly smile became a flat line. Anger pulsed behind his eyes.

So the rumors were true. She gasped and covered her mouth. "No," she whispered. "Tell me it's not true, General. Tell me what I've heard is lies."

Deacon looked down at his hands. "My son is a criminal, Miss Pemberton. He chose to save a group of murderous rebels over his own people. He has deserted the Gray Elite."

Her heart flip-flopped. She deflated into the chaise, letting her breaths go shallow. "Why would he... I don't understand."

"Neither do I," Deacon said, his voice strong. "Ivaline, I need to ask you a few questions. This is a serious matter. Do you feel up to it?"

Ivaline pretended to consider this strange request. He had questions for her, and she had questions for him, though hers would not be so blatant. She calmed herself, took several deep breaths, and quickly found that girl deep inside that could lie and charm.

"Yes, General," Ivaline said, hand resting over her heart. "I will help in any way I can."

"I'm glad to hear it," Deacon said, his grin wolfish.

Raven stood on the Belt as they crossed the border from Rhynwier into Tinatun. They flew above the clouds, and a dome of endless blue stretched above them. Below was a sea of puffy white clouds. Through the occasional gap in the clouds, Raven spotted the thick green of the forest, the serpentine aquamarine river, and thatch villages. She couldn't see the ocean, but she could imagine it. Endless blue-green, sparkling in the sun.

The *Orion* traveled into the mountainous coast of Wayward Point, tucking between a cluster of spiky peaks.

Raven, Zander, Thalame, and Malik climbed onto a smaller airship that would take them down to the coastal air docks. Conrad followed a step behind, but as he started to step over the gangplank, Malik barred his passage.

"What? I'm not invited?" Conrad asked, looking between Malik's ringed fingers and to his stoic expression.

"Not to the stronghold," Malik said firmly. "You have been barred from the Wraiths until you can prove yourself with your patron Sister."

Conrad's grin fell, and his shoulders deflated. Malik's glare did not lessen, and Conrad took careful steps backward on the gangplank, until he stood on the berth. He held Malik's glare the entire time, casual mischief twisted into something serious and unreadable. Malik closed the door and snapped orders at the pilot. The engines rumbled to life.

Raven met Malik's stare, and she suspected he had other reasons for not wanting Conrad to come. Within his glare, he wore a severe warning not to say anything.

She didn't.

The ship dropped out of the air docks and into a gorge underneath. Raven's stomach, heart, and lungs dropped with it, only to lurch back into place as the ship started to fly. The airship nimbly navigated through the mountains and over the forests and villages.

Raven tried to hold herself steady. She would be meeting with the Wraiths, an order older than the kingdom, an order full of magicians and secrets. Raven wished Rosaria had come with them, but she'd stayed behind to keep Ezra company. Luckett had him placed in a holding cell belowdecks, because she didn't want the risk of having a Gray Elite wandering about her ship.

And for Ezra's safety, Zander had added. Plenty of Crusaders had ill feelings toward the Gray Elite. Rosaria would make sure none of them took out those ill feelings on Ezra.

The pilot navigated them through the rocky opening to the hidden air docks of Wayward Point. The air docks had been built inside a cavern, catwalks and berths secured over the ocean by thick steel cables and pitons thicker than a grown man's arm. It felt strange to come back, Raven thought as she stepped onto the gangplank. It felt like a lifetime ago she and Conrad had departed from these docks, bound for Moorin. It still smelled like seaweed, mildew, and cheap ale.

Malik led them through the network of catwalks and out of the air docks. The path led down the cavern wall and wound around it—just above high tide—and out of the cavern mouth and to the rocky beach on the other side. The path led up along the beach and to a fork divided by palms. Raven vaguely remembered this. One path would take them into the outskirts of Wayward Point. It had been the path Malik had taken to bring her to the air docks. He did not take that path now. He chose the second.

The second path wound through the jungle of palms, scraggly bushes, and squat trees. The path narrowed and in some places, became as steep as stairs. Raven slid on the sandy rocks several times, and each time, Zander's hands flattened against her back to steady her. He didn't tell her to be careful, to watch her step, or to walk slower. He only prevented her from falling.

The path wound through cliffs, between cliff sides so close together, Raven had to walk sideways, underneath skinny waterfalls that splattered her face with drops of cool water, underneath vine-strung bluffs, and through the roots of one massive tree. Finally, after an hour of hiking, the path opened up to a small gulf. Cliffs rose on all sides, save for the narrow opening that led to the sea. A village of thatch and jungle wood nestled into the cove. Some houses had been built over buoyed docks, others had been built into the branches of the ancient trees, and others had been built onto the rocks.

The chittering of birds echoed through the cove. More than one waterfall cascaded from the top of the cliffs, and into the cove, the sound echoed until it sounded like a gentle roar.

As Malik led them through the village, Raven's stomach tightened; the village was empty. She heard no voices, saw no people. But fresh footsteps remained in the sand, several sets of them. The air smelled of roasted fish, overripe fruit, and smoke. People lived here, but where had they gone? It gave Raven the impression that she had disturbed something, like she had intruded upon something sacred.

"They've added more huts since the last time I was here," Zander said, his voice low, cautious.

"We've had more magicians in the past ten years than we've ever had," Malik said. "Thanks to the Gray Elite, magicians are desperately trying to get out and survive. Some choose to stay here and fight with us."

Malik led them toward the cliff at the back of the cove. The moment they crossed underneath the shadow of the cliff's ledge, the temperature dropped. Raven felt something else, something within the air, as if the world had fallen away from beneath her feet and she had walked into another world. The sensation sent every hair on her body standing on end.

As they continued, the shadow revealed the massive structure at the back of the cove, a stone temple carved from the cliff itself. Three stone dragons perched on three stone gables, each with vicious eyes and wings poised for flight. Pillars lined the front of the temple, each pillar carved with elegant depictions of trees, stars, sea life, and people. As they approached the temple's wide front steps, Raven could see that every inch of the stone had been carved. Whorls, runes, and stories had been etched into every surface.

Malik started up the steps without hesitation and then paused at the massive stone doors. No handle, no knocker, not even a peephole, but they were clearly doors. Of course, she reminded herself, Wraiths had magic.

Everything about this place—the otherness, the strangeness—it had to be magic. It radiated from the sand and stone, from the very air. Despite the chill working its way through her body, despite how her legs trembled and her knees felt like sand, despite how much she wanted to turn around and run back to the sunlight, Raven followed Malik up the stairs.

Her brother wore dire seriousness as he asked, "Are you ready?"

Raven took a deep breath. No. "Yes. I'm ready." For what, she didn't know, but she hadn't come all this way just to stand at the door like a coward.

Malik didn't knock. He didn't even touch the doors. The doors opened on their own, swinging inward, revealing a darkness as thick as ink.

Her unease doubled.

Malik walked inside first, his form vanishing into the darkness. Thalame set a reassuring hand on her shoulder and then followed Malik inside. He vanished too. He did not remove her fear and unease.

Steeling herself, she stepped across the threshold. Her boots echoed on the stone floor. Soon, the darkness swallowed her too. She couldn't see Malik or Thalame. She couldn't hear them. She heard footsteps behind her—Zander.

The massive stone doors shut, and the darkness was complete.

She heard only silence. Raven's heart hammered hard in her chest, once, twice—torches burst to life, flooding the chamber with bright gold light. Raven flinched at the brightness and shielded her eyes with her arm. She stood in a large square room of stone. The torches hung on iron brackets. In the middle of the ceiling, chains held a circular dish aloft. From that dish, gold flames flickered and danced, illuminating more than regular fire. Magic, she realized.

The chamber rose two floors. The second floor was a veranda that stretched around the chamber, and standing on that veranda were at least thirty people. Some were dressed in dark clothes like Wraiths, others wore simple clothes, and others looked as though they belonged on the beach. The people from the village.

A bronze-skinned old man stood on the other side of the first floor, his charcoal beard and matching hair braided with gold and silver beads. He wore gray robes tied loosely with a golden sash. His feet were bare. His black eyes took them in under an unreadable expression.

"Grand Master Deikun," Malik said with reverence. He bowed deeply.

Zander and Thalame stood on either side of Raven, and as they mirrored Malik's bow, she quickly mirrored theirs.

A beat passed, and Raven's heart tried again to escape up her throat.

"Three of our own, come home," said Deikun, his voice deep, harsh, and lilting with a sharp accent Raven had never heard. "And you have brought a guest."

Zander and Thalame straightened, and Raven copied. She found Deikun staring at her.

"I bring fresh blood," Malik said.

Raven bristled.

"Ah." Deikun did not have to speak loud; his voice carried. His dark eyes took in Raven. At first, his gaze merely searched, but then it sharpened. "Interesting blood you've brought before me, seeker."

Whispering came from the veranda, the gentle murmur echoing delicately off the stone, and it made Raven glance up. Indeed, most looked down at her. She swallowed, steeled herself, and met Deikun's gaze.

The grand master stepped closer, his bare feet silent on the stone, his hands folded behind his back. "You hold magic I have rarely felt before," he said to Raven. He halted in front of her, bringing with him the smells of the sea. His dark eyes studied her again, and then he held out his hands. "Your hands."

She cautiously set her hands into his. His were bony, age-spotted, and wrinkled, but sturdy. He closed his callused fingers around hers. Her magic responded, like blood rushing to her head. It brought a sudden wave of nausea, and then it stopped. Her magic settled back into its safe place, as did the sense that she might empty her stomach on the grand master's robes.

"Interesting, indeed." Deikun beheld her with a new curiosity. "Your magic is strong, but wild and untamed. Ferocious but precarious." His eyes narrowed. "Unnaturally obtained."

Panic, quick and hot, surged through her bones. The grand master could tell all of that from a touch?

The panic and fear must have shown on her face, for Deikun said, "It is not a crime, magician. Do not worry. There are no repercussions waiting for you here. This is not a trial, nor am I a judge."

Deikun released her hands and folded his behind his back. The whispers along the veranda silenced.

"You have passed the first test," said Deikun, his voice soft but loud. "You have found us, come of your own freewill, and have proven your magic. However, the next test is not as simple."

Malik took a step forward, and the words on Deikun's tongue vanished. By the shift in whispers along the veranda, Raven gathered that Deikun was not supposed to be interrupted.

"Grand Master," Malik started, his panic subtle but present. "We didn't bring her here to become a Wraith, we—"

"I know why you have come," said Deikun, his voice strong and steady, speaking over Malik easily.

Malik bowed again.

"You have come here for answers. You have come here, thinking that I have those answers. I will save you the trouble, seeker. I do not have the answers this magician seeks."

Raven felt the wind go out of her. Malik tensed. Zander let out the faintest of gasps. Only Thalame seemed to be holding himself steady.

"The Sisters know far more than I," Deikun said. "And it is in this magician's best interest to seek out that wisdom on her own."

"Seek it out on my own?" Raven repeated.

"Become a Wraith," Deikun answered. Zander started to speak, but Deikun held up a hand. "This is a decision she must make on her own."

Without confiding in her friends first, all three of whom were Wraiths.

But if she could find answers to her power, to controlling it, by becoming a Wraith? Several long beats passed. Malik glanced over his shoulder at her, urgency in his eyes. She blinked. He then nodded toward Deikun—it took her a moment to realize Deikun waited for her to speak. For her answer.

"I'll do it," Raven said. "I'll become a Wraith."

Malik's urgency faded into calm. On either side of her, Thalame and Zander stood still as stone.

"Are you ready?" asked Deikun.

Raven nodded. "I am ready," she said, her voice quiet in the vast space.

"And confident." A small smile tugged at Deikun lips. Winkles stretched from ear to ear. "Even if it is only in words."

He knew her fear too, then.

"To be afraid is not a shameful thing," Deikun said. "Fear keeps us humble. Fear keeps us alert. It reminds us of our own limitations and vulnerabilities." He cleared his throat. "The Trial begins immediately."

Zander, Thalame, and Malik all gasped; the sharpness of the sound stirred her own panic anew. Along the veranda, nervous whispers surged and rattled Raven's resolve. Had she chosen the wrong answer?

Zander met her gaze, worried and panicked. Thalame didn't look any better. Malik looked as though he had swallowed something too hot.

Had she known what the grand master had meant by the Trial, she would have felt the same. Likely more.

Every Wraith had gone through the Trial, alone and without guidance, as would Raven. Deikun and Malik escorted Raven out of the temple at once, to a rowboat tied to a dock. Zander and Thalame could not come, mostly because of the rowboat's size. Raven sat with her back to the stern, Malik sat beside her, Deikun sat at the bow, and Elizi—a young woman with rich brown skin and emerald eyes—sat in the middle.

The boat held no oars, and before Raven could ask how they planned to row a rowboat without them, Elizi held her hands over the sides of the boat. The water rolled beneath the boat, and they glided across the cove. Raven's gasp brought a smile to Elizi's face. Magic—she controlled the water underneath them, making oars obsolete. They glided through the cliffs and into the sea, smooth as glass. Gulls flew across the opening, wings white in the sun, calls bright. The briny sea breeze felt cool against her cheeks, even as the sun warmed her.

"Minerva's gulls are a symbol of protection against bad weather." Deikun watched the birds fly out of sight. His eyes settled on Raven.

"I hope so," Raven said.

Elizi steered the rowboat farther and farther from the mainland, and as it shrank, a nervousness set Raven's bones on fire. Her magic mixed with her fear, but she banished it as best she could. She could do this. She had done so much already. She could handle the Trial of the Wraiths. Whatever it was. She had her magic, her wits, and her will to survive.

They rowed farther out to sea, and then at last, she heard the crashing of waves against sand and stone. She turned her head, holding onto the stern for fear of falling into the water. They approached an island no bigger than a small village, on which sat the ruins of an ancient fort. As Malik brought them closer, the derelict state of the fort became clearer. Once, it might have been as grand as a castle, its towers and turrets and battlements made for protection. But over time, walls had collapsed, towers leaned, and battlements crumbled. Moss and ivy had taken over much of the outside. Despite the ruined state, a good portion of the fort still stood, windows dark and empty.

"This is what remains of Fort Agnar," said Deikun. "It belongs to no kingdom or country. Its origins are beyond our history. It comes from a time long before, another kingdom, another war. Within its walls are hidden treasures. You must retrieve one of these treasures and then explain its value to me. You have one week's time to complete this task. No outside help is allowed. No tools. No advice. You have your magic and your mind."

"Good thing I ate a full breakfast this morning," Raven said.

Malik frowned, but a small smile twisted the corners of the grand master's lips.

The rowboat approached a wooden dock that had seen much better days. Several of the planks had rotted away or fallen into the shallow water below. Elizi glided them closer and angled Raven's side of the boat against the studier part of the dock.

"This is where we part," said Deikun. "In one week, we will return to this spot to fetch you. If you do not return, we will assume you dead. No one will fetch your body from the ruins."

A chill ran through her at those words. She glanced at Malik; worry had wormed through his stoic mask. Now, she understood why they had been nervous at her answer—she might die. She glanced at Deikun, but his expression betrayed no emotion. Raven swallowed her fears, gathered her wits, and climbed out of the boat. The weathered boards of the docks creaked viciously under her boots. She took another step, testing the board before she put her weight fully upon it.

"Do you understand, magician?" asked Deikun.

"Find the treasure, don't die, and be back here in a week." Speaking her mission aloud made it sound simpler, and she felt a sprig of hope. She could do this.

She turned back to Deikun and Malik, both looking serious and dire. Elizi, at least, didn't look so grim.

Raven gave them a confident grin. "I'll be fine. What if I finish before the week is up?"

"You have a week," Deikun repeated. "No more, no less."

She nodded. "Yes, I understand."

Deikun nodded, his lips a straight line. "May the Sisters look upon you with favor, magician."

The boat glided away from the dock and started back to the mass of greenish blue mainland.

"I'll see you in a week!" Raven called from the dock, waving. She stood there a while, watching, but neither the grand master or Malik turned around or waved. Elizi was busy with the water.

Every Wraith had taken this Trial. Of course, Raven had no idea how many magicians had taken this test and failed. That would not be her. She could do this. She could become a Wraith.

A week. She had a week to find treasure hidden somewhere within the fort, figure out its value, and not die in the process. She had a week to survive on this island with no help.

She could handle a week. She had her magic, her ebony-handled dagger, and a will to survive. Her mother had said a will does incredible things if strong enough. The grand master had said no tools, but he hadn't told her to leave her dagger, and she wore it proudly on her waist. Weapons must not count, then. Even if they did, she might not even need a dagger with her magic.

Raven steeled her will and straightened her shoulders. She marched along the sandy path to the fort. She followed the winding path with her eye first, the overgrowth, the gravel, the loose pale sand, to what had been the front doors of the fort—grand wooden doors reinforced with iron bars that had long since fallen from the hinges. A wall had fallen on the other side. She wouldn't be getting in through the front doors. She trekked around the weedy island until she came to a hole—it looked like a pillar had fallen on the other side, knocking a sizable chunk out of the wall.

Raven waded through the weeds and climbed onto the fallen stones. The sunlight illuminated the room beyond, but darkness prevailed farther in. Raven climbed through the hole. Inside, the darkness lingering under forsaken furniture and crumbling stone looked thicker, heavier. This chamber had been subject to the elements for a long time. Vines had squeezed between stones, mold and moss grew along the walls, and water had streaked the stones.

It wouldn't do for shelter. Summoning a flame in her hand, she started for the dark corridor on the other side. The crashing of the waves became distant. Her footsteps echoed. She heard scurrying, rats likely. The mildew and moss turned the air dank and humid.

Beyond the exterior walls, the fort looked relatively sturdy. The thick stone ceilings and walls held and didn't look as though they would collapse if she breathed too hard or stomped too close. The chambers without windows had remained unscathed, only musty and damp and dusty with disuse. Rugs and tapestries had been eaten away by mildew and time to the barest of discolorations on the stone floor. Iron torch brackets had thick knots of rust. Paintings had molded, the colors leeched and frames rotting.

Raven wandered through several rooms and chambers and corridors until she came to what looked to have been the base of a tower. The roof was intact, the walls stood straight, and it had a hole that had once been a window that overlooked a stretch of sandy beach and the endless ocean. Thanks to a fallen pillar on the outside that angled over the window, rain hadn't fallen inside. With the natural light streaming in from the window, she didn't need her flame—she let it go.

If Raven had to spend a week here, she would need a base of operations. This chamber looked as good as any. A quick trip of the chamber's edges proved no hidden nests of mysterious critters or worrisome mold. The remains of a campfire suggested others had used this spot to camp as well. She would need shelter, food, and clean water. With her shelter secured, that left two vitals.

She would need drinking water first. Back in Silver Glen, they had old stills that stole the pure water from the dirt and grime that lurked in the lakewater. Of course, the mechanics and smiths had tools to craft such a device. Raven had only her fire. She knew the basics—let the sun do the work. She needed something to hold the seawater, something else to catch the vapor, and something to catch the clean water. She didn't have time to scour the island for parts.

She climbed through the window and to the shore. The loose sand gave in under her feet. The idea struck—sand. She walked to a wide stretch of sand and knelt. She summoned her flame on the sand. At first, she didn't think it would work, but she felt the sand starting to give in. She urged her flame to burn hotter.

By the time she had crafted the sand into a rudimentary glass still, sweat dripped down her face, and her magic whined for rest. The still was small, uneven, and a bit lumpy where bits of sand hadn't melted, but the basic shape was there. Raven used an old tin cup from the tower chamber and filled the base of the still. She set it in the sunlight.

Her dry tongue couldn't wait for the sun. She heated the water with the dregs of her magic. She watched the vapor gather on the top, more and more of it, until drops fell into the collection cup. Drops at a time. She dislodged the glass collection cup from the still with a clink; it was barely more than two gulps.

It was better than drinking seawater. In all of her books, nothing good came from drinking seawater.

She gathered palm fronds, coconuts, and driftwood, anything she thought might be of use. The sun heated the air and the humidity stuck her clothes to her skin, though the sea breeze made it bearable. As much as she wanted to, she couldn't strip—she had nothing to manage a sunburn.

By the time the sun began to set, she had a bed made, coconuts stored, and a firepit for when she didn't feel like using her magic.

As the sun set, as the colors of the sky streaked with dark golds, mauve, and indigo, Raven felt good about this Trial. She stood on the rocky shore as the colors brightened and then faded into twilight. She had removed her boots, trousers, and corset and relished the feeling of the cool sand under her bare feet and the sea breeze on her legs. As the sun sank, the temperature sank with it, though not by much.

Conrad had been right. The sunset over the ocean was breathtaking.

As the glow of twilight finally faded, Raven returned to the tower using her flame. She settled into her makeshift bed. As she had expected, it was not very comfortable.

If every Wraith had taken this Trial, it meant one of two things: either this old fort had a plethora of hidden treasures to be found, or Deikun replaced a treasure when someone found it. The latter implied that Deikun knew exactly where the treasures were and what explanation she needed to come up with for each one.

It didn't matter. She could handle it.

She would become a Wraith.

She slept terribly. The fronds did little to soften the stone floor, and each nighttime sound had her pulling her eyes open and summoning a fire—but each time, only the empty room greeted her. No monsters, no giant rats, no creeping spiders. Only shadows. By the time the sun began to glow, Raven gave up on getting any more sleep. She searched the island for a suitable stick, then used her magic, dagger, and stones to focus the end of the stick to a point. She found a fallen pillar that stretched into the sea, and she made way to the end of it. The warm salt water lapped over her ankles.

She crouched and waited, spear poised.

Raven could remember going fishing with her father. She'd been young. He had taught her how to wait, how to aim not at the fish but above it. It had been in the days when she didn't know what job she would grow into, when she still thought she would grow into the leading role her father held so effortlessly. It took a few dozen failures, but Raven speared a fish. After a small hoot of victory, she carried the fish back into her shelter, sparked a fire on the driftwood, and roasted the fish. She drank from the still and refilled it.

After breakfast, she started the dreadful and exciting work of exploring the ruins for treasure. Like a pirate, she told herself. Using her magic as a torch, she delved deeper into the shadow-laden corridors. While the sun and weather hadn't touched the interior walls, the dank and damp had. Some corridors had collapsed, others had puddles of filmy green water, and others had splotches of mold inching along the stones. She avoided the mold and stagnant water when she could, and when she couldn't, she held her shirt over her nose. Growing up in an underground mine, she had learned to avoid mold. It could be harmless, but it could also be toxic.

At least she wouldn't have to worry about burning off her magic—she would need all of it to make it through this nightmarish fort.

Despite the dank, the air reminded her of the Wraiths' stronghold. The air felt different, alive somehow, but steady. Indifferent. Her mind drifted over the word, *haunted*. More than once, Raven had been looking one direction, only to see the barest glimpse of movement from the other. She would whirl around, flame in hand, but she never saw anything or anyone. She heard rats scurrying, bats skittering, and gulls calling, but she never saw them. The absence of life bothered her. It felt worse than the mines, utterly closed off and forgotten by the world.

Had the grand master meant it when he said no one would fetch her body? At the time, she had agreed without thinking about what those words implied—that others had not returned, that their bodies hadn't been fetched either, that those bodies remained in the very ruins she exploded.

She shivered. She stopped looking so closely at the shadows after that. She didn't want to stumble across a body.

She wandered for what felt like hours, up and down crumbling staircases, through fallen archways and corridors, crawling through tiny passages underneath fallen columns and pillars, through decrepit chambers and rooms and closets. She had gone deep enough that no windows allowed her light. Water dripped endlessly, mimicking footsteps. The sea breeze whistled through impossible drafts, sounding like whispers.

Her sleeplessness caught up with her too soon, her stomach started to growl, and she hadn't a clue about how to get back to her camp. But she kept going.

She kept walking.

Kept wandering.

Even though she questioned her sense of direction—that crumbling archway looked familiar. Had she passed it before?

Exhausted, hungry, thirsty, and frustrated, Raven jumped the last four steps of a crumbling staircase to a corridor she hadn't seen before. Stone pillars lined the walls, and between each was a faded mural. Once, the hall might have been beautiful. An iron chandelier had once hung from the ceiling but now crumpled in a heap of rusted metal on the floor. The murals themselves, however, looked mostly intact.

Raven brought her flame closer to the first mural. The shadows lifted, the dust burned away, and the picture became one that she knew. She had seen it on maps in her mother's office—the continent—Gracita, Rhynwier, and Tinatun. But, it was not the same as she had seen. The three kingdoms were not named, and in the southwest corner of the map, where on every other map was nothing but open ocean, was a great land mass. Raven inched closer; there were no lines dividing kingdoms, only land.

At the top of the mural, beyond the northern mountains, a face overlooked the world. A man's face. His robes braided with the stone frame of the mural, and two carved feet rested at the bottom, touching the floor. Words in a language she had never seen before traced around the frame, the characters elegant and curving.

Raven felt a chill race through her bones. She knew who it was. The old god, the one the Gray Elite had tried to erase.

Raven stared into the stone eyes of the lost god; her breath quickened, and her heart stammered. She brought her flame to the next mural. The old god hovered above the mural as he did in the first, but this time, the continent had been divided into four kingdoms. The lines were not the same as the current borders, but the shapes were relatively the same. From his hand, four seeds dropped into the heart of each kingdom. Inside each seed, a symbol was carved: in Rhynwier, sky; in Gracita, stone; in Tinatun, water, and in the fourth kingdom in the southwest, a flame. The first three symbols decorated the walls of the Temple of the Three Sisters in Silver Glen, but Raven had never seen the fourth.

The grand master had said these ruins came from another time. He knew about these murals. He had to know.

In the next Mural, the seeds had grown into women. Raven's breath caught in her throat—she knew them. The seed of earth had become Solen, Goddess of Stone and Metal. From her, gears and tools grew. The seed of sky had become Wilyn, Goddess of the Forest and Stars. From her, trees flourished and flowers bloomed. The seed of water had become Minerva, Goddess of the Sea and Wind. Around her, snake-like creatures wove in and around.

The three sisters that she knew. They had come from the old god.

And then, in the southwest of the mural's map, the seed of flame had become a woman Raven had never seen before. A fourth Sister. From the fourth Sister, books and scrolls grew. A monster had been carved around her, fangs and bat-like wings. A dragon. Smoke billowed from its nostrils.

But it was not the books or scrolls or dragon that worried Raven. It was the face of the fourth Sister. It had been scratched from the mural, leaving a jagged dent in the stone where her face should have been. She doubted it had been from time—no other part of the murals had been damaged. Only the slice over the fourth Sister. Someone had purposefully carved her away.

Her eyes lingered on the fourth Sister. Four Sisters, not three. What had happened to the fourth? Why had history forgotten her? Had the Gray Elite erased her from history like it had the old god? Zander had once told her they wanted the Sisters gone too, and that they would succeed if left unchecked. Had they already erased one?

Raven pulled her lip between her teeth. Adding a fourth Sister felt blasphemous, yet something about it felt...right. Something deeper than her bones didn't balk at the idea, like her magic knew the fourth Sister had been real. Her magic accepted it, knew it.

"Magic works in its own way," Conrad had once said. "It doesn't work like human laws do or the way humans think it should. It does what it wants, however it wants to do it."

In the next mural, the old god remained at the top of the map. The Four Sisters stood in their kingdoms. Trees and stars spread around Wilyn; machinery spread over Solen's land; ships dotted the water around Minerva; and books stacked around the fourth Sister. The dragon had risen from the water, its wings spread, a flame shooting out of its mouth, reaching Solen's land.

Raven gasped—her flame nearly went out. She brought her light closer to the mural. There, where Solen and the fourth Sister collided, was an etching of what at first looked like a canon. The more Raven looked at it, the more she knew what it was: Altair's Augur.

The augur had been created between Solen and the fourth Sister?

Raven half ran and stumbled to the next mural. Altair's Augur had been carved with flames, and a hole had been carved where the old god had once been. His face, his hands, his braided robes, his feet—gone. Because of Altair's Augur. It had been used against him.

Her breath caught in her throat. What kind of power could erase gods?

Solen had not been happy. On the mural, she held her head in her hands. Wilyn and Minerva lifted their hands, water and stars in a flurry.

A hole had been carved in Solen's land. Raven shuddered. Legends told of Altair's Augur power and how it had destroyed an entire city in a single blast of blinding white light.

In the next mural, the Three Sisters combined their powers of earth, sky, and water. Vines of their magic swirled between them, a great storm. Lightning bolts struck the fourth Sister's land, killing the dragon, burning the books, and in the final mural, the map looked as Raven knew it. The fourth Sister was gone. No land existed in the southwest, only vast seas.

The fourth sister had been erased, just like the old god, just like the Gray Elite wanted to do to magic. But the Gray Elite had not erased the fourth Sister; the Three Sisters had. Raven returned to the mural depicting Altair's Augur, the collaboration between Solen and the fourth Sister. The fourth Sister's fire powered the machine, encircled it on the mural.

Even after the fourth Sister vanished, her fire remained with the augur. The centrum—it came from that power of Fire.

The same Fire that Raven now possessed.

Raven felt the world shift under her feet. She collapsed on the stone ground, breath catching, heart thudding. The world grayed. Darkness edged her vision.

She held the flame of the missing fourth Sister?

Deikun's words echoed through her mind, *unnaturally obtained.* Rosaria had said her magic was wild and untamed and violent.

She reached deep into her magic. It didn't feel like it could power such a machine. It didn't feel like the power of a goddess. Perhaps the centrum hadn't taken all of the fourth Sister's magic. Maybe it had left a fraction of it.

A chill shook her bones. Again, she felt like an intruder. She had taken a Sister's power.

Raven sat until the world righted itself and the darkness retreated. Her stomach grumbled and clenched with hunger. Raven tore her eyes off the mural and continued down the hall. She needed to find her way back before she collapsed from exhaustion—she would think of these things from the relative safety of her camp.

The Mural Hall led into another old part of the fort, what looked to have once been barracks or a meeting hall. The fort's lower halls didn't seem to have an organized layout, and the fallen walls, crumbling pillars, and water-logged stairwells didn't help.

Raven wandered for the majority of the day, and somehow she made it back to her camp in the tower. The sun had already started to set. Rather than fish, she used her magic to split a coconut. She stared listlessly at the gilded waters as she ate her fill of coconut meat and milk. She collapsed into her bed, not minding the stiff stones.

Her mind churned, her muscles ached, she felt bruises forming, and she hadn't seen anything she would consider treasure. That meant she would have to go back into the maze and hunt again.

But, tomorrow. Right now, she needed sleep.

It didn't take long to relax.

Raven hadn't spent so long by herself in... She didn't know how long. She liked the silence, the peace, but she longed for the company of the others. She missed Conrad's humor, Thalame's cynicism, Rosaria's heartfelt logic, Ivy's cleverness, and Zander's...everything. Thinking of them all, the air around her felt miserably empty.

Two days gone, five left. Plenty of time to hunt down treasure. And then she would be back with her friends.

On the morning of the third day, rather than going right into the fort, Raven explored more of the island. She burned her excess magic as she explored. The sun on her skin felt marvelous after a day spent almost entirely in the dark. She found evidence of humans, ancient and not so ancient—weathered lean-tos, frayed bits of rope, carvings that signaled three days, four days, and five days. Magicians on the Trial, she realized. Had they simply gotten lost and not returned to mark the sixth day, or had something happened to them?

She found a flattened piece of land that might have once been a farm, the remains of old pig pens, and a small gulf. In the base of the gulf, the wooden planks of a dock had long since rotted away into nothing. In the shallows, skeletons of old boats were half-buried in the silt and sand. Further out to sea, she spotted the remains of large boats, masts broken, hulls cracked. All sunken and forgotten.

Scattered along the sunken boats, she spotted what looked fearfully like bones. Human bones...skulls and ribs and spines. Sailors who went down with the ship. Bones scattered this side of the beach too. Half-buried in the sand. Leaning against what remained of the interior battlements, broke ribs and fractured skulls.

Had the fort been left to rot, or had something happened? The evidence—the sunken ships, the collapsed walls and corridors, the bones—suggested the fort had been subject to an attack. No repairs had happened. Whoever had held the fort had either lost or fled, never to return.

Raven meandered past a pile of bones, one of which still had a spearhead stuck in the eye socket. So many bones, so many people. Death had struck this island hard and left its mark.

Raven continued scouring the island, and around midday, she came across a berry bush growing in the shadow of a palm. Without deer or other wildlife to eat them, the berries remained untouched. She plucked one. It looked like a grape, only larger. The skin was a pale and translucent cyan. She'd never seen a berry like it, nor had she heard of a berry like it. She squeezed it and let a few drops of the juice land on her arm. The drops felt cool, but she felt no tingle, no pain, nothing. The drop rolled down her arm and to the ground.

In her favorite book, Leon Stark had proven berries to be safe or poisonous by rubbing the juice on his skin. If the juice irritated the skin, they were poisonous.

Her skin remained unharmed, albeit sticky.

And with no one to disprove that theory, she accepted it. She gathered a large handful of the sea-colored berries. On the way back to her tower, she plopped one berry at a time onto her tongue. They were bittersweet like a cranberry, juicy like a grape, and a bit tart like an apple. By the time she reached the window of her tower, she had eaten them all.

She put her hand on the windowsill and started to hoist herself through when her stomach gave a frightening lurch. She doubled over, half-falling onto the sandy ground. Her insides clenched, knotted, tearing her apart from the inside out and—

She emptied her stomach onto the beach. Her vision swayed, but she spotted cyan berries in her vomit.

The edges of her vision blackened. Clouds swirled low over the fort, funneling toward her tower in vicious shades of bleak gray and toxic green. The fading sunlight danced off the thickening clouds, dimming with every blink until only shadows remained. The wind picked up, pulsing in time with a growling thunder. Raven stumbled to her feet but collapsed onto a dry strip of sand. The sun-warmed sand turned to dust under her fingers. The dust snaked up her wrists, and talon-tipped fingers poked through.

Screaming, she fell backward and shook the dust off her skin.

The water slowly encroached on the beach, swallowing the land like it had the fourth Sister's island, higher and higher—Raven scrambled for her tower. The water wouldn't get her there! She fell through the window, leaving the water and sandy monsters behind. She crawled onto her bed of palm fronds.

The berries had not been all right. Sleep. She needed sleep. She shut her eyes, the treasures forgotten, the hunt pushed aside, the Trial paused. She needed to wait out the reaction.

She'd be fine. She'd be fine. She'd—

A hand grabbed her ankle and tugged. Raven kicked at the hand. The motion shook her roiling stomach and squeezing organs. The hand tightened its grip, the bony fingers biting into her skin, cutting through the leather of her boots.

She kicked at the hand with one foot and pulled on her other, but the hand didn't budge. "Stop," she whined. She pushed herself onto her hands, forced herself to sit up, intent on throwing up on whoever had come to annoy her in her weakened state.

But the words dried up on her tongue. A skeleton lay at the foot of her makeshift bed, fibers of old clothes hung in dirty tatters, eyes empty and dark, bones old and paled with time. Its bony hand clutched her ankle.

She swore it smiled, and underneath the howling wind, it laughed.

Raven screamed.

She kicked at the skeleton. The toe of her boot hooked into the eye, yanking the skull from the spine. It clattered against the wall. The rest of the skeleton didn't seem to mind—still, it laughed, a deep, raspy sound that came from everywhere. She clamored to her feet and stomped on its wrist, shattering the bones. It released her, though the laughter didn't cease.

All around the tower, skeletons rose from the ground, squeezing through the minute cracks in the floor, bone by bone. They crawled toward her as their bones pulled together, as if held by invisible tendons. Some wore sword belts, the leather dry and cracked. The skeletons stumbled onto feet, some wore boots, others did not, and some only had one boot. Some had cracked skulls, fractured bones, missing fingers or ribs. They wore ratty uniforms, but none Raven had seen before—dark trousers and shirts, tarnished silver buttons. The soldiers who had died here.

Ghosts. The dead come to throw the intruder from their home.

"No!" Raven shouted. She darted to the window, but a skull blocked her.

A skeleton hoisted itself up into the window, and a dozen more pushed to be next. They climbed out of the sand, out of the water, covered in seaweed and algae. She stumbled back as the skeleton reached for her, and her back hit the bony rib cage of another. A skeletal hand landed on her shoulder.

Screaming, Raven summoned her magic. Fire erupted from her palm, blasting the skeletons through the window. The fire scorched the stone, licked at the vines and moss, and seared the air around her. A skeleton grabbed her shoulder—she turned and smothered the tower in orange streaked white flames. The skeletons fell apart before her, turned back into the dust in the heat. A hand landed on her shoulder—another skeleton crawled through the window.

She blasted it back, but more lurched forward to take its place.

Her shelter was no longer safe.

She darted into the corridor. Skeletons came from every doorway, corridor, and window, falling from ledges, squeezing through the cracks and between fallen pillars, turning from dust and slivers to skeletons once more.

Raven ran and blasted them out of her way, blasting and running, knocking anything and everything from her path.

Still, they kept coming.

There had to be somewhere safe. She refused to die like this, poisoned and attacked by the dead.

She skittered around a dark corridor, her flickering flame dancing shadows over the stone walls, and there, at the far end, stood a woman. She glowed bright against the dank walls, her brown skin luminescent and dark curls escaping from her hood. She smiled at Raven and motioned for her to follow, but Raven thought she had been down this corridor the day before. The way the woman wanted her to go ended in a dead end.

The skeletons came closer.

Raven bolted after the stranger, down the dead-end corridor. The stranger seemed to vanish into the wall, and as Raven skidded to a halt, she noticed the narrow gap where the stone had shifted and broken. Raven crouched; she could not see the other side. Skeletons scraped against the stone behind her. With no other way forward, Raven crawled through the dark passage.

It came out into a half-collapsed corridor. On the other side, the strange woman stood. Raven straightened, and summoned a weak flame in one hand. She could barely see through the thick darkness. The glow of the woman seemed to take all the light her pitiful flame gave off, absorbing it.

The skeletons were right behind, clamoring against the stones, crawling through the narrow corridor, bones scraping against stone. Their low growls echoed off the stone, more chilling than any beast of the forest.

The strange woman glided down the dark hall, and Raven ran to keep up with her. She ran, ran, and ran—and then the floor vanished.

For a moment that seemed longer than it was, Raven was suspended in complete darkness. The dank air whipped past, and then—*splash*. Cool water engulfed her and doused her flame. She sank. Her clothes absorbed the water in an instant, soaking her to the bone.

Heart pounding, flame extinguished, she knew only black water.

The water muffled all sounds. She did not know up from down. She couldn't breathe. Her lungs burned, her panic flared, and as she reached out, she felt only stone.

Deeper she sank.

She would drown down here. Die like all the other fools who thought they could become a Wraith.

Dankness, everywhere. Impenetrable.

She would die. She would...

No.

She would not die down here. Raven refused to believe it. There had to be a way out of this, a way up or down or something. Her magic responded, to her determination or desperation, and she felt a tug. And, lungs threatening to burst, she followed it. She swam through the darkness with only her magic to guide her. An invisible path led her down, down, down, and then to the left, and then over, and then up, up, up—

She broke through the surface of the black water and took a gasp of dank, soured air. Again, she saw only darkness, but without the water, she summoned her fire.

She had come up in a half-submerged, lopsided corridor. The walls tilted to the right. The inky water reflected her flame like liquid gold. She climbed out and onto the soggy, mossy floor. Moss hung from the ceiling and clung to the walls. Mildew and spongy plants grew in every crack it could find. Water dripped endlessly.

Raven glanced at the way back. The rippling water was black as ink. The ceiling had collapsed, blocking the way out, unless she wanted to dive back into the water.

No way she was going back that way. She turned back toward the corridor. She had not been in this part of the ruins during her hunt. She didn't even know what part of the fort she'd gone to. It didn't matter. If she couldn't go back, she had to go forward.

But... Sisters.

She took a deep breath and then another. No more skeletons crawled out of the stone. It seemed their pursuit did not extend beyond the water. Standing on wobbly legs, her clothes and boots soaked through, she started down the lopsided corridor.

She kept one eye out for treasure and the other for a way out. She saw no more skeletons or ghosts or whatever they had been.

Raven moved slower than before. Her stomach clenched every few moments, and though she thought she might, she did not vomit again. She came to the end of a corridor and found a lopsided painting, the color faded and the frame rotting. Through holes in the canvas, she could see a thicker shadow behind it. The decaying strips of canvas gently moved. She yanked it off the wall—an easy feat—and revealed tightly spiraled stone steps. The steps rose up and out of sight through the darkness.

She held her flame aloft and started to climb. She had to duck slightly to keep her head from hitting the top of the stairs above her. Her flame shoved away the closest shadows, but they remained at the edge of her light. She thought for a foolish, hopeful moment that maybe Zander could see through the shadows—she didn't even know if he had that power, let alone use it so far away. Just the thought that he might be closer gave her a small comfort, despite the stretch of sea between them.

The stairs ended at another passage hidden by a painting. She shoved against the back of the painting, and the rusted fastenings gave with a vicious *creak*—the painting fell into the corridor beyond.

She stepped through and into a room full of shadows. No windows allowed in natural light, and by the look of it, no light had touched this part of the fort in a very long time. Raven's flame flickered against the coiled shadows, startling them away. The stone was darker, the stones themselves bigger, and the air danker. This part of the fort looked older. She stepped into the room; her flames illuminated a collapsed desk and rotting bookshelves, books and scrolls molded and sinking inward with time. A mural took up the wall across from the desk, the art style identical to those she had found during her hunt.

Stepping closer, she lifted her flame toward the stone. The mural depicted the continent as she knew it, three kingdoms and three Sisters. The old god hadn't been etched onto this mural; neither had the southwestern kingdom or the fourth Sister. Altair's Augur was gone. Gears and machines flourished around Solen; ships and sea life bloomed around Minerva; and trees and flowers grew around Wilyn.

And... Sisters. Raven brought her flame closer to the mural, to the hooded figure of Wilyn. Curls escaped the hood, and a kind smile stretched her lips.

Just like the strange woman who had guided Raven away from the skeletons.

Raven stared at the hooded figure of Wilyn. Had the Sister helped her, or had she been hallucinating? Had any of it even been real? Those skeletal hands had certainly felt real, and she had plunged into water—her soaked clothes proved that much.

Raven shook the thoughts from her mind. Too much to think about, too soon. She left the office and kept wandering, through half-rotten halls, lopsided corridors, and leaky ceilings. The temperature sank, and the already cool water soaking her clothes turned frigid. Still, she wandered.

Finally—shivering from cold, chafing from wet clothes, stomach growling—Raven came to a knocked-down wall. Through the holes, she spotted a familiar glow of sunlight. Distant, but sunlight nonetheless. She climbed through and into something of a throne room. A crumbling arcade lined the room. The ironwork torch brackets had rusted and flaked, most of them gone. Old pots held molded soil and long dead flowers, the stems shriveled and black. At the far end sat an old, ornate stone chair. A throne.

A skeleton sat on the throne, bones pale as moonlight, shoulders slumped. Raven shivered from something other than the cold. Though the ruler of this fort might appear dead and gone, she had the distinct feeling of being watched.

The glow of sunlight came from behind the throne, through another wall punctured by a fallen pillar.

Raven started across the throne room, toward the sunlight—as she moved, the angle of sunlight shifted, and a beam of light glinted off an ornate saber that rested across the dead ruler's thighs. Raven approached with caution, watching for movements of the white bones. The saber, unlike the rest of the fort, shined like new. The steel was spotless. A bejeweled handguard held a dozen small pearls and emeralds. Her flames reflected in the ruby on the pommel.

Treasure.

Raven paused before the dead ruler and ran her finger along the flat side of the blade. Smooth and cool, not a spec of rust. Someone had indeed placed this saber here recently. Had the grand master come all this way to put this saber here? Or had Malik done the chore?

Before she took the saber, she wandered into the adjoining room. It looked to have once been a meeting room, attached to the throne room within easy reach of the king. Just inside, a bejeweled shield rested against the wall. Not far from it, a golden bow rested on the wall.

Three ornate weapons. Three treasures?

Further exploration of the room led her to another secret passage, one whose painting had rotten away and left the room beyond exposed. It looked to have been used for storage. Resting on three separate barrels were a goblet, a lute, and a lantern. Each too shiny and new and smothered in jewels to have belonged to the fort itself. Six treasures placed in the same room.

She doubted the hider of the items would have been so careless, meaning they intended for her to find them all at once. Yet the grand master had told her to pick *one*.

She understood. She had to not only find the treasure room but pick a treasure and then explain its value. It was a test of survival and of person.

But which treasure?

Raven thought back to the murals she'd found, to the Sisters, and to all of her stepmother's stories of the Sisters and Mel's teachings. These objects had meaning.

The sword and goblet belonged to Solen, Goddess of Stone and Steel. The sword stood for those who wished to protect, those unafraid of violence, those willing to make change. The goblet stood for those who protected and healed from the inside, with food and drink.

The shield and lantern belonged to Minerva, Goddess of the Sea and Wind. The shield for those of unwavering faith, unafraid of sacrifice, those able to withstand the tempest. Those of inner strength. The lantern lit the way for those lost at sea, for those lighting the darkness for others, those who uncover secrets, those of the guiding light.

The arrow and lute belonged to Wilyn, Goddess of the Forest and Stars. Her arrow stood for stealth, for the silent protectors, for those who worked not for glory but for results, from the air and shadows. The lute stood for those who brightened the darkness within, those who bring joy in times of darkness.

And by picking a treasure, Raven would be picking a Sister.

Was there a wrong answer? If she picked the wrong treasure, would the Wraiths turn her away? Picking the sword might imply that she hadn't searched thoroughly and found the others. It might imply her shortsighted and inpatient.

Raven gathered all the treasure into the sunlit room—after carefully removing the sword from the skeleton, which did not move. She arranged them on the floor. Each glittered in her flame, rubies and diamonds and pearls. Each would be worth a fortune.

She heaved a sigh. Each object had its own set of traits. Depending on which she chose, it would imply that she had those traits. The object would reflect her strengths and weaknesses. But, what were her strengths and weaknesses? She didn't know. Logically, the shield would be the most awkward to get out. The goblet might be the easiest. Picking the shield might suggest stubbornness. The goblet might suggest laziness. She didn't like either of those.

The longer she stared at the treasures, the more uncertain she was. Her empty stomach played games with her mind. Though the outside air warmed the room, her clothes were still wet and cold. As the sunlight began to tilt toward the west, she gave up. She had time to make this impossible decision.

She wandered back through the throne room and through the corridors. Finding her way back to her shelter wasn't as hard as she feared. By the time she returned, the sun sank to the west, turning the ocean liquid gold.

She encountered no skeletons or ghosts.

Scorch marks darkened the walls like claw marks, and the room smelled like smoke. Too tired to dwell on it, she arranged what palm fronds remained, stripped herself of her wet clothes, and collapsed.

She slept deeply and woke to the grayed light of an overcast dawn. Over a breakfast of clean water and coconut, she mulled over what had happened. The berries, the skeletons, the ghost—she didn't know what to make of it all.

And which treasure should she pick? She feared what her choice would tell the grand master about her.

She fingered her dried clothes. They were stiff from stagnant water and stunk of mildew. She couldn't wander around the fort naked. Well, she could, but she didn't want to. She took the time to gather enough clean water to sate her thirst and rinse her clothes. It took a while to gather enough water, but she considered it worth it. She carefully used her magic to heat the water from the threads. One wrong move, and she would turn her clothes to ashes and have a very awkward meeting when the grand master returned to fetch her.

Once her clothes were dry, she wandered back to the throne room. She got lost only three times. Strangely enough, the corridors and halls were beginning to make sense.

The treasures remained where she had put them. She sat down, determined not to leave the room without an answer.

She left several hours later without an answer.

She spent the rest of the day cleaning up the mess she'd made of her tower and gathering a fresh armload of palm fronds and coconuts. That night, spearing for fish in her underthings, Raven glanced up at the sky. Inky clouds floated between her and the stars.

The experience of the adventure is the real treasure.

Raven inhaled sharply as her mother's voice resounded in her head as clear as if she stood on the rocky beach. Her mother, who had flown all over the world. Her mother, who had chosen herself above others. Her mother, who had flown at top speed to save the people Raven cared about. Her mother, who had once done this very Trial and become a Wraith.

Raven no longer felt anger toward her mother. She felt something far warmer: fondness and admiration.

Despite everything, Luckett was still her mother. And like it or not, she and her daughter shared a remarkable number of qualities. Didn't Raven choose herself over others when she went to catch the thief with Zander? Hadn't she picked adventure over safety in the mines? Hadn't she picked herself when she ran away from the Dwellers? And when she agreed to become a Wraith, she had thought of herself, her future, and what she wanted.

Despite everything, Raven was still her mother's daughter.

She had always been this way. She had always been her mother's daughter.

And her mother's words repeated in her mind as she cooked fish over the newly arranged firepit, as she picked the meat from the bones, as she fell asleep with the starry sky within her view.

Raven returned to the treasure room every day but hesitated to take anything.

At the end of her seven days, Raven returned to the dock at dawn. The rowboat appeared first as a speck and grew closer with every blink. She kept her hands behind her back. Grand Master Deikun, Malik, Elizi, and—Raven's breath caught at the sight of the fourth person in the boat. It was Zander. That he had come to see her made her heart swell.

The past week had been refreshing but also lonely.

Raven held her chin high and her shoulders steady. The boat glided to the dock and paused. Zander quickly looked her over—thankfully she had taken the time to bathe that morning. She hadn't had soap, but it had been better than wearing a week's worth of grime. Zander brought his sapphire eyes up to hers. Thoughts churned behind them. He had a lot he wanted to say, but he knew now wasn't the time.

The grand master gracefully climbed out of the boat and stood on the sturdy part of the dock, barring her exit into the boat.

Suddenly, her choice didn't feel so good. What if she had chosen wrong? What happened when someone failed the Trial? Would he kill her and be done with it?

"It is good to see you alive, magician. What treasure have you recovered?" His eyes were steady and curious.

Raven steeled herself by envisioning her mother. Then she brought her empty hands in front of her, palms up. Deikun stared at her hands, mouth tilted down, then at her. She met his stare, unafraid. In the boat, Zander, Malik, and Elizi looked horrified.

"You did not find a treasure?" Deikun's voice came out firm, but a twinkle in his eyes told her he suspected otherwise.

"I found them all," Raven said, her voice steady as her posture. She had gone over this speech a dozen times that morning. "The sword to cut down. The shield to defend. The arrow to strike from afar. The lute to entertain. The goblet to drink. The lantern to expose. I found them all, but none are the treasure that I chose."

Deikun lifted his brows. Behind him, Zander shifted in the boat, causing it to gently rock. Malik put a steady hand on his shoulders. Zander blinked at Raven; his sapphire eyes were stars in the daylight. She had missed those stars.

"The experience of an adventure cannot be defined in an ornate object," Raven explained.

The grand master tilted his chin in curiosity.

"I learned that my magic can help me see where my eyes cannot and to hear what my ears cannot. I learned to trust my magic. That experience cannot be measured in gold or jewels."

A long moment passed. The grand master blinked at her, and for a terrifying moment, she thought she had made an error—then he smiled.

Deikun threw his arms out, and said, "Welcome, magician, to the Wraiths."

Raven wanted to fall to the ground in relief, but she held her shoulders straight. She allowed a smile to creep over her lips. Zander sighed in relief and ran a hand through his hair. Malik released a held breath, a subtle action.

"Let us return," Deikun announced, and he climbed back into the boat.

Zander held his hand out for hers, and she accepted his offer as she eagerly joined them. She sat beside Zander while Malik sat beside the grand master. At Elizi's command, the boat gently glided away from the island and toward the mainland.

"How did it go?" Zander could likely smell the week on her skin, her hair, but he didn't say anything. Of course, having gone through the Trial himself, he understood exactly what she felt.

Raven met his eyes. She felt utterly exhausted. Worry over her choice of treasure had kept her tossing and turning. Everything ached from the wandering and exploring, and the strange skeleton chase. Her back ached from sleeping on a hard stone floor. And now that the survival had been taken from her shoulders, she felt beyond exhausted and spent.

"Fine, I suppose," Raven told Zander. "I'm tired and hungry."

Deikun gave her a knowing smile. "There will be a celebration dinner tonight in honor of your successful Trial," he told her. "After that, you will enter the temple for your Choosing. Once Chosen, you will be formally inducted into the Wraiths."

At the thought of a celebration dinner, her mouth began to water, but that there was more to becoming a Wraith sent her nerves rattling.

"My Choosing?" She looked helplessly from Deikun to Malik to Zander.

"It will be explained when the time comes," said Deikun. "Before that, we celebrate."

Neither Malik or Zander further explained, so she asked no more. Whatever the Choosing was, it couldn't possibly be worse than the Trial. So Raven let herself relax. Before her Choosing, she would celebrate. She would bathe, eat, and rest. She would be prepared for whatever came next.

Zander nudged her shoulder with his. She had unknowingly closed her eyes. She found the stars of his eyes and smiled at him to let him know that she was ready. For anything.

The boat glided between the cliffs and into the gulf. A gentle murmur had settled over the village since the last time Raven had seen it—a chatter of voices and life. Their boat paused against the dock, and Elizi tied it off. Deikun led them along the sandy path and to the shadowed temple. To Raven's surprise, Wraiths gathered in front of the temple; they stood on either side of the steps, leaving a path for the grand master. Deikun paused just inside the shadow of the cliff.

"A new Wraith will soon join us," he announced, his voice strong.

A single cheer came from the crowd, a single word from every mouth—a word Raven had never heard. Just as the cheer filled the air, it vanished.

"*Jul,*" Zander whispered. "It's an old word. It means success, happiness, and congratulations."

Deikun led Raven to the stronghold. Wraiths surrounded her, shaking her hand, offering smiles and congratulations, whispering kind words and praise. It felt so different than before. Where the Wraiths had been cold and indifferent, they were now warm and welcoming.

"There was a real chance you wouldn't make it back," Zander said as they started up the steps.

Deikun opened the doors to the stronghold with a wave of his hand. Unlike before, the torches were already lit.

"No one wanted to get close to you and then have you die."

It was such a morbid thought, but she understood.

Deikun turned and said to Malik, "See that the celebrations are set into motion for tonight."

Malik nodded and started back outside.

"Zander, see our newest member to the guest chambers," Deikun said. "They should be ready for you."

Zander nodded and offered his arm to Raven. She slipped her arm into his, and he guided her through a stone archway and into a darkly lit corridor. The corridor had been carved from the stone, though the walls had been carved with decorative lines and patterns. Fires burned in plates held aloft by carved hooded figures, spread just far enough to leave a line of shadow between each one. It smelled of smoke and stone, not unlike the mines of Silver Glen, but also of something else; something sweet she couldn't quite identify.

Magic, the childish part of her mind whispered.

She wanted to believe it, so she did.

"How many don't come back?" she asked. Her voice seemed to echo, but at the same time, it seemed to sink into the very stone.

"It's hard to say," Zander said grimly. "One in five, maybe. Not everyone can survive being alone for a week with nothing but the ocean. They either starve or drown or fall."

"I didn't see anyone," she whispered. Bodies, she meant, but she didn't want to voice it.

Zander's expression darkened. "If they aren't there when the grand master goes to get them, he sends a retrieval team. I know he says no one will get your body, but he sends someone. I... I went on a few during my training. We scour the old fort for bodies. It's not fun. Worse than the Trial."

She bit her lip. "I'm sorry."

"I've always said that we should at least warn magicians before tossing them onto an island," Zander said. "I thought I would have time to warn you, but..."

"I jumped in head first," she said, sighing.

Zander laughed. "Yeah, but apparently, I was wrong to worry. Of course, I knew you'd do it. And without breaking anything or getting some strange infection too."

"How would you know that?"

"You shook hands with three healers that I saw," Zander said, grinning. "They would have sensed anything wrong immediately."

Thalame had patted her shoulder, now that she thought about it.

"I learned how to scavenge in Silver Glen," Raven said proudly. "My father taught me how to fish, and luckily I prefer my food slightly burned." She started to mention the berries but paused.

Zander caught the hesitation and frowned. "What is it? Did something happen?"

"Well...yes and no."

He pulled her to a stop.

Half laughing, she said, "I found a berry bush."

Zander's brows came together and, in the next heartbeat, shot to his hairline. His mouth formed an O. "Rae...tell me you didn't eat them."

"Oh, I ate a handful," she said, her tone light.

Zander paled.

"I threw up immediately and saw skeletons coming out of the stone."

Zander gawked at her like she had gone mad.

"I found the passage that took me into the treasure room on my mad dash to get away from the skeletons," she said, poking his dropped chin.

He closed his mouth. She did not tell him about the ghostly vision of Wilyn. It felt too personal.

Zander let out a low laugh and continued down the corridor. "Sisters, Raven. You could have poisoned yourself beyond healing with those. They're called shade fruit. They only grow in the shade in the topics. They're powerful hallucinogens. I've heard shade is used a lot in the southern islands of Tinatun, but it's a diluted formula, not the straight berries."

"I felt horrible for several days." Raven had lived through that fight too. She had beaten the poison, beaten the Trial, and she could beat whatever this Choosing was too. "Can I ask you about what happens next?"

"I'm forbidden to tell you," Zander said plainly. "What? Don't give me that look. It's the truth. I swore an oath, Raven. A *magic* oath."

She pouted but didn't complain.

Zander guided her up a staircase and into a short corridor with a handful of dark wooden doors. He guided her to the last door. "This is the guest wing. No one else is staying up here, so you've got the place to yourself. Everything you need should be inside."

"Where will you be staying?"

"I've got a room a corridor away," Zander said. "You'll get your own room after your Choosing and the induction ceremony."

"You have a room here? Even if you're never here?"

"It's not really *my* room," Zander explained. "It's in the hall where the other Wraiths sleep." He stepped closer, mouth a straight line. "But I have a place here, among the Wraiths. As does every magician who has become a Wraith; as will you."

"That sounds nice," she said.

They stood alone in the corridor. The stone soaked up the sound, and it felt as though they were the only people for leagues. Raven glanced at the door to her guest room, then back to Zander's sapphire eyes.

He cupped her cheek. "I'm glad you made it back."

"I'm glad you were there to meet me," she said.

He leaned in, but she leaned away. Zander blinked, hurt flashing across his face.

"And I will kiss you twice after I wash the grime off myself." She smiled at his pout. She didn't give him a chance to argue. She patted his chest and let herself into her guest room.

It was a simple room. A candle burned on the bedside table. A narrow bed stood against the wall, made up with plain linens. A wooden folding screen divided the bed from the rest of the room. A washing basin stood on a stone pedestal underneath a carved clamshell; a rope hung underneath it. She tugged on the rope, and chilled water fell from the clam and into the basin. She released the rope; the water stopped flowing.

She didn't have the mind or patience to marvel at the inner workings. She pulled the rope and filled the tub. She found soap in the cabinet and used her magic to heat the water. She left her dirty clothes in a pile on the floor—Oh! A bath had never felt so good! She washed herself twice for good measure, relishing the feeling of the water, the soap, the softness of the skin left behind.

A drain at the bottom of the tub let the water flow out of sight. Towels had been stocked in the cabinet as well as a few essentials. After toweling off, Raven found a set of plain robes, not unlike the Wraiths wore, only unadorned and unarmored. She ran her hands over the simple material, soft and supple.

A Wraith. Her, a Wraith!

So much had happened in such a short period of time, her mind grappled to keep up with it all. For so long, every day had been the same. Now, every day was a surprise. And it had left her exhausted. She reclined back on the bed, wearing just the towel, intent on only a few moments' rest.

She woke sometime later to a knocking at the door.

"Raven?" came Zander's voice. "Are you in there? Raven?"

"I'm here," she said groggily, straining to sit up. Oh, she could sleep for days more. Her limbs begged to remain unused, but she sat up anyway.

The towel had gotten shoved to the floor sometime during her nap, leaving her naked and tangled in a mess of sheets. The handle on the door turned, and she grabbed the edge of the blanket and covered herself just as Zander stepped into the room.

"I came to see..." His words faded as his eyes fell on her. He blinked several times.

"You came to see?" Raven asked, chuckling at the wording. A mad blush heated her skin.

"...if you were awake," Zander said, each word carefully spoken. He dragged his eyes over her and finally met hers. "Dinner is ready, and it would be inappropriate to start the celebration of your success without you."

She maneuvered her body with the sheet, setting her bare feet on the floor. The sheet rose up her thighs. Dinner sounded marvelous, even more so than another nap. She lingered on the bedside, clutching the sheet to her chest. Zander stood dumbfounded in the doorway, and she relished it—she had gotten so few chances to stump him.

"I will be in the corridor," Zander said quickly. He stepped out and shut the door.

She dressed in the robes she'd found earlier and braided her wild hair over her shoulder. She dusted off her leather boots and tucked her ebony-handled dagger into the left one. The familiar weight settled against her leg.

She found Zander leaning against the wall with his arms crossed and one leg propped up. He wore fresh Wraith robes of dark indigo and gray.

"Your arm." Raven nodded to his mechanical arm. In the robes, only his brass hand was visible. "You've made progress."

Zander made a show of stretching his arms—both of them—in unison above his head. He brought his hands back down and flipped his mechanical wrist just so—with a delicate whirl of gears, the compass in his palm opened and quickly settled on north. "It's working like a dream," Zander said. "What about you? Considering you had an entire week to work on your magic?"

"I told the grand master the truth." She shrugged. "My magic helped me, but not just to cook dinner and clean water. It...guided me, if that makes sense."

"Can't say," Zander said. "Magic's odd like that. Everyone's magic is a little different, and considering yours is extremely different, it's impossible to say anything for certain."

Raven huffed and set her hands on her hips. "Enough talk. You mentioned food."

Zander extended his human arm for hers. She threaded her arm in his, and he guided her through the corridors and to the main chamber of the stronghold. Tables had been arranged from wall to wall, each laden with fruit, roasted meat and fish, breads, and sweets. Her mouth watered. Wraiths lingered around, chatting and laughing. The doors of the stronghold were open, and from somewhere in the village, music played.

A celebration.

Zander guided her toward the main doors, and on the way, she snagged a small loaf of dark bread with cinnamon and sugar baked in, a wooden skewer of pineapple, and a skewer of roasted pork. The sun hadn't yet set over the ocean, and the entire world seemed alight in bright golds and yellows and ambers. The shadow of the cliff extended over most of the village and gulf, but it did not dampen the spirits. Music sang from everywhere, strings and flutes and drums.

As Zander led Raven toward the gathering, a great shout of "*Jul!*" rose around them, and with her present, the celebration started.

Raven danced, ate her fill, and met as many other Wraiths as she could. They had heard stories of her from Thalame and Zander while she had been at her Trial, and all that she had done to agitate the Gray Elite. Everyone had heard about the melted Colossus by now, and everyone wanted to meet the girl who had done it. She found it both flattering and exhausting, but having slept and replenished her spirit with food and drink, she didn't mind. Luckily, the Wraiths had no qualms about her eating and greeting at the same time.

The sun sank, the stars glittered, and she danced on the beach. Though she would have liked to dance all night, her exhaustion caught up with her. When she could dance and eat no more, Zander guided her back into the stronghold.

Once in the relative calm of the corridors, she slipped her arm out of his and instead slipped it around his middle. She hugged him close, pressing her face into his shoulder. He smelled like the beach, like wet sand, woodsmoke, and briny sea breeze, but like him, dark and powerful.

"Have fun?" Zander asked.

She nodded against his shoulder.

He set his mechanical arm around her waist and stroked her hair with his other hand. She could stay like this for a long time.

"The Choosing isn't that bad," Zander whispered. "I was terrified before mine. I thought it would be worse than the island, but it wasn't. It's not bad at all."

"I don't want to talk about that right now," Raven said, though his words did provide a sense of comfort for the following morning. She pulled her head off his shoulder but didn't lean away.

"What do you want to talk about, then?"

She closed the gap between them in a heartbeat, pressing her mouth against his. She broke apart just long enough to say, "Nothing." She kissed him again.

Sisters, how she had missed Zander. How she had thought about him. How she had thought about this.

He pulled her closer and deepened the kiss. She ran her hand along the stubble of his jaw, down the contours of his throat, and to the folds of his robes. Having done up her own, she knew about how they worked, the hidden ties and clasps. She tugged the soft material away from his throat, and as her fingers graced his collarbone, he shifted—he pushed her against the wall. Her gasp was lost in the heat of his mouth. He laced his fingers with hers and pinned her hands above her head. He kissed her deeply, a kiss long overdue.

He pressed his body into hers. Her gasp evaporated on his lips. She nipped at his bottom lip, and a low moan escaped the back of his throat. He kissed her neck, his breath hot. Heat seared across her skin and through her bones, something other than her magic. Something hotter, something brighter. She needed more. She wanted more. Of this, of him.

She slid her calf along his. Up, down, then back up a little higher, a little higher, and then she hooked her leg around his waist. A low growl came from the back of his throat, rumbling against her skin. His teeth scraped along her jaw, nipped at her ear.

"Now would be the time to stop," Zander whispered, his voice husky. "Unless you want me to haul you to the nearest closet."

His voice sent a shiver down her back. She thought of a closet, dark and private, the cold floor against her back, of his... She hooked her other leg around his waist. He released a heavy sigh against her throat. He gave a single thrust of his hips into hers, to accentuate his meaning. To accentuate hers, she squeezed her legs tighter.

"Raven." His breath left his throat in a gasp, a sigh—she didn't know.

"If I wanted you to stop, I would have punched you by now," she said, shocked at the huskiness of her own voice.

Zander tightened his arms around her. In a swift motion, he pushed off from the wall, cradling her in his arms. He carried her into the guest corridor, into her room, and kicked the door closed. He laid her down on the bed. He removed his cowl and tunic, one tie and clasp at a time, leaving his chest exposed. She trailed her fingertips along the scars that crisscrossed his bronze skin, painting a story for each one. Fire burst through her veins as she touched him; the heat pulsed at the faintest brushes of his fingers and against her skin as she tugged at her robes.

His lips, his hands—he moved in such ways that had her seeing fantasies she'd never dreamed of! Her senses overheated. Everything blurred together and sharpened at once: the soft rustle of their robes hitting the floor, the thud of boots, the clicking of his belt unbuckling, and his skin against hers.

And the world exploded into stars and blinding colors.

Zander collapsed beside her. As the euphoria eased into something warmer, something steadier, Raven rolled onto her side. She waited for the feeling of being bare to make her blush, but it never came. Zander lay beside her, just as bare. She nestled her head onto his shoulder, and his heart beat under her cheek. She found his hand and laced her fingers with his.

Raven woke up to a gentle motion. She rolled over to see Zander sitting on the side of the bed, stretching his arms across his chest. His human arm flexed. His metal arm held, steel joints moved flawlessly, clicking and whirling. The scars along his shoulder had healed to pale bronze. The skin and metal met as if the metal had always been there.

His back held as many scars as his chest, and Raven absently traced her finger over one that slashed over his side. She dropped her hand back to the bed as he stood. He leaned over and pressed a kiss to her forehead, then started to dress. He picked up her robes from the floor and tossed them onto the bed.

She made no move. She hugged the pillow closer. She hadn't slept so well in what felt like months.

"I'd love to spend the morning cuddling," Zander said, buckling his belt, sapphire eyes rolling over her. "But, you've got an important meeting. It's bad form to be late to your Choosing."

She groaned, rolled onto her back, and stretched. Granted, she felt remarkably better than she had yesterday morning. Zander started to fill the basin, and Raven pulled on her robes. As she secured the clasp across her middle, she caught Zander watching. He wore that calm, arrogant smirk of his, the one that had left knots in her stomach from the first moment she'd seen it. Not that she would tell him that.

He splashed cool water on his face and tied back his hair; Raven combed hers and braided it back.

"You ready?" Zander asked into her neck. He punctuated his words with a kiss on her pulse.

"As ready as I can be," Raven said. "Though, are you sure they won't mind us being a little late?" She'd rather stay in here with him a while longer.

"As tempting as that is, it's not the Wraiths you've got to worry about today." Zander stepped away. "There's always tonight, and the night after that."

She hummed. Tonight seemed awfully far away. Changing the subject, she asked, "How's your arm?"

"It's still not quite one hundred percent." He thrust his metal arm to the side, fingers splayed. She heard the subtle grind of gears. He curled in his metal fingers and his human fingers; the metal took a heartbeat longer to respond. "Every day is a little better."

"Give it another week," Raven said.

He'd made so much progress in what time he'd had. Another week, two, three? He would be back to normal. Or, as normal as a metal arm could be.

Zander flexed his fingers again and then wiggled them at her. The tiny gears clicked, the joint of his wrist whirled. He stroked his metal thumb against her cheek.

"I could get used to this," he said.

Warmth spread through her limbs. "Your arm?" she asked, smirking. "You'd better. I don't think you can get the other one back."

He chuckled, but she saw it—a glimpse of something darker. "I meant I could get used to you. Waking up next to you. Seeing you first thing in the morning." He stepped closer, and that dark something vanished.

"Zander, are you turning sentimental on me?" She smiled; she couldn't help it. Zander had always been the tough guy, the snarky one. "Don't tell me you're going soft."

He snaked his arms around her and pulled her into an embrace. He kissed her temple. "I've not had a lot to be sentimental or soft about." His kiss found its way to her lips.

Say it, a little voice in her head said. *Say it. Say it. Say it.*

Her lips parted, she inhaled—a knock sounded on the door.

"Raven?" Malik called.

Zander let out a soft, disgruntled sigh.

"I'm awake," she called back.

The door started to open, and she and Zander stepped out of each other's arms. Malik looked as though he had slept well. Color brightened his cheeks and his eyes. He wore the robes of the Wraiths, as well as his rings and several fine silver chains around his neck. Each glinted in the candlelight.

"She's on her way to the Choosing," Zander said.

"It's not that." In a blink, Malik's gaze turned dire. "I'm actually looking for you, Zander. Deikun called an emergency meeting."

"What happened?" Zander asked.

"He didn't say," Malik said. "Only to spread the word."

"All right," Zander said.

Malik left, and Zander and Raven quickly readied. She straightened her robes and tightened the laces of her boots. She didn't know how to get ready for her Choosing. She double-checked to make sure her dagger was in place. Zander then led the way to the main chamber. Several other Wraiths had gathered for the emergency meeting, all in their armored gear. Tense whispers floated through the room. The tables remained from the celebration the night before, and platters of biscuits, bagels, and fruit had been served.

Raven and Zander sat at a table beside Thalame, and she took a large bite from a biscuit. Tiny seeds flecked the inside.

Grand Master Deikun stood at the end of the chamber, at a table with a few older Wraiths. Slowly, Wraiths filed in from the adjoining corridors. The hall gradually filled. At last, the grand master stood. Silence issued.

"As most of you know," started Deikun. He did not shout, yet his voice filled the room. "Raven completed the Trial and must attend her Choosing." An agreeable murmur followed. "But we have other news this morning. There is a Gray Elite caravan crossing into Tinatun to the west, transporting magicians. I am sending a small team to disrupt the caravan and retrieve the captive magicians. The scouts have reason to think they are sending the magicians to the coast to be shipped south. The Wraiths will not allow it."

A few of the Wraiths stood. Volunteers for the mission, Raven realized.

Zander stood, and her heart skidded.

"Your arm good enough, mate?" Thalame remained seated—he had once told Raven he didn't like fighting.

"My arm is more than good enough." Zander flexed his metal fingers. "This is my chance to prove it."

"Are you certain?" came the steady voice of Deikun.

"Yes," Zander said, bowing his head. "Allow me to prove my recovery on this mission."

Deikun held Zander's gaze a long moment, then nodded.

"Zander?" Raven started to stand, but Thalame put a hand on her shoulder.

"You're not a full Wraith," Thalame whispered. "The grand master wouldn't allow it. You've got to be Chosen first."

She bit her lip. She hadn't planned on being separated so soon.

Deikun scanned the volunteers. "All right. Those willing, meet me after breakfast in the Crystal Chamber."

Zander sat back down. "It'll be fine, Rae. This sort of thing is typical Wraith business. Nothing special. I can't go with you to the Choosing anyway, and they tend to last a while. I'll be back before you are."

She blinked; she hadn't planned on going anywhere either. Would the Choosing take place on another island? In the heart of the forest? Underground?

"You'll be fine." Zander nudged her knee with his. "It's not bad."

"Would you have told me that about the Trial?"

"No," he said. "I would have told you how horrible it was, and that you could die."

"So, there's no chance I'll die in the Choosing?"

"No."

"None at all?"

He shrugged. "I'm sure there's the smallest chance. If you somehow find a way to die during the Choosing, I'll be impressed."

Breakfast ended, and Malik motioned for Raven to follow. Zander stood, but rather than follow the other volunteers, he followed Malik.

"Don't you need to go with them?" Raven asked.

"In a few minutes." Zander laced his fingers with hers.

They followed Malik through a set of doors in the very back of the hall and down a spiraling stone staircase carved from the cliffside. The walls were smooth, too smooth to have been carved by tools or human hands. Sconces along the ceiling held flames, but she smelled no smoke, saw no candles. A chill ran up her spine as she realized why this place looked so familiar. It looked like the smooth stone of the Temple of the Three Sisters in Silver Glen.

Malik was leading her into a temple.

Her skin prickled.

The stairs ended before a grand set of stone doors, carved in the same fashion as the murals she'd found on the island. The carvings depicted the Three Sisters, their talents, their objects, and their elements. The mysterious fourth Sister was absent, and in her place on the door was a tree whose roots spread over the edges of the door. Had the doors in Silver Glen held such a tree? She couldn't remember. It felt like a lifetime ago that Mel had led her into the temple.

Malik paused before the doors, the flames casting his face in shadows.

Zander kissed her cheek and said, "You'll do fine, babe."

She blushed; she'd never been called *babe* before. "And I'll see you when I'm done? Babe?" It didn't sound as romantic when she said it.

132

Zander smiled and kissed the back of her hand. "Of course."

Say it. Say it. Say it.

Raven watched Zander go up the stairs and out of sight, and those words jumbled on her tongue. She swallowed them. When they met again, then.

"Ready?" Malik placed his hand against the seam of the doors.

She took a deep breath. "I'm ready."

The doors began to open. And she steeled herself to face her Choosing.

Raven stepped through the stone doors and into a dark chamber. The darkness swirled thick, like it had when she had first stepped into the Wraiths' stronghold. A magical darkness, meant to blind and hide. The doors began to close, and she glanced back at Malik. He stood on the other side, but he did not wear the same worry he had when he left her on the island. The light shrank into a sliver that divided her body in halves, then vanished as the doors closed.

For a terrifying heartbeat, she stood in total darkness. Alone. She repressed a shiver as she remembered the black water she'd fallen into, the darkness, the pressure, the inability to breathe—she took a gasping breath of the cool, cavernous air.

She would not drown. There was no water here.

And she had her magic. She brought a flame to life in her palm, dousing the back of the stone doors in bright red-orange. The stone was smooth. She turned to face the chamber; her light did not reach very far in, but it uncovered enough. She stood in a hall of plain stone walls and a gently curved ceiling.

With no other way to go, she started walking. A few steps in, torches burst to life on either side of her—eliciting a yelp of surprise from her. The flames were dull silver, ghosts of flames that had once been. The torches hung on iron brackets, the ironwork heavy and out of style. The torches brightened the corridor better than her flame, so she let it go out.

As she reached the edge of the torches' light, the next set burst to life with the same ghostly glow. The torches remained lit behind her, and when eight sets of torches burned, a multitude of torches burst to life at once.

She had reached the temple.

It looked identical to the one in Silver Gen. Three massive statues, one of each sister, stood at the cardinal points of the room. Each had been carved from the Sister's chosen stone: sandstone for Minerva; limestone for Solen; and marble for Wilyn. In the center of the chamber stood a circular platform, the edges carved with elegant lines that never intersected.

The Wraiths used a temple for the Choosing? Her heart thudded hard against her ribs—had the temple in Silver Glen once been used for the same purpose?

"Come forward," three voices spoke in unison, each female, each strong, and each proud. There was no mistaking the sound; the voices filled the room.

The Three Sisters.

A chill like Raven had never felt raced through her entire body. She forced her shaky legs forward, stepping onto the platform. Her legs shook too much to stand, so she sat. Her bones felt like they would rattle into nonexistence.

"A new face comes to us," said a voice from her left, from Solen's statue. Her voice was deep and somber, strong as steel.

"Another seeks to become a Wraith," said a voice from her right, from Minerva. Her voice was smooth and fluid, deep as the ocean.

"Another comes to be Chosen," said a voice in front of her, from Wilyn. Her voice was buttery and soft, a wind through the trees. Raven had the eeriest feeling that she had heard it before.

She could feel eyes on her, though she could not see anyone. She glanced into the eyes of Wilyn, but she saw only shadowed stone. But the Sisters were here, a part of them, somehow. That reality shook her deeper than she knew possible. The Sisters were real. And they were talking to her.

And in their silence, she realized they were waiting for her.

"Yes," she said, unsure of what else to say. "To be Chosen."

Her voice did not echo as theirs did, nor did it fill the chamber. She had never felt more insignificant.

"You have survived the Trial," said Solen.

"You have proven your worth of skill and persistence," said Minerva.

"You have shown your determination to live," said Wilyn.

"And now you have come to be Chosen," they said as one, the eerie cadence resounding.

"To be judged of character and mind," said Minerva.

"To be weighed of spirit," said Solen.

"To be Chosen by one of us," said Wilyn.

"To become a patron," they said together.

Raven swallowed. To be Chosen meant to be chosen by a Sister, a patron.

"But she has questions," added Solen.

"About that which has been erased," said Wilyn.

"About that which you now possess," Minerva said, her voice neither accusing nor mean.

"Speak," they said together.

Raven's hands shook. She balled them, but it didn't help. They knew about the murals, about what she had uncovered, and they knew the truth about her magic—that it wasn't hers. She swallowed.

"The murals I saw during the Trial," Raven said softly, her voice neither echoing nor brave. "There were four of you."

"Yes," Minerva said, regret in her voice. "Our forgotten Sister. Our father made four of us. From the depths of the ocean, he birthed me. From the deepest cavern, he birthed Solen. From the heart of the forest, he birthed Wilyn. And from the core of a volcano, he birthed Aeon."

"To each of us, he gifted a kingdom," said Solen. "And, for many years, we lived in peace. Our peoples thrived."

"But Aeon grew greedy and restless," said Wilyn. "She and her people were gifted with knowledge, and they wanted more."

"They wanted war," added Solen, her voice dark with remorse. "They sought to take."

"Aeon's people created a machine that would destroy any in their way and fortify them as the strongest kingdom of them all."

A deathly silence fell in the chamber.

"Altair's Augur," Raven whispered.

"Her people turned on her," said Solen. "But she allowed it. Her power became the machine, and war ensued. Many lives were lost. The era was darkened with fear."

"Our father sought to stop her, but she turned on him. Her people turned on him," said Wilyn.

"Our father could not stop her, so we did," said Minerva.

"Between the three of us, we stopped our sister and her people," said Wilyn.

"Her kingdom sank to the bottom of the ocean," said Minerva.

"Her name, erased," said Solen.

"The machine, hidden," said Minerva.

"Her power, contained," said Wilyn.

Again, silence thickened. Raven flattened her palms on her thighs. With every word, every piece of the story, her insides churned and shook. "Her power," she whispered. "It was contained in the machine."

"Her power became yours," Wilyn said, her voice soft, not unkind or accusing.

Raven felt that power tugging under her skin. She hadn't burned it off that morning. "I didn't mean to take it," Raven said.

"We know," Wilyn said. "You sought to keep the power away from those who would use it. You did not intend to use it yourself. You have become a vessel for Aeon's gift of fire. It is now yours."

"You chose to keep the world safe over your own safety," Minerva said proudly. "Without knowing what might happen to yourself."

"Your acts are commendable," Solen said.

"It shows a will to protect others, even strangers, and the world," said Wilyn.

"It is a will we wish more had," said Minerva.

Silence again fell, and Raven felt a question bubble up her throat. "In the ruins," she started, almost afraid of the answer. She cast her eyes toward Wilyn's statue. "I saw a woman. She helped me."

"She looked like me," Wilyn supplied. "Aeon. It would not be unthinkable that a part of her exists within the power that resides within you. A shadow of Aeon. She helped you survive?"

"She did," Raven said, nodding.

She thought of the hooded woman. It had been Aeon, the Sister whose face had been taken from the murals. The Sister who had been wiped from history for her greed and ambition. And a piece of that Sister resided within her magic? Raven looked at her hands. She hadn't felt anything, but then, she realized, that voice she hadn't heard in so long. It had been that sliver of Aeon. Something within her magic seemed to confirm it.

"She is not you, and you are not her," said Minerva. "Do not let that worry invade your senses. She cannot control you, though her power is now yours."

"Yours," echoed Wilyn. "Not hers."

"What you choose to do with it," said Solen, "time will tell."

"But now it is time for us to make a choice," Minerva said.

"To Choose," the three of them said together. "Let us begin."

The temperature in the chamber dropped. The blue light dimmed. The very stone seemed to hum with power. Raven felt the presence around her—all around, comforting and invasive. It felt heavy as water, soft as starlight, and strong as steel. Into her thoughts, her heart, her being.

A judgment.

She felt their voices, their words, their thoughts.

Solen admired her determination and her will in the face of danger and adversity. Minerva admired her bravery and her will to protect those around her. Wilyn admired her creativity and inner strength. Raven felt the Sisters confer amongst themselves, around her, about her. She felt the air changing and moving as light through water. She had proven herself in the eyes of each Sister. Any would gladly have her, but only one could Choose her.

The undulating air changed, then stopped. She felt the change, the difference—a decision had been made. And all at once, the presence vanished from around her. She gasped for a deep, much-needed breath. Had she even been breathing?

"Raven," came the soft, starry voice of Wilyn. "I Choose you as mine. I will be your patron. For your creativity, your passion, your desire, your ambition, your thirst for adventure, your strong heart."

"Do you accept?" said the Sisters as one.

"Yes," Raven said without thinking. "I accept."

"Welcome, Wraith," said Wilyn. Her Sisters echoed.

To be addressed as a Wraith felt unreal and fitting. Raven thought of Zander and Thalame, how powerful and dangerous they looked in their dark robes, leathers, and steel. The thought of herself in such a position felt tantalizing and empowering.

"Welcome, child," said Wilyn. "*Gorar gachy u kiwo*. May the stars forever guide you."

Raven felt a chill—her stepmother had often chimed those same words.

"Proceed the way you came," said Minerva. "Your new family is waiting for you."

"But be on guard," said Solen. "For choices lay on the horizon, both easy and most difficult."

"And remember," Wilyn said. "We are always there."

The air lightened and thinned. The silver light returned to its original brightness, which now felt too bright. Raven blinked; her eyes felt gummy, as though she hadn't opened them in some time. She climbed down from the platform; her limbs felt stiff and tired. Once on the temple floor, she stretched before heading down the corridor. The silver torches were still lit. As she proceeded toward the door, the torches went out behind her.

As she approached the doors, the last set of torches went out. For a terrifying moment, she stood in absolute darkness. Then the stone doors began to open.

Elizi sat on the bottom stair, cleaning a set of throwing knives. At the sight of Raven, she jumped to her feet. She dropped the cleaning rag and handed Raven a canteen. Raven gratefully accepted it. While she took a long drink, Elizi gathered the knives, which soon vanished into her robes. Raven corked the canteen and handed it back to Elizi. A quick glance around the chamber told her Malik hadn't stayed.

"How do you feel?" A faint accent sweetened Elizi's words. "You've been in there for a little more than a day."

Raven blinked. "What? A day? No, that's not possible."

"Time moves differently inside," said Elizi. "Time moves differently when the Sisters are speaking. You must be starving."

Raven put a hand over her stomach. "I don't feel hungry."

"It'll catch up to you." Elizi winked. "Come on. I'll walk you back to your room and send word for something to be brought up."

Raven rubbed her face as Elizi led her back up the stairs. An entire day had passed? When they entered the stronghold, the chaos of the celebration had been replaced with a calm murmur. No sooner had she sat on her bed than a tray of bread, hard cheese, and fruit appeared on her bedside table.

"Need anything else?" asked an older woman with freckles along her nose and charcoal in her dark hair.

Raven blinked. Elizi had disappeared.

"Don't worry." The older woman offered Raven a motherly smile. "I felt odd for days after my Choosing. It's like you're still walking through a dream."

"Yes, it does feel like that." Raven reached for the bread. Still warm. "Have the Wraiths who went to meet the Gray Elite caravan returned yet?"

The woman frowned. "No, but I wouldn't worry about it. It would have taken them several hours to get there, maybe longer. They'll return soon. With new faces, I hope."

Raven nodded. "Thank you."

"You are welcome," said the woman before she left.

Raven tore pieces of her bread and set them onto her tongue. She would tell Zander about her power's origin when he returned. She felt too weak to do much else. She ate her fill and then collapsed onto her bed. The pillow still smelled like Zander.

Raven woke feeling remarkably well rested. She took her time washing and dressed in a fresh set of deep plum and black robes that someone had brought up while she slept. The robes were silken and light as feathers, but strong and durable. They lacked the steel plating and weapon hiding spots of their typical gear, but she had only her dagger to wear. Someone had taken the tray too. She must have slept soundly for them to not have bothered her.

She stretched. Oh, she felt stiff. How long had she slept? Coupled with the time spent in the Choosing, her limbs felt leaden. Still, she was a Wraith. A Wraith! That knowledge sent a feverish excitement along her stiff limbs.

Raven made her way through the corridor and into the main room. She silently prided herself on not getting lost. The main doors were open, letting in glorious late afternoon sunlight. She made her way through the doors and down the sandy beach. The sunlight gleamed off the gulf in dazzling yellows and crystalline blues. To one side, a group of Wraiths jumped from a cliff halfway up the cove's wall and into the gulf below. On the other side, a group of older Wraiths sat in the shade, weaving baskets.

"Raven?" Malik appeared beside her. He wore fewer necklaces but just as many rings. His eyes searched hers, anxiety in his own. "You're awake."

"You're upset," she said.

Malik blinked, then half laughed. "You've got our mother's way of knowing things other people don't want to talk about."

"Not *other* people," Raven said. "You. You only have three faces: serious, mildly happy, and upset."

The corners of his lips twitched upward. "I can't argue with that."

"Is there something you want to talk about?" Raven asked. It seemed like a sisterly thing to do, and something a friend would do. And she felt incredibly light, like she could do anything, even help her half-brother with his problems.

"No," Malik said flatly.

"Let me rephrase," Raven said. "Is there something you *need* to talk about?"

He sighed. "No."

Raven held her gaze on him. She hadn't anticipated him telling her his deepest darkest secrets, but she hadn't anticipated a blunt refusal either.

"Walk with me." Malik held out his arm. She strung hers with his, and they started a slow meander along the gulf's shore. "I know we're family. I've never had a sister before. It's just been me for a long time, and I've not used to having people around. Especially those who care about my wellbeing."

"Our mother said she left you when you were little," Raven said, her voice low, not wanting to say something insensitive out loud.

"She did," Malik said. "Because she was a Wraith and because I had magic, she left me here. I grew up with one of the older Wraiths, a basket weaver." He glanced to the group of Wraiths weaving baskets. "I didn't understand why my mother didn't want me. I assumed I wasn't good enough for her. I grew up by myself. Because I had magic, I couldn't wander freely. And Wraiths come and go. I had few children my age, and I spent most of my time alone or with the Wraiths too old to go on missions. I learned a lot about magic from Deikun, and when I proved to have the gifts of a seeker, he took me under his wing."

"That sounds more exciting than growing up in a mine," Raven said. "My father didn't let us go outside without a reason, because he had this wild notion that we would get snatched by wandering automatons or Gray Elite soldiers."

"Yet you still ran back there to save them," Malik said.

Raven nodded. "I did. I might be resentful toward the people of Silver Glen for their backwater ways and old fashioned ideals, but they are still family. Of a sort." She hugged his arm. "I used to dream of flying through the clouds on an airship. Strange how it worked out."

"I knew my mother was a pirate, because the Wraiths told me," Malik said. "I always thought she would come back for me one day, and then she did, and I didn't know what to think about it."

"You don't sound happy about it," she said.

Malik sighed, considering. "Luckett is a great woman, but her mothering skills are...lacking." He offered her a small smile. "I remember your father. I remember the day I met him. I thought he was the greatest man in the world, because he could lift me above his head."

Raven felt her chest tighten. It felt strange to consider a time when her father, her mother, and Malik were together—before she was born. Her father...who was still up in the sky. Her thoughts snapped toward the sky.

She asked Malik, "Have you heard anything from the *Orion*?"

"I've kept Luckett updated on your Trial and Choosing." Malik glanced up, then quickly back down. "I only assume she relayed that information with your father, but Sisters only know what she told him, if she told him."

Malik paused underneath the shadow of a palm. "I remember the day we headed to Silver Glen, because your father wanted to. Because Mother was carrying you. I remember thinking that we would be a family. That everything would be as it should. But I was a child and foolish. You know how it turned out."

Raven pulled his arm closer, and by extension, him. "Wanting a family isn't foolish," she said. "Not even a little."

"It is when your mother is Bailey Luckett." Malik added in a hasty mutter, "And you share her taste in men."

"We're family," Raven said. "You said so."

Malik tore his eyes from the gulf and met hers. He looked bothered, but less than he had before. "Thank you, Raven. You have our mother in you, but you've got your father in you too."

"I accept that," Raven said. "I admire them both for their strengths." And she understood their faults, to a degree. "I wonder how they're getting along up there."

Malik let out a small, delicate laugh. "The *Orion* is a big ship, but Mother has a way of taking up a lot of space at once."

"As does my father," she added.

Malik cast his eyes back toward the gulf, toward the ocean visible between the cliffs, the expanse endless and blue.

"The team that went to find the Gray Elite caravan is late," Malik admitted, eyes on the ocean. "There are a hundred things that could have delayed them, but I don't like it. It might be my anxiety catching up to me and making me paranoid."

"Could something bad have happened?" Raven asked quietly.

"Something bad can always happen," Malik said with certainty. "But Wraiths are trained for bad situations. And, in all the time I've known Zander, he has repeatedly proven to be one of the toughest Wraiths out there. He fights with ferocity. I trained with him a few times, and he is a terrifying opponent."

She nodded, thinking of how his shadows had surged toward her, how they had taken down those automatons so effortlessly.

A boat rowed through the gulf's mouth, a fresh catch of fish on board. A few Wraiths waited by the dock, ready to help.

"Conrad is getting impatient," Malik said. Had Raven imagined the hitch in her brother's voice on the other boy's name?

"Is he here?" she asked, glancing around.

"No," Malik said quickly. "He cannot step into the village. He's been exiled." Malik sighed through his nose. "But he has been pacing by the gate every day, annoying the guards to no end, asking about you."

Raven glanced toward the path that led through the brush and palms to Wayward Point.

"He said he wanted you to see him when you returned from your Choosing," Malik said.

"He said?" she repeated. "He told you?"

Malik's face flushed deep scarlet. He looked away, and the panic of embarrassment flooded into his eyes.

"You went to see him?" she asked, curious. Before Malik could answer, she saw the answer in his eyes. Her smile turned wicked. "He came to see you? I thought he couldn't step foot into the village?"

"He shouldn't," Malik corrected, voice low. "The punishment for defying his exile is death, but only if he gets caught. Any Wraith can deliver the punishment."

Raven looked Malik up and down. Conrad had violated his exile, and he had gone to Malik. Yet Malik hadn't delivered punishment. He had broken the rules for Conrad.

"I thought you were the straight-laced type," Raven whispered.

He cleared his throat. "Have you eaten yet? I came out of my Choosing ravenous. I ate enough for two in my first meal."

Chuckling, she allowed the diversion in conversation.

Malik took Raven back to the kitchen, where he snagged her bread and cheese. While she ate, he led her through the village. Wraiths worked to repair huts, tend to gardens, and clean fish—only they used magic. Malik explained that jobs were given based on a magician's talents. Elizi had ferried almost every magician to the Trial since her induction. One Wraith could whisper to plants and make them grow faster. One man turned green fibers into dried rope in a few moments. It seemed every Wraith had a place in the village.

"We don't all stay here all the time," Malik said. "Wraiths travel all over, seeking magicians. Some follow the guidance of their patron Sister."

He introduced her to Wraiths as they approached, and now that she had gone through her Trial and Choosing, they could tell her about their own. She hadn't been the only one unprepared for a week's stay on an island, and she hadn't been the only one to eat the shade fruit. Other unfortunate Wraiths had seen ghouls rising from the waters, thought the island sinking, or felt spiders crawling under their skin.

No one else admitted to seeing a ghost guide, and Raven didn't volunteer that information.

The sun gradually sank, pulling its golden light across the gulf's calm waters. The waters turned molten, the shadows under the cliff thickened, and torches were lit in the village. Dinner was served, and Raven ate enough for two. She sat beside Malik and Thalame, but she kept one eye on the doors. The team sent to intercept the Gray Elite caravan hadn't returned.

Dinner ended, and Malik walked her back to her room in the guest wing. By the time they came to her door, exhaustion had settled into her bones.

"That strange feeling goes away," Malik said. "I remember feeling odd for days after my Choosing. It felt like a lucid dream."

"Is it because of what happened during the Choosing?" Raven whispered. "When the Sisters did...whatever they did?"

Malik shook his head. "I don't know. It's old magic, and no one alive understands what exactly happens."

Raven reached for her door, and Malik turned to leave.

"Do you think the team will come back tomorrow?" she asked.

Malik didn't answer immediately. "Odds are, yes. Goodnight, Raven."

"Goodnight."

When he left, Raven sat on the edge of her bed and clutched Zander's pillow to her chest. It didn't smell as much like him as it had the night before. His absence felt stronger this time, and she didn't like it.

The next morning, Raven meandered through the Wraiths' village. The day's work had begun. She didn't see Malik or Thalame, and her feet took her along the path that wound through the forest, up the cliffside, and toward Wayward Point. Few clouds marred the periwinkle sky, and the humid air clung Raven's thin robes to her skin, but the briny breeze blowing off the ocean was cool.

She came to the border of the Wraiths' village, signified by two stone pillars worn by time and weather and half-smothered in moss and vines. Walking through, she didn't spy any guards in the greenery, but she knew they were there somewhere.

Not far on the other side, a shadow fell into step beside her. A glance told her it was Conrad. Beads clinked in his braids. He wore the breezy clothes of Wayward Point, a thin sleeveless tunic and trousers the color of sand.

"About time," Conrad said. "I was starting to think they'd locked you down there."

"Malik was right," she said. "You're impatient."

"It's boring over here when all the Wraiths and excitement are over there," he said, pouting. He bent forward, searching her face. "What's wrong, little bird?"

"What makes you think something is wrong?"

"You and your brother share several expressions," Conrad said plainly.

She sighed. "Zander went on a mission to disrupt a Gray Elite caravan, and they're not back yet," she said in a single breath.

"Ah," he said, as though it explained it all. They walked for a while in silence, navigating the brambles and tree roots and bushes. As the path evened out enough they could walk side by side, he added, "I'm sure they're fine."

"How can you be sure?" Raven asked.

"How can you be sure they aren't?" Conrad asked with the same indifference as Malik. "Many things don't go as planned, and sometimes we have to improvise. You saw that with your own eyes in Moorin. There might have been more prisoners than they thought, and traveling with a crowd without attracting attention is hard."

"I hadn't thought about that," she said.

They came to the fork in the path.

"Do you have business to attend to?" Conrad asked.

She shrugged. "No. I just needed a walk."

"Good, then come and walk with me, little bird. I need the company, and I want to hear all about your Trial and Choosing." They started toward Wayward Point, and his grin widened, and his eyes grew curious. "Tell me, did you find the shade fruit?"

She laughed. They meandered through the outskirts of Wayward Point's oldest residences, and she talked. Conrad listened. She withheld the part of Aeon's ghost and the truth of her power. She didn't know what to think about it yet, and she wanted to talk to Zander about it first. As her story came to an end, they passed a small garden where a group of older women sat in a circle, each at a washboard, chattering in Tinatunian.

"You're lucky your magic helped you during the Trial," Conrad said, his words low as to not carry. "My magic doesn't heat water or cook fish. I knew how to start a fire and basic survival, but those berries got me. I started seeing mermaids calling me out to the sea. I swam out to sea, nearly drowned, but somehow managed to find dry land."

She grinned. "If it weren't for those berries, I might not have found the treasure."

"I can't believe you had the stones to come back empty-handed." Conrad shook his head at her. "And that old man let you in anyway." He harrumphed. "I brought back the lute."

"Can you play?"

"Not a single note," Conrad said. "But I like music, which was my answer, and people always forget about their troubles and dance. Music is a language everyone understands."

"Did your Choosing take a whole day?"

"Most of them take at least a day," Conrad said. "Time doesn't flow the same for the Sisters as it does for us, at least not when they commune. I think the longest Choosing lasted three days. The poor boy was nearly dry as death. Mine took about a day. It was exhausting in a different way, listening to the Sisters pick apart my qualities."

"Wilyn Chose me," Raven said. A prickling of panic seized her next thought. "Am I allowed to tell you that?"

Conrad shrugged. "I've never been told otherwise." He looked her up and down. "It fits. You did gravitate toward the sky. You have a strange love of airships. You like the stars."

"Some of that might be true," Raven said.

"It's legend that Wilyn has a soft spot for dreamers and hopeless romantics," Conrad said, winking.

"Then I would be among friends."

"Indeed, little bird." Conrad laughed. He glanced out to the sea. "Minerva Chose me, although she also threw me back out to the sea."

"Can you blame her?" Raven asked.

Conrad sighed deeply. "Legends say that Minerva is the stern one," he mumbled. "They also say she has a soft spot for pirates and treasure hunters, but I'm not so sure of that."

Because Conrad had stolen a treasure map from the Wraiths' archive.

"Do you regret it?" Raven asked. "Stealing the map, I mean."

"Yes and no," Conrad said, considering. "Yes, because I got kicked out of the best club on the continent, and Malik only glares at me now. No, because I found places so fantastic, I couldn't have dreamed them up. I know I am among the few humans to have stepped in certain places in the past one thousand years."

The huts parted, and they had a breathtaking view of the white sand beach and Linila Bay.

He sighed and looked to the endless sea with longing. "I've had incredible experiences on the sea during my exile, found myself, discovered far more than I intended. So...I suppose my final answer is no. I do not regret what I've done, because it's made me who I am."

Raven lifted her chin to the breeze. The salty air brushed her hair out of her face and away from her neck. Everything she had done, gone through, survived, had helped make her who she was. If she had stayed in Silver Glen, if she and Zander had returned there, if she had just stayed in the Dwellers' treehouse, so many things would have happened differently.

"Minerva told me to help you when we first met," Conrad admitted. "Well, she didn't say those words exactly. She told me to put that wooden coin in my pocket before I left to steal that stupid box, because someone would need it. She told me to go to the arena that day, because there was someone she wanted me to see. And I saw you." He chuckled. "If it weren't for that little bit of divine intervention, who knows where you would have ended up."

"I suppose I should thank her," Raven said.

"I should too," Conrad said. "I'm glad she sent me here. I almost ignored her, you know. Though, I feel like a better man for it all, and think of the adventure we've had! I know where I'd be had we not met. I'd be slumming it up on some ship headed southwest."

Raven's heart thumped hard. "What's to the southwest?"

Aeon's kingdom had been to the southwest, the kingdom her Sisters had sunk.

"Scattered islands and ruins, mostly," Conrad said casually, eyes drifting over the ocean's horizon. "It's a trove of adventures and treasure."

They wandered into Wayward Point's thriving market. Conrad bought two iced juices, one for each of them, and Raven brought hers to her lips just as a familiar voice drifted over the crowd in Tinatunian.

Raven didn't taste the passion fruit or citrus; she only felt sharp panic and fiery rage.

"You're looking pale, little bird." Conrad's eyes bored into hers with concern.

"That voice." Raven glanced over the crowd. Her eyes settled on the speaker, a Tinatunian woman in her twenties, smile broad and careless.

"Do you know her?" Conrad asked.

Raven felt rage bubble and boil under her skin. "That's the woman who sold me."

Raven balled her fists and felt flames licking her skin. She envisioned a dozen deaths for the woman who had saved her, then sold her—Nia. At the woman's name, her rage sprang—Conrad's fingers folded around her forearm. A sharp pain flickered down her arm and into that place deep inside where her magic slept.

A short gasp escaped her lips, and her magic shorted out. She turned a wide-eyed gaze to Conrad.

"Not here," he warned. "Magic upsets people when displayed openly. It also attracts the wrong kind of attention. Don't forget, not everyone looks kindly on the Wraiths."

"How did you—"

"We all have our talents," Conrad said, his voice rushed and low.

His seeker abilities to detect magic had shorted out her own.

She huffed, because she knew he was right. She turned her attention back to Nia, but she had already vanished into the crowd. Raven scanned the faces, but she didn't see Nia or the two other scavengers who had sold her into slavery.

"Come on, little bird." Conrad ushered her away. They returned to their walk of the market. "Take some deep, calming breaths."

She humored him by taking an exaggerated breath. Conrad offered her a small smile. They turned a corner into an alley and then onto a small side street.

"I didn't think I would ever see them again," Raven admitted. "I've thought about what I would do and say to them over and over, but...I hoped I'd not have to."

"Wayward Point does have its dark alleys," Conrad said with a heavy sigh. "Slavery just happens to be one of them."

"Is all of Tinatun like this place?"

"No." He shook his head. "Unlike Gracita and Rhynwier, Tinatun is divided into smaller provinces that act as their own kingdoms. This province is the least ruled, because the southern kings and queens don't like the Gray Elite. The southern peoples refer to their northern corner as the wild country. The wayward son, if you will." Conrad chuckled. "King

Olino has openly hung pirates and gutted slavers, but since they are confined up here, and he's on the southern tip of the kingdom, he does not care."

Raven saw the distraction he offered, the chance to ask more about the vicious southern king and how Conrad knew such things. He offered a story while steering her away from the market. A part of her wanted to take the bait and forget about those scavengers, but another part knew she couldn't be the only unfortunate girl sold like meat. She had to do something, but what? What could she possibly do against an industry?

"You're looking glum," Conrad said in a sing-song tone. "Are you thinking those bad thoughts again?"

"I want to do something."

"I suppose we could hog-tie them and send them out to sea."

"Not just about the scavengers, but about the whole industry. Burn down every slaver hut or something."

"I don't have any advice on that, but I know what you need. Something cool to drink."

Conrad pulled her back toward the market and to a little tavern that sold cold drinks in coconuts. He bought her one but did not buy himself one. She sat at one of the little tables.

"Why don't you stay here and enjoy the drink," Conrad said, eyes across the market. "I've got someone I need to see about...something."

"Someone and something?"

Conrad winked. "It might not be strictly...Wraith approved or legal."

She frowned.

He sighed and said lowly, "It's a lead on old pirate treasure. I had a friend looking into it, and he's back. I need to catch him before he sells the information to someone else or gets himself killed in a bar fight. Both are likely."

She half laughed. She sipped loudly from the coconut, and Conrad vanished into the market. The coconut helped; she tasted sweet rum and something salty and sweet mixed with the coconut milk. As she sat there, she let her mind wander over foolish plans of revenge against the scavengers, against the slavers, against anyone who thought slavery fine. She had never felt such a strong sense of vengeance before, but she had never been tricked and damned. She had never experienced that side of humanity before, and she wanted to make sure no other lost girl or boy was tricked like she had been.

She hit the bottom of her coconut too soon, but she didn't want another. She could feel the loose feeling under her skin, the sense of detachment. It had not made her worry go away, but she cared less about it.

Conrad had not returned. She didn't see him in the market crowd either. The coconut vender spotted her—he had that look about him of one hoping for another sale. Raven stood, discarded her coconut, and started to meander through the busy market. She walked past the carts and stalls and stores with the same sense of amazement she'd felt when she first came to Wayward Point. She spotted scarves in every color and fabric, tropic clothes designed for heat, jewelry of every metal and stone and shade, food on sticks and food in melons. Voices chatted away in Tinatunian and her own tongue, the languages mixed together in a blur of sound.

She meandered past a tavern. The outside wall was covered in posters, including wanted posters. Raven had no intention to stop, but a familiar face among the others pulled her to a halt. It was a girl. The harshly drawn lines made her look vicious and beautiful, and the heavy lines of her eyes made her look clever and smart.

But it was the name under the poster that gave her pause—Raven Thane, wanted for the attempted assassination of General Oliver Deacon and other crimes.

She gawked. She knew about her bounty, but she hadn't seen a wanted poster.

She felt eyes on her. The guard by the tavern door looked her up and down. His eyes shifted to the poster. Before he could make a connection, Raven turned her back to him and started away. A few stalls down, she spotted another wanted poster. She pretended not to notice. She made a lap of the market, and she spotted no less than twenty wanted posters wearing her face.

Conrad's chime of laughter came from her left, and she turned down the alley. Footsteps followed—bare feet on the sandy ground. Her heart humped. Conrad wore boots. She walked a little faster. So did her stalker.

Before she reached the other end of the alley, a hand grabbed her wrist and whirled her around. Her panic flared, and it took a heartbeat for her to recognize the Tinatunian man who had grabbed her—one of the scavengers who had sold her. His black eyes pierced hers, and a wicked smile spread over his face. Her panic turned into rage.

"You," Raven spat.

"*Wawuw gai lu!*" he spat.

"I still don't understand." Raven started to summon flames.

"Look who found her way back," came a drawling female voice on the other side of the alley. At the sound of the voice, Raven's flames sputtered. Nia strolled into the alley. The other scavenger walked a step behind, wooden club over his shoulders. "You cost me money, girl."

Raven put her hand over her heart and asked innocently, "I cost you money? Hmm. I distinctly remember you walking away with a bag of tokens, marks, and piks when you sold me." Raven heated her wrist under the scavenger's hand—he yelped and yanked his hand away.

"*Aggi*," the man spat, cradling his hand.

"You are one of them." Nia looked down her nose at Raven.

"And you are no longer a threat," Raven spat back. "But you have piqued my interest. How did I cost you money?"

"I bet against you in the *Chjelhu Tal*," Nia said. "Half what we were paid for you. I thought he would rip you apart."

"And you bet wrong," Raven growled.

"Maybe." Nia chuckled. "But the Gray Elite will pay ten times what I got for you the first time."

Raven harrumphed, taunt on her tongue, when the scavenger behind her grabbed her arm. He pressed something smooth and cold against her neck. A stone. A needling sensation started where the stone met her skin and traveled inward, through her bloodstream, through her bones. Her panic reared, and she reached for her magic—flames sputtered. Pain flared in the place of her magic.

A cry ripped through her throat. Darkness surged on the edges of her vision, dark and cold and gripping.

She collapsed to the sand-packed ground.

The scavengers blurred above her. The sun turned them into shadows. Hands grabbed her, lifted her, but the darkness consumed her.

Raven came to against something hard. She blinked. Darkness swayed within her vision, and her body wobbled. The wooden ceiling came into view. She was lying on a stone floor in a windowless room. The only light came from a lantern in the hall, on the other side of an iron barred door.

"...when we've done half of the work?" came Nia's voice. One of the scavengers spat something in Tinatunian. "We want half the bounty."

A male voice sighed. "Fine. Half. But you'll wait here until the Gray Elite come to pick her up. I'm not shoving out any coin to you scumbags until I've got my half."

"She's not going anywhere," Nia spat. "We got her with a rune. She won't be using her *aggi* magic anytime soon."

The darkness retreated bit by bit. Raven could see the shadows of her captors in the hall outside the door. She reached for her magic, but it did not respond. The inferno had been reduced to a flicker.

A rune... She remembered seeing stones with runes painted and etched on them in the market. Is that what they'd done to her? The rune had shoved her magic out of her reach. It wasn't impossible; the Wraiths had been painting and tattooing runes to burn off excess magic, but this rune hadn't burned off her excess magic. It had stomped on it, suppressed it.

She tried to get up. They had tied her hands and ankles with rope.

The darkness faded from her vision and her mind. She could hear other people in other cells. Other prisoners.

"Fine," Nia spat. "We wait, and we get half."

"Fine."

A door slammed, and several sets of footsteps trailed into another room.

Raven let out a groan. What would Conrad think? Would he think she'd gone back to the stronghold without him? She couldn't count on him to save her, which left her on her own.

And they had sent word to the Gray Elite.

It will not hold you, said the voice in her mind, the ghost of Aeon.

Raven sighed. "And what do you want me to do about it?" she hissed at the voice. "I'm tied up and can't use my magic."

I can help you. Allow me control. I will bring you the revenge you desire.

Raven didn't like the sound of those words, yet she wanted revenge on those slavers, on the whole slaving industry for not only what they had done to her, but what they had done to so many others.

"Fine," Raven whispered.

A beat of silence, and then her magic flared through her bloodstream, burning off the icy remains of the rune's strange magic. Flames erupted from every pore, breathing through her skin and hair and clothes. The ropes on her wrists and ankles disintegrated. Flames spread through the fibers of her robes and spread across the dust and dirt and sand. They snaked up the wooden walls and reached across the iron door. They moved on their own once they touched the wooden walls, spreading up and down along the old dry wood. The flames raced to the ceiling, converging and spreading without mercy, without prejudice.

Screams sounded over the crackling wood and creaking stone. Panic filled the air. The other prisoners. Raven pushed herself over the burning stones and to her feet. No one deserved to be trapped like this.

She moved through the flames, her flames, and they licked at arms and legs but did not burn her. Her flames shoved the iron cell door out of its frame and raced along the hall, ripping doors from the other cells. At her command, the flames arched, leaving a path between them for the prisoners. They crept through the flames, fearful and worried.

They run like cowards!

Her flames consumed the building. They raced over the walls, the ceiling, the floor. They devoured everything.

See what we can do?

Raven stood among the flames, feeling the heat against her skin. The building crackled and groaned. Her flames consumed it all.

"Raven!"

She knew that voice, and she gravitated toward it. She walked through the wall of flame and into the cooler air of Wayward Point. The cool air seemed to steal her very breath.

"Raven?" Hands grabbed her shoulders. She blinked, and Conrad's worried face appeared in front of hers. "What happened?"

He pulled her away from the burning building. Something snapped—she gasped for breath. The flames had gone wild, and it was no longer her flames that consumed it, but the fire her's had sparked to life. It licked up the walls and reached into the air. Dark smoke trailing into the sky.

And people had stopped to watch.

"You might want this," Conrad said. He held his tunic in his hand.

Raven blinked—the flames had singed her robes, leaving them hanging on by tatters. She stood nearly naked. Something warm and slippery crawled under her skin, and a fierce blush turned her a deep shade of red. She hastily pulled his tunic over her head.

"We need to get out of here," Conrad said.

Already, people were hauling buckets of water to put out the fire. It didn't matter. Conrad pulled her away. He weaved through alleys, leading them farther away, until they left the chaos behind. When he paused in a quiet alley, Raven sank to the ground.

Conrad paced in front of her.

"What happened?" she asked after a time.

Conrad jerked to a halt and looked at her with wide eyes. "What happened?" A mad grin stretched across his face. "Little bird, you burned down one of the most profitable slave huts in Wayward Point. Extra points for doing it naked. You're insane, you know that?"

"I'm starting to question it," she said.

His grin waned. "Why is that?"

She looked down at her hands. How could she explain Aeon's strange influence? "It didn't feel like I was...me. It felt like someone else was controlling me."

Conrad tilted his head. "Hmm. Odd, though I've heard stress does strange things to people."

Raven inhaled deep. She didn't remember it clearly. She remembered waking up tied and helpless and then...fire. Power.

Conrad heaved a sigh. "Your turn. What happened?"

She told him about the wanted posters and the scavengers.

"I can't leave you alone for a minute." Conrad crossed his arms. "Come on, let's get you something else to wear."

He held out his arm, and she took it. He guided her away from the burning building as if it didn't exist. Raven soaked in the calm, desperately wishing her panic away.

"I suppose I shouldn't be surprised," Conrad said after a while. "You have spent a considerable amount of time with me. From here on out, little bird, you must promise to spend more time with your brother. Either to have his dire sense of the law rub off on you, or to have your chaotic whims rub off on him."

"Will the Wraiths be mad at me?" she asked.

"It's hard to tell," Conrad said. "You saved people, but you also made a scene."

They stopped at a small shop on the outskirts of the market, and Raven picked out a thin skirt that tied at her waist and brightly colored cropped shirt like she had seen many of the women wearing; much of her skin remained exposed, but the important things were covered. Conrad paid the merchant, who hadn't said a word about Raven's state of dress. Conrad then pulled his tunic back over his head.

"Did you find your friend?" Raven asked as they started away from the market.

"I did." Conrad's smile widened, and his eyes glittered—he had good news. He opened his mouth to tell her about it when Elizi slid out from an alley.

"There you are." Elizi stomped over. "I've been looking for you. I have news. Aside from whatever stunt you pulled." She motioned to the pillar of gray and black smoke.

Raven's heart plummeted. The Wraiths had already heard of her blunder? Had Elizi come to deliver the news of her exile?

"What other news?" Conrad asked, leaning forward.

"I take it you haven't heard, then," Elizi said. "Malik told me to find you when the news reached us. It's our missing team. It was a setup."

Elizi pulled a piece of folded paper from her robes and handed it to Conrad. He snatched it before Raven could and quickly unfolded it where she could see it. It was a wanted poster. Like her own, it bore the seal of the Gray Elite.

"By order of Emperor Renald the Fourth," read Conrad, "the public execution of the magician and assassin known as the Revenant will take place in the town square of the city of Kusmerk, tomorrow at sunset."

The Gray Elite had added a drawing of a masked figure with empty eyes and dark clothes.

The Revenant—Zander.

Raven couldn't breathe. She read the wanted poster again and again. The words blurred together, drowned out by her pounding heart and screaming mind. The Gray Elite had set the caravan up as a trap, and now they had Zander. They knew who and what he was, and they were going to kill him.

Conrad spat a curse. "The Gray Elite knew the Wraiths couldn't resist a crate of magicians so close to Wayward Point." He crumpled the wanted poster and threw it at the ground.

"You need to head back," Elizi said to Raven. "People are looking for you in new vigor."

"Come on, little bird." Conrad led her by the hand toward the stronghold, keeping to the side streets and alleys.

Once on the outskirts, they broke into a run. She forced her legs to move faster, over the sun-dried sand, through the trees and rocks, despite the stitch in her side and burning lungs. They neared the boundary pillars to the Wraith's village, but Conrad didn't slow down. They passed through. The guards didn't stop him.

By the time they reached the stronghold, her lungs felt like fire, and her side threatened to rip itself open. A group had gathered by the steps on the stronghold; Grand Master Deikun stood on the steps, worry creasing the skin between his brows.

"You shouldn't be here," came Malik's hiss. He appeared through the crowd and grabbed Conrad's arm. His eyes were wide with fear, not rage.

As if summoned by Conrad's presence, the grand master appeared beside Malik. Her brother's eyes grew wider still.

"This isn't about me," Conrad said to Malik. To Deikun, he said, "You're sending Wraiths after the others. I'm going."

The grand master considered him a long moment, then nodded. "If that is what you wish."

"It is," Conrad said with more determination than Raven had ever heard.

"I'm going too." Raven had hoped to say it with as much resolve as Conrad, but her voice fell flat and breathless.

At her, the grand master looked less enthused, almost pitied.

"It was a trap," Raven started, before the grand master could argue with her. "The Gray Elite set it up to catch Wraiths. They're going to execute Zander, and it's likely another trap they've set up for me. They know I'll go after him, and that's what they want."

"If that is what they want, then you shouldn't go," Malik said.

"It's why I should go," she countered.

Malik frowned. "Why risk yourself by going?"

"Because I want to make sure they know exactly who they're dealing with." Venom dripped from each word. The fury from before returned, hot and bright and powerful. This time, she controlled the fury. Flames danced around her hands. "I will make sure the Gray Elite never think about bothering me or Zander or the Wraiths again."

"Those are bold claims," said Deikun. Her flames reflected in his dark eyes. He didn't look enthused or impressed, though many Wraiths standing behind him did.

"Yes, they are." Raven nodded. She let her flames go out, but she could still feel the power. "I refuse to stand by and hide while Zander is killed because of me. I would rather let them kill me. I would rather die trying to save him than do nothing while he is hurt."

Again.

Conrad squeezed her hand. "And we have just a few hours to prepare. It will take us half a day to get there, and I would prefer not to be fashionably late."

"You will have to leave before dawn," Deikun announced for them all to hear. He glanced over the gathered. "Conrad and Raven cannot do this alone."

Hands shot into the air. Malik's curled fists shook at his sides.

"He's not a fighter," Conrad whispered to Raven, nodding toward Malik. "But he hates to stand by while others go fight."

Raven understood that feeling completely.

"The team is selected," the grand master announced over the crowd. "Those of you will get your rest. Your things will be packed and ready for you come the hour of departure."

Raven headed for the stronghold, as did several others, to sleep in the stone-walled rooms that held no sunlight so they would be ready to leave before dawn. Conrad followed her, and no one stopped him.

They would get there in time. They had to. Or Zander's head would roll, and she refused to allow that. If he died, if the Gray Elite killed him just to get at her, she would burn everything in Gracita to the ground. And she knew Aeon would help.

Raven just wished she knew if she wanted the forgotten Sister's help or not.

Raven couldn't sleep. A young Wraith brought her fresh robes, but she pretended to be asleep. Her new robes had plates of dark steel, hardened leather, and hidden pockets—the combat robes she had seen in Moorin. Along with her new robes, a tray of bread and butter, nuts, and dried berries rested on her bedside table. Raven tossed and turned. Her feverish magic churned under her skin, itching to incinerate any Gray Elite who dared to hurt Zander.

Was the thirst for vengeance her own or Aeon's?

In truth, she didn't know.

A knock sounded on her door, shattering what shallow sleep she had managed to find. Raven sat up as Elizi entered, her face solemn.

"It's time," said Elizi, her voice light as birdsong and as steady as the moon.

Raven did not trust her own voice to be as strong, so she said nothing. She sat up and tore a chunk of bread off with her teeth. It had gone stale.

"They're meeting in the hall when you're ready." Elizi departed without a sound.

Raven washed in cold water. She needed the shock. She ate what she could stomach, forcing her meal down. She would need her strength. She dressed in her new robes. Steel plates and hardened leather protected her vitals and made her feel heavy, but invulnerable and sturdy. She braided her hair back and tucked it under the hood.

Standing in her own Wraith gear, fire dancing under her skin, she felt a sense of power she had never felt before. She could save Zander. She would save him. She and the team of Wraiths going with her. The Gray Elite wouldn't see them coming.

She headed to the main hall. Conrad appeared beside her, dressed in the same dark robes. The next several moments blurred together. Malik appeared, worried but stoic. Thalame had volunteered to go, and he wore the same dark robes. He had gathered healing supplies along with daggers.

Along with Raven, Conrad, and Thalame, five other Wraiths had volunteered to go. The eight of them sat together in the hall, and Raven tried her best to listen as Deikun fed them the details. Kusmerk had been built over a series of bridges that stretched over the southern Gladia River. It meant there were few ways into the city and a lot of things could go wrong.

"The Gray Elite chose their location wisely," Deikun said grimly. "They will be patrolling the city."

Raven studied the hand-drawn map of Kusmerk spread over the table. Zander had once told her about a city built over a river, a feat by the Gray Elite to prove themselves above the laws of nature. The Gray Elite had wanted to prove their engineering and machines could do the impossible.

We will show them the power of nature.

In that moment, Raven agreed.

"Kusmerk also sits just within the border of Gracita," Malik added. "So you will have to sneak across."

"Sneaking across the border is one thing," said Thalame, crease between his brows. "But then we've got to find a way into the city once we're inside. You can bet all the piks in Wayward Point, they'll have the border guarded, as well as any way in or out of the city."

"You leave that to me," Conrad said, winking. "Kusmerk may look tough, but it's only tough on the outside."

"Now's not the time for vague nonsense," one of the other Wraiths said.

"I agree," Deikun said to Conrad. "What is your plan?"

Conrad sighed in defeat. He pointed to the map, his finger just below the city's edge. "Boats still have to pass underneath, and for the accomplished smuggler, the tangle of pipes and steel beams and maintenance halls are perfect for coming and going without going through all the trouble of the main gates."

"That'd work," Thalame said. "Assuming no one is afraid of cramped spaces?"

No one objected.

The door to the chamber opened, and a Wraith escorted two familiar faces. Raven jumped to her feet. Brent and Niall looked at the stronghold with a mixture of awe and uncertainty. Brent's gaze fell onto Raven, and relief replaced his worry.

"These are the two I told you about," Malik said to Deikun.

Thalame stood next, confusion on his brow. "What did I miss?"

"I reached out to our new friends regarding the situation," Malik said.

Niall paused at the table, eyes taking in the map. His gaze met Thalame's, then Raven's. "And we have the very thing that might save your necks—and Zander's."

Raven blinked at Brent.

"We've been busy." As Brent moved, the light shifted off the goggles around his neck. "Niall and I have been working on several projects, and Malik came by yesterday and told us what happened to Zander and what you were planning on doing."

"And this seems like the perfect time to test out something that we've been developing," Niall grinned.

"Unless you've got something that can get us to Kusmerk without being seen..." Thalame's brows rose. His confusion fell into a knowing smirk, along with a devilish twinkle in his eyes—one that Niall returned.

"That's right," Niall said.

"Did I miss the part where you announced it?" Conrad looked between Thalame and Raven.

"It's better if we show you," Brent said, excitement coursing through his every action.

They followed the tinkers out of the stronghold and to the gulf, to the shore, to a little boat.

"It's a boat?" one of the Wraiths deadpanned.

"No, this is the boat that will take you to the real surprise," Niall said plainly. "It wouldn't fit here in the shallows."

The Wraith sighed, as did Conrad.

Niall, Brent, Raven, Thalame, Malik, and Conrad went first—because only so many could fit in the boat at once. They rowed out of the gulf and to the open ocean, just a short way from the mouth. Raven spotted the dark shadow under the water first, then she spotted the thing above the shadow. She first thought it sea-foam covered driftwood, but as they rowed closer, it became a metal hatch. It had been painted the same pale green of the sea around it.

"What is it?" Raven asked, leaned over the side of the boat to see it better. The boat tilted, and Conrad pulled her back.

Niall hooked the oar on the hatch and pulled the boat right beside it. He smiled proudly and said, "Brent and I call it the *Barnacle*."

Raven gawked. Her friends—all that time spent scheming and thinking and building—they had built the perfect way into Kusmerk. A submersible machine.

"Would you like to look inside?" Niall's eyes were bright and his smile wide.

"Yes!" Raven said at once.

Niall knocked on the hatch. A few moments, then it opened from within. A familiar face appeared, her flaxen hair tied back, brassy goggles perched on her head, and her simple dress exchanged for fitted trousers, plain white shirt, and buttoned vest.

"Sweets?" Raven asked, delighted to see her friend.

"Hello again." Sweets leaned against the hatch's side. "What brings you all out to sea?"

Raven gathered herself and straightened her shoulders. "Permission to come aboard."

Sweets grinned. She ducked back down into the hatch, leaving it open, and Raven heard the *thunk-thunk* of boots on a metal ladder. Niall motioned for Raven to go first, and she eagerly climbed out of the boat and into the hatch. Her boots *thunk-thunk*ed as she climbed down into the *Barnacle*'s interior.

The submersible gently swayed, an unsteady but steady sensation. The *Barnacle* was larger on the inside than she thought it would be. The body was the size of a large bed, with benches that folded into the wall. Stubby brass lanterns were mounted on the walls, glowing bluish green. The brass and steel walls had been bolted and welded from oddly shaped scraps and gently curved to form the oval shape of the *Barnacle*. A narrow door in the back led to the engine room, a series of pipes and gauges and buzzing. With the eerie green light, the maze looked maddening.

Raven pressed her hand against the metal wall. She could hear the water moving on the other side, a deep, constant movement, like low-rolling thunder that never ended.

Conrad started down the ladder. His quick eyes took in the submersible, and he grimaced. "Cozy," he mumbled.

"I thought you loved the sea?" Raven asked.

"I'd rather be above the water," he mumbled.

"Think of it as a ship meant for deep sea," Niall said from that hatch. His voice echoed slightly.

Thalame climbed down next, looking more enthused as Conrad. "This is what you've been working on? How fast she go?"

"This baby isn't about speed," said Brent from above. "Not yet anyway."

Raven stepped into the bridge. Two seats had been welded to the floor and padded with brown leather. Sweets sat at one of them, arm thrown over the back of the seat.

The dashboard was filled with gauges, levers, switches, and dials—a colorful blend of brass and steel and iron. She spotted pieces of salvaged automatons. The steering wheel had been crafted from small automaton arms, bent at the elbow. The front of the *Barnacle* had two thick windows, through which Raven spotted a school of fish fluttering in the water beyond.

The green light of the lanterns filled the space, but the sunlight through the water made it glow; an undulating net of sunlight bathed the bridge and Sweets.

"Sisters," Raven breathed as she watched the fish weave back and forth, the sunlight glittering off each scale and tailfin.

"I know," Sweets said. "When Brent told me what they were working on, I didn't think it possible. But look at where we are now."

"The Gray Elite may have problems," came Conrad's voice behind Raven. He stood in the doorway to the bridge, taking in the view. "But they do know how to build a machine. If only they weren't so arrogant and hellbent on proving themselves superior to everything else. Let that be a lesson, little bird." He winked.

Niall slid down the ladder. "Malik went back for the others. I offered, but he refused to come down. He looked a bit green too."

"He isn't a fan of the ocean," Conrad explained. "He has a fear of drowning, and he likely looks at this contraption as a coffin."

"A tour while we wait?" Niall motioned toward the small space.

Niall started with the lanterns. They did not hold candles; they held glowing crystals. Niall called them sunstones, a strange mineral-rich crystal from Tinatun's southern islands that soaked up the sun and radiated the light. The sunstones in the *Barnacle* held sunlight for two days, he said.

"We'll have plenty of light, but we have a limited air supply. We'll have to resurface every so often to replenish or suffocate," said Niall. "And the more people on board, the faster we'll go through that supply."

Conrad frowned. "This is starting to sound like a coffin."

The second boat arrived, and everyone except Malik climbed down. Conrad volunteered to go with Malik for the supplies. Malik did not turn down his company. Raven watched him vanish through the hatch, wondering what the two boys might have to say to one another when no one else could hear.

Thalame leaned into the bridge, grinning. "This is just what we needed. You came through again, mate."

Niall shrugged. "If it hadn't been for Brent, this idea would have never made it out of the workshop, let alone into the water."

"So, the new plan is," Thalame started, leaning against the bridge door, "we swim right underneath Kusmerk. We get in, grab Zander, and get out. The Gray Elite will never know we were there."

Raven frowned. "That will put a dent in my dramatics."

Thalame chuckled. "Can't say I'm sad about that. Your dramatics tend to endanger us all and piss off the Gray Elite."

"Speaking of dramatics." Sweets swiveled to see Raven better. "I heard you melted an automaton? A big one?"

Raven shrugged. "It might be true, but I don't like to brag."

Sweets's grin widened.

Water splashed from above—the rowboat and their supplies had returned. Whatever conversation Malik and Conrad had been having ended as the hatch opened.

"I'll tell you about it when we get back," Raven told Sweets. "Or Conrad can, he's a better storyteller than I am."

Raven stood aside while the Wraiths handed down the supplies. They had brought a fraction of the supplies they originally packed; they had planned on going over land, but the *Barnacle* had shortened their trip considerably. Supplies secured in the small hold, they bid farewell to Malik—he would be returning to the stronghold along with their rowboat. The sunlight squeezed out with a heavy clank as Brent closed and sealed the hatch.

Brent took to the engine room, and Niall sat behind the wheel. Sweets remained in the bridge's second chair.

"Ready when you are," Niall said into a brassy speaking tube beside the captain's chair.

"All systems go," came Brent's tinny confirmation from the speaking tube.

"Here we go." Niall pulled a lever. A *thunk* resounded through the *Barnacle*. A gurgle started below Raven's feet, and that gurgle burst into a roar. Raven tensed, but the roar settled into a purring buzz, one she had grown familiar with on the *Orion*. It was the sound of an engine working like it should.

With a few more levers and fluctuating gurgles, the *Barnacle* began to move. They dove deeper into the ocean until the sunlight dulled and the ocean opened up to a darkness below them. It reminded Raven of the night sky, endless and dark, only it had no stars or clouds. Only monsters and sunken kingdoms lurking at its depths.

Niall guided the *Barnacle* out to sea so they could move faster. He explained that once they entered the river, they wouldn't be able to move as fast. The engine would make too much noise, and even this deep, they didn't want to risk cavitating too much.

Raven resisted the urge to pace the length of the submersible. She settled on tapping her nails against the steel. They had a huge head start when they previously thought they would be short on time, and she reminded herself of that. They would have plenty of time to get to Zander. They would save him. She repeated those words over and over, but still her gut clenched, and her stomach twisted itself into unseemly knots. She watched the sea life go by, the schools of fish and bigger fish.

"Ever see a mermaid?" Conrad whispered, but he had spoken loud enough that others could hear him.

"Are they real?" she asked.

He winked. "According to pirate lore, they live in clans. Some live in the deepest depths, some in the shallows, and some in waterlogged ruins. They collect treasure from sunken ships and hoard it in their dens, like dragons, but cunning and shrewd. Legends tell that pirates and merchants of old made deals with a select few mermaid clans, dealing for lost treasures, and when I first set sail, I thought I would be the first of my generation to strike such a deal with a mermaid clan."

"Did you?" Raven whispered.

Conrad shrugged. "Mermaids are shrewd as they come, distrusting of humans, and firm believers in revenge. If I had, I would not tell you."

She pouted. "But, if mermaids exist, then that means I could find them for myself."

"You could, and you might live to tell the tale." Conrad smirked. "Legends suggest that mermaids are less hostile toward females."

"As they should be," Raven said.

Conrad laughed. "I suppose you're right."

"We're coming up on the river," said Niall.

Raven leaned forward to see what Niall saw. Ahead, the river plunged into the ocean. Niall guided the *Barnacle* toward the river's end. They rose toward the surface. The sound of the engines grew as they fought the current. Niall gently pulled a lever, and the engines worked harder. It took several long, loud moments, but they managed to enter the river. When they had gone far enough upstream that the current wouldn't sweep them into the sea, Niall calmed the engines.

"It'll be slower, but smoother," Niall explained. He relaxed in his chair, as did Sweets.

"And in a few hours," added Thalame, "we'll be underneath Kusmerk."

"Might as well make yourselves at home," Sweets added. "Apologies for the sparse interior. I wanted to add a few couches, but Brent said we didn't have time."

"We didn't!" came Brent's echoing voice from the speaking tube.

A few hours, Raven repeated to herself. Just a few hours. This time tomorrow, they would be celebrating another victory against the Gray Elite.

Compared to before, the *Barnacle* moved terribly slow—too slow. Didn't they realize Zander's life hung on the line?

"And we've plenty of time to prepare," said Conrad. "I've been to Kusmerk before, and I can give you something of a layout of the underside."

Conrad drew a map of Kusmerk's underside in the air. Raven couldn't picture it—smuggler ports, hidden berths, and maintenance tunnels. Her mind painted a dark, dangerous picture, and her resolve shuddered. Sisters... Was this how Zander felt when she had vanished from the treehouse? Lost and confused and overwhelmed? At least she knew where he was and how to get to him. She had just vanished. No word, no posted execution, no secret messages—he hadn't found a lead on her until they arrived in Moorin.

She couldn't imagine what it would feel like if Zander would have just vanished without a trace, if she had no idea of where to start looking, or how he'd vanished or why—just thinking about it made her anxious. If he had done to her what she had done to him...her nervous system would have likely imploded.

The sun filtered through the river and shimmered in beams as the *Barnacle* glided through the water. The light angled toward the west, gilding the surface of the river in shades of bronze.

Would the Gray Elite really execute Zander? Would his father not step in to save him? Or had General Winchester thrown his son aside? Raven took a deep breath to calm her nerves, an action that did not go unnoticed by Conrad or Thalame. Conrad continued to explain Kusmerk, and Thalame started to reach for her—to calm her emotions.

"No," Raven whispered.

Thalame hesitated. "You sure?"

"You can't hold my hand once we get there. If I don't take control of it now, I won't be of any use when it matters."

Thalame's hand returned to his side. He looked impressed by that answer. "Good on you, then. Let me know if you change your mind."

She nodded, though she knew she wouldn't change her mind. She needed to be in control. She needed to help them. They would need everyone to get Zander and themselves out safely. She took another deep, calming breath.

"There it is," Niall said from the bridge.

"Incredible," whispered Sweets.

Raven's cloud of thought shattered, and she jumped to her feet. She leaned into the bridge. There—a dark smudge on the other side of the water's surface. Kusmerk. It arched over the wide river, shadowing the water underneath it. Niall brought them closer to the surface. The smudge sharpened into a city. In Gray Elite fashion, many of the buildings ended in spirals and steeples. The buildings blended together in brightly colored steel, blues and purples and greens and golds. Kusmerk looked like a compact version of Moorin.

The ride had been smooth, as Niall had predicted. They had crossed the border into Gracita without detection. She knew stealth was the better approach, but a part of her still wanted to go in blazing and leave a trail of destruction behind her. She wanted there to be no mistaking who had come for Zander and who had bested the Gray Elite.

She wanted to burn the whole city to the ground.

Raven banished that line of thinking. She didn't know if it was her own or Aeon's.

"All right, here comes the slick maneuvering." Conrad moved into the bridge behind Niall's chair. There wasn't much room for him and Raven, but she didn't mind his proximity.

"You ready back there?" Niall said to the speaking tube.

"Ready," came Brent's reply. "Engaging silent running."

All but the smallest propeller shut off, and the *Barnacle* slowed to a crawl. They seemed to drift upstream, low enough to avoid detection and slow enough to avoid startling the fish. Like the engines, no one inside spoke. Soon the shadow of the city overtook them, leaving them with only the sunstones' glow.

Conrad navigated Niall through the dark undercarriage of Kusmerk. Above them, over the gushing of the river, came the muffled sound of a bustling dock—crews preparing ships, goods being loaded and unloaded, sailors lounging and laughing, orders being shouted, and somewhere a hurdy-gurdy played.

Kusmerk's grand bridge had three arches. The center arch allowed for ships and barges to pass through. The eastern and western arches were reserved for docking ships and business. Smuggler's Way was tucked into a corner of the eastern arch, a few berths hidden from obvious view and guarded by thugs. One of those berths would be a perfect place for the *Barnacle* to surface and wait.

Raven held her breath as Niall and Conrad navigated the near-total darkness of Smuggler's Way. In the glow of the sunstones, she could just make out the algae-covered stone walls. The *Barnacle* eased into one of the narrow berths and came to a halt.

"This is good," Conrad whispered.

"Shut her down," Niall said to Brent.

The *Barnacle* slowly rose through the water until the hatch broke the surface. Conrad volunteered to get out first, and no one objected. Conrad climbed up the ladder, and halfway there pulled a pistol from his waist. One of the Wraiths—Jack—stood on the ladder behind him. His magic commanded metals, and should the smugglers shoot first, Jack would halt the bullets midair. Conrad opened the hatch and climbed out. Yellow lantern light spilled into the *Barnacle*.

"It's ten tokens to park," came a gruff male voice from above. "Even if you ain't got no ship."

"The sea brought me in, not the wind," said Conrad. Coins jingled. "Here's for the berth."

"Aye," came the voice, a pitch friendlier. Footsteps carried it away.

Jack climbed out next, and Raven followed. Her boots landed on a wooden dock. They were inside the arch, between the stone and metal pillars. Lanterns and torches illuminated the space, albeit poorly. A wooden dock ran above the water, mismatched and stained and patched. A few other ships had docked; none looked friendly. The air smelled strongly of stagnant water and sweat. Smuggler's Way had a quiet air about it, though Raven could hear the distant clatter of the docks, shouting voices, stomping boots, and wind-rattled riggings.

Conrad nudged her. "Hood up." He pointed to the stone wall of wanted posters. Her own looked back at her.

Raven tucked her braid into her robes and pulled the hood over her head. She adjusted the silken cowl to be able to pull it up quickly over her nose and mouth if she needed to.

Conrad led the way down the narrow docks of Smuggler's Way. Few people lingered, but those who did wore pistols and short swords. Most wore hoods. Others still wore no shirt at all, openly displaying an upper body covered in tattoos. Luckily, no one seemed eager to give or get attention, and Raven fit in just fine among the underbelly. That thought both excited and despaired her.

Smuggler's Way opened to a broad and brightly lit corridor of berths. The ships were cleaner, and the crews were louder. At the end of the corridor, sunlight flared in the main archway, sparkling off the surface of the river. Conrad led them through a nook in the stone, through an alley between warehouses, and then down another. They paused at a metal door which read **MAINTENANCE SHAFT 5**. Conrad opened the door, revealing a ladder that led up into darkness.

"Unguarded?" Thalame whispered.

"I'm sure it's guarded by smugglers," Conrad whispered back. He then winked. "Or ghosts."

Conrad climbed up first, then Jack. Raven glanced up. The ladder led up through nearly complete darkness, and already she couldn't see Conrad. Jack was quickly fading into the dark too. Raven thought of Zander and started up. Thalame started up after her. The darkness closed in around her with every rung until she could barely see them. She made sure to leave space between herself and Jack; she'd rather not get kicked in the face.

They climbed and climbed, and then a squeal of metal on metal sounded—light spilled down the ladder. Raven winced in the sudden light.

"Here we are," Conrad said.

The ladder led into a maintenance room full of pipes, big and small, running horizontally along the ceiling, the walls, and the floor. Water gushed through the pipes, along with steam and Sisters knew what else. A constant sound of rushing and gushing filled the space, a monotonous whisper.

Conrad started down a narrow passage between walls of pipes, and they followed behind, single-file. He led them up a series of steep iron-grate stairs that might as well have been ladders, through corridors made of pipes so narrow, they had to walk sideways, and they steadily climbed up through the city's internals. As they trekked, the *thunk*ing of gears echoed without harmony. Steam engines pulled water from the river and pumped steam through pipes; for a city as big as Kusmerk, she couldn't imagine how many engines were needed or how much steam ran underneath the city. She had seen the maze that ran through the *Orion*, and three *Orion*s could easily fit within Kusmerk.

Up and up they climbed through the pipes. Raven felt like a rat, climbing between work spaces and rooms, underneath and beside human workers and automations. She heard the workers behind walls of pipes, working, whistling, and talking. Conrad never slowed and never lost his path, and it left her wondering how many times he had infiltrated Kusmerk this way.

Finally, their path led to a steel hatch. Conrad stood underneath it, leaning on the steep stairs, and knocked once, waited a beat, knocked twice, waited a beat, and knocked again.

A deadbolt slid back on the other side. The hatch opened; a woman stood on the other side with a pistol aimed at Conrad's head.

Raven's heart skipped a beat. In front of her, Jack's hand tightened into a fist. Despite knowing he could stop a bullet before it struck any of them, it didn't stop her panic.

"The weather is wonderful this afternoon," Conrad said calmly, as if no one threatened his life. "Not a cloud in the sky."

"Though Minerva knows we could use rain," said the woman.

"May the Sisters be kind," Conrad replied.

The woman removed her finger from the trigger and pointed the pistol skyward. "Hurry up, then."

Conrad climbed out.

Passwords, Raven realized. Conrad had given one to the man at the dock and another to this woman. They guarded Smuggler's Way.

Raven followed Jack though the hatch into a wooden-walled room full of barrels and crates. Conrad led them into a hallway and then into a low-key tavern. No one paid attention as they slipped into the barroom. The smell of grog and ale and fried food filled the air. The barroom itself had stone walls and hanging globes for light. Few windows let in the waning daylight, and each had a tight iron lattice. The bar itself was made of planks resting over thick barrels.

The clientele looked like smugglers, or other such criminals and lawbreakers. As the Wraiths made their way in and took to one of the booths, Raven realized that she didn't mind the crowd. Something like relief had gone over her that she did not have to act a certain way, that these people didn't care.

"All right," Conrad said with a sigh. He leaned back in the booth. "We've got several hours before sunset, plenty of time to relax and plan and then get into place. Tea anyone?"

"I could use something a lot stronger than tea," Thalame grumbled from beside Raven.

"Then you'd be useless," Jack deadpanned.

"Tea is fine," Thalame said, sighing.

"Barmaid?" Conrad called.

With an order of tea that came with a differently patterned china cup for each person, the team went over their plan once again. They had gone over it several times in the *Barnacle*, and each time made Raven feel slightly more prepared. Their plan wasn't perfect or without holes; there were too many unknowns to make a solid plan. As Conrad had explained, "Every plan needs room for adjustments and improvisations."

Zander would be executed in the Greens—a large public square. He would be in the open and exposed, more fitting for the dramatic show the Gray Elite advertised it as. However, as Thalame explained, "The more public an execution, the easier it'll be to get to Zander, but the more complicated our escape will be."

"Can't have it both ways," Conrad had mumbled to Raven.

Raven sipped her bitter tea and watched the sunlight fade too fast.

At last, when the afternoon light had turned golden, Thalame suggested they head out. "Better to be early than too late," he said grimly.

Raven couldn't bring herself to respond, so she nodded.

A horrible thought seared through her mind—what if they arrived too late?

The team followed Conrad out of the tavern and onto the narrow streets of Kusmerk. They had come up on the eastern side of the city. Lamps of stone and wrought iron lined the main streets. Lamplighters worked to get them lit before full dark, leaving the city with streaks of light and puddles of darkness. Conrad led the way, Raven walking a step behind him. Thalame maintained a steady presence at her side. She knew he did it on purpose. He was giving her the opportunity to lose her panic and dread, and a part of her wanted to grab his hand just to be able to think straight. She didn't.

Gulls and crows cawed overhead, blurs of gray and black in the darkness above the city. Conrad led them through narrow alleys strung with sagging silk streamers and clotheslines. Raven spotted a drain at the end of nearly every street, catching rainwater and whatever else, and each had an echoing trickle that gave the eerie impression that the city's innards were hollow. She knew otherwise; they were a mass of pipes and tanks.

They passed a group of sailors hurrying "to get a good seat," and Raven's heart plummeted.

Raven looked to the fading blue of the sky. Wilyn's Star had not yet appeared. She didn't know how the patron Sister thing worked, but in that moment, she asked for Zander's safety.

Conrad led them to the Greens, a large patch of too-green grass and thin birch trees located in the center of Kusmerk, directly on top of the largest archway. Shops lined the Greens, and most had already closed. At least a hundred people had already gathered, and countless more filed onto the Greens. Chatter filled the late summer evening as if they had gathered to watch a show, not a young man's execution.

Conrad led them around the Greens and into an alley parallel to the Greens. Raven caught glimpses of the Green and its crowd in the narrow gap between buildings.

"Why are there so many people?" Raven spat.

"Everyone's heard of the Revenant," Conrad whispered. "The Gray Elite have made sure everyone sees him as a horrid villain. It's made him quite popular."

"Now's not the time," Thalame said. "Joke when we're safe and on the way out of here."

As per their plan, they split up. They would surround the square. Raven went with Conrad, Jack, and a Wraith named Karl. They went along the northern side of the square. The closer they came to the center of the Greens, the thicker the crowd. People lounged on balconies and rooftops, ladies fanned themselves, and men sipped drinks like they had gone to a bar rather than an execution. Their breezy chatter drifted through the alleys, punctuated with bursts of laughter.

Rage burned under her skin. Monsters. All of them. Seeking out death like a game, a show, something to gawk at.

Conrad paused behind a three-story building of lavender-colored steel. He picked the lock on the backdoor, and they slipped inside. The shop was dark, closed for the event. Judging by the sterile setting, neatly stacked papers, shelves of ink bottles and quills, and shined floors, they had entered some sort of office space. Conrad led them up the back stairwell. They didn't encounter anyone one the stairs, but two men occupied the roof. Both wore fine suits and drank from crystal tumblers. They stood near the edge of the roof, looking down at the unfolding event.

"...told her I'd be watching from the office and invited her, but she scoffed and rolled her eyes," said the taller of the two men. "Said she'd rather watch from the street level."

174

"On the street where she belongs," said the shorter man, chuckling as he sipped his drink.

Conrad and Jack worked in perfect sync—in a blink, the two men were unconscious. They hadn't even spilled the drinks. Jack and Karl dragged the two men into the building. Raven didn't ask what they planned on doing with them. At the moment, she didn't care.

Conrad stepped up to the edge of the roof, lips parted to speak, but as he gazed down, the humor evaporated.

Her heart slammed against her ribs, and she dashed to the edge to see what he saw—her heart sputtered and stopped cold.

A wooden platform had been erected in the middle of the green. A dozen Gray Elite stood on the platform, and twice as many stood guard on the ground. An executioner in all black stood on the platform with a ceremonial ax resting over his shoulder. The fading sunlight glinted off the decorative metal.

But it was the boy kneeling in the center of the platform that made her heart stop. Zander—his mechanical arm had been torn from his body; metal scraps and wires dangled from his shoulder. Shackles chained his remaining wrist to his ankles.

The sight tore through her chest like it had been her own body ripped apart. His magic had allowed him to feel the arm too. He would have felt the arm being ripped apart. She couldn't breathe—her breath balled in her throat and stayed there.

Burn them. Burn them all. They deserve it for what they have done.

Rage bubbled and burned under her skin like a violent storm just waiting for the clouds to part. In that moment of blind rage, she agreed with Aeon. Those Gray Elite, those who had hurt him, deserved no less than her fire. They had hurt him just to get to her, to hurt her, to spite her.

"Oh, that's not good," Conrad said.

His voice brought Raven out of her rageful stupor. Blinking, she turned to him. He pointed downward with his eyes.

"See those automatons?"

She followed his line of sight. The guards on the ground she had initially believed to be Gray Elite were not. They were not human. Red eyes gleamed underneath Gray Elite caps. Each figure had the body shape and rigid posture; each had the same waxy beige skin tone.

"They're the same as the ones in the factory," Raven whispered.

"Oh, good," Conrad said sarcastically. "I was worried these were some new and improved auto-man with better marksmanship."

The automatons scanned the crowd with eyes of pale red. The crowd had put a distance between themselves and the humanoid automatons; no one wanted to be too close. The automatons also formed a protective circle around Zander.

Raven quickly counted. "There's so many of them," she whispered.

"Indeed," Conrad said.

When they had faced the humanoid automatons in the factory, the Wraiths had had the element of surprise and had outnumbered them. Now, the automatons outnumbered the Wraiths—and were armed with pistols.

Raven opened her mouth to voice her concerns when another thought struck and spilled out first, "I thought they could detect magic?"

"They can," said Conrad, his voice grim. "They would have sensed us the moment we entered the Greens. Most of the Wraiths have let their tattoos fade, and there won't be any mistaking what we are."

And Zander had let his tattoo fade. Had that been how they found him?

"It's more than we anticipated," whispered Karl.

"They don't seem interested in us," said Jack. "I'm a little offended."

"Because they don't want just any magician," Raven said bitterly. She swallowed and steeled herself. "They're after me."

"And they wouldn't risk losing you by chasing after any magician that distracts the automatons," Conrad finished.

More and more people arrived on the Greens to watch the execution. The moments ticked by faster than Raven wanted. The sun slowly slid to the west, turning the sunlight molten. Karl had left to see if he could talk with the other teams—thankfully, they had arrived early enough to do so. Raven tapped her fingers against the rooftop while Conrad paced. Jack glared at the automatons.

Hundreds of people had come to see Zander executed.

Burn them all.

A horn sounded—the crowd silenced. A broad-shouldered Gray Elite stepped onto the platform. He moved with a predator's grace and arrogance. He had sandy hair and a broad jaw, and even from this distance, she felt the coldness of his stare.

"General Deacon graces us with his presence," Conrad muttered.

General Oliver Deacon sauntered to the center of the platform. He said something to Zander, who tilted his head upward. Whatever Deacon had said, Zander spat at the general's feet. Deacon didn't react. Instead, the general sauntered away from Zander and spoke to the Gray Elite soldier. The soldier nodded.

"They're getting ready to start." Conrad's dark eyes scanned the crowd and the rooftops on the other side of the square, looking for the other Wraiths. Worry reflected in his eyes and his words.

Her thoughts churned fast—hers and Aeon's, but she didn't feel like arguing with a ghost.

Deacon stepped back onto the platform, ready to address the crowd.

"I have a new plan," Raven said quickly. A reckless, foolish, desperate plan.

"I'm all ears," said Conrad.

"You might not like it," she admitted. The sun touched the top of the western buildings, shading half the square and gilding the other.

"People of Kusmerk," boomed Deacon's voice.

"I don't have time to not like it, little bird," said Conrad. "Talk fast, or your boy's head is going to roll."

"For too long, the Revenant has terrorized our cities and murdered our people," boomed Deacon's voice. The square had gone utterly silent, and at the mention of the Revenant, agreeing boos echoed. "And today, the Revenant will face justice!"

A cheer sounded around the square.

Raven raced down the stairs of the office building and burst out the backdoor. Even as she moved, her plan sounded horrible. So many things could go wrong. Deadly wrong.

She bolted as silently as she could. Deacon was still talking, riling up the crowd against Zander, recounting his crimes and notable people he had assassinated. She didn't know how much longer Deacon would talk, and she wasted no time. She ran to the western side of the square, behind the platform. Because Deacon and Zander both faced away from her, fewer people had chosen the western side to watch. It left the alleys mostly clear, and those who lingered were looking at Deacon, not her.

She started through a crowded street and shouldered her way to the front. With the gilded evening sunlight, those she shoved didn't have a clear view of her face. A few muttered unkind things, but she ignored them.

She didn't care about these people, not when they hungered for Zander's blood.

Did it ever occur to you that the boy deserves such a death?

Raven slowed to a meander to garner less attention. This way, she appeared as just a girl wanting to get a better look.

He has killed people.

Raven mentally shushed Aeon's voice. She didn't want to think about these things. Not right now. She knew Zander had done things that, legally and morally, warranted execution. But that didn't matter when the Gray Elite used him as bait for her. She doubted they would care about his crimes if they had no means to use him to get to her.

And, she didn't care about legality—she cared about Zander.

She stepped onto the cushy grass of the Greens. People stood in clusters, nearly elbow to elbow, and it made shoving her way closer harder. The unkind words came with more venom.

"Should have gotten here earlier," spat one woman in an old frilly dress. She shoved Raven back.

We don't have time for this.

Raven grabbed the woman's wrist. Heat surged from her own. The woman shrieked, yanked her hand away, and before she could say or do anything more, Raven vanished into the crowd. The woman moped and whined, stealing attention away from Raven. She should have felt bad for it, but in that moment, she felt little else besides anger.

She came to the edge of the crowd, or as close to the edge of the crowd as she could squeeze. People had packed themselves so tightly together, she couldn't elbow her way through. She'd already gotten called every demeaning name she knew and a few she didn't. The two young women she had pushed between both glared at her with enough venom to kill lesser wills. Raven ignored them. She could see the circle of humanoid automatons. Their pale red eyes kept watch, but none had signaled her approach.

Someone's elbow nudged Raven in the back, and she took a step forward. Her heel hit the edge of the drain between her feet.

"And today we close an era of panic and issue in an era of peace," came Deacon's voice.

"He certainly likes to hear himself talk," mumbled a tall man in front of Raven. "Why not get on with it already? I'm losing business."

"What's he waiting for? We skipped dinner to be here," said someone else.

The realization hit Raven hard—Deacon was stalling.

And she had fallen for it.

The absurdity of it all shattered her building panic and played into her rage. She laughed, stealing the attention of those around her.

Improvisation, like Conrad had said.

"The general is waiting for me," Raven said casually to the two men standing in front of her. "And for your own safety, I highly recommend you get out of the way."

The tall man half laughed, and the other muttered a curse under his breath.

"Suit yourselves." Raven grabbed the edge of the tall man's jacket and set it aflame.

He began to scream and writhe. He knocked people over in his desperate attempt to remove his jacket. He fell into the space between the crowd and the automatons, stomping his jacket into the grass.

Raven brought a flame to each hand. At once, the crowd around her scrambled to get away, stumbling over each other.

Like rats.

The automatons noticed, but none moved. She felt their pale red eyes on her. Waiting. One of the soldiers on the platform turned.

The executioner raised his ax. The steel caught the gilded light.

Together.

"Deacon!" Her voice rang out across the Greens, powerful and raw. As it coursed through the air, she heard another underneath her own, deeper and threatening—Aeon's.

At her call, everything stopped. The square went silent. Deacon slowly turned, not at all surprised. With a wave of his hand, the executioner swung down the ax. A scream ripped from her throat, and fire sizzled under her skin. The flames in her hand shot skyward, the red-orange burning white. The grass under her feet wilted and melted, the strong stench of burning hair filled the Greens.

The ax thunked into the platform in front of Zander.

Deacon's smug grin widened.

"On alert," Deacon ordered.

The eyes of the humanoid automatons flared blood red, and in one swift motion, each drew a pistol. A hundred pistols cocked, each aimed at her.

The crowd had begun to scream and panic. They flooded the alleys and streets in their desperate flight from the Greens.

"I didn't think you'd come." Deacon nodded to one of the Gray Elite, who yanked Zander to his feet. Zander awkwardly turned—he could barely move in the shackles.

Zander's sapphire eyes met hers and widened. Bruises spotted his face and vanished into his torn shirt. His bottom lip had split. He gently shook his head at Raven. He knew his odds; he knew hers.

She hadn't thought about her odds. She hadn't let herself consider failure.

Water sloshed under her feet, gurgling through the tangled mess of pipes snaking throughout Kusmerk's innards, to the thousands of grates, taps, and faucets scattered throughout the city. Steel creaked and groaned.

"You know what we want," Deacon said.

"I'm well aware," Raven said. "Unfortunately, I don't have it anymore. No one does. It's gone."

Deacon considered her.

The grate under her feet clattered as steam pushed against the underside. The automatons' red eyes were focused on her. They saw her.

They sensed her magic. Yet they waited for their master's order. Raven didn't know how many pistols were aimed at her; she didn't want to know. If she played her game right, none of those bullets would hit her.

A crowd had lingered, watching from what they believed to be a safe distance. Raven saw them on the edge of her vision—she didn't take her eyes off Deacon.

"Can you blame me for not believing you?" Deacon said, still looking like he had won.

Columns of steam began to issue into the air around the Greens. Shouts of panic sounded from across the Greens, and the lingering crowd began to flee. She pushed her magic further; the steam thickened and gained momentum. Steam shot through every grate in the Greens. Deacon remained impassive, even as several of his soldiers glanced around nervously.

The stone under their feet creaked dangerously. A low rumble shook shop windows and streetlamps, making the flames within flicker.

Deacon's smug grin flattened.

The ground under their feet trembled, and the mild panic of the crowd grew into something wild. Raven pushed her magic to the edges of the arch, pipe to pipe. The first pipe burst with a thunderous bang, echoing through every alley. A series of bursts followed, metal clanking and gears sticking.

The automatons started toward her. A wave of bullets popped; she summoned a wall of fire in front of her, burning white hot. Bullets melted as they hit the flame. Bystanders were not so lucky; grunts of pain and shock rattled through the crowd behind her.

"We want her alive!" Deacon roared over the panic. "Cease fire!"

The automatons came toward her. She sent her wall of fire toward them. This time, she knew what she was doing. This time, she was in control. She encapsulated the automatons, and they melted as the larger one had, only faster. Her magic burned at her command, hotter and faster and brighter. Her white flames met the gilded air, turning the dusky square a devastating gold.

She felt it under her skin, in her being. Aeon's fire. The power of a goddess. It flowed through her bones, her blood, her skin. It was her.

I once thought I was unstoppable.

The automatons didn't understand; they continued to march toward her, stumbling into the molten remains of the others. The crowd ran, gasping, crying, shouting, desperately fleeing. Their panic and fear fueled her power, and her fire burned higher. The fire under the square continued through the pipes, melting the metal, and the entire bridge trembled. The ground cried and whined, stone crunching, metal giving. The Gray Elite thought they would defy nature? She would show them.

I too sought to show them all my power.

The ground shifted. The stone gave a thunderous crash as a building on her right came tumbling down. Its neighbor followed, sending plumes of gray dust into the sky.

The bullets started again. She brought her fire wall up, but not in time. A bullet seared into her upper arm. Pain exploded inward. A scream ripped from her throat. She glanced at her arm, sure that her entire shoulder had been blown off. It hadn't. The bullet had caught a soft spot between the hardened leather and steel plate. Half an inch higher, and the bullet would have deflected off the steel.

Another bullet bounced off the steel on her other arm, and then another buried itself in her thigh. The pain seared down her leg. Screaming, she collapsed onto her knees. Her flames faltered. The white flickered and shifted back to red-orange. Hot but incapable of melting automatons. Pain overtook her senses. She tried to summon that power again but couldn't.

The haze over her awareness ebbed. Her distraction had worked: Zander was gone from the platform. Conrad had gotten to him in time. The executioner lay dead or unconscious. His clean ax lay on the ground by the stairs. By the warped bullets peppering the ground and the lack of blood, Jack had done his part.

And Raven had done hers. However stupid it had been.

Pipes burst, and steam hissed from the Greens. The ground shook. Metal creaked and bent. Stone crumbled. Her flames had caused catastrophic damage to the city's undercarriage. She fought to keep those flames alive, but with every pounding heartbeat, her flames shrank.

Automatons stepped through her flames, pistols raised.

Panic raced alongside the pain. They wouldn't kill her. Not her. They needed her. Deacon had said so.

She collapsed from the pain, and her magic collapsed with her. Her flames snuffed out all at once, and the steam began to cool. The automatons surrounded her, washing her in their blood-red light.

"Subject detained," said the flat, emotionless voice.

Raven couldn't think straight, not between the pain and the blood quickly soaking through her robes. Still, she knew her odds were not good.

Raven gasped for her next breath. Between the automatons and through the thinning steam, she saw the extent of her display. Several buildings had collapsed. The ground continued to tremble and shake, and the stone and metal underneath creaked and rumbled.

"We need to get out of here," commanded a Gray Elite, a voice she didn't know. "This place is coming down."

"Start the engine!" boomed Deacon.

Raven couldn't move. Her bullet wounds oozed hot, sticky blood. The pain burned in a different way than her fire, a horrible way. It made the rest of her feel cold. With every heartbeat, the world dimmed, and her vision tunneled.

"Keep her alive!" barked Deacon, much closer now. His voice proximity sent a tremor down her spine, and the coldness rattled her nerves.

The general appeared beside the automatons, his glare vicious and his sneer vile. As he looked down at her, his grin turned victorious.

"And you thought you could win?" Deacon asked.

The world tilted, and she shut her eyes. Deacon barked orders at the Gray Elite, but the words blurred in her ears. Hard metal hands hauled her off the ground, away from the Greens. Raven felt blood seeping, felt it fleeing her body and leaving it a husk. She knew then, even if the automatons put her down, she wouldn't be able to go anywhere. She wouldn't be able to move.

Deacon was ordering his men into place, whatever that meant.

Raven waited for the Wraiths to jump from nowhere, to swoop down like the ancient beings they took their name from, to save her. Thalame would heal her, and then Zander would yell at her for endangering herself. Conrad would congratulate her on her dramatics. She would tell Zander she loved him.

But no one came.

The automatons carried her to a waiting airship, the engine purring. Balloons held it aloft, safe from the shaking ground.

"Hurry up! This place is coming down!" came a shout. Behind them, stone crumbled, and metal snapped.

They hauled her into the ship like cargo. As the automatons carried her over the gangplank, she saw the Greens. The bridge had started to crumble inward, exposing its mangled innards. Even as she watched, pieces of grass and entire trees and forgotten umbrellas vanished into the hole. Debris clattered into the maze of pipes. She imagined the hole going straight through, and things splashing into the river far below.

They entered the airship, blocking her view.

The automatons tossed her into a cell. Her body hit the steel floor, and pain radiated anew from every inch, every bone, and every fiber—a scream scratched the insides of her throat. Black stars danced across her vision. As her vision cleared, she blinked in time to see a barred door slam.

"The prisoner is secured," came a female voice.

"Get us out of here!"

The engines rumbled as the ship ascended, then evened into a purr.

Deacon appeared on the other side of the bars. He folded his arms behind his back and straightened his shoulders. "You think you've outsmarted me? You think I wouldn't be prepared for your little magic friends to come save that boy?" He chuckled.

It took all her effort to say, "They got away."

Though she had planned on getting away too.

"This wasn't about him or the Wraiths." He leaned closer to the bars. "This is about me getting what I want. What I want is the stone you stole from me."

He reached into the pocket of his jacket and pulled out the little iron box that had once held the centrum of Altair's Augur, the box she had emptied before giving to him. He clenched the box, then threw it at her. The iron smacked the wall beside her head and clattered to the floor.

A part of her magic recoiled. It remembered the box, being trapped.

"I was worried about where you would hide the stone, never mind how you managed to retrieve it without hurting yourself," Deacon said. "I didn't know how I'd track you or your friends down, and then your friend just happened to make a scene right outside my own front door." He chuckled, and his smile turned devilish. "You've had it all this time. I want it back."

"I'm not sure I can give it back." Raven gasped. Each word was hard to form. She had the feeling that if she died, the power would also go with her.

Deacon frowned. "That is yet to be decided."

Her blood seeped too fast. Darkness crept at the edges of her visions and on her thoughts, a gnawing sensation to rest.

"And if I die along the way?" she managed to gasp.

Deacon scoffed. "You'll live."

The general stepped aside, and a medic in white, gray, and yellow appeared. The medic stood by as Deacon opened the door. Raven closed her eyes and took a breath.

"Don't let her die, or I'll throw you from this aircraft," came Deacon's distant voice.

"Sir."

The door opened, footsteps approached, and Raven could barely open her eyes as the medic knelt over her.

And her world went black.

She dreamed of a temple made of volcanic stone. She knew the place; she knew the temple. She knew she need not fear an eruption, for the volcano would not disobey her. She sat in her tower, surrounded by books and scrolls. A light rain fell, pitter-pattering on the hibiscus flowers that grew on the mountainside. She reclined on her cushions and drew her legs closer. Her silken robes floated about her.

She reached her slender hand through the window. The cool raindrops splashed against her brown skin, cooling the incessant heat underneath. Below, the sun-drenched city stretched to the coast. Her people moved about the city, dots from this distance.

Footsteps sounded on the stone stairs. Who would dare intrude without a proper introduction? Her answer came as the dark-headed scholar fumbled up the last of the stairs. He bowed his head and mumbled his apologies in his soft voice.

"Altair? You've returned."

"I arrived this morning, my lady, and the news I bear could not wait. You were wise to send me to seek your sister's input. She has moved us along considerably."

She smiled. She had doubted her sister's helpfulness. It didn't matter. As Altair spread his latest diagrams on the table before her, chattering in his eager way, she felt a surge of pride. Their creation would change the world. She could feel it in her bones.

Thunder shook apart the world, ripping it at the seams. The temple crumbled, the books turned to dust, and the ocean washed away the village.

Raven sucked in her next breath—she woke. She blinked her eyes open. Everything ached. As the deadened sleep wore off, she became aware of the epicenters of the aching—two bullet wounds, one in her shoulder and one in her thigh.

She tried to summon her magic, but it didn't come. Flames flickered underneath her skin and died.

"Easy." A man in a Gray Elite uniform appeared beside her. He set a strong hand on her good shoulder and gently pushed her back onto the cot. He didn't look menacing. He had a boyish face and kind eyes.

"What happened?" Raven whispered.

The medic's brows rose. "What happened?" he whispered back. "You sank the Greens into the river."

Reality slammed into her senses. The execution, the Wraiths, Kusmerk. The Gray Elite had been waiting for her. She had been captured. Zander had been rescued. Deacon had taken her into an airship.

"Steady, now," said the medic.

She was no longer lying on the hard floor of the cell. She had been moved onto a canvas cot. Her arms and legs were secured. Heavy bandages wrapped her shoulder and thigh. Granted, she felt remarkably better, however she did not feel good; she felt groggy and wobbly, and she had to focus on breathing.

"Did I sink the whole city?" she asked.

"No, just the Greens. From what I've heard from the officers, most people made it out on time. But Kusmerk now has a hole in it. We barely made it out."

Raven took a deep breath.

"I gave you a serum to help with the pain and another to offset infection," said the medic, his tone professional. "You'll be a little wobbly for a while. I also gave you an experimental serum that disrupts magic, which will add to that wobbly sense. I've never used it. I'm not a magician, but I've been told it's like being under water."

That explained it, then.

The medic started to say something else, but Deacon's commanding voice boomed from somewhere in the ship. The medic's lips pursed, his shoulders straightened, and any emotion vanished from his face. As he stood, Raven noticed the porthole on the other side of the ship. The sky outside was dark, inky blue.

Deacon didn't appear. The medic changed her bandages, assured her that she would heal fine, threw a blanket over her, and then left her in the cell. Raven didn't mind. She didn't feel like forming sentences or thoughts. She didn't feel like anything at all. Over the rumble of the engine, she heard

186

people talking. She recognized the cadence from the *Orion*—orders and information passing between pilot, captain, and crew.

The dark blue steadily brightened into the pale glow of dawn. The crew stayed clear of her cell, though a humanoid automaton stood on the other side of the doors. It watched her with pale red eyes. Guarding, not detecting.

Raven shifted her stare to the steel ceiling of her cell. As the serums wore off, the pain slithered back, but her thoughts un-muddied. That dream—it hadn't been a dream, had it? The temple had felt familiar, so had the man named Altair. She knew what she wanted to think, but it seemed ridiculous. Had she truly dreamed of Aeon and Altair? They had been talking about the augur. The diagrams Altair had laid before her had been of the cursed machine, hadn't they?

And it had, for better or worse, changed the world.

A dark bitterness agreed with her.

The glow of dawn brightened imperceptibly. She did not see Deacon. Each time she opened her eyes, the daylight appeared more yellow. They had sailed all night, or maybe even several days. She didn't know.

Gradually, the hum of other airships joined them in the sky. The rumbling doubled, tripled. The engines shifted, the daylight dimmed, and the sound echoed—they had entered an air dock. The airship rattled as it docked, then the engines quieted.

Deacon's commanding voice ordered the crew to, "Hurry up."

The medic appeared at her door again. Deacon stood behind him, glaring down at her like something nasty he'd stepped in. The medic prepared a syringe.

"What's that?" she asked, her voice breathy and dry.

"For the pain," the medic answered, though he did not look her in the eye as he said it. He injected the syringe into her uninjured arm. She felt the serum enter her system, cool and slippery. Whether for pain, infection, or anti-magic, she didn't know. It entered her bloodstream, and she felt its effects at once. Tendrils of unbearable exhaustion slithered through her bones and muscles and mind. She couldn't keep her eyes open, and in a few heartbeats, didn't want to.

A deep sleep settled over her body, and she welcomed it.

Raven slowly became aware. Her body felt sluggish and cold. She was moving. She blinked—a pair of Gray Elite soldiers carried her on a stretcher between them. Both wore impassive expressions. They were carrying her through a corridor of dark wooden paneling and arched ceilings and curling ironwork light fixtures. At first, she thought of Winchester house, but this house looked different. A different house. Still, the style resembled Lenhala. Deacon had taken her all the way to Lenhala.

She couldn't see where they were going. Her grogginess clung to her senses like a wet blanket. They went through a wide doorway and down a staircase. She didn't see any windows or even the glow of daylight. Old-fashioned sconces gave them the only light. Had they gone underground?

Humanoid automatons stood guard in the hall. The sconces exaggerated the shadows on their waxy faces and made their pale red eyes glow brighter.

They carried her down the corridor and through a narrow door. Bookshelves towered on either side of her, filled with tomes and glassy baubles and diagrams. Someone spoke. Their words melted together in her mind, though she knew she understood them. Deacon appeared beside her. He glanced down, his face impassive and bored—but his eyes gleamed. He thought he had won.

In that moment, Raven didn't know if he had or not.

Deacon motioned the soldiers forward. They carried her into a birdcage elevator with brass bars twisted together into an elegant arch. A globe hung from the center, bathing them all in dull yellow light. Deacon joined them, and the doors shut with a small clink; the gears had been oiled to silence. The birdcage began to descend with a *click-click-click* of a dozen head-sized gears, visible through the scrolling brass. The elevator came to a stop, the doors slid aside, and the Gray Elite carried her into a stone-walled corridor. With the flip of a heavy switch, mounted globes came to life along the corridor, their wiring exposed and hanging between each. Each globe flickered every few seconds, leaving a constant wiggle in the illumination.

The stone corridor went on—Raven used the time to fight the serum weighing her senses. With every heartbeat, her awareness solidified.

They went underneath a stone archway, the stones engraved with strange symbols she had never seen before. The echo of Deacon's footsteps shifted; he entered a larger chamber. They passed through the archway, and the ceiling on the other side rose into darkness. Because of the stretcher, she could only see above her. She spotted carvings on the gray stone wall, the lines slightly darker than the stone around it. Whorls and interlaced symbols like those on the archway decorated the stone as far as she could see in every direction.

She spotted a particular symbol on the wall, and in a flash of memory, she remembered it—she had seen similar symbols at the ruined fort, and on the books and scrolls from her dream of a kingdom that no longer existed. This chamber belonged to the same age.

That knowledge seared along her spine like lightning.

They set the stretcher down on what felt like stone. They unbound the straps on her shoulders, her arms, and then her legs. It didn't matter. In her sluggish state, she wouldn't be able to get away. Her numb legs barely twitched under her command. She would only fall on her face if she tried to run.

"Put her in the cage," commanded Deacon. His voice still sounded water-logged.

Gray Elite lifted her off the stretcher and carried her up a short set of stairs, onto a platform, and then into a cage no larger than a carriage. Rather than metal, the cage consisted of pillars roughly carved from clear crystal and obsidian. Some of the pillars twisted; others did not. The obsidian and crystal twisted together at the top of the cage.

They laid her on the floor. Her hands flopped to the cool floor, and as her skin came into contact with the obsidian, she *felt* it—a monstrosity of twisted obsidian and crystal loomed above her, taking the majority of the massive chamber. The sudden sensation overwhelmed everything else. She could feel the whorls carved into the obsidian, feel the lines, feel the symbols they created, feel the ancient magic it evoked. In the darkness, she could not see it, but she didn't need to see in order to know what it was. Altair's Augur. She felt its presence like a building storm, a great devouring beast of magic and metal. It yearned for her energy, her magic—its missing piece.

Raven gasped for breath she hadn't realized she needed. Her lungs expanded with gratitude. She blinked several times. The crystal pillars of the cage glowed a faint yellow. With every heartbeat, the yellow glow brightened elsewhere within the chamber—in the crystal of the augur. The pale energy flowed like water.

She could feel the augur's strange magic. It was...groggy. Her presence had stirred it from a deep, ageless slumber.

"Interesting," came a drawling male voice.

"Indeed," came Deacon's voice.

"The centrum has truly sunk into her flesh?"

"It would appear our sources were telling the truth." Deacon chuckled. "Sometimes the truth is stranger than fiction."

Raven recognized the first voice. She knew it. She tilted her head to the side, toward the voices. Deacon and a second man stood on the other side of the cage. Deacon wore his Gray Elite uniform. The second man wore a finely made suit of dark gray. He looked down at her with cruel sapphire eyes, cold and indifferent. She knew him at once. Brigadier General Winchester, Zander's father. She blinked. Winchester stood beside Deacon like he belonged there, as if they weren't on opposite sides of a war.

"Oh, don't look so surprised," drawled Winchester. He smirked, looking so much like Zander yet vastly different at the same time. Zander may have his father's eyes and bronze skin, but he had never looked at her with such coldness.

"But you're a Hawk." Raven's voice came out scratchy and pitiful. Whether due to the machine or the serum, she didn't know, but it felt like her entire being was slowly leaking into the obsidian.

Winchester let out a controlled sigh. "Yes, yes, I suppose I am. But when it comes to an opportunity like this, a smart man seizes it."

Deacon nodded.

A hand squeezed around her lungs as realization set in. Winchester had betrayed the Hawks for power.

"What about your rebellion?" she asked.

Winchester chuckled. "The rebellion would never have won," he said with such assurance that it chilled her. "They were playing a game without an end. In the end, it's about power."

"And you would throw your son aside for it?"

Winchester glared at her, the coldness barely punctuated. "Zander made his choices, despite my warnings and guidance. If he chose to throw himself aside, then it is hardly my fault. I offered him a role in the new era, and he chose to rebel. I had the princess, and I would have put her on the throne. It would have appeased the Hawks, even if she had no political power. Besides, I still have one son who listens to me."

"We will put an end to this fruitless squabble." Deacon looked up at the augur. "It took some time, but we were able to configure this machine to hold a human instead of a box. Our little genius did a marvelous job."

"Oliver," Winchester warned. He pulled a golden pocket watch from his jacket. "We cannot be missed."

Deacon sighed. "You're right. Wouldn't want the uppers to suspect anything." He leaned in closer to the cage. "Sit tight. We will return soon."

The two men started away. Raven tilted her head as far as she could to see. Deacon left by the corridor they had carried her through. Winchester left through the opposite side, through a corridor that looked strikingly similar to the other.

And she was alone.

Alone with Altair's Augur and a body numbed with mystery serum. She supposed it could be worse. She just couldn't quite imagine how.

Raven didn't know how long she lay there. She and the machine had reached an equilibrium. It no longer tugged on her magic, but she tugged back. She felt the machine looming, felt it whispering in a language she somehow knew—wordless, silent, and persistent. It spoke sweetly, tenderly, and it needed her. She needed it.

This is what I have done. My creation.

"Is it what you thought would happen?" Raven asked the silence.

No. But I shouldn't be surprised. I should have seen it coming. I lost myself in my dream for power, my desire to change the world.

A soft footstep caught her attention, softer than either Deacon or Winchester. She sluggishly pulled her arm from over her eyes and turned her head. A short, narrow figure approached from the shadows. It took a long heartbeat for Raven to recognize the straw-colored hair.

"Ivy," Raven gasped. A surge of relief like she had never felt pulled her onto her feet. She clutched the pillars separating her from her friend. The obsidian felt cool to the touch.

Ivy, not Ivaline Pemberton, approached the cage. She wore slim-fitting trousers and a pale green vest over her dark blouse. She loosely crossed her arms, scanning the obsidian and crystal cage with indifference.

"Ivy?" Raven asked.

Ivy brought her eyes from the cage and finally looked at Raven.

"You have to get me out of here before they come back," Raven said.

"It took a while to figure out the right proportion of crystal and obsidian," Ivy said, her voice distant and clinical. She ran her fingers along the faintly growing crystal. "This is the fourth attempt. I never asked how much the materials cost. I didn't want to know."

"Ivy?" Raven's voice hitched on her friend's name. That joy of seeing Ivy turned to cold caution in a flash. "What are you talking about?"

"Because there's so little knowledge available about the magical properties of the materials," Ivy said, "I had so little to go on, so there was a lot of trial and error."

Raven blinked. She shook her head. Maybe the lingering effects of the serum were disrupting her mind. "Ivy," she said, rubbing her eyes. "I don't understand... Just... I need to get out of here. They gave me something to mess with my magic, I don't know what it was, but I need to get out here. There's got to be something around here to get this door open."

Ivy didn't move. She took a careful step forward. The kohl had been wiped hastily from her eyes, leaving streaks behind. It made it look as though she had been crying, but her eyes held no sadness. She did not approach the door.

"Ivy?" Raven asked.

"I can't do that."

"Why not?" Raven's heart sputtered in her chest, fear of what Ivy might say. She thought of what Deacon had said about the cage, about their *little genius*. "Ivy? What have you done?"

Ivy's blank face fell slightly. She inhaled and released it slowly. "I made a choice."

"And you chose *them*?" Raven whispered. She gave Ivy a moment to correct her, and when she didn't, Raven's hands tightened around the obsidian bars. "How could you choose them over your friends?"

"I chose myself," Ivy spat.

"You can't possibly believe a thing Deacon says," Raven said. "He's lying to you. Whatever he's promised you, he won't give to you. As soon as he gets what he wants, he'll get rid of you."

Ivy's eyes ran along the bars of the cage, all emotion erased. "Building it wasn't easy, you know. But I've watched Niall work so many times that I figured my way around the tools. He never wanted my help. He didn't think I could be anything other than Ivaline the Spy, gossiping and spreading rumors and pretending to be useful while everyone else went out to save magicians and sneak around." Her tone was light, almost bored. "That's what everyone else thought too. Thalame refused to train me like he trained you. He said I didn't need to know how to fight. He said I shouldn't get in situations where I had to fight."

Raven swallowed. She hadn't known that. She had assumed Ivy already knew how to fight like most of the other Dwellers. It had never occurred that she didn't.

"Thalame cares about you," Raven said. She had seen it on his face.

Ivy rolled her eyes.

"When we stopped at the treehouse and you weren't there, it was all over his face," Raven said.

Zander often wore that same face, worry underlined with the desire to keep her safe. And, like Zander, Thalame's plan had backfired.

Ivy let out a grievous sigh and took a step closer to the cage. She put her hand against one of the obsidian bars. "Obsidian is always cool to the touch. It doesn't soak in body heat like other materials. I could stand here and hold my hand against the same place for an hour, and it would still be cool to the touch."

"Ivy," Raven pleaded. How long before Deacon or Winchester came back? "It's not too late to change your mind. We can escape and contact the others before anyone notices."

"I was never useful." Ivy wasn't looking at Raven. Her eyes remained on the obsidian. "I'm not a magician. I'm no assassin. While my closest friends joined the Hawks or the Gray Elite or went south to become Wraiths, I was bedridden. When I was sick, I prayed every day for the Sisters to grant me magic too. Then I could be someone important, do something grand, just like my friends."

"You are important," Raven tried to tell her.

"When Zander told me about the Dwellers, I jumped on the chance to be a part of something bigger than myself. When my health returned, I did all I could to be useful. I recruited Niall from a Gray Elite sweatshop. I convinced Thalame to join after we saved him from a Gray Elite stronghold. I opened lines of communication between the Hawks, Gray Elite, and the Dwellers. But then other spies showed up, and other scouts, and then I wasn't as important."

"Ivy—"

"And then *you* showed up." Ivy brought her cold gaze to Raven. "I thought you would be different. Another girl for me to talk to. Another non-magician who might understand."

And Raven did understand, but her words failed her. She understood what Ivy felt, about uselessness, about being replaceable. She did not understand how Ivy could betray her friends so easily.

"And you had to go and find magic for yourself," Ivy spat, her tone spiteful. "And then I was alone again. The useless one who couldn't do anything but talk."

"You're not alone, Ivy," Raven said. She thought she had been too. "You have everyone in the treehouse. You have friends who would understand."

Ivy frowned. "They all think I'm just a frilly spy, good for nothing but gossiping. I could fight if they let me. I could be useful if they just gave me a chance."

The very chance that Deacon had provided. Raven felt spikes through her chest.

"How long?" Raven asked.

Ivy drew her hand away from the obsidian. She took a leisurely step toward the abandoned stretcher. "I was tired of being treated like a helpless little girl who couldn't do anything but bat her eyelashes. It felt like everyone stopped treating me like Ivy and started thinking I was really Ivaline, and that too much stress would send me to my deathbed." She heaved a sigh. "The Dwellers, the Hawks, the Wraiths...they all treated me like some precious doll that couldn't be taken down from the shelf. But the Gray Elite didn't see me that way. Deacon said I could be helpful. He gave me a chance, and I took it." Her straight-line lips twisted into a scowl. "Then I had my own secrets. I could choose what to tell the Dwellers, what to tell the Hawks, and what to tell the Gray Elite. I controlled what everyone heard. I controlled what others figured out and when and how."

And that control had given her the sense of power she craved.

Raven couldn't believe it. Ivy, sweet and smart Ivy, her friend and confidante, had betrayed them. She had been leaking information to the Gray Elite—to Deacon—and keeping information from the Dwellers—her friends. All because she had tasted power and wanted more.

"I messed up the blast on purpose," Ivy said after a beat of silence. "Back when Zander got thrown into the Hawks' dungeon and you and Thalame disguised yourselves and went in after him. I got left behind, again, to be the distraction. I purposefully messed it up so the Gray Elite would find the lair." A flicker of guilt came over her face. "No one told me to do it. I wanted to see what would happen. It made the night more interesting, wouldn't you say?" She offered Raven a half-smile.

Raven swallowed. Ivy had always had the capability for betrayal. Deacon just got her to switch sides.

"And when Thalame's word came that you had absorbed the centrum's power, and that's where your magic came from, I wanted to see what happened," Ivy said. "Deacon added another strand to the web."

"You told Deacon," Raven said.

"He tried not to act surprised," Ivy said, shrugging. "He thought you used the centrum to melt that Colossus. You did, just not in the way he assumed."

"And you just happened to tell him where and how to get me to expose myself," Raven added bitterly.

Ivy tilted one shoulder in a slight shrug. "I may have given him a few suggestions. I'm sorry to hear about Zander's arm, and his new arm. It was supposed to be a sneak attack, but the Gray Elite aren't as stealthy as the Wraiths. There was a struggle."

Raven seethed. The image of Zander kneeling on the execution platform—mechanical arm ripped from his body, the defeat in his eyes—evaporated any feeling of sympathy she had toward Ivy. Had she ever been a friend?

"But why help them and not us?" Raven asked.

"Because the Gray Elite have the upper hand," Ivy said like it was obvious. "What are a handful of rebels and magicians going to do against an empire of machines and soldiers?" A flicker of emotion came over her eyes. Ivy huffed, blinked, and the emotion vanished. "I've lived in the shadow of magicians all my life. Growing up, my father always talked about changing things, about Princess Rosaria, about Zander, about Ezra, all these great people who would be the face of the new era. I was never part of that. I was the sickly useless girl who couldn't do anything. I was never good enough. I never had anything interesting enough to say to please my parents. I couldn't save kingdoms or protect magic or usher in a new era." Ivy's breath had gone ragged. She took a deep breath, then another. "I *will* help usher in a new era. They were wrong."

"Yeah, they were. We were too," Raven said.

"It doesn't matter," Ivy said bitterly. She crossed her arms. "What's done is done. After the meeting with the Gray Elite, Deacon plans to show everyone just what his secret project can do. As we speak, an airship battalion is on their way from Moorin, just as your pirate friends are rushing to Lenhala to save you. They won't make it in time."

"You might be surprised," Raven said, though as the words left her mouth, her heart sputtered.

"They claim that rebels took out Kusmerk," Ivy said. "You did, kind of. You put a serious hole in the top of the bridge. Of course, the Gray Elite claim the rebels orchestrated it, and that the rebels are heading toward Lenhala on an airship. That's the same airship Deacon plans to test out Altair's Augur on."

Her heart sank. The *Orion*?

"Your friends are on that ship," Raven warned.

"No, *your* friends are on that ship," Ivy spat. "They were only my friends when they needed me. I was a means to an end, a line of communication."

"That's a lie, and you know it!" Raven's voice cracked. She banged her fists against the obsidian. "Deacon has poisoned your mind with all his talk, Ivy! Of course Thalame cares about you! Zander and Niall and I care too. You can't let that lying scum tell you what you should be thinking. Don't listen to him."

"Shut up!" Ivy covered her ears and turned her back to Raven. "Just shut up! You don't know what you're talking about! You don't understand!"

"Ivy—"

Ivy let out a disgruntled cry and stormed out of the chamber, through the dark corridor Winchester had gone down. Her footsteps echoed, then vanished.

And just like that, Raven was alone again. Alone with the augur. Moments passed, and Raven sank to the floor of the cage. With the silence, she felt the pull of the machine. It beckoned, yearned, and whispered in its strange, ancient language.

Zander gripped the railing of the Belt. The *Orion* raced through the sky. The wind shoved his hair away from his face. This side of the clouds made it impossible to know what was happening on the ground. A mechanic had patched his left arm, removing the dangling wires and twisted metal. The shoulder joint remained; his magic had accepted the socket, making it a part of him. They were throwing a new one together. It wouldn't be anything special, Niall had warned. Zander didn't care. He would give up his other arm to have Raven safe and sound on the Belt beside him.

"There you are," came Niall's voice. The tinker jogged down the Belt with a simple hobbled-together arm of steel scraps and brass. Niall stopped before Zander, panting. He'd likely run all the way from the workshop. Breath gathered, Niall held up the arm.

"Let's go." Zander motioned toward his left shoulder.

Niall braced Zander's shoulder with one hand and readied the arm's attaching joint against the socket. Zander gripped the Belt.

"On three," Niall warned. "One, two...three."

He thrust the arm into the socket. Bolts snapped into place, and Zander's magic raced up and down the arm, searching for the nerves he no longer had. A grunt of pain erupted from his throat, and his grip on the Belt turned white-knuckled. It felt like his arm was slowly waking up after being numb, the nerves and skin tingling and itching. With every passing second, the tingling subsided, and the strange numbness returned to the metal.

"How is it?" Niall asked.

Zander lifted his new metal arm and tested his range of motion. The wrist clicked too loudly, but he didn't complain. His metal arm moved a beat slower than his flesh and bones arm, but his other had started out slower too. It had become more responsive with every day. But they didn't have days.

"It'll do," Zander said. It didn't have all the extras the other had had, the compass, the compartments, the utility fingers.

"I met Thalame on the way up here." Niall leaned onto the railing. The wind caught his short braids and tossed them in the wind. "He sent word to Ivy in Lenhala, but he hasn't heard back."

"What?" Zander yanked his eyes from his arm to Niall.

"Our scouts came back and said they couldn't find her." Niall looked grim. "I don't know what it means, whether she ran into trouble on her own or something prevented her from getting to the scouts."

"It could be anything," Zander said. "Ivy's resourceful. She might not have been able to get to the scouts on short notice."

Niall nodded. "Thalame's not convinced. He's worried something happened."

Zander sighed through his nose. He had little right to condemn Thalame's thinking. He'd done the same when Raven hadn't come back to the treehouse that day. He had unwillingly envisioned her death a hundred different ways. Horrible scenarios had tortured his mind for days, until a whisper came of a girl fitting her description came from Wayward Point, then again from Moorin.

And then she was alive, the Wraiths thought her a traitor, and he thought he would have to end her life after all of that.

No, he couldn't tell Thalame not to think those things. He knew Thalame couldn't help it.

"There's more news," Niall said.

"Good news, right?" Zander deadpanned.

"Hardly. There's a Gray Elite Battalion heading for Lenhala."

Zander's breath left him, but he forced his exterior calm. He looked to the northwest, toward Moorin. If the Gray Elite thought a battalion necessary, what did they think was going to happen?

"They know we're coming," Zander said. "They either think we're coming in guns blazing, or they want us to think they're coming in guns blazing."

"We're not equipped for that kind of battle," Niall said. "Malik suggested to the captain that she send a small team of smaller, faster ships instead, but... As you can see, we are still heading to Lenhala."

"The Gray Elite threatened her daughter," Zander said. Luckett, he had gathered from his time with the Crusaders, held a grudge.

Niall looked skyward. "They are preparing for an attack anyway."

"We did say we could start a war." Zander counted on his fingers. "We stole the centrum, we made a fool out of Deacon, we rescued Rosaria, we destroyed that Colossus, we broke a pirate captain out of prison... Did I miss anything?"

"We rescued the Revenant from execution," Niall added darkly.

Zander ignored the tone. None of his friends had been pleased when they discovered that dirty little secret of his. "I'm not going to stand by and let them have Raven. I'd rather start a war. Besides, this is what the Hawks wanted all along. To push the Gray Elite into open war, to either win at last or lose and not worry about it anymore."

To win or die trying.

Niall frowned. "I don't like how you're thinking."

"Neither do I." Zander sighed and flexed his ten fingers. His new mechanical hand worked a little better than it had only moments ago. "Hopefully, if the Sisters are feeling kind, this will all be over quicker than we think, and we can all be laughing about it on the beach."

"All of us," Niall repeated.

Zander didn't comment. Niall knew just as he did that the odds of them all surviving whatever came were not very high.

But the odds had never stopped Zander before.

As soon as the official word came that the Gray Elite had sent a battalion to deal with the incoming rebel ship, Ivy had gone straight to the Hawks' lair. The new lair was an old inn downtown, a few notches up from their dungeon lair. It had an old sewer entrance, and with a few adjustments and simple construction, they had it connected to the old passageways.

The Hawk standing guard at the sewer entrance knew her; he offered her his hand. She took it because she wanted them all to think her a delicate lady. She didn't know why, but why break the charade without good reason?

Hawks and their associates lounged in the main floor's bar, pretending to drink. She didn't see Winchester among them, so she made her way upstairs to the meeting suite. She found him looking over maps of Lenhala and the surrounding countryside, including the escape tunnels the upper crust knew about—or rather, the tunnels the rich and important could afford to know about.

Ivy gently knocked on the door.

Winchester glanced up from his maps. He looked eerily like Zander. Sometimes, Zander's eyes went just as cold and detached.

"Yes?" Winchester asked, his tone that of a gentleman.

Ivy shut the office door, signaling the start of the meeting. She had seen Deacon do it. It was another power play. She refused to wait for him to invite her inside. Winchester said nothing. He straightened and folded his arms behind his back. She had his attention.

"I've just received word from the Dwellers," she said.

Winchester's brows rose. He had never been able to detect the Dwellers' spies, and it irritated and fascinated him.

"They know about the battalion," she said. "They're heading this way anyway, just not as fast, along with the pirate band known as the Crusaders."

"I didn't think pirates cared about our wars," Winchester said.

She shrugged. "I don't know why or how it happened or if it had anything to do with the battalion. Maybe they are rethinking their approach."

"What is your opinion on the matter?"

"I think bringing a sky city to an air fight is a horrible idea," Ivy answered. "I think they know that too. Smaller ships would work better. Especially considering they don't know where their target is."

Winchester hummed and looked back down at his maps. "The battalion is on course. Any pirate ship will be severely outgunned, and any smart pirate would know that. Of course, they'll have magicians on their side."

"Word is the Wraiths want nothing to do with this war," Ivy said.

Winchester glanced up.

"Kusmerk threw a wrench into those plans, but if what the scouts say is correct, few Wraiths are with them. Most returned to Tinatun to avoid the fighting."

Winchester offered a small smile of victory. "Those pacifists will hand the war to us. Anything else?"

"I went to see her." Ivy tried to look sad and guilty. It wasn't hard. Raven hadn't been happy when she'd realized what Ivy had done.

"And? Are her accommodations to her liking?"

"She didn't mention them," Ivy said, "although I'm sure she wouldn't mind a lantern or maybe a blanket. The tunnels are a bit chilly and dark."

Winchester gave a single huff of a laugh. "I will look into it."

His tone meant he wouldn't.

"That's all," Ivy said.

"Thank you," Winchester said.

Ivy let herself out in the hall, leaving the door open as she had found it. Only after she'd left the Hawks' den behind and stood within the cellar of Pemberton House did she release an aggravated breath. The role of Ivaline fell away like a damp towel. Ivaline would be ill today, she decided. Ivy didn't want to be in the city or deal with the gossip of the approaching battalion. Something told her it would be best to be inside.

A hot bath gave Ivy time to think. To go over all she'd said to Winchester, and all she hadn't said. She didn't know what had possessed her to take her message to Winchester. She didn't have the brain for strategy or the patience to consider all possible outcomes. She'd always been one to throw the dice and see what happened.

Ivy returned to the tunnels and made her way to the augur. She hated the machine. It was too big and too quiet, but not normal quiet. It was the quiet of a held breath.

The single lantern barely glowed, leaving the augur's chamber mostly dark. The machine itself emitted a strange glow but gave off little to no light. Raven had fallen asleep, curled on her side. Ivy replaced the lantern with another. She lit the candle within, brightening the platform. It would have a good day and a half of light in it.

Ivy tiptoed to the cage. Raven didn't move. As she'd suspected, her recommendation of a blanket had gone ignored. Ivy pulled the folded blanket from her satchel and tucked through the pillars. She started back to the surface. She didn't want to be in this cursed place any longer than she had to.

A few steps off the platform, she heard a shuffle. Ivy paused. A beat of silence passed, and then she glanced over her shoulder. Raven had tugged the blanket around herself. Ivy hesitated in case Raven said something. She hadn't prepared anything to say, and the panic her lack of preparation had caused bothered her. Raven didn't speak. She didn't move.

Ivy turned back and continued away, not minding if her steps echoed.

Raven dreamed of forgotten places. She dreamed of scattered islands and coral reefs, connected by bridges both high above the water and underneath; towering bookshelves of battered scrolls full of ancient knowledge since lost; temples of volcanic stone and cities built on sandy coasts.

She walked through a library with shelves three times her height. Windows let in clear sunlight and the briny sea breeze.

She walked along sand-packed streets. A language drifted on the breeze, one no longer spoken. The syllables were crisp and sing-song.

She walked through the market. Goods exchanged hands, fish and fruit and woven thread and silks in every color.

She stood in the dark chamber with Altair's Augur. She set her hand against the obsidian. The clear crystal began to glow pale yellow, then brighter, until it hummed with power. Her power. Her flames became white-hot starlight when it passed through the channeling crystal—a small slip of her sister's knowledge had led her to that discovery. Her power—and her, by extension—rushed through the crystal. She saw her target—the offending city that had slaughtered her people.

Her power burst from the machine, and the city vanished in a dazzling display of light. No rubble, no debris, no bodies. Gone.

It had been the final mistake.

Footsteps stirred Raven from her dream. It took a moment to realize the footsteps came from the present, not her dream. She blinked her eyes open, but sleep tugged on her awareness.

Voices were speaking lowly, too far away to understand. She knew the voices—Deacon and Winchester. She was too tired to care about what they said. How long had she slept? The shift between her dream and the present felt like a rift, and she was lost somewhere in the middle.

Ivy hadn't returned to talk since that first meeting, but Raven knew she'd visited. She had brought fresh candles so Raven wouldn't have to be in total darkness. Raven pulled the blanket closer to her chin. She wanted to go back to sleep. Her dreams were so much more pleasant than the augur's dark chamber.

But she felt the change in the air. It thrummed with tension and apprehension.

Deacon and Winchester continued to talk. Then, footsteps marched closer.

"We will find out," said Deacon.

"Are you sure it will even work with the centrum in this...state?" asked Winchester.

"We are about to find out," said Deacon, his voice cold and hungry.

Boots marched onto the platform. Raven turned her head to see Deacon standing before the platform. Winchester stood behind him, observing everything with his cold indifference. Deacon placed his hand on a panel she couldn't see, and then an eerie hum filled the chamber.

The augur came to life. The steady equilibrium she and the machine had reached shattered, and the machine ripped her magic away from her. Her energy pulsed through the crystal. She felt her body, lying in the cage. She could feel her throat stretching, hear herself screaming. She felt the machine—the crystals and magic. The machine whirled and sang, the ancient magic thrumming through the obsidian pillars. Her magic evoked the countless runes etched into the stone. The magic intensified; the thrumming grew stronger. The entire chamber hummed with a vicious, dangerous power.

Raven no longer felt herself. She felt magic and power. She was the device; the device was her.

Her being erupted into stars and white starlight. She rushed upward, guided along by the crystal paths, contained by the obsidian. Up and up, and then out. The sky above was blue. She was in a tower, contained. But she could see. A battle was happening. Airships littered the sky, guns firing in all directions.

Her power rushed up the crystal channelings, filling the containment. The containment began to swivel, guiding her.

And then, in a blast of light, she shot from the tower and into the battle.

She saw it all at once: the Gray Elite ships of white and yellow, the hobbled together pirate ships, the ships bearing the seal of the Hawks. Smoke and gunfire littered the air. The battalion had arrived. Hundreds of smaller airships, pristine and armed, zoomed and hummed. The battleship, a terror of steel and cannons, hung on the edge of the fight. Guns flashed. Ships were spiraling, engines smoking, balloons popped, wings torn.

Deacon had aimed the augur east, and she saw her planned destination. In the far distance, almost hidden by the clouds, was the *Orion*.

They would have her destroy her own family?

Her father was still onboard, as well as her stepmother and Lena. Luckett would be commanding her fleet from her office. All the people from Silver Glen. All her friends. The Crusaders.

She came close enough to the *Orion* to see the red of the Belt, the snapping of the rigging in the wind, the portholes. The young man with bronze skin and dark hair standing on the Belt, sapphire eyes wide.

No. She wouldn't let them control her. She would not allow Deacon to hurt anyone else. She would not allow him to use her to do it.

This power was *hers*.

And it obeyed only her.

She twisted herself, curving away from the *Orion*. She soared to the west, straight for the Gray Elite battleship.

She didn't catch the name on the steel hull. She didn't see the panicked faces of the crew as the blinding white light tore through the steel and leather like a blade through water. She felt it happen—the grand explosion, the utter obliteration, the seamless death and destruction. She felt the horror of it all, she felt the beauty in it.

She felt overwhelming exoneration and relief, and then everything blurred. Her magic had been expended. The augur calmed. The thrumming lessened.

Raven slammed into her own consciousness, her body still in the augur's cage, and her grogginess shattered into understanding. Lives had just been lost. She had killed people. She gasped for breath and curled into herself. It felt as though her bones had shattered and her blood had turned to sand.

Still...she had saved those she loved. She had turned her power onto the enemy instead.

The words did not make her feel better.

With every thudding heartbeat, the feeling went away. After her bones stopped hurting, she rolled onto her back. Deacon stood on the other side of the cage, looking smug. Winchester stood behind him, face blank.

"That is interesting." Deacon looked at her with the eyes of a madman. "Tell me, what did that feel like? Did it tear the magic from you? Do you remember it?"

"I was there," Raven said, her voice raw. "I was in the sky."

Deacon's grin turned devilish. He barked out a laugh. "You saw the whole thing, didn't you? We heard it, even from down here. I've never heard such a sound. A songbird of war. Tell me, did you see the looks on their faces as you killed them?"

"I didn't look," she said. A fragment of the wild flight slithered through her senses, the weightlessness, the utter power.

Deacon looked utterly delighted. Winchester, however, frowned. Raven met Winchester's skeptical eye. Did he suspect? The corners of her mouth tilted upward.

"What did you do?" Winchester asked.

She laughed; it came out a dry croak. "You don't know?"

"We are underground," said Winchester.

Deacon's mad grin fell. He looked between her and Winchester. "What? What did you do?" He grimaced. "The taste of power too much for you?"

She couldn't keep her lips from twitching into a smirk. "Too much for your fleet."

She watched her words sink into Deacon. His face fell, eyes widening. Winchester remained stony. From down here, they couldn't hear the peppering gunfire or the constant whirling of engines. They had only heard the blast—they hadn't seen it.

Deacon slammed a fist against the cage. "What did you do?"

She grinned. "Go upstairs and find out."

Deacon growled and again slammed his fist against the cage. Winchester started toward the far tunnel at a clipped pace. Deacon spat a curse, then he started toward the other tunnel.

Then both men were gone.

Raven reached for the blanket from where it lay across the cage. She felt horrible, like the augur had ripped her magic away and then stuffed what remained back into her body. When she reached inside, she found only embers.

Zander had always heard that in the moments before death, when the body realized what would happen and as the mind accepted the inevitable, one's life flashed before their eyes. But as he stood on the Belt and watched the beam of deadly light rush toward the *Orion*, his mind blanked. No memories came forward, no fears made themselves known—his mind hit the realization that he would die and cease to exist.

Altair's Augur would erase him and the *Orion* and everyone on board out of existence.

The beam, white as moonlight, gleamed off the Belt. The beam cut through the clouds, evaporating them into nothing. Zander felt the heat of it on his skin.

And then, by the grace of the Sisters, the beam *turned*. The light curved like a dove in mid-flight and surged toward the Gray Elite battleship. Zander took a shaky breath. Through the hole in the clouds, Zander watched the beam strike the battleship. In a dash of light and fire, the battleship was gone. The few remaining pieces fell to the ground.

Realization settled as his mind began to think again—the Gray Elite had fired the augur, but if Raven had the centrum— His breath caught. *Raven.*

Zander raced along the Belt and through the ship, toward the air docks. Sisters, let him be wrong! He ran himself breathless, but he didn't stop. He threw himself into the doors of the air docks and raced along the catwalks. He scanned the air docks for—

"Someone's in a hurry," Conrad said without turning around to look at Zander. He was fastening the special vest that pilots wore during combat, something the pirates had borrowed from a Gray Elite cache. He tightened a strap across his chest and glanced over his shoulder at Zander. His long braids had been tied back. His usual humor was gone.

"I'm going with you," Zander said at once.

Conrad's stoic expression betrayed no emotion. He knew Zander had been barred from combat due to his injuries. He knew the captain would be furious if he allowed Zander to go.

"You saw that light." Zander nodded toward the open dome where gunfire echoed like birds.

"I did." Conrad tightened the strap across his left shoulder. "I'm assuming we suspect the same?"

Zander stepped closer to Conrad. "It came from somewhere high. That's where she'll be. That's where we need to go."

"Are you sure?"

"She's down there," Zander whispered, urgency in every word. "Sisters only know what they did to her to get her to agree to something like that, if they didn't force her into it."

Conrad nodded, tightening a strap across his stomach.

The crew that had been prepping Conrad's small fighter ship backed away, giving the thumbs-up signal. Conrad climbed into the cockpit. As he started the first engine, he glanced at Zander with raised brows.

The crew released the ship from the rigging. Conrad's ship began to plummet. Zander rushed forward—amid the shouting and cursing of several Crusaders—and jumped. He fell through the air and landed with a thunk on top of Conrad's ship. He hooked his hands on the steel rods used to hook the ship into the air docks. Through the cockpit's window, Conrad was laughing.

The ship fell through the open air for a terrifying and exhilarating moment before the engines came to life. Zander let out a whoop. He had never felt a rush like this!

The engines *click-click*ed through a series of pitched purrs before settling into a constant roar. Conrad flew them toward Lenhala, toward the gunfight in the sky, and Zander held on with everything he had. The whipping air stung his eyes and tore at his hair. Conrad seemed to take his passenger into consideration; he did not twirl or pivot like the other Crusaders. They nimbly dodged while shooting; Conrad skirted the worst of the fight.

Zander had never seen an air fight. He'd heard about them from his father, from school, from other Gray Elite—but he had always heard it from the Gray Elite's side of victory. Hundreds of sleek metal ships zoomed around each other, peppering the air with gunfire, trying to knock the enemy from the air. The air rang with a constant barrage of bullets against the metal, the scream of engines pushed to their limits, the crunch of metal. Pieces of metal tumbled from the sky as ships were hit. The streets of Lenhala far below were empty; the people had either evacuated or gone underground.

A Gray Elite Buzzer went down—it filled the air with the worst screech Zander had ever heard.

Conrad steered them to the north. It didn't take long for Zander to see why; he aimed for an old watchtower, a remnant from when the City Watch guarded the city under the king's command. The tower had the right trajectory, and as Conrad circled the tower's open top, Zander's heart skipped a beat and then burned.

A mass of black stone and crystal had been partially uncovered. The black stone and crystal extended into a cannon—the barrel of the augur. It could be nothing else. That would lead him to Raven.

Zander knocked on the cockpit and pointed. Conrad angled them closer. Zander readied himself to jump. This time, his legs shook. Conrad wouldn't have the air space to catch him if he judged the distance wrong.

A bullet seared the air by Zander's cheek. He wrenched his head back, almost throwing himself off the ship's other side.

A Gray Elite Buzzer headed straight for them, and it opened fire. Conrad yanked the ship to the side, turning it to hide the engine under the thicker steel. Conrad maneuvered them around the other ship's gunfire. Zander flattened himself against the hull. The Buzzer came at them again.

It was guarding the tower. Zander spat a curse. That confirmed it—the Gray Elite were hiding something in that tower.

Too bad Zander already knew what it was.

Conrad and the Buzzer circled one another, trading bullets back and forth, and Zander felt his meager breakfast threatening to come back up. Conrad jerked the ship to the right, forcing Zander to hold on tighter or be thrown—something in his mechanical wrist popped. Zander felt the arm lose grip, felt the mechanism slacken, felt his magic shift within the bolts and gears.

One arm or five—he didn't care how many limbs he had to lose to get Raven out. Even if it killed him. She had risked everything to save him, and he would do the same for her.

Conrad shifted the other way, diving back toward the tower. Zander readied himself. He would have a small window. Conrad rolled the ship to avoid gunfire—Zander held his eyes on the tower, even as the world swiveled around him.

For all his shortcomings, Conrad could pilot the hell out of a ship. Zander vowed to buy him a tankard of the best ale if they both survived this.

The tower came closer. Conrad brought them in as close as it could, and Zander jumped. Bullets peppered the air. A few ricocheted off the fighter and sank into the stone of the tower. Conrad raced off, luring the Buzzer after him.

Zander's boots hit the stone ledge—for a terrifying moment, his weight pulled him backward, toward a deadly fall. Two Gray Elite stationed in the tower aimed their pistols at his chest. He thrust his weight forward and rolled onto the landing. As he rolled, he stole the soldiers' shadows. The Gray Elite fired. The bullets deflected off Zander's shadow shield. He commanded the shadows up, and in less than a heartbeat, he had the soldiers out cold.

He took a shaky, ragged breath.

He lifted his metal arm. Something had snapped in the mechanism. His fingers took twice as long to make a fist, and twice as long to uncurl. The little finger stuck out.

"Shit," he spat.

He dropped his arm. He couldn't do anything about it now.

He turned his attention to the partially uncovered cannon and yanked the tarp off. The mass of obsidian and crystal had been carved with ancient runes, most so complex and intricate, they made him dizzy. Obsidian entombed the crystal of the barrel, but beyond it, the two twisted together in thick ribbons. The crystal glowed a faint yellow. The cannon was aimed at the *Orion*, and it had fired—he had witnessed the blast—but the beam had altered course mid-flight.

Raven had done it. He knew she had. Somehow.

Somewhere in this mess, was Raven.

Zander put his hand against the barrel of the augur. After seeing what it had done to the battleship, every fiber of his being told him not to stand in front of it. He flattened his palm against the crystal. From his training as a Wraith, he knew obsidian did not react to magic while crystal absorbed it. The crystal would have channeled the magic while the obsidian kept it from leaving the desired pathway. His own magic reached into the faintly glowing crystal. Magic residue remained. He had felt the magic before—in Raven.

Her magic slowly crawled down the crystal. It headed below the tower.

He circled the tower's landing. On the far side, he found a trap door that led into a dark, narrow stairwell lit by scattered lanterns. Zander started down quietly. He sent his shadows ahead of him, testing for squeaky steps, feeling for signs of life. The lamps provided plenty of shadows too. With so many shadows, he didn't need light—he could move in near total darkness. That skill was what had made him the Revenant.

Another lifetime, he told himself.

Halfway down the tower, three Gray Elite started up from the street level. Zander halted. In the narrow stairwell, he had few options and little time to decide.

"This is stupid," one of them whined.

"Nah, I saw that ship drop something."

"Bloody waste of time," growled another.

Zander exhaled a breath of relief—he recognized none of the voices. He peered over the railing. He didn't recognize their faces either. That would make his job easier.

He readied himself, cleared his mind, and jumped over the railing. The Gray Elite noticed—as they drew weapons, Zander summoned a cocoon of shadows around himself. He landed on the stairs in front of the Gray Elite. Several bullets zinged off the shadows and landed in the stone. His shadows grabbed the closest soldier, knocked the saber from his hand, and sent him tumbling down the stairs. The saber clattered on the tower's bottom.

The shadows engulfed the second soldier. Zander grabbed his wrist and twisted, breaking his grip on his pistol. His shadows snapped his neck.

Zander maneuvered for the third Gray Elite. His shadows danced around him. The soldier had backed up several stairs. He fired—the bullet zinged off the shadows. Zander lunged. The Gray Elite came at him. In a regular fight, the guy might have had a chance. Zander didn't have time for a regular fight, not with Raven's life on the line.

The soldier slumped on the stairs, dead or out cold, he didn't know.

A bullet passed through a gap in the shadows. It banged off the metal of his arm. The impact sent a shockwave of pain through his shoulder and into his fingers; he grimaced, and his shadows quivered. The soldier he had knocked down the stairs now stood, aiming a pistol, a landing below. Zander threw his arm up—the second shot fired. The bullet careened through his weakened shadows and crashed into his metal palm.

The bullet tore through his metal hand, his wrist—shattering the metal on impact. Zander screamed—he felt the shattering through his entire being. His shadows dissolved. His metal arm fell limp against his side. Pieces clattered on the stairs, clinking and rolling, falling through the dark center of the tower.

The Gray Elite sneered. He aimed the third bullet at Zander's head. "Not so tough now," said the Gray Elite. He squeezed the trigger.

Zander summoned a shadow shield. The bullet zinged against it and fell to the floor. He formed a shadow spear and sent it at the Gray Elite. He didn't look—he looked at the stone above the soldier as the spear tore through flesh and bone. He didn't need to look. He heard it. He felt it through his magic. In his opinion, feeling it was worse than seeing.

The tower went quiet again. Zander let his magic fade and continued down the stairs without looking at the bodies he'd left behind. More bodies to leave behind him. Zander made his way to the bottom of the tower—an office. After a careless search, during which he didn't care if he shattered or broke anything, Zander discovered a secret passage behind—of all things—a painting.

It led into an old stone passage. Zander climbed through. It gradually declined, the sound softened and grew stale. Underground. It reminded him too much of the Hawk's lair, always gloomy and dank.

The passage ended in a sparse chamber lit with a single lamp. A brassy birdcage elevator had been built within the stone. A tangle of wires and gears were exposed—an obvious addition of the Gray Elite. Zander wrenched the elevator's door open. A panel held two buttons: up and down. Neither worked. Someone had turned the power off. Someone did not want anyone going down without permission.

Fine. He'd go the old fashioned way.

He used his magic to unscrew the hatch in the corner of the elevator's floor. Underneath, steel tracks, gears, and chains lined the darkness as far as he could see, for hauling the elevator up and down. Easy. Zander eased through the door and jumped onto the chain. It swung dangerously for several moments, during which his metal stub of an arm proved utterly useless.

As a Wraith, he had learned to climb impossible things. He'd climbed the steep cliffs of Wayward Point wearing nothing but trousers. If he could scale a slippery cliff during a thunderstorm without shoes, he could rappel down a chain in the dark with one arm.

His mechanical arm hung from his shoulder, dead weight. Every once in a while, a piece would fall and clink against the chain.

Still, he kept going.

He could do this. He had to do this.

His arm and thighs and back began to ache and burn. His hand slipped on the chain, and his entire body tensed.

And then, his grip faltered. His fingers spasmed.

And he fell through the dark elevator shaft.

Panic, hot and fluid, surged through his limbs. He reached for the walls, the chain, anything to stop his fall. His shadows reacted—his magic burned through the last of his rune, singeing the skin around it. A gasp of pain escaped his throat, echoing off the shaft.

Without the rune to dampen his magic, his shadows surged.

Zander latched onto a stone shelf. His hands found purchase, and his fall ended. His feet and knees slammed into stone.

After a terrifying moment, he allowed himself a breath.

And he realized he could feel his hands on the stone shelf—both of them.

A creak came from above, and in fear of being crushed by the elevator, he maneuvered his way down the stone wall and to the bottom of the shaft.

He landed on the stone floor of the shaft, and in the pale light that came from the elevator room beyond, he could see his hands—one of flesh and bone, one of shadow and scrap metal. His magic had created an arm for him, using the bits of broken metal for bones. He felt it too. Not like flesh and bone, but like his magic.

"Sisters," Zander breathed.

The elevator room was empty. A single lamp burned on a simple wooden table. The yellow light reflected off his new arm, making it look like a thousand flames danced within the shadows, and glinted off the protruding bits of steel and bronze.

He allowed himself a smirk and turned his new hand over in the light. He didn't even know his magic could do that. If he had, he would have had an arm days ago.

He tightened his shadow fingers into a fist. Oh, he could work with this.

Rosaria climbed into the airship behind Ezra. A Wraith who'd introduced himself as Jack only moments ago followed her. According to Ezra, Jack had been one of his contacts when smuggling magicians out of Gracita and into Tinatun. She had never met Jack, but if Ezra trusted him, then she would too.

Ezra situated himself in the pilot's chair. This particular ship had two leather-padded seats facing the dashboard of ramshackle gauges and mismatched dials, and then a third seat positioned sideways behind the co-pilot's seat. Rosaria, knowing next to nothing about flying, sat in the third seat. With a steel wall to her left and the back of the co-pilot's seat on her right, she felt moderately safe. Jack plopped into the co-pilot's seat.

The boys went through their list of jargon. Rosaria only half listened. She didn't care for flying. She knew what was about to happen, and her heart sped up and her skin broke into a sweat.

"We're ready to fly," Ezra called to the Crusaders waiting on the berth.

The Crusaders released the rigging. Rosaria dug her nails into the leather. She sucked in her next breath. The ship tipped forward and then fell out of the air docks. Her stomach rose into her throat, but she managed to withhold her gasp.

Ezra showed no fear. He wore his Gray Elite mask, calm and in control and ready for anything. He switched on the engines, the freefall ended with a swooping that echoed through her ribcage, and then they were flying toward Lenhala.

"Never gets old," said Jack.

Rosaria wanted to argue. She could go the rest of her life without falling out of another airship.

Ezra guided them the long way around the war-struck city. Even with her minimal view of the fight, she could hear it. The banging of guns and cannons, the smashing of metal, the scream of failing engines, the impact of fallen aircraft into the city below. Into her city. By the grace of the Sisters, if their plan worked, she would have a monstrous mess to clean up afterward.

They skirted the southern side of the cliffs, where age and weather and nature had left the rockface pocked with roots and sheer drops. Three large waterfalls cascaded down the cliffside and into the river far, far below.

"I hope you've got your info right," Jack said.

Ezra flashed him one of his winning smiles, but Rosaria saw what he hid underneath: fear and weariness. Then he steered them straight toward the leftmost waterfall.

Rosaria's heart plummeted. They raced toward the waterfall. The hum of the engine echoed off the cliffs. Water speckled the window, and the roar of the falls overtook all other sounds. The bow entered the falls—she gasped, anticipating the horrible crushing of metal against rock—the airship flew through the waterfall and into a long cavernous chamber lit by cloudy gaslights. The floor of the cavern had been painted in yellow and white: a Gray Elite airstrip.

Ezra brought the airship down, cut the engines, then turned around and grinned at Rosaria. "I told you I knew where it was."

Rosaria exhaled—it came out somewhere between a laugh and a groan. She couldn't fathom a response over her hammering heart. She wasn't cut out for these harrowing acts. Nevertheless, she banished the worry and panic from her face and met Ezra's smile with one of her own.

"I never doubted you," she said breathlessly.

"I did," Jack said. "Several times, and I might have wished a plague onto your house."

Ezra laughed and unhooked the leather belts holding him into his seat. Jack followed suit. Rosaria fumbled with her belt as Jack began unlatching the main door. Ezra took a small step in front of her in the moment before Jack pulled the door open, hand on the pistol at his side.

The door squealed open.

"Halt!" came a deep male voice.

Crossbows clicked. Pistols cocked.

"We are not enemies." Ezra stepped in front of Jack and revealed his empty hands. "It's me, Ezra Deacon."

"Hold your fire," came a voice that pricked against Rosaria's mind. "I can vouch for him."

"Exit your craft," said the deep male voice. "No sudden moves. Hands where we can see them."

Ezra exited first, followed by Jack, and then Rosaria. She mimicked their stance of hands up, fingers apart. A group of ten or so men and women stood around their airship, all aiming to kill. Some wore Gray Elite uniforms, others wore plain clothes, and others still wore hobbled together leather armor that looked like something the Hawks would have worn. Rosaria took it all in, just as the soldiers took her in. An arcade went along both walls of the long cavern, and she spotted several airships at the far end, poised for an easy takeoff.

"Make sure there's no one else," spat the man with the deep voice. He stood a head taller than Ezra and three times as wide. A scar traced a vicious line down his brown face.

Three soldiers entered the airship and began searching. Ezra held himself perfectly still, and Rosaria did the same. She had been through worse, she told herself.

"It's clear," came a female soldier from behind them.

The three soldiers did not return to the others. They remained behind.

"You vouch for them?" the first man asked.

"Yes." A younger man stepped forward beside the first. He held a pistol, but he did not hold his finger over the trigger like the others. The young man met her eye, and a small smile came over his lips. "This is Captain Ezra Deacon, Wraith Jack, and Princess Rosaria Whisehunt."

At her title, a murmur grew and dissipated within the span of a heartbeat.

"Bertrand," Rosaria whispered, more so to herself than to anyone.

Bertrand nodded. "I am glad to see you made it out of Moorin, Your Highness." He turned his attention to Ezra, and his expression turned dire. "We'd heard you'd been killed."

"I almost was," Ezra said. "My father discovered my treachery. I defected."

"And now you've sided with pirates?"

"Yes." Ezra wore no humor.

"This is Colonel Havelock." Bertrand motioned to the large man. "He has been leading this pocket of resistance."

Havelock returned his pistol to its holder and bowed his head at Rosaria. "It is an honor to meet you at last, Your Highness. It is our goal to return you to the throne."

Rosaria returned the bow, though she didn't have to. It felt disrespectful not to. Despite her questionable upbringing, Mrs. Winchester had taught her to always be respectful, even if the other person didn't deserve it.

"Let us speak elsewhere," Havelock said. "We have much to discuss and little time."

Havelock led them into the caves and to a meeting room. Askew wooden chairs circled an old and stained table as if a meeting had ended not that long ago. Introductions were quick. Havelock had served the Gray Elite faithfully until his daughter showed signs of magic. The Gray Elite warranted her death, but Havelock refused.

"As far as the Gray Elite know, my wife left me and stole my daughter," Havelock said without remorse. "They have been living in a small town in Tinatun. My daughter joined the Wraiths."

"Elizi," Jack said, nodding. "We've met."

Havelock nodded. "Is she here fighting?"

Jack hesitated, then nodded. "She is."

"If my plan goes the way I want, we will no longer have to hide our magicians." Ezra leaned onto the table, and the kind boy Rosaria had grown fond of vanished. A stern commander took his place, an unsettling replica of General Deacon. "My friends are fighting as we speak. Pirates, Hawks, rebels, and a handful of Wraiths. While they have the attention of the fleet, we are taking back the palace."

Havelock frowned, but he didn't interrupt.

"When the Gray Elite falter, Rosaria will be poised to reclaim her rightful place as queen," Ezra continued.

Just hearing those words spoken aloud sent a shiver along Rosaria's spine. She had often daydreamed of what it would be like to become queen, but those thoughts had never gained traction. She'd always known how slim her chances of becoming queen were.

"And you think that's going to work?" Havelock asked.

Ezra glanced at Rosaria. Havelock's stern stare followed. She held herself proud and firm. They all thought her a queen, and she needed to be one.

"Have you heard of the white fire?" Rosaria asked.

"Just old rumors," Havelock said. Skepticism furrowed his brow.

"It's not just rumors." Rosaria held every eye in the room, and the attention unnerved her. "There is an ancient Temple of the Three Sisters within the palace. It contains the white fire. It went out the day my parents were murdered. Only someone of royal blood can relight it, and by doing so, I will connect with the kingdom as my predecessors have done. It will magically tie me to the land, and it is the final push we need to cast the Gray Elite out of our kingdom."

"And having magic fire on our side will win this war?" asked Jack.

"It isn't just magic fire," Rosaria said. "It is a symbol. Anyone within sight will know that the Gray Elite have lost the palace and that I have claimed the throne and my kingdom."

"Anyone who served under your father will know it by sight," Havelock added lowly, remorse curving his words.

"Relighting the fire will also strengthen the magic of any magician in the city," Ezra added.

"It will give us more fire power," Jack added.

Havelock studied them for a long moment. "And I'm guessing you want our help in getting into the palace?"

"Correct," said Ezra.

Havelock retrieved a rolled map from a wooden cabinet and spread it over the table. It was a map of the palace and the surrounding streets, marked by countless pens and pins, leaving it nicked and endlessly illegible. Rosaria recognized the map from those she had seen growing up, the outer palace wall, the gardens, the rectangular palace itself. She had never thought of the palace as home. She had been too young when her parents died and her life had been ripped apart. Winchester house had been home. Over the past year, her life had been turned upside down over and over. Winchester house didn't feel like home anymore.

"We should be able to get in through the old Wraith quarters on the southeast corner of the palace grounds." Ezra pointed to the faded little building on the map. He glanced at Rosaria. "According to Zander, that's how you escaped that night."

The night General Winchester had taken her from the palace before the assassins could get to her.

Havelock hummed. "Right... We have a place not far from there. Two streets from the south wall."

"Which is why I came to you," Ezra said. "We don't have a lot of time. A storm is raging above, and we need to be ready when it calms."

"All right," started Havelock. "Give me half an hour. I'll grab a team, and we will meet you at the lift."

Bertrand led them to the lift room, a barren cave, save for the dusty gaslights and the birdcage elevator. Another rebel brought them canteens of fresh water and a small ration each. Without proper seating, Rosaria sat on the floor and leaned against the cavern wall. Ezra sat beside her.

"Ro," Ezra whispered, eyes on the lift. "On the chance that this mission goes wrong, I need to say something."

"This mission will not go wrong," she said firmly, though her own doubt quivered. There were a thousand things that could go wrong.

He offered her his charming boyish smile. "I wish I had a sliver of your confidence."

"I wish I had as much confidence as you think I do." She returned his smile. "But I also have something to ask of you."

Ezra's smile flattened. "Ro—"

"It's nothing morbid," she assured him. She held her open hand between them. He didn't hesitate to set his palm over hers and lace their fingers. "When this is over and I am queen, I will need a court of people I trust. I will also need an ambassador to the Gray Elite. I doubt our little coup will go over well with the emperor. I'll need someone clever and even tempered and brilliant with words."

Ezra blinked once. "Is this really the time to be thinking of things like this? We can find someone once the dust settles, and I'm sure—"

"I'm talking about *you*," she said, smiling.

His eyes widened, then guilt darkened his face. "I'm a defector. The Gray Elite wouldn't listen to me."

"They would if you are my ambassador," she said. "You defected because you did not believe in the Gray Elite's mission any longer. You saw the greater good and reached for it without worrying about the consequences for yourself. They will understand."

He half laughed. "Our views of the Gray Elite aren't quite the same."

"If not, there's always room in the court for a king consort," she said, squeezing his hands.

He blushed. He put his hand over his heart. "My lady, are you asking me to marry you?"

"Oh, I am merely suggesting," she said. "Should either of us ask such a thing, it would have to be under much more romantic conditions."

"I will keep that in mind," Ezra said.

They shared a quick, chaste kiss.

"What did you have to tell me?" Rosaria asked.

He grinned. "I was going to say I love you."

It was her turn to blush. "I would have said I love you too."

He started to speak, but the door to the little room opened and their rebel friends marched inside. Each had come armed and ready, daggers, pistols, sabers, and crossbows.

"You two ready?" asked Havelock.

"Yes, sir," Ezra said, standing.

"I'm ready." Rosaria stood.

Half the team went up first, and the second half, which included Ezra and Rosaria, went after. As the lift rose, Rosaria prayed to the Sisters for victory. She asked for confidence and guidance. The Sisters had long ago looked upon the people of Rhynwier with grace, and she prayed they would once again.

The elevator room had a single locked door. Zander's shadows slipped through the keyhole, and after prodding the tumblers, formed into the key. Unlike Raven, Zander couldn't easily blast through solid objects. He'd always preferred the stealth route.

The door swung open to a long, empty, sparsely lit corridor. He started down, feeling like an intruder. The tunnel reminded him of the one he'd found under his father's house, the tunnel that had gone to the augur's chamber. It likely connected to the other tunnels, including the one that led to Altair's Augur. That is where they would have taken Raven. They couldn't have activated the augur any other way.

The tunnel led steadily down. As he had imagined, other tunnels connected to it. It opened at the end, and his footsteps—as quiet as they were—echoed into the massive chamber beyond. The ceiling rose, carved with thousands of ancient runes, just like the augur's cannon.

His eyes fell on the monstrous machine that took over most of the room. Altair's Augur, a tangle of obsidian and crystal. It still hummed, still faintly glowed. It lifted the hair on his arm and on the back of his neck. Unlike the last time he had been there, a cage of obsidian and crystal had been crudely attached to the machine. Within the cage, a brown-haired girl lay unmoving.

Zander rushed up the platform's steps and collapsed by the cage. He grabbed an obsidian pillar with his human hand and grabbed a crystal bar with his shadow hand. At once he felt the leeching of his magic into the crystal—he wrenched his hand away. Where his shadow hand had touched the crystal, it glowed a faint blue. He set his shadow hand on obsidian instead. It felt cool.

"Raven?" he asked.

She didn't move. Her peachy skin had paled to a ghostly white, yet her chest gently rose and fell.

"Raven, wake up ," Zander pleaded.

She twitched. Her inhale came a little sharper.

"I'll get you out," he said.

Zander circled the cage. A heavy lock hung from the small door, and his magic cautiously entered the keyhole. As he found the right tumblers, Raven rolled onto her back. Her lips parted. His shadow-key found the right combination, he wrenched the lock from the door, and he crawled inside. He pressed his human hand against her cheek. Warm. A gentle exhale escaped her mouth and hit his thumb. He found her pulse. Alive. Zander released a breath of relief.

The strange leeching sensation he'd felt when he had touched the crystal radiated from all sides of the cage.

"I won't let them take you from me," Zander whispered.

He scooped Raven into his arms. The energy shifted as they exited, like the machine was trying to pull them back in. Not him, he realized, her.

They must have somehow used Raven in place of the centrum, harnessing her power as if she were the centrum. Which, he supposed, she was.

Outside the cage, the augur shuddered with her absence. The deep rumble shook the cavern. Zander felt a sharp panic tingle up and down his spine—he had heard that shudder before. He had thought it an earthquake. Someone had been tampering with the augur.

After the shudder, the augur whined, each tone lower than the one before. The augur gave a final, desperate whine.

"Tough shit," Zander spat at the device. "I need her more than you."

"I don't know about that."

Zander froze.

His father stood in the archway of the same corridor he had come through. He wore an immaculate suit of dark gray. General Winchester looked his son over, sneering. He looked like he always had, dark hair short and combed to the side in Gray Elite fashion, his shoes shined and spotless.

"I was starting to wonder if we would ever see each other again." His father sauntered into the chamber, his sapphire eyes roaming along Zander's arm of shadows and metal scraps. "You've been busy. I heard you were wounded in Moorin, but no one could tell me how badly."

"I lost my arm." Zander shrugged his shadow shoulder as much as he could while holding Raven. "Not that you'd care about that."

General Winchester's brows rose. "Would you believe me if I said I'm glad you're alive?"

"No," Zander said flatly, although a part of him desperately wanted to.

General Winchester shrugged. "Then, why would I tell you that if I knew you wouldn't believe me? Although, your mother will be ecstatic about your health. I'll make sure she knows."

Raven stirred in his arms. She took a deep breath, expanding her chest. Zander didn't dare take his eyes off his father. He reached out to her with his magic—hers responded. Her warm flame met his cool shadow halfway. The two energies laced together. With every passing heartbeat, her magic grew stronger. Replenishing.

"She's quite the catch." General Winchester nodded toward Raven. He didn't take his eyes off his son either. "Attractive and powerful."

Raven's magic curled around his, tightening in warning. A heartbeat later, he heard footsteps. Something was coming toward them from the opposite corridor. By the *thunk*ing footsteps, an automaton. Raven's magic released his own.

"Divide and conquer," Raven whispered, her voice hoarse.

"I'll take the old man," Zander whispered back.

General Winchester cocked his head, narrowing his eyes.

He'd wanted to punch his father for ten years. Since he'd shipped him south to become a Wraith, since he'd forced him into the role of assassin, since he'd stopped treating him like a son and, instead, a pawn.

Zander and Raven moved as one. He set her feet on the floor; she jumped from his arms. Zander gathered his shadows and went after his father. She and her flames surged down the opposite corridor. A squeal of metal sounded as the automaton halted.

General Winchester dodged his son's first punch. From within his suit jacket, he pulled out a small metal cylinder. With a click, the cylinder shot forward and extended into a steel cane. Zander dodged the first blow, but not the second. The steel cane thwacked him hard on his human shoulder, padded by the leather of his robes. It still stung.

Zander met his father's cane with a long dagger. Back and forth, they traded blows. Zander was fast, but so was his father. Before and after the Wraiths, General Winchester had trained with his sons, making sure both exceeded Gray Elite expectations. He trained with them as Hawks too. Despite his age, his father had kept up with his fitness.

But Zander had the advantage. He had his magic, his Wraith training, and the fierce determination to beat his revenge into his old man. The cane thwacked against the dagger. Zander started to feint to the left, preparing to go right with the dagger, and his father read those steps—as his father blocked his right side with his cane, a shadow-fist collided with his father's jaw on the left.

General Winchester stumbled back, and Zander let out a bark of a laugh. His father scowled and came back at him. Zander threw another shadow-fist, this time into his father's gut. His father stumbled backward into the wall of the corridor. His split lip bled onto his suit.

Zander had something witty on his tongue, but the stone around them gave a terrible shudder. General Winchester's eyes widened, as did Zander's. The shudder trembled through the stone, loosening rocks and dust. It did not come from the augur. It was no earthquake. The sound came from within the stone—the cavern was collapsing.

Zander ran one way, and Raven ran the other. As much as she wanted to look back at him, to make sure she hadn't imagined him, she didn't. She held her gaze straight ahead, at her target. They would have time for a better reunion when this was all over.

She met the automaton in the cavernous corridor. It stood seven feet and slim, its waxy skin a reddish brown. She didn't give it a chance—she engulfed it in flames. Her magic had dwindled from the augur's use, but she had enough. She pushed herself to burn hotter, and the red-orange flames flashed brilliant blue.

She felt her flames dancing around the automaton, licking its waxy flesh-like skin, but the automaton remained. She pulled her flames back. The flames danced red-orange around her fingers. The automaton still stood, not even singed.

"It's flame resistant," Ivy chimed from farther down the corridor. She stood in simple clothes, a hooded jacket pulled over her blonde hair. "Took ages to figure out."

Her magic guttered out, and she dismissed the flames around her hands. Sensing the window, the automaton came at Raven. Without her magic to rely on, she had few other options. She pulled two hidden daggers from her back—Deacon had disarmed her of the obvious weapons, but he hadn't searched her very thoroughly. She managed to dodge the automaton's grasping hands and used the right arm for leverage—she launched herself at the automaton's humanoid face. She didn't allow herself to think; she acted.

She had planned to pop the head off like she had seen other Wraiths do, however she lacked the grace. Her feet found no purchase on the waxy skin, and she slid right off the shoulder. She thrust one dagger into the automaton's shoulder, and as she tumbled off, her weight slammed into the hilt. The dagger sank into the waxy skin and caught in the mechanisms within, ripping it from Raven's grip. She smacked into the floor with the grace of a dead bird, but just as Thalame had taught her, she rolled and bounced back to her feet.

She had left a gash on the automaton's chest, exposing steely bones and mechanical insides.

"They ordered you to be captured alive," Ivy said like it was obvious. "They didn't mention uninjured. For your own safety—"

"Shut up," Raven spat. "I'm not going to just give up like you did."

Ivy frowned but held her tongue.

The automaton moved as if it hadn't been wounded, yet she spotted the twitch in its left side. It moved slower than the right. It came at her again. She dodged, but the automaton's fist smacked into her shoulder. She yelped and tumbled backward.

Any other Wraith would have popped the stupid head off. Raven didn't have years of training or the acrobatic skills the other Wraiths did.

Raven gathered her remaining magic, and as the automaton started toward her, she blasted everything she had into the gash on its chest. Blue flames erupted inside the automaton, melting whatever they touched. The automaton stumbled toward her, its arms and legs twitching, its internal workings crunching and squishing. Raven felt her magic squeezing, but she pushed her flames deeper, hotter. Gears melted. Joints twisted. Wires snapped. Her flames sliced through the engine and to the metal heart.

The automaton collapsed. Its fire-proof waxy skin slumped; the molten innards oozed from the seams.

Raven doubled over, panting.

"I hadn't thought of that." Ivy looked at the melted automaton with a clinical expression.

Raven glared at Ivy, her friend who'd betrayed her, who had built an automaton with fire-proof skin. She had something snarky to say—a crash sounded from above, echoing with a mighty thud through the stone.

"The air fight is more intense than the Gray Elite anticipated." Ivy brought her eyes to Raven. "They underestimated the *Orion*'s speed and the number of enemy ships, and then you dealt them a serious blow when you destroyed the battleship."

"I chose my side," Raven said firmly. "And I intend to fight for them until we win or I'm dead."

"I admire your tenacity," Ivy said, sounding just like the girl Raven had met in the woods all those weeks ago: optimistic, admirable, and kind.

"I wish I could say the same for you," Raven said. "It's not too late. You can still come with us. Turn on the Gray Elite."

The corridor shook. The very stone groaned and whined. Loosened rocks tumbled from the ceiling. Ivy's eyes widened. She took a step back, then another, and then bolted down the corridor.

"Ivy!" Raven shouted. She started after her.

The roar shook the tunnel; stone cracked. Ivy skidded to a halt, but only just in time. The ceiling collapsed, sending rocks and debris tumbling into her path. Ivy stumbled backward, smacking her head on the stone floor. She groaned and curled inward, but did not get up.

"Ivy?" Raven skidded to a halt beside Ivy's unconscious self. She pushed flaxen hair away from Ivy's temple. She didn't see a wound, but she had learned from Thalame that head injuries were never to be taken lightly.

The cavern shook dangerously. More rocks came loose. The walls shed layers of stone, knocking out the power to the lights and plunging parts of the corridor into darkness.

Raven shook Ivy's shoulder. Ivy came to, but her unfocused vision swam over Raven.

Raven pulled on Ivy's arm. "Come on!"

Ivy stumbled to her feet and leaned heavily on Raven. They ran as fast as they could back toward the augur. Ivy mumbled something, but Raven couldn't understand it over the rumbling of the cavern.

Zander met them by the augur. He'd taken a few blows but nothing bad.

"Ivy?" Zander looked the girl over. "Never mind, we've got to get out of here. Now. Give her to me."

Without waiting for permission, Zander hoisted Ivy into his arms.

"This way's blocked!" Raven said, pointing behind them.

Zander motioned her toward the other corridor, and they ran. Ivy told them to turn right at the fork, not left, and Zander listened to her without hesitation. Raven's heart squeezed. Even after all that Ivy had done, Raven still wanted to believe her.

The corridor gradually rose. The shaking lessened, but Raven could hear stone falling in the chamber behind them, crashing and shattering on the ground, clanking against the augur. She knew in her bones, it would take a lot more than a collapsing cavern to break the augur.

Zander guided them through the maze of stone corridors, steadily rising. When the walls no longer rumbled, they slowed to a walk.

"Where's your father?" Raven asked.

"He ran when the cave started to shake." Zander glanced behind them. "Sounds like it's really coming down."

"Something crashed on the ground above, something big," Raven said.

The tunnels led into a musty cellar, and a wooden staircase led them into a house. Zander kicked the door to the cellar closed. The dark paneling, red walls, and elaborate metalwork looked familiar, and as Zander led them into a lounge, it dawned on her. He'd led them to the Winchester house. Zander locked the lounge door behind them.

Raven meandered through the dainty furniture and to the tall windows. She pulled aside the heavy maroon drapes. Lenhala smoldered. Plumes of white and gray smoke billowed into the sky from the south, enough to shade the northern part of the city. The smell penetrated the lounge, smoke and burned metal and gunpowder. She could hear the constant *pop, pop, pop* of the air fight still raging.

"It sounds much worse from here," Raven whispered.

"It sounds much worse in the air," Zander said.

He set Ivy on the couch. She'd fallen unconscious along the way. Then he joined Raven at the window. The reflection of his shadow arm undulated like sea water, shimmering and dancing in the sunlight.

He whispered, "What the hell was Ivy doing down there?"

"Ivy sold us out," Raven said. The words felt like poison.

Zander's reflection gawked at her.

"I didn't want to believe it either. She came to see me while I was locked up down there. She told me that she'd led the Gray Elite to the Hawk's lair on purpose. She told Deacon that I had the centrum. She made the cage for the augur. She suggested Deacon use you against me."

"And Deacon knew exactly how to find us," Zander added. Gloom darkened his expression.

Raven turned from the window and meandered to the sofa. Zander sat in the chair beside her, glaring at Ivy.

"I couldn't just leave her down there," Raven said. The thought had never crossed her mind. "I know what she did was wrong, but she's still Ivy."

"You made the right choice." Zander held his hand out to her, and she took it.

They sat there for a moment with the air fight raging in the skies.

"It's a mess out there," she said.

"War isn't supposed to be fun." Zander took a deep breath. "I can't believe you took down Kusmerk like that."

"It wasn't the original plan."

Zander half laughed. "That's what Conrad said."

"I improvised," Raven said. "My goal was to get you out. And it worked."

His small smile vanished. "And got yourself captured."

"That wasn't part of the plan either, but…" She sighed. How could she explain what happened in Kusmerk? "I wasn't entirely myself. My magic wasn't—isn't—entirely mine."

Zander frowned.

She explained it to him as best she could, how the centrum had once belonged to the fourth Sister, Aeon. She told him about Aeon, how her thirst for power had created the augur, how the augur had started an ancient war, and how her Sisters had struck her and her kingdom down.

"Aeon's power was fire, and it was somehow contained in the centrum," Raven explained. "And that power became mine, but it's not *just* mine. A sliver of Aeon remains, and she…took over in Kusmerk."

"You're…possessed?" Zander raised a brow.

"I don't know. It's strange, but since they used me in the augur, I haven't felt her presence. It's like the machine took that sliver of her away."

Zander held her under a piercing gaze, thinking. She shifted her own to the window. How many Crusaders had gone down? How many had been her friends?

"Rae?" Zander asked softly.

"I'm sorry," she said. "I know what I did was reckless. I just… I was thinking about you, not myself."

He tugged on her hand, pulling her attention back to him. "It'll be okay."

"And your arm?" Raven said, looking at the shadow-metal.

He flexed his shadow hand. The shadows moved like smoke but held the shape. "That's another story. I'll tell you about it later. Right now, we need to dust ourselves off and figure out our next move." He reached into his robes and withdrew a small black metal cylinder. "This is a flare. It lets friendly ships know that we need a pickup."

"Let's go." Raven stood. The floor wobbled, and at first, she thought it part of the battle. Zander grabbed her arm to steady her, and she realized the dizzy spell had been solely her.

"Easy." Zander stood, keeping his grip on her arm. "You sit with Ivy. I'll be right back."

Zander left, and Raven slumped in the chair. She missed the *Orion*. She missed the white sand beaches of Wayward Point. She missed calm and not having trouble following a step behind her.

Soon, she told herself, she would be lying on the sand with a coconut drink. Soon, this would all be over. Soon—because she knew they weren't done yet.

Zander returned a few moments later with a black bag. He set it on the table and pulled out a few small cloudy bottles and bags of dried meat and fruit. He uncorked one of the bottles and handed it to Raven, then opened the other for himself.

She sniffed it. It smelled cool and vaguely familiar. She took a drink. As it washed down her throat, a tingling sensation oozed into her limbs. The sensation settled, and she felt better, like she'd rested for several hours.

"What is this?" she asked. The bottle wore no label.

"Rejuvenation potion." Zander took a swig of his own. "It replenishes your magic and takes the sting off the depletion."

She'd taken a similar potion after their rescue from Moorin. She took another drink, finishing the small bottle.

They ate what they could. Despite how little she had eaten, she didn't have an appetite. By how Zander picked at his food, he didn't have much of one either. Ivy remained asleep. If she pretended, Raven didn't know. She didn't care. She felt like lying down for a long time too.

When Zander deemed their time up, he lifted Ivy into his arms, and they headed into the grand Winchester gardens. The sky gleamed in the late afternoon, the sunlight turning the smoke grayish gold. It smelled like gunpowder and molten steel, and though the air fight had calmed, sporadic gunshots still rang out. Raven glanced to the sky, but no airships battled over them. The fight kept to the southern parts of the city.

Despite the stench of the fight, the gardens smelled of ripening fruit trees and fresh soil. The bioluminescent flowers had dulled, their pedals folded as if in sleep.

Zander led them into the open patio and handed Raven the flare. She pried the tab off and yanked it back; blueish green smoke started to drift upward.

"Toss it up," Zander instructed. "It'll agitate the smoke and make it brighter."

She heaved and tossed. The smoke turned a vibrant sea green.

The flare reached the apex of the toss, and as it began to fall, a bullet zinged through the air—it hit the flare, knocking it out of the air and knocking it across the garden. It landed in the fountain. The smoke stopped.

General Deacon stepped out of the atrium. "Not so fast."

Gray Elite emerged from the garden—from behind trees, bushes, and under leafy camouflage—a hundred soldiers, at least. Each had a pistol or crossbow aimed at them. Raven sucked in a breath of surprise. They had been hiding in the garden? Of course, from the augur's chamber, the tunnels likely only led a handful of places.

"You're predictable," Deacon spat. He sauntered toward them. His usual smugness had been replaced with rage and disgust. "I knew you'd end up here. It's the only location you could have summoned a ship from."

"Wasn't hard to deduce," Zander added lowly.

Deacon scowled. "You've lost." He waved in the air. His Gray Elite moved closer in, but no one fired. "If you haven't noticed, the Gray Elite have proven superior yet again. Your pirate friends haven't the ships or the soldiers."

Raven glanced to the sky, to the guns and crossbows aimed at them, to the fallen and silent flare in the bottom of the fountain.

"I'm not so sure about that," Zander said. "From what I heard, your fleet was surprised. Not to mention that battleship that went down. To a bunch of pirates, of all things."

"Because of her." Deacon glared at Raven. His rage turned sinister and mad. "And with that kind of power at my disposal, the Gray Elite will overcome. This battle will be but a bump in our triumph over magic and rebels."

He said *magic* with more malice and bitterness than Raven thought possible.

"No, it won't." Raven steeled herself and straightened her shoulders. She took a step forward. Guns and crossbows followed her, more focused on her than Zander. "I control my magic, not you." Not Aeon. "You saw what I did. You will never have control of the augur. No one will, because it listens to me."

Deacon raised his pistol and aimed it at her head. He cocked it.

The sound reverberated down her spine, but she held her chin high and said, "And if I'm dead, the power is gone forever."

Deacon hesitated. She didn't know if the power would vanish with her death, but she spoke it as if she did. She knew Deacon couldn't afford to take that gamble. She couldn't either.

The Gray Elite didn't shift. They waited for their general's command. Then, the air filled with the roar of an incoming airship. Another followed.

A small battle boomed—bullets zinging off metal, engines whirling and straining with the stress. Raven dared not take her eyes off Deacon.

The air exploded—one of the ships went down. It landed beyond the garden; the impact shuddered through the ground, shaking the trees in the garden and making the water in the fountain sputter and ripple. Metal ripped apart on impact, stone fractured, and glass shattered. A new plume of blackened smoke rose into the air, tinged with red.

Raven's heart hammered. Had that ship been Gray Elite or Crusader?

A ship flew over the garden, the victorious ship—and to Raven's utter glee, it bore the ramshackle metal shades of the Crusaders.

Raven laughed. "You've lost," she shouted to Deacon.

"And, if our timing is right," Zander added, "Rosaria will be relighting the white fire any moment."

Deacon's fingers flexed over the grip.

"I'm assuming your silence means you didn't foresee that coming?" Zander asked, his tone every bit the arrogant boy Raven had first met all those months ago.

"It doesn't matter," Deacon said. "It'll go out when she's dead. Just like her parents."

The Crusader ship doubled back. It fired a few warning shots into the tops of the trees, sending branches and fruit in every direction. The Gray Elite closest jumped out of the way, several yelping. The Crusader ship came back, circling the garden.

"That would be our exit," Zander mumbled.

"Shoot it down!" barked Deacon.

Half the Gray Elite aimed upward and fired. The shots shook the garden air, and Raven held her breath as those bullets smacked against the hull of the ship. Some sank in, some bounced off. The ship continued to circle.

Raven's eyes were on the sky. In her moment of distraction, the Gray Elite surged forward. The airship dove closer. A door opened, ropes descended, and pirates slid down the rope and to the ground. Each pirate let out a mighty war cry. Bullets and bolts banged and thwacks, hitting flesh, tree trunks, and the ground. Zander dropped to the ground, holding Ivy against him, and brought shadows on either side of them.

Deacon grabbed Raven and yanked her from the fight. She grabbed his hand, intending to burn him alive or until he released her, but Deacon had both strength and skill. He twisted her around, and her back slammed against his chest.

"Don't try it," he growled. He pressed the barrel of his pistol against her temple. "Unless you're willing to test your theory. I've got no problem with throwing your dead body into the machine."

He cocked the gun. She released her hands.

He started to walk backward, toward the house, and she had no choice but to walk with him. The fight unfolded in the garden. Bodies and blood and bullet shells. The airship circled overhead.

"You think you can make me do what you want?" she asked. "I'll just destroy something of yours again."

"And I'll destroy something of yours if you do," Deacon countered. "You think we don't have a dozen battleships waiting to head this way? The *Orion* will crash to the earth, and everyone on board will be killed. You think we don't have armies of automatons waiting for the order to march through Rhynwier and slaughter every last one of them?"

She heard the sounds—bullets and bolts tearing through flesh, yelps of pain. Bodies hit the ground, one after another. But as Deacon pulled her onto the back porch of the Winchester house, she saw something else—most of the bodies wore gray and yellow. Crusaders outgunned the Gray Elite.

Two Crusaders took watch over Ivy, and Zander joined the fight. He blasted two Gray Elite out of his way, searched the garden for Raven, and with a fearsome cry, charged for Deacon. Zander halted before the patio with death in his eyes.

"Let her go!" Zander's shadows curled around his hands like talons.

"Careful." Deacon wiggled the pistol he held to her head. "You wouldn't want me to do anything drastic."

Zander let his shadows fade. He straightened, took a breath, and drew Birdie. He aimed at Deacon, but she saw trepidation on his face. Zander could shoot a deer between the eyes at a hundred yards, but he wouldn't risk shooting her. Deacon pulled Raven closer. Zander's grim expression didn't wave, but his finger over the trigger did.

"Don't want to shoot her, do you?" Deacon taunted.

Raven tried to reach out to Zander with her magic, with that indescribable invisible force, like he had done in the augur's chamber. It took a moment to find that strange sense within herself, and another to send it out to Zander. Then, a cool wave of magic responded to her own—Zander's cool shadows. He didn't take his eyes off Deacon.

Trust me, she told him.

Zander swallowed. He took a slow inhale and blew his breath out. His magic responded, *Okay*.

Raven shifted her hand to her stomach. Deacon couldn't see her hand under his own arm, but Zander could see it clearly. She splayed her fingers wide—the countdown. Just like they used to do.

"You're not going to accomplish anything by taking her," Zander said, though his concentration flickered.

Raven put one finger down, *four*. Then another, *three*.

"Altair's Augur is mine!" Spittle flew from Deacon's mouth.

Raven put another finger down, *two*. Zander's finger settled over the trigger. Her heart hammered. She thought of how her mother would handle this, how Conrad would handle this. She steeled herself and put another finger down, *one*.

The fight in the garden had slowed, and those remaining were surrendering.

She inhaled, and as she curled her final finger toward her palm, as the countdown hit zero, she let her weight drop. Deacon's grip faltered and slipped; Birdie fired. The blast ripped through the air, and she felt the impact as the bullet hit Deacon. His arm slackened, he fell backward, and she tumbled to the ground with him. They hit the patio.

Raven rolled to the side, away from the body. Deacon looked skyward. He'd taken the bullet right between the eyes.

Zander appeared at her side, looking her over with wide eyes. He touched the sides of her head, searching for an accidental bullet wound. The assassin had vanished, and her Zander had returned.

"I'm fine," she said, though her quivering voice said otherwise. Her ears were ringing from the blast, but it faded with every heartbeat. "A refreshing cup of tea would be nice, but I'm okay."

"Sisters," Zander breathed, pushing his hair out of his face. "I aimed a gun at you."

"You fired a gun at me," she added.

He holstered Birdie and helped Raven to her feet. He then wrapped his arms around her and pressed a desperate kiss to her temple.

A redheaded Crusader jumped onto the patio and looked Deacon over. He nudged the body with the toe of his boot. "Safe to say he's dead, yeah?" he said in a rough accent.

In the garden, the Gray Elite were either dead or captured. The redheaded pirate let out a cry of victory—a cry echoed across the garden.

"We won," Zander breathed into Raven's hair. "Let's get the hell out of here."

Zander pulled Raven toward the hovering airship. She held onto him. If he let go, she would surely collapse. The bodies, despite them being mostly enemies, churned her stomach. Blood and gunpowder stained the air. The already wilted-looking flowers had been trampled.

A second Crusader ship appeared in the sky, and rope ladders fell from the doorway. Zander helped Raven onto one of those ladders, and he climbed behind her. Raven spotted Ivy—a Crusader carried her on his back. Ivy hung on, which meant she had woken up again. Once inside the ship, Raven slumped against the far wall. Zander sat beside her. They sat close to make room for all the others.

"What now?" she breathed.

"Well, with the general dead and Rosaria in position, our chances of winning just rose considerably," Zander said.

"I thought we already won?"

"We won this fight," Zander said. "We took down Deacon, but he's just one of countless power-hungry wolves in the Gray Elite."

The airship started away, and one of the Crusaders threw a flare out of the door. It spewed golden smoke. As they circled back around, Raven spotted at least a dozen golden flares following suit—a signal.

"We let the others know the general is dead," Zander said. "And our princess knows it's time."

The airship flew over the palace. Raven felt the white fire before she saw it. Her magic swelled, and she felt as light as air. From Zander's subtle intake of breath, he felt it too. Before she could question the strange sensation, she saw it. In the palace's center tower, a white fire burned.

"I've only ever read about the white fire," Zander breathed. "It boosts magic and protects it."

"It also ties the ruler to the land," said a man in Wraith gear from the cockpit. "Every magician in the kingdom will know that a queen has risen, and that this century of war is over."

They circled the palace several times, as did several others, before heading back to the *Orion*. From the air, Raven saw the devastation. The southern part of Lenhala smoldered. Airship crashes spotted the district, buildings had collapsed with the impact, and several fires had spread.

"What about all the people?" Raven asked. Smoke billowed from a high rise, and most of the windows had been shattered.

"Evacuated," said Zander. "Anyone with Gray Elite connections knew about the incoming attack and fled or hid early. Sirens warned everyone else."

Raven nodded at the news. She felt a strange numbness. She had heard the battle, the engines, the gunfight, the crashes, but seeing the ruins left behind gave her a different kind of pitting.

They flew back to the *Orion*. It remained hidden on the other side of the clouds and a layer of smoke. Their airship nimbly rose into the air docks, and the crew rushed to fasten it into the rigging. The air docks buzzed with activity, ships in repair, pilots limping along the catwalks, and medics tending to those who couldn't wait. One of the Crusaders from another ship carried Ivy along the catwalks.

Only she and Zander knew of her treachery. The Crusaders would tend to her injuries.

A medic rushed along the catwalk, sweaty and out of breath. He motioned to Raven and asked, "You hurt?"

"No." Raven looked to Zander, to his shadow-metal arm. He shook his head at the medic.

The medic rushed to help others, and Raven and Zander retreated through the *Orion* and to the Belt. Raven leaned onto the railing and took the deep breath she'd needed days ago. Zander joined her, and her eyes wandered over his shadow arm.

"How did you know you could do that?"

"I didn't until I did it." Zander flexed his shadow fingers. "It takes energy, but without the rune, I can handle it."

"And if you grow tired?"

Zander released his control. The shadows dissolved, exposing the damaged metal arm. The hand and wrist and part of the forearm had been shattered. A few pieces of metal fell onto the Belt.

Raven pretended to consider it. "It's not as attractive."

"I'm sure the mechanics can build me another." Zander brought his shadow arm back. "But since they're probably busy with damaged ships, I can wait."

Zander offered her his human hand. She took it. She felt the gentle caress of his magic against hers.

"Can you feel that?" he whispered.

"Yes." She responded to his touch with her own.

Zander's eyes softened. "According to the Wraiths, to touch someone else's magic with your own is more intimate than skin."

"It feels that way," she said.

When their magic touched, it felt like their souls connected. She felt his being, his essence—she couldn't describe it. And by the softness in his eyes, he could feel hers.

She stepped closer. "What would happen if... I mean, what if our magic were to be touching, and then we were also touching...in other places?"

A mischievous grin spread over Zander's face, and a warm tingle surged down her spine and into her toes. He kissed her, a kiss full of desire and longing. He pulled away, but not far. His warm breath hit her lips.

"This is nice," she said, cheeks heating, "but I was thinking more of bedroom touching."

Zander laughed, his breath husky and deep. "I was too, but I don't think that's appropriate for this part of the ship."

She laughed in return. She leaned into his chest and wrapped her arms around his middle. She felt bruises lining her arms and legs, but she ignored them. She had more pressing matters.

"Zander," she started. Her magic caressed his.

"Hmm?"

"I love you," she whispered.

His magic threaded with hers, and his lips found her temple.

"I should have said so weeks ago," she added.

"I love you more than I thought myself capable of loving anyone," he said, lips against her temple. "I knew there was something about you when I met you in Silver Glen. You kept staring at me like I was some wild mongrel that wandered into your house."

"You were," she said, laughing. He'd looked it too.

He hugged her closer.

A bell sounded—the official victory. The last of the Gray Elite ships had retreated, and the surrender had been made. Even from this part of the ship, a resonant cheer could be heard.

Raven and Zander made their way to the air docks to be among the crowd welcoming their pilots back. Most stood along the mezzanine—out of the way—and whistled as each ship came in, as each pilot exited, while the mechanics and medics scrambled from ship to ship. Mechanics tended to the worst of the ships; medics tended to the worst of the injured. The lesser injured were carted along the catwalks and to the hospital. She found Malik on the mezzanine, looking pale and nervous. He couldn't stand still; his fingers twitched on his arm, his feet tapped, and he swayed back and forth in agitation. He stared at each ship as it came in, waiting for the pilot. She didn't need to ask who he was waiting for.

"I'm sure he's all right." Raven gave his arm a sisterly squeeze of affection, like Lena had done to her so many times. "He's a good pilot."

"One of the finest," Malik said dryly. He cleared his throat. "A ship will be ready shortly to take you down to the palace, if you wish. Several Wraiths are already there."

"That's good," Zander said.

One by one, the berths filled.

Among the last to enter the docks was a ship with a smoking hole dangerously close to the engine. It wobbled as it docked. Malik's breath hitched, and he started along the catwalks toward the ship. No one told him to stand back.

Raven remembered Ezra limping out of his damaged airship, bleeding and barely conscious. She found herself holding her breath as Malik approached the ship. The crew checked the hole by the engine first, and medics stood ready for the pilot. The cockpit slid open, and Conrad ungracefully climbed to the dock. He wobbled but remained standing. He bore no obvious wounds or blood stains; he looked unenthused and weary.

Malik pushed his way to the berth. Conrad gave him a tired smile, but Malik didn't give him the chance to say anything—he threw his arms around Conrad's neck.

Raven released a breath of relief.

"What?" Zander asked. "You think Conrad wouldn't come back?"

"I had considered it."

Zander chuckled. "He's too stubborn and clever to die, or the Wraiths would have done him in years ago."

She laughed, and it felt joyous on her lungs.

Conrad and Malik parted. Conrad's lips moved. Malik frowned, looking like he might slap him—instead, he kissed him.

Zander nudged Raven and gave her a knowing smile.

"Mother did say Malik and I had similar tastes in men," Raven said.

He raised a brow. "And what tastes are those?"

She took a long moment to look him up and down, considering. "The bad ones."

He smirked, and butterflies let loose in her ribcage. "Bad as in good, or bad as in bad?"

Raven only smiled and laced her fingers with his.

Raven had fallen asleep to thoughts of a new era. She woke to Zander's gentle breathing and her darkened cabin aboard the *Orion*. Zander slept in Rosaria's bunk; Rosaria had opted to stay in the palace with a few trusted companions, including Ezra. She had a few Wraiths with her, so Raven wasn't worried for her safety.

She climbed out of her bunk. Zander slept on his stomach, and his human arm dangled off the side of the bed. She couldn't see his other arm. A mechanic had removed the broken bits of metal. They hadn't replaced it—Zander had told them not to. When he had explained what had happened with his magic, Niall and Brent had shared an expression. They had a plan, but neither told Zander what it was.

She washed her hands and face, pulled on her Wraith robes from the day before, and tiptoed into the corridor. Despite the early hour, the airship buzzed with activity. Raven made her way to the holding cells belowdecks, past the purring engines, past the mechanic workshops and smiths. The holding cells were on the lowest part of the ship. The Crusader guarding the iron door was leaning against the wall, puffing on a sweet-smelling cigar. Two pistols hung off his hips, and two daggers crisscrossed his back. Gray streaked his black hair and his beard. An old scar stretched from his cheekbone to his jaw, and the hair didn't grow there.

"I want to see a prisoner," Raven said.

"Awful early," he said.

"The sun is up," Raven said.

He chuckled. "You're starting to sound like the captain."

Raven shrugged. The news of her being Luckett's daughter had made the rounds. The Crusader unlocked the heavy door and pulled it open—it gave a vicious squeal of metal on metal.

Raven walked into the holding cells. It was a corridor of plain steel and iron, lined with iron-barred doors. Dirty globes hung from the ceiling. No windows allowed in sunlight. The holding cells were not friendly or welcoming, and Raven hated them. She reasoned that those thrown into the holding cells had done something wrong and didn't deserve to sit in a friendly, welcoming place. Thankfully, most of the cells were empty.

Ivy's cell was at the end of the corridor. Thalame leaned against the iron bars of the cell, looking like he hadn't slept. He had been busy tending to the wounded all night, and he had still been at it when Raven had gone to bed. Ivy sat cross-legged on the cot. She wore the same trousers and blouse as the day before.

"How are you?" Raven asked Ivy.

"I'm awake," Ivy said. She didn't have the same cool demeanor as she'd had in the cavern. She sounded defeated and tired. Her voice was hoarse. "Thalame said he fixed my head."

"Concussion," Thalame said to Raven. Dark circles hung under his eyes. The way he said it made Raven think it had been much worse than a concussion, but she didn't push him for the truth.

"Raven, tell Thalame to go get some sleep," Ivy said. "He's being grumpy."

Thalame grimaced and left. Several cells down, he muttered something too low for Raven to hear. The iron door creaked open and closed once more.

"He's persistent." Ivy gazed at the ceiling. "He said he'd forgive me if I apologized."

"Did you?"

Ivy shook her head. "Not yet."

Raven scowled. "Why not?"

Ivy's gaze slid to Raven. "I don't feel sorry."

Raven wanted to shake her friend until she felt sorry for what she had done, all the trouble she had caused. All the lives she had cost.

"You look mad," Ivy deadpanned.

Raven's rage bubbled. "Of course I'm mad! Your stupid decisions got us in this mess. If you hadn't sold us out to Deacon, none of this would have happened. They wouldn't have known where to find Zander, they wouldn't have caught me, and they wouldn't have used me to…" Raven sucked back a hot rush of tears. "I killed people. They forced me to. I don't even know how many people."

Ivy stilled.

"And you're pretending like it was nothing," Raven spat.

"I suppose this means you won't be asking me to apologize like Thalame."

Raven wanted Ivy to feel sorry for what she had done, but by the empty expression on the girl's face, she did not. Yelling would not help things, despite how much she wanted to scream at Ivy.

"Thalame will wait until you are sorry," Raven said, her words threaded with the tears she had pushed down. She wiped at her eyes with the back of her hand.

"Will you?" Ivy asked softly.

"I don't know." Raven sniffled and swallowed the rest of her tears. "You know, if anyone else had done what you did, they would have been tried as a war criminal and executed."

That punctuated Ivy's stony expression. Her brows rose, and her lips twitched.

"I don't know what Luckett is planning on doing with you." Raven let those words sink in. Luckett had not been happy with having Ivy on board; however, Ivy's fate in Lenhala would have been much worse. "I only asked her not to throw you overboard."

A moment passed, then Ivy said quietly, "Thank you." Another long moment passed, and Raven turned to go, when Ivy spoke again, "Do you think Thalame hates me?"

"No," Raven said at once. "I think he might love you." Raven didn't know for certain what Thalame's feelings were, but in some way, whether platonically or romantically, he did care for Ivy.

"Is that so?" Ivy sighed. "He's not very good at showing it."

Raven didn't feel like talking about boys with Ivy. She didn't feel like talking with Ivy at all. She had come to see her because she knew, deep down, she needed to. "We're friends. We care about you, despite the horrible decisions you've made, and despite how much it doesn't feel like it right now."

Ivy sighed and returned her gaze to the ceiling. "Like you're friends with Conrad? He's a pirate and a thief and a liar. He's been kicked out of the Wraiths for stealing. I hear there's people in Tinatun who want him dead."

"Yes, like I'm friends with Conrad, only he never stabbed me in the back."

Ivy didn't say anything.

A horn sounded within the ship—the signal to switch shifts in the engine room. She'd only heard it a few times; it didn't sound in the upper parts of the ship.

Raven stepped away from the bars.

"I'm thinking about moving to Wayward Point when this is all over," Ivy said casually, eyes on the ceiling. "I could use a beach after all this."

After a long pause, Raven started back to the upper deck. They had a lot of things to do in the next few days, and she didn't have time to nag Ivy. She could wait for the other girl to feel remorse.

Raven headed up to the captain's office near the bridge. Her mother had requested—a bit aggressively—for Raven to join her and Malik for tea.

A week passed in a blur of news and gossip. Raven made several trips from the *Orion* to Lenhala's new royal palace, where Rosaria and her inner circle of trusted companions oversaw the rebuilding of Rhynwier. The people had started to return to their homes and business. Teams swept the city for debris and bodies.

With the Gray Elite's retreat and subsequent surrender, Rosaria reclaimed her throne. Her ragtag team of Wraiths, rebels, and Hawks became her Royal Guard, led by the newly appointed Captain Havelock. The Hawks had sworn allegiance to her immediately, though Raven had noted the absence of Zander's father. Zander noted a few other Hawks who had failed to show. Rosaria also extended a welcome to those of the Gray Elite who wished to remain in Lenhala; it was their home too, she had reasoned.

The Gray Elite had not been happy about the entire ordeal. The emperor had sent a delegation to speak with Rosaria three days after the official surrender. Raven had attended as a Wraith, alongside a few others, as security for Rosaria. The emperor offered a treaty, which Rosaria picked apart during the meeting. Rosaria had borrowed a few of the Crusaders scouts and spread rumors that she had taken control of Altair's Augur. They said it curved upon her command and destroyed the Gray Elite Battleship at her will. It made the delegation nervous. Rosaria demanded the Gray Elite and its automatons leave Rhynwier, and she asked for peace between their two peoples.

It had been a dreadful meeting full of politics and court-trained smiles and duplicitous words, but Rosaria had navigated her way with ease and grace. Luckily, all Raven had to do was look intimidating. Her dark robes with plated steel and hardened leather made her part easy to manage.

By the end of the first week, Raven was exhausted.

It would be a long road uphill, as Rosaria had claimed. She had ten years of Gray Elite tyranny to undo, hundreds of villages to help rebuild, and an economy to piece back together.

The day of Rosaria's coronation dawned bright and clear. The growing court had been hard at work cleaning and preparing the palace. Many Wraiths came in their full gear, Raven and Zander among them. Rosaria entered the throne room in a simple gown of ivory and a cape of gold.

She made her way through the throne room to the newly crafted throne; behind it, a portion of white fire burned in a silver cask. Captain Havelock stood on one side, and Ezra Deacon stood on the other. Ezra had traded his Gray Elite uniform for a suit of brown and ivory. An aged woman—one of the few scholars to have escaped the palace massacre and newly appointed Chief of Council—held the crown while Rosaria recited an ancient oath of justice and loyalty.

Then the old woman placed the crown upon Rosaria's head.

"May the Sisters look upon your rule with grace." Her frail voice wobbled and tears lined her eyes. "Rise, Queen Rosaria Whisehunt."

Rosaria stood. The crown gleamed in the midmorning sunlight streaming in through the tall windows. As she stood, every knee in the room bent.

The new era had dawned. Raven felt it in her bones. It tingled on her skin. Everything would be changing.

Following the coronation, Queen Rosaria gave her first speech from the palace steps. Hundreds had come to see her. She spoke of a bright future, renewed independence, and a thriving economy. Magicians would no longer be hunted. Automatons would no longer replace human workers. The Gray Elite would have no power over the people. Along with the Wraiths and the Hawks, Rosaria would usher in an era of peace and prosperity. They would rebuild Lenhala and all the villages and cities that had once dotted the kingdom. They would become the mighty and brave kingdom they once had been. They would rebuild the kingdom the Gray Elite had tried to slay.

Rosaria's first act as queen was to lift the ban on magic and magicians. For her second, she appointed Ezra Deacon as her ambassador. She ordered the automaton statues removed and commissioned new statues of the Sisters. It stirred mild unrest, but Rosaria announced that those upset by the change in leadership were free to leave, for Rhynwier would return to the Sisters.

The Order of the Hawk returned to the surface and stood behind Queen Rosaria. Some had even found old uniforms bearing the royal coat of arms—a hawk in flight. The old Wraith quarters would again house

Wraiths, and the ancient order agreed to set up a headquarters in Lenhala. Elizi had volunteered to oversee the new faction.

The evening after the coronation, Raven stood in the vast palace grounds and bid farewell to her friend from Silver Glen. Most had come down from the *Orion* to see their new queen crowned, but now it was time for them to go home. Luckett had offered to ferry them. Most had already returned to the *Orion*. Raven had wished luck and happiness to Brent and Sweets, who hadn't decided if they were going to stay in Silver Glen or travel.

Only Raven's father, stepmother, and sister remained on the ground. A Crusader ship waited to take them back up to the *Orion*.

Lena hugged Raven tight, as did her stepmother.

"You take care of yourself," said her stepmother.

"And write every week," Lena added. "I want to hear about all of your adventures."

"As long as you write back," Raven said.

Her stepmother and Lena climbed aboard the waiting airship. Her father stood with his arms crossed, looking as commanding as ever.

"You'll always have a home in Silver Glen," he said. "No matter how much time passes or where you go."

She nodded. "Thanks, Dad."

Samuel's gaze shifted over her shoulder. Footsteps sounded against the grass, and then Zander appeared at her side. For a long moment, the two men stared at one another.

"You mind yourself." Samuel extended his hand to Zander.

"I will, sir." Zander shook his hand.

"Take care of her," Samuel said to Zander. He turned to Raven and added, "Take care of him."

"You make it sound easy." Raven smiled at Zander.

"You know," her father started, eyes on the horizon, "without the Gray Elite and their automatons, there's no need to hide so far north or in the dank mines. There are plenty of places to make a new home."

Samuel brought his eyes back to Raven, and she saw something within them she had never seen before—a twinkle of excitement, a glimmer of the sky sailor he had once been.

"Wherever you end up, send us a letter," Raven said. "We can't visit if we don't know where to go."

"That I'll do," her father said.

"Bye, Dad," Raven said.

"See you, Samuel," said Zander.

Her father huff-laughed, then took them both in an embrace. He kissed his daughter's head, then joined the others in the airship. Raven watched it rise through the clouds to the waiting *Orion*.

Raven inhaled and released a calming breath.

"What do you think?" Zander asked.

"I think it's strange watching my family fly away, but at the same time it feels..." She didn't know the words to use. "It feels like my father is allowing me to grow up."

A crash came from the far side of the grounds, where a team of royal guards were busy taking down an automaton statue. One of the statues had fallen into the grassy earth, barely missing one of the guards. A beat of silence passed, and then laughter rang through the yard.

"We've got a lot of work to do," Raven said.

Zander sighed. "Can't say I'm looking forward to it."

While the *Orion* took the people of Silver Glen home—wherever home ended up being—Raven and Zander remained in Lenhala to help the Hawks and Wraiths rebuild. Magicians no longer had to hide, and over the next several weeks, magic shops dotted the city. The Wraiths offered to start a school for magicians, just like there had been one hundred years before, to teach young magicians how to control their gifts.

Zander and Raven—being Wraiths—had beds in the Wraiths' new headquarters. Being friends with the queen, they were offered quarters in the palace. Raven hadn't hesitated to pick the palace. The room she and Zander shared had come with a large amount of dust, dirty floors, and a musty smell of disuse. It also had a beautiful view of the grounds.

Three weeks into their stay at the palace, three weeks of cleaning, rebuilding, organizing, discussing, and taking down Gray Elite emblems, Raven collapsed into the cushy bed and groaned into the pillow. Her wet hair flopped around her face. She hadn't the energy to braid it back. She'd barely had the energy to pull on one of the summer nightdresses she'd accumulated. The one she chose was pale blue with a calf-length pleated skirt and short sleeves.

Zander stepped out of the grand bathroom they'd spent an entire day deep cleaning. He wore only a towel around his waist, and his real hand and his shadow hand worked to tie his wet hair into a knot behind his head.

"I don't think I'll be able to sleep on anything other than silk again," she whined.

Zander chuckled. "There goes that camping trip into the mountains I was planning."

"Just pack silk sheets." She turned her head to see him. They had been so busy, she'd barely seen Zander more than a few minutes at a time and in the evenings when they were both exhausted.

Zander was sorting through his side of their walk-in closet. He pulled a gray sleeping shirt over his head. It fell to his knees. He looked exhausted and bothered. While she had spent the day with Rosaria, Zander had gone to the Winchester house to sort things out.

"Any word of your father?"

"No." Zander deflated. "They haven't found his body among the dead, so he's still out there. I bet he slipped out with the other refugees going to

Gracita. With him presumed dead, the estate falls to my mother, but she doesn't want it."

"Do you want it?"

"No," Zander said without hesitation. "She's already passed it to Baxter, who has claimed innocence of our father's double dealings. Baxter claims to be a Hawk and loyal to the queen."

"Is he?"

"I don't know," Zander whispered. "Baxter grew up with Rosaria too. She sees him as a brother. Regardless of what he is, Ro won't throw him in the dungeon." Zander rubbed his face. "It's fine. I don't want an estate. I'd end up selling it. At least my brother will get use out of it. My mother says she's going to stay with relatives in Moorin, but it's a lie and everyone knows it. She's going to go wherever my father is." He let out a grievous groan. "It doesn't matter. If my old man wants to stay over there, I don't care. Sisters... How could I have been blind to his true nature? How could I not know he doubled-crossed the Hawks?"

"He saw a chance for power." Brigadier General Winchester had said as much to her. "He didn't think the Hawks had a real chance."

Zander leaned against the thick bedpost. "If I did half the things he did, would you still follow me around?"

"First," Raven started with a pointed tone, "I do not follow you around. We happen to share a path most of the time. Second, if you did half the stupid stuff your father has done, I would have punched you ages ago."

"I expect no less." Zander's expression became dire. "I expect you to keep me from becoming my father. I don't want to end up like him."

"Only if you keep me from becoming mine," she said.

His brow furrowed. "What's wrong with your father?"

"Oh, don't get me wrong, he's a great father, but he's a stick in the mud."

Zander chuckled. "He's protective."

"*Overprotective*," she corrected.

"He doesn't want anything to happen to you, and neither do I," Zander said. "I know you can take care of yourself, and now he does too. At least you can most of the time."

She let out a soft laugh and shut her eyes.

"Don't fall asleep yet." Zander strode to the bed and trailed his shadow fingers along her shoulder blades.

She hummed her disapproval. "We can do that tomorrow."

He laughed, low and husky. "Not that. I've got something else planned. Come on. Get up."

She reluctantly pushed herself into a sitting position. Zander stood by the balcony doors. Heavy brocade curtains hung over the windows and the doors. It had taken days for the musty smell to dissipate, and some magic.

"Do I need shoes?" Raven asked.

"Nah."

Zander opened the balcony doors and stepped out. Raven followed. The stone was cool under Raven's bare feet, and a gentle breeze blew from the north, pushing the stale smoke to the south. The royal grounds stretched on, dark and green and teeming with cicadas. Stars littered the sky. With the lights of Lenhala dimmed, the stars glowed brighter.

Raven looked around the balcony. It looked exactly the same as it had before. She glanced over the balcony to the grounds. They also looked the same.

"And we're out here because...?" Raven frowned at Zander, and her next words dissolved. Zander stood with his shadow arm behind his back and his human hand extended.

"We're out here because we have a dance we never finished," Zander said. "I promised we would dance under the stars, and this seems like the right place. I don't think I can find anything nicer than a private suite in a palace."

Raven didn't have words. She'd almost forgotten all about that. She gave him a tired, happy smile and slid her hand into his. Zander swept her into his arms, and they danced around the balcony. Her pleated skirt fluttered as he twirled her. Without music, they invented their own rhythm.

Zander spun her away and then back in, meeting her lips with his own. Raven traced her fingers along his clean-shaven jaw and tilted her head, deepening the kiss. His arms tightened around her middle. All the things she had been worried about seemed farther away.

He mumbled against his lips, "Still too tired?"

She grinned. Yes, she was exhausted, but too tired? "Not anymore."

Zander pulled her back into the bedroom, kicking the balcony doors closed. They collapsed into the silk sheets in a tangle of limbs and laughter. Raven had gotten used to Zander in the past few weeks, and he hadn't been able to make her blush as easily.

After, Raven snuggled into his neck. Zander hugged her close. A beat of silence passed, and within it, Raven fell asleep. In the next moment, sunlight glowed behind the closed curtains. Zander slept soundly beside her.

Raven lay there a while, taking in the sight of the grand room, the golds and creams. She woke to the same view every morning, but a part of it still didn't feel real.

On the way to breakfast, a courier intercepted Raven. He handed her a letter.

"Who's it from?" Zander asked.

Raven ripped the letter open and read it over quickly. "My mother." She read it again, slower. "They've returned to Lenhala. My father and the others have relocated, and Mom wants to know if we need a lift."

"What do you think?" Zander asked, brows raised. "We *have* been in Lenhala a while."

"Hmm... I think I need to eat before I make big decisions." Raven tucked the letter into her pocket.

They had eaten breakfast every morning in a small parlor that overlooked the eastern grounds. Rosaria and Ezra were already seated, and royal guards stood by the doors. After tea, Raven relayed her mother's message to Rosaria.

"The city's restoration is going well," Rosaria said. "I don't want you to feel like you have to stay here. You've already done beyond what I could have asked. If you wish to travel with your mother, you have my blessing. Only, mind the piracy. I can't allow it when it's blatant."

"I will take your warning to my mother." Raven turned to Zander. "While staying here has been amazing, I want to see the rest of the world."

With their queen's permission, Zander and Raven boarded a crusader airship that afternoon. She watched the city of Lenhala shrink from the porthole, the towering buildings and homes in the middle of repair, steadied with scaffolding. Then, they punched through the clouds. The *Orion* waited for them, looking like a dream. The afternoon sunlight glinted off the steel rigging, the crimson Belt, and the sky-blue balloons.

Once aboard, they made their way to the Belt.

Far below, on the other side of the wispy clouds, Lenhala gradually drifted west as the *Orion* drifted east.

"Well, what do you want to do now?" Zander asked, leaning onto the railing. "We probably have ten minutes before your mother sends for you."

Raven took a long moment to think it over. What did she want to do? She looked out over the horizon, endless in every direction.

"I want to see what else is out there," Raven said. "I want to see the coast of Rhynwier. I want to see how far the beaches stretch in Tinatun. I want to see if there are sea monsters and mermaids in the southern seas. I want to see how high the mountains go. I want to see everything."

"Everything?" Zander raised a brow. The sun glided his dark hair in shades of gold. "That is a tall order. Luckily, we happen to have use of a sky city. And, from what I hear, the captain likes you. She might take requests."

Raven grinned and leaned away from the railing. "Then let's go request our next adventure."

She grabbed his hand and tugged him back into the ship. As they made their way to the bridge, she couldn't stop smiling. All those years of daydreaming, and she couldn't wait to see what adventures she and Zander might find together.

Acknowledgments

When I penned the first scene of Raven's story, I had no idea where it would go. This series somehow came about, in a blaze of inspiration I don't understand, and here we are. At the end. It fills me with a strange combination of success and sorrow, because while I finished a series, I have also finished my journey with Raven and Zander.

First and foremost, this story and its characters would have never seen the light of day had it not been for the amazing team at Authors 4 Authors. Rebecca, Renee, Brandi, and Kari—it has been such an incredible blessing and an honor to share this story with, to work with you, to grow as an author with your guidance. I'm not the same author I was when I first submitted my too-long and wordy epic fantasy back in 2018, and it is mind-blowing to go back and see the difference in my writing. I have you all to thank for taking my words and making them sparkle. Thank you from the bottom of my heart, as cold and stony as it sometimes is.

To my mother, I could express my gratitude every day for the rest of your life, but it would never be enough for all you've done for me. All the tantrums you've withstood. All the late-night typing from my mechanical keyboard that you've somehow ignored. All of my daydreaming and whining. You were always the first to buy my next book, even if you had no plans on reading it. Yes, I know they're stacked on your dresser in order that you bought them. I love you regardless, and always will.

And of course, to the readers who gave Raven a chance, thank you. For giving this unknown, small-time author a chance, for giving this series a chance, for making it through the journey alongside me. Thank you, thank you, and thank you.

About the Author

Beatrice B. Morgan lives in southern Illinois. When she isn't reading or writing, she is most likely playing a video game. She is a night owl, caffeine addict, yoga enthusiast, dog person, hopeless romantic, optimist, and shameless Ravenclaw.

Follow her online:

bbmorgan.com
Twitter: @BBMorgan_W
Facebook: @BBMorganBooks

ALSO BY BEATRICE B. MORGAN

STARS AND BONES:
Thief in the Castle

The notorious Juniper Thimble is destined for execution. Caught stealing the king's crown—in addition to her long list of crimes—she has only one way out. Juniper must survive the biggest, most deadly con of her life, commissioned by the king himself. Disguised as the crown prince's lover, she is forced to protect him with her life...literally. Guarded by a surly squire, relentlessly attacked by demons, and surrounded by mysteriously disappearing servants, Juniper must dispatch the threat to the prince's life before they find out who she really is.

books2read.com/thiefinthecastle

Authors 4 Authors Publishing

A publishing company for authors, run by authors, blending the best of traditional and independent publishing

We specialize in speculative fiction: science fiction, fantasy, paranormal, and romance. Get lost in another world!

Check out our collection at https://books2read.com/rl/a4a
or visit Authors4AuthorsPublishing.com/books

For updates, scan the QR code or visit our website to join our semi-monthly newsletter!

Want more heart-pounding YA? We recommend:

FYR

by Lisa Borne Graves

At seventeen, Toury arrives in Fyr, where magic is power, a prince's love is deadly, and female autonomy is a dream. Formerly a loner and burden to her adoptive parents, she ruins her chances of a fresh start by offending an ogler who just happens to be the prince.

Alex, the Prince of Fyr, is no novice when it comes to pressure. He has to face his father's ailing health, the expectation to marry soon, and the hidden necromancers trying to take over the realm by exploiting his dark curse. At least there's hope in a cheeky savior, but Earth girls aren't so easy.

books2read.com/fyr

www.ingramcontent.com/pod-product-compliance
Lightning Source LLC
Chambersburg PA
CBHW011511100726
47899CB00010BD/3321